PRAISE FOR THE NOVELS OF
*NEW YORK TIMES* BESTSELLING AUTHOR
## JoAnn Ross

### OUT OF THE MIST

"The story's robust momentum and lively characters make this a fun, energetic read."

—*Publishers Weekly*

"A wonderfully engaging story and terrific characters."

—*Booklist*

"If you enjoyed the Callahan Brothers trilogy, you're in luck. *Out of the Mist* is Book One of JoAnn Ross's Stewart Sisters trilogy, and this one definitely sets the bar high. . . . Her characterizations are stellar and the setting of the beautiful Smoky Mountains comes alive with her evocative words."

—*A Romance Review*

"Ross weaves the search for the missing family treasure and the growing attraction between two creative spirits with aplomb in this charming romance."

—*BookPage*

"Fun, funny, sexy, and entirely enjoyable. Think *To Catch a Thief* with a twist—a Scottish twist. A great premise, a marvelous setting, delightful characters, including an incredibly sexy Scotsman, and a terrific romance—what more could a reader want?"

—Susan Lantz,
Romance Fiction Team Captain, America Online

"A great afternoon read. Ooh, those Scotsmen! . . . characters are believable, even the quirky family members, and the setting is beautiful."

—*The Old Book Barn Gazette*

### RIVER ROAD

"Skillful and satisfying. . . . With its emotional depth, Ross's tale will appeal to Nora Roberts fans."

*—Booklist*

"The romance . . . crackles, and their verbal sparring keeps the narrative moving along at an energetic clip. Readers who have read the first book in this trilogy will be heartily entertained; those who haven't will rush out to buy it after savoring this delightful entry."

*—Publishers Weekly*

"Highly entertaining reading—this is major fun!"

*—Romantic Times*, Top Pick

"A delicious read with a vast array of zany characters to keep you glued to the pages."

*—Rendezvous*

### BLUE BAYOU

"[An] atmospheric contemporary romance. Ross is in fine form . . . plenty of sex and secrets to keep readers captivated."

*—Publishers Weekly*

"The opening chapter in what promises to be an exceptional and emotional trilogy. . . . Ms. Ross [creates] refreshing and rewarding reading experiences."

*—Romantic Times*, Top Pick

"*Blue Bayou* brilliantly spirits us to the hot and steamy Louisiana bayou. . . . The touching love story, intriguing plot, and unforgettable characters create a marvelous read you can't put down."

*—The Old Book Barn Gazette*

### LEGENDS LAKE

"Sexual sparks fly. . . . Similar to Nora Roberts's Irish trilogies."

*—Publishers Weekly*

"[A] marvel of exquisitely crafted prose. . . . I couldn't turn the pages fast enough."

—*Affaire de Coeur*

"This irresistible tale is a must read."

—*Rendezvous*

### FAIR HAVEN

"[An] impressive blend of tender warmth and fascinating characters . . . [with] a colorful dash of the supernatural."

—*Romantic Times*

"As magical as Ireland itself. . . . A masterpiece of writing from the heart. Storytelling at its all-time best."

—*The Belles and Beaux of Romance*

### FAR HARBOR

"A profoundly moving story of intense emotional depth, satisfying on every level. You won't want to leave this family."

—CompuServe Romance Reviews

"A wonderful relationship drama in which JoAnn Ross splendidly describes love the second time around."

—Barnesandnoble.com

### HOMEPLACE

"[An] engrossing story of love's healing power. . . . A great read."

—*The Old Book Barn Gazette*

**Also by JoAnn Ross**

**Available from Pocket Books**

# JoAnn Ross

## Out of the Blue

**POCKET BOOKS**
New York  London  Toronto  Sydney

This book is a work of fiction. Names, characters, places and incidents are products of the author's imagination or are used fictitiously. Any resemblance to actual events or locales or persons, living or dead, is entirely coincidental.

An *Original* Publication of POCKET BOOKS

 POCKET BOOKS, a division of Simon & Schuster, Inc.
1230 Avenue of the Americas, New York, NY 10020

ISBN: 0-7434-6474-5

First Pocket Books printing March 2004

10  9  8  7  6  5  4  3  2

POCKET and colophon are registered trademarks of Simon & Schuster, Inc.

Cover design by Lisa Litwack
Author type by Jim Lebbab
Photo of house © Mark Tomalty/Masterfile
Photo of tree © Zefa

Manufactured in the United States of America

For information regarding special discounts for bulk purchases, please contact Simon & Schuster Special Sales at 1-800-456-6798 or business@simonandschuster.com

# Out of the Blue

# Prologue

*There is no witness so dreadful, no accuser so terrible, as the conscience that dwells in the heart of every man.*
—Polybius

*It is justice, not charity, that is wanting in the world.*
—Mary Wollstonecraft

The moon over New Orleans was a thin silver sickle, the dense night air scented with salt and the musk from the surrounding swamps; Lucas McCloud lay prone on the roof of the building, the familiar weight of a Remington rifle pressed hard against the hollow of his shoulder. His cheek rested against the wooden stock. Lucas didn't know how long he'd been in the same spot, in the same pose. He'd learned to be silent, still, and patient. And disinterested in anything but the target that kept moving in and out of the night scope's crosshairs.

The French Quarter had glowed with red twilight when the hostage team had arrived at the small shotgun house. Now the only light came from the neon flash of the strip joint across the street. There should have been streetlights, but they'd probably been shot out by criminals who preferred no audience for the indecencies human beings could perpetrate against one another.

Lucas didn't mind the dark; the night scope didn't need much light. He didn't mind the waiting. Nor did he have any interest in the conversation taking place between the team negotiator and Lucas's target, who, on a murderous spree, had already killed four people, including a Louisiana state trooper, and had now taken a nineteen-year-old college student from Baton Rouge hostage.

If Lucas heard the conversation, he might make the mistake of getting emotionally involved, which would only complicate what he was paid to do. It was important to keep his work in the abstract, to not allow the slightest tinge of doubt to creep into his mind. And brooding about the results afterward was only asking for trouble.

The rifle was an old friend. When he'd first arrived on the roof, he'd loaded a total of five rounds to satisfy the Bureau's desk jockeys: four in the magazine, one in the chamber. He had no intention of using the four in the magazine. *One shot, one kill.* It was the marine sniper motto, one Lucas had lived by during the Desert Storm war.

Focused as he was, he was aware only on the most distant level of the others involved in this Code Red situation. The Containment Team had secured the outer perimeter, restricting the target area. The Rescue Team, whose specialties were firing on the move, room entries, and evacuating hostages, waited inside the perimeter along with the Arrest Team.

As members of the FBI Hostage Rescue Team, Lucas and his spotter provided observation and intelligence at the crime scene, along with their more obvious duty of precision suspect neutralization. A damn stupid euphemism for taking the life of another human being, he'd always thought.

His spotter, Jack Barnes, a fellow former marine scout, sat in a folding chair nearby, calmly drinking coffee. Lucas never drank caffeine; it jangled the nerves, something a guy in his business couldn't allow. Barnes's job was to listen to the ongoing conversation on the earphones. When he got the green light from the team on the ground, he'd pass the order on to Lucas, who'd bring the Remington's hammer down and bring an end to the standoff.

Moody blues floated seductively on the night air; Lucas didn't notice.

A rat scurried through the shadows, his eyes shining in the thin slash of moonlight. Lucas didn't care.

He watched the target pacing back and forth in front of the window, phone to his ear, a shotgun in his hand. Even without sound, Lucas could sense that the tension level was cranking up inside the house. It wouldn't be long now.

He squinted and ordered his mind to stay cool and collected. The New Orleans humidity could affect bullet trajectory, but he'd adjusted for that. His finger caressed the trigger as he steadied his lungs and slowed his heart, seeking the stillness deep within himself as he waited.

*One shot. One kill.*

# 1

*Seven years later*

It was the holiday season in New Orleans. The green St. Charles streetcar was packed with last-minute shoppers as it clattered past historic homes garlanded in white Christmas lights; the mood was festive, bustling, and decidedly contagious.

As she left the car and drifted into the French Quarter, Lark Stewart couldn't remember feeling so happy. So free.

Cheerful carols of wise men and herald angels blended with the cacophony of jazz and blues pouring from the open doorways on Bourbon Street. Lark exchanged Christmas greetings with a group of tourists laden down with packages. Caught up in her enjoyment of the season, she didn't notice when several of the shoppers excitedly turned to watch as she continued strolling beneath the famed cast-iron balconies from which more lights sparkled. Nor was she aware of camera shutters clicking madly away when she paused to study a display of T-shirts and Mardi Gras masks in a storefront window.

A pair of earrings caught her attention, drawing her

into the store where she handed a ten-dollar bill to a bored teenager who possessed even less holiday spirit than the Grinch. Undeterred by the girl's unwelcoming attitude, Lark left the store with small green trees flashing gaily from her earlobes.

A block away, she entered an Irish pub where a Loreena McKennit wannabe was pulling off a heartfelt rendition of "A Wexford Carol." Believing her sparkly new earrings were drawing the stares, Lark pasted a vague smile on her face as she made her way through the crowd and ordered a Coke from a bartender who looked as if he'd just gotten off the boat from the Auld Sod.

"It's on the house, Ms. Stewart," he said when she tried to pay.

"I'm sorry." Her smile slipped slightly. "I believe you have me confused with someone else."

A look of surprise flashed across his ruddy face, then, as if catching on to a joke, he winked. "Right." He put a glass in front of her. "Well, it's on the house, anyway. Merry Christmas."

"Merry Christmas to you, too," she said cheerfully. New Orleans was such a lovely town, with such charming people. Maybe she'd just settle down here instead of going on to . . .

Where?

An image wavered on the far reaches of her mind. A bus with a vista of the blue-tinged Smoky Mountains painted on its side, headed down the road to . . .

Lark shook her head. It didn't matter, she decided, focusing on the singer who, while not possessing Loreena's extraordinary voice, still hit all the right notes.

As she sipped the drink, a memory flashed through Lark's mind. She'd been here before. *The pub was an Irish outpost in the French Quarter, not the least bit flashy, with a small wraparound bar, dart boards on the wall, and the soundless television tuned to a soccer game.*

*The moment she entered the pub's smoke-hazed darkness, her gaze was drawn immediately to a small wooden table in the back of the room, where Lucas McCloud sat hunkered over a pint of Guinness.*

She took a deep breath, screwed up her courage, and made her way through the crowd.

"So, have you seen the ghosts?" she asked with an abundance of false cheer.

He glanced up, his midnight-dark eyes remote. He didn't seem all that surprised to see her. Nor did he offer a word of welcome.

"I read about them in a guide on the way down here." She pulled out the extra chair and sat across from him. Their knees touched beneath the small table. If she had her way, there'd be a lot more touching before the night was over.

"There are supposedly five ghosts living in the courtyard. One's the wife of a former owner; another's a different owner who appears to be searching for something. The third and fourth are yet another former owner who killed either his secretary or his servant—just which is a little unclear—because she wouldn't have an affair with him. Then he killed himself.

"And the fifth ghost is a little boy who got separated from his mother in the Quarter and died. The story goes that his spirit wandered in here, looking for her, and the other ghosts took him in."

Nothing.

He'd gone back to staring into the Guinness as if the secrets of the universe could be found in the dark, foam-topped depths. But she hadn't come all this way to be ignored.

"That's so tragic and sweet at the same time, don't you think? I'm working on a song about it. I'm having a little trouble getting the bridge right, but—"

"What are you doing here?"

He was so different. And it wasn't just the marine haircut that had left him with nearly a shaved scalp, save for the little patch of black on the top of his head that made him appear larger and far more forbidding than the boy she'd fallen heart over heels in love with. He'd never been all that talkative, but now he'd turned dark and moody. Definitely not encouraging.

Lark reached out and covered his hand. She'd always loved his hands, loved the way they looked, so dark and strong against her fair skin, loved the way they felt stroking her eager body, creating rivers of flame.

"That should be obvious. I came to see you." She hitched in a breath before he could counter with the argument she'd heard before. "And because I refuse to believe you really don't want me."

His answering laugh was harsh and humorless. "And people actually believe you're the shy Stewart sister."

"I am. But not with you." Sensing the faint crack in his armor, she linked their fingers together. "Never with you, Lucas."

"No." He turned their joined hands over. His thumb began tracing absent little circles on her palm. "Not with me." He sighed heavily, like a man with the weight of the world on his shoulders. "I'm shipping out."

"I know." His sister, who'd moved to New Orleans with her new husband, had called to tell Lark he'd surprised them with a visit before heading off to war. The moment she'd hung up,

*Lark had, without a moment's regret, blown off a meeting with a record producer she'd been trying to convince to give her an audition for the past two years, and rushed to Louisiana.* "You've changed."

"Nobody stays eighteen forever."

"Thank God." *She'd cried for weeks after he'd left Highland Falls. Her heart had been broken. All the way here from Nashville, Lark had assured herself that this time all she was risking was her pride. Unfortunately, her heart was still as vulnerable to this man as it had been in her teens.*

"I'm not asking for forever after, Lucas." *She touched her free hand to his cheek and felt the muscle clench beneath her fingertips.* "If this one night is all we're destined to have, then it'll be enough for me."

*There was no one on this earth who knew her as well as Lucas McCloud did. He shook his head slowly, obviously aware that she was lying. She wanted much, much more—and they both knew it.*

"My hotel's around the corner," *he said.*

"I know." *Nearly weeping with relief, she managed a faint smile.* "I didn't want to carry my suitcase all through the French Quarter, so I asked the bellman to take it up to your room."

"Why am I not surprised?" *His tone was dry, resigned.* "I doubt there's a man on earth who could resist you."

"It's not that way. He's a sweet old fellow who has to be at least eighty, if he's a day."

"No matter. A woman like you makes a man remember things he'd thought he'd put behind him."

*As Lucas had left her behind.*

*No! She wasn't going to dwell on the past. Nor was she going to think about the future. There was only now—this stolen moment in time with this man she'd always loved. Would always love.*

"Possibly he was remembering," she allowed. "But only because I reminded him of his wife. He was in the South Pacific during World War II and they spent their last night before he shipped out in the Fairmont Hotel in San Francisco."

*His lips curved in a quick slash of a smile that reminded her of the boy who'd pulled her beneath the water in the pool behind Firefly Falls the summer she'd been sixteen. When they'd come to the surface together, arms and legs tangled, a dizzying sensation had swept over her, making her so weak, he'd ended up carrying her out of the water. As she'd looked up at his handsome face, Lark had wished she could remain in his arms forever. Five years later, she felt the same way.*

"It figures you'd know a total stranger's life story within two minutes of meeting him." *His dark brown eyes warmed with the gentle fondness that had won her heart. Strain began to melt away, replaced by familiar desire.* "It's that connection with people that's going to make the world fall in love with you."

I only want *you* to be in love with me. *Prudently, she kept that thought to herself.*

*Later, she couldn't remember the walk from the pub to the hotel. She did recall, in vivid clarity, the way he'd lifted her into his arms, and with his mouth hot and hard on hers, carried her across the threshold, just as a groom would carry his bride.*

*Their first coupling had been hot, quick, and stormy. Then, passions too long denied satisfied, Lucas slowed the pace, using his hands, lips, and teeth to drive Lark to the brink again and again, until she was writhing on the tangled sheets, begging for release.*

*And still, when it finally came, it was not enough.*

*They made love as if there'd be no tomorrow. Which there*

*might well not be. A soft, rosy lavender light was slipping between the slats of the hurricane shutters when Lark finally drifted off to sleep, her head on his chest, his arms holding her close.*

*He was gone when she woke up. The only proof that he'd been there was the stiffness in her muscles and a brief, almost terse good-bye note left on the pillow atop of pair of marine-issue dog tags.*

*Her first thought had been panic: if Lucas was killed in the war, without the identification, how would anyone recognize his body? The note had relieved that fear, assuring her that he had an extra set—although it wasn't officially allowed, apparently "everyone" did it. Then, proving that he'd been thinking of her, as she had him, he admitted that he'd intended the tags for her all along.*

*He did not promise to marry her when he returned home from the Gulf. He didn't even sign the note with love. But the tags spoke volumes, and as she slipped them over her head, the metal feeling cold against her bare skin, Lark vowed to wear them until he returned to her safe and sound.*

"You sure you're doing okay?" the bartender asked, jerking her back to the present. He was looking at her strangely in the blue neon glow.

"I'm fine," Lark assured him not quite truthfully, as she realized, with a slash of concern, that the U.S. Marine she'd spent that night of hot, unbridled sex with so many years ago was the sole memory of her life.

The bartender gave her another long, silent look, then wiped his hands on a towel and went to the end of the bar. Lark watched him pick up the black house phone, but with his back turned toward her, she couldn't hear him above the singer. The conversation was brief, then he was back, refilling her glass with another spritz of Coke.

His smile was reassuring when he slid the drink across the bar, causing her prick of concern to fade away. Everything would come back to her. All she had to do was relax and enjoy this perfect stolen moment in this perfect City That Care Forgot.

But a few minutes later, a pair of uniformed police officers appeared at her elbow. One was a woman about Lark's height of five-feet-five, with the kind of toned body that came from working out, and sleek dark hair. Her uniform looked custom-tailored and her black leather cop shoes had a spit shine. The other cop was male, taller than his partner, his winter blues looking as if he'd slept in them.

"Lark Stewart?" the female cop asked. Her green eyes, as she looked straight into Lark's, were as hard as her body.

"I'm sorry." Lark felt something inside her shift. "I'm not Lark Stewart."

"*I'm* sorry." The man's kind, rumpled face echoed his words. "But I'm going to have to ask you to come with us, Ms. Stewart."

A headache she'd forgotten about while riding the streetcar began to pound. She lifted a hand to her temple, felt something sticky beneath her hair and stared at the red stain on her fingertips.

It was only after she was outside, and the nice cop had warned her against bumping her head on the roof of the patrol car, that Lark noticed, in the flashing red-and-blue strobe of the emergency light, the scarlet blood spattered across the front of her beaded white gown.

# 2

The nightmare jerked Lucas from a tortured sleep. He sat bolt upright in bed, drenched in sweat, the bedding kicked into a heap on the floor, reliving that deadly Christmas Eve seven years ago.

God, what he wouldn't give for a drink! The smooth slide of bourbon, the cool splash of beer, the tang of tequila, numbing his mind, blocking out images too painful to remember. The problem was that there was a point before blessed oblivion set in when the memories attacked from all sides, like a team of snipers.

"You don't drink alcohol." Sometimes saying it out loud helped.

He took a deep breath and managed to slow his pulse enough to keep it from pounding against his eardrums. Even awake, he was still sweating; the four walls of the bedroom were closing in on him.

Fighting off the temptation to slide back into the bad old days, he crawled out of bed on unsteady legs, pulled on thick wool socks, then grabbed his jeans off a chair and yanked them on. He layered a flannel shirt over a thermal one, jerked on his boots, shrugged into the jacket hanging on the hook by the door, and went outside.

Ice crystals sparkled in the snow and in the bracing mountain air that cleared his head. A full moon hung low in the sky, lighting his way as he walked through the woods, but Lucas could have made his way blindfolded. He knew this mountain intimately, the way a longtime lover knows the curves and valleys of a woman's body.

His nerves were still buzzing like high-voltage power lines in morning fog as he waded through the snow. Forcing his mind to dwell on more positive images, he paused beside the frozen stream where he'd shot his first buck. He'd been twelve years old and had worked mowing lawns in the summer, shoveling sidewalks and driveways in the winter, delivering *The Highland Herald*, and bagging groceries at the Tartan Market, along with going to school.

He'd been underage for the market job, but since locals believed in instilling children with a strong work ethic, no one in town was about to turn him in. Lucas was the oldest of five children and the only son of Jed McCloud, a part-time truck driver for the Stewart family distillery. The Stewarts, who were the closest thing Highland Falls had to royalty—even living in a massive stone reproduction of a medieval castle—made premium whiskey from a secret recipe an ancestor had brought with him from the Scottish Highlands. Highlander's Pride had driven the local economy for more than two centuries.

Having been driven off their land in County Clare prior to the American Revolution, Lucas's ancestors had arrived in a region that became populated mostly by Scots. The McClouds were farmers, with broad backs as

strong as their will. Lucas's father, claiming a strong dis-
taste for working from dawn to dusk, falling into bed
before dark, then rising again before sunrise the next
morning to begin the entire cycle all over again, had broken with that tradition.

Besides hating the hardscrabble life of an Appalachian
farm, Jed McCloud wasn't much happier behind the
wheel of a delivery truck. Though none of his get-rich-
quick schemes ever worked, he wasn't embarrassed about
the financial or legal problems, blaming them on bad
luck or unfair competition. He was a glib man who used
his Black Irish good looks and practiced charm to win the
trust of both men and women. Especially women.

He was also a binge alcoholic who possessed a violent
side that few but his family knew about. Once, Lucas had
flattened a tire on the family's rusty old pickup to keep his
father from driving drunk. Enraged when he'd discovered the vandalism, Jed made him change the tire, then
had broken his ten-year-old son's arm.

After getting a neighbor to watch his younger sisters,
Lucas walked the two miles to the hospital. The nurse at
the reception desk called his mother, who arrived from
her job fixing corpses' hair at a funeral parlor in
Asheville, just as the doctor was encasing his arm in a
heavy plaster cast. The pungent, antiseptic odor of the
ER didn't quite overcome the smell that clung to Paula
McCloud's hair and clothes. On the Saturday mornings
when Lucas collected his paper route money, he'd
noticed that other mothers smelled of flowers or cookies.
For as long as he could remember, his own had smelled
of death and embalming fluid.

"Don't worry, Lucas," she'd assured him. "Your father won't remember what you did tomorrow."

*Don't talk. Don't feel. Don't tell. If you ignore it, maybe it won't hurt as bad.* Denial had been the family motto.

Lucas heard a rustling of bushes. A white-tailed deer came browsing among the trees, returning Lucas's thoughts to the day of the buck. He'd just turned twelve when Harlan Boone, Highland Falls's sheriff, had shown up at the Tartan Market with a shiny new Winchester. The instant Lucas took the rifle from the leather case, it felt absolutely right in his hands. Going into the woods at the edge of town, they shot at tin cans until dark.

"Hot damn," Harlan had said as Lucas sent can after can flying off tree stumps. "You've got yourself a natural talent for shooting, son."

He didn't know it at the time, but that afternoon would determine the course of Lucas's life. Target practice became an obsession as he honed his skill, and three weeks later, on the opening day of hunting season, he was out in the woods with the sheriff when a four-point buck appeared from out of the mist. The older man passed the shot to Lucas who, with adrenaline coursing through his veins, raised the Winchester and jammed the stock against his shoulder as he'd been taught.

His hands weren't as steady as they'd been when peppering Del Monte and Budweiser cans, and the weight of responsibility felt even heavier on his shoulders as he realized that if he made this shot, his family would have meat for the long winter. He took a deep breath. He hadn't yet developed the ability to slow his heartbeat, but he managed to calm his nerves.

The buck was posed in the crosshairs like a glossy photograph from the cover of *Field and Stream*. Lucas pulled the trigger with the steady movement he'd been practicing. The shot rang out, cracking like broken glass through the morning air, echoing over the rounded mountaintops. The buck's knees crumbled and he fell right where he'd been standing.

The sheriff slapped his shoulder. "I knew you could do it, boy."

Lucas's chest swelled at hearing such rare words of praise, but when they reached the fallen deer, a sharp pang of regret for having taken the life of such a magnificent animal robbed him of his earlier thrill.

Harlan sensed Lucas's ambivalence. "If God hadn't meant for you to bring venison home to your mama, he wouldn't have given you the talent to shoot, son."

The affirmation, stated in a mild, matter-of-fact way, made Lucas feel better. But killing the buck had also driven home the realization that all life was valuable, and that anyone who took it upon himself to snuff out a life ought to be damn sure he could live with the consequences.

Which Lucas had done. Until that night on the New Orleans rooftop . . .

"Don't go there." Surely there was *some* memory that wouldn't send his mind back through that labyrinth of tragedy.

A figure clad in a black motorcycle jacket and filthy, oil-stained jeans appeared in front of him, his lips twisted in a snarl. *What's the matter, McCloud? Guilt hanging a little heavy these days?*

The man, whose mocking eyes gleamed like flames, was one of several ghosts who'd haunted Lucas over the years—among them an enemy soldier who'd ambushed a tank unit on the Iraqi-Kuwait border, a sicko white supremacist who'd climbed into the belfry of a Portland, Oregon church and began taking target practice at African-American third graders jumping rope on the playground of a neighboring Catholic school, and a father of three who'd held his children hostage at gunpoint because he'd believed his wife was having an affair with the contractor remodeling their den. Those ghosts had always lurked in the shadows, waiting for Lucas in his dreams.

But not Aaron Bragg. There'd been a time when Bragg had taunted him ceaselessly, night and day. Since Lucas had dried out two years ago, he'd managed to keep the mass murderer at bay. Most of the time.

"Go to hell, Bragg."

*Newsflash, McCloud, I'm already there.* His breath was rank; his yellow teeth flashed in a wolfish smile. *And I'm saving you a place right next to me. Think of it, Special Agent: me and you, spending eternity together.*

He barked a coarse, deep laugh that sent a flurry of startled birds into the air from the winter-bare branches of a nearby tree.

Then, with a mocking wink, he faded away into the mist, leaving behind the stench of death.

"Sick son of a bitch."

Hoping that the flames in hell were as hot as those fire-and-brimstone tent revival preachers always hollered about, Lucas doggedly forged on, following the stream until he reached a frozen, shimmering, pale blue water-fall.

A bittersweet memory of Lark Stewart, her smooth flesh warmed to gold by the high summer sun, her hair a wet, shiny chestnut sliding down her bare back as he'd carried her from the pool, strummed a deep, almost painful chord. A week later he'd left Highland Falls, deserting the girl he'd loved.

More guilt roiled in his gut. Feeling the woods beginning to crowd in on him, Lucas headed back toward the house with Lark's latest hit single, "Born to Be Lonely," echoing in his mind.

Was she being arrested? And if so, for what? Lark had never been a coward, but she was afraid to ask. Afraid of the answer.

Unfortunately, the two cops weren't volunteering anything.

She pressed a hand against her fear-knotted stomach and struggled not to be sick. Despite the hot air blowing from the dashboard of the police cruiser, she was suddenly so, so cold. She rubbed her arms in an attempt to warm up, but it didn't help.

Not jail, Lark realized with a surge of relief as they pulled up in front of the building. *A hospital.* She touched her fingers to her forehead again and wondered why she couldn't remember what had happened to her.

The emergency room was a large, brightly lit human beehive. Apparently not everyone had gotten the news that it was the season of goodwill. An old man—homeless from the looks and smell of him—sat in a molded plastic chair, his hand wrapped in a filthy, blood-soaked rag as he patiently awaited his turn; a young woman lay on a gurney, silently weeping as a team worked on her battered face; and behind a curtain a baby in obvious distress screamed.

A tuxedo-clad man and a woman dressed in scarlet sequins and draped in diamonds had apparently indulged in too much holiday cheer. The driver had plowed into a tree along Lakeshore Drive, causing their Mercedes's airbags to inflate. The woman, still obviously drunk, cursed like a longshoreman while the doctor treated her superficial facial burns.

Confused and terrified, Lark was pulled into the frantic activity; her ruined dress was cut off her, then a team of doctors and nurses took her vital signs, checked her from head to toe for injuries, and sent her off for X-rays and a CT scan.

"Other than a concussion and some nasty scrapes and bruises, there doesn't seem to be anything physically wrong with you," reported the neurologist who'd been called in to examine the brain scan.

Lark would have been relieved at her words were it not for the female cop who'd remained with her during her time in the ER and was still there by the door, uniformed arms crossed.

"Why can't I remember anything?"

"It's not unusual to have short-term memory loss following a head injury." The neurologist's professional smile was meant to reassure. "However, your memory loss goes beyond that, since there's seemingly a loss of identity."

She tapped a plastic ballpoint pen against her metal clipboard. "I don't want to make a diagnosis without running a battery of psychological tests, but there's a possibility you might be suffering a hysterical reaction. Or a fugue."

"I don't believe I'm hysterical." The fact that she'd been thrown into such a surreal situation and wasn't screaming suggested she was normally a calm, even-tempered person.

A young man wearing blue scrubs appeared in the doorway. "You're needed back in the ER, STAT, Dr. Thompson. The EMTs just brought in a jumper, and Dr. Burke's tied up with a head injury from a rollover on I-10."

"I'm sorry," the doctor told Lark as she sprinted from the room. "We'll have to continue this later."

Lark was wondering what she was supposed to do next when two men, clad in dark suits and trench coats, appeared in the open doorway.

"Ms. Stewart?" asked the taller man, a trim African-American with graying hair.

"I'm sorry, I don't know." She was no longer certain of anything.

"Then you'd be . . . ?" The second man's French Cajun accent did nothing to soften his tone.

"I'm really not sure." Her throat tightened; Lark swallowed to dislodge the lump. "The doctor said something about a fugue, but other than the musical kind, I've no idea what that is."

"It's a form of temporary amnesia, often triggered by stress or trauma," the first man said. "In our business, we run across it every once in a while. I'm Detective Wayne Jordan, New Orleans PD." He flipped open a wallet, flashing his badge. "This is Detective Dave Deveraux." He nodded toward his partner, whose grim-faced ID photo reminded Lark of the Most Wanted posters in post offices. "We're here in regards to the shooting of Daniel Murphy."

"Shooting?" Her brain couldn't process the word; it was as if he'd started speaking Swahili. She shot a look toward the patrol woman, whose unblinking expression gave nothing away.

"Daniel Murphy was shot in Pirate's Alley around midnight," Detective Jordan's baritone voice echoed oddly, as if he were speaking from a cave in the bottom of the sea.

"That can't be."

Lark felt the blood draining from her face. She began to shake as reality flooded back with dizzying speed. Dear God, it *was* possible for your entire life to pass in front of your eyes! She *was* Lark Stewart. And Danny was one of her closest friends.

A Nashville veteran and longtime studio musician, Danny had been with her from the beginning.

They'd met while recording demo tapes, and it had been his idea to record their own CDs while waiting for a major label to discover them. It had also been Danny's idea to form a small band and go out on the road, singing in the arenas that couldn't afford big stars, selling their CDs after the shows.

It hadn't been easy and they certainly hadn't traveled in luxury, but as it turned out, getting away from Tennessee had proven good for her, eventually allowing her to overcome the need to always look over her shoulder. It had been like having a big brother to tour with, since Danny—who, at six-feet-five made an imposing presence—had always been there to protect her.

He'd also always made her laugh and kept up her sagging spirits as the battered old bus wound its way across America on what he'd dubbed the "Mud and Dust Tour" of rural county rodeos. When their fortunes improved, about the same time she'd married a former rodeo bronc rider, she'd moved to her own bus with her husband, who became her manager.

But she'd dearly missed her "big brother's" sunny company, and after separating from Cody, she'd gone back to traveling with the band.

"How is he?" she asked, still trying to focus. "Where is he?"

"He's in surgery," Detective Jordan revealed.

"They're trying to remove the bullet from his skull," Deveraux tacked on.

The idea was incomprehensible. Lark's vision blurred and her stomach, which had been tied up in knots since the two cops had taken her out of the pub, clenched. When she doubled over, Jordan grabbed a metal basin from a nearby counter and stuck it in front of her just in time.

"I'm sorry," she managed weakly, after she'd finished throwing up. She was afraid, shaken, and embarrassed.

"It happens," the detective answered matter-of-factly as he took the basin away, wetted a paper towel in the metal sink and handed it to her.

"Are you claiming you don't remember the shooting?" Deveraux asked with open skepticism. His lips were a thin blade.

Lark's mouth tasted as if she'd been sucking up Mississippi Delta mud. Her headache had turned blinding. She dragged her fingers through her hair in a nervous gesture, and flinched as they brushed over the bandaged abrasion.

"That's exactly what I'm saying," she said with a calm she was a long way from feeling.

"Yet you were seen leaving the arena with him after your show," Jordan reported. Unlike his partner's voice, there wasn't a hint of judgment in his tone.

*Concentrate!* Lark desperately tried to focus, which was difficult to do with the angry static buzz in her brain. "I remember doing the concert." The energy generated from the sold-out crowd in the New Orleans arena had been contagious.

Seven months ago she'd taken control of her life, divorcing her unfaithful husband and throwing out the flash and dazzle theatrics Cody had insisted she incorporate into her act, returning to just standing on the stage, playing her flattop acoustic guitar backed by a five-piece band. From the first concert, the revamped show had drawn raves from reviewers and fans.

"A friend of Danny's was playing in a new blues club on St. Peters," she recalled. "I was still jazzed from the show and knew I wouldn't be able to sleep. Since I never eat before a performance, I was starving. And the club's supposed to have the best ribs in town."

"It does," Jordan agreed. His dark eyes were encouraging. "What next?"

A vision swirled just barely out of reach, as if viewed through a blurry camera lens. She struggled to bring it into focus. "We took a cab to the Quarter."

She could suddenly see it so clearly: the Creole Queen blazing with lights on the Mississippi, the Café du Monde, draped in heavy sheets of yellowed plastic to protect customers from the weather, the faithful arriving at the St. Louis Cathedral for midnight mass.

"Then what?"

*Good question. Think, dammit!* Lark frowned in concentration and focused hard, which increased the stabbing pain in her head, and drew a blank.

"I don't know . . . I bought some earrings." She lifted an absent hand to her bare earlobe.

"They were put in a properties envelope when you were admitted to the ER," the cop at the door finally spoke.

"Then I went into a pub and ordered a Coke." There was no point in sharing memories of having been there with Lucas McCloud. That was so long ago, it could have been another life. "I wasn't there very long—perhaps five minutes—when two police officers arrived, told me I needed to come with them and put me in the back of their patrol car." Ice skimmed down her spine at the memory. "The blood all over my dress . . ."

She couldn't say it. Dreaded thinking it. Lark drew in a deep breath, then tried again. "Was it Danny's?"

"We won't know for certain until it gets back from the lab," Jordan said. "But since your wounds are fairly minor, the best guess is that it's the victim's blood."

*The victim.*

Surely this was some horrible nightmare! Lark squeezed her eyes shut, then opened them again, desperately hoping to find herself in bed on the bus. But she was still in this ice-cold room with laminated charts of the human body tacked onto pea-soup colored walls.

Just when she thought things couldn't get any worse, a brunette in her twenties opened the door, and the tension in the room immediately thickened.

"This is Police Officer Farrell," Jordan introduced the uniform-clad woman.

"From the Scientific Criminal Investigations Division," Deveraux added in his just-the-facts-ma'am tone.

"Or SCI, as those of us who work there refer to it." Officer Farrell's smile was the warmest Lark had witnessed from the police thus far. "I still think New Orleans would have made a lot sexier spinoff to that TV show than Miami." She placed a small kit on a wheeled table. "Our French Quarter is much more atmospheric than all those pink buildings."

"Officer Farrell will be testing you for residue," Deveraux informed Lark, brusquely cutting off the pleasantries.

"Residue?" Surely he couldn't think . . .

"Gunshot residue," Jordan explained. "It's standard police procedure to test everyone involved in a crime, Ms. Stewart. The sooner we can eliminate you as a suspect, the sooner we can go about apprehending the suspect."

His encouraging words were at direct odds with Deveraux's grim, suspicious face. Lark wondered if she should ask for an attorney, then immediately dismissed the idea. The police needed to capture whoever it was

OUT OF THE BLUE 27

who'd shot Danny, before he attacked another innocent person.

Lark felt a distant pain in her hands, looked down and saw that her nails were digging into her palms. She held out her hands palms up, as instructed, and fought for strength as she battled tears.

# 3

Knowing there'd be no more sleep tonight, Lucas went to work in his shop, an old barn built by his great-grandfather.

A few years ago, he'd begun making furniture to give himself something to do besides drink. After he'd sent a piece as a wedding present to his sister Rachel, who'd gotten herself engaged to a Wall Street banker, she'd shown off the chifforobe to all her friends. To Lucas's amazement—and occasional vexation—a demand had instantly arisen for his work.

As he planed a farm table he'd built from recycled wormy chestnut he'd found at a salvage yard in Charlotte, the phone rang. Middle-of-the-night phone calls never meant good news.

He scooped up the receiver. "McCloud."

"Lucas, this is Zelda Stewart. I'm so relieved you're home!"

"I usually am at"—he glanced at his watch—"two in the morning."

"Is it two? I was so upset, I didn't stop to calculate the time difference. I'm stuck out here on an island in the middle of the Aegean and need your help."

"My help?" He doubted he'd seen Lark's aunt more than half a dozen times in the seven years he'd been back in Highland Falls. Why the hell had she picked him, out of all the people in the county to call?

"It's Lark. She's in trouble."

He felt the blow, low and sharp, as if he'd been hit in the gut with an ax. "What kind of trouble?"

"That's just it, dammit—I don't know. But I have this dreadful feeling that something's gone terribly wrong."

Zelda Stewart's *feelings* were legend in these mountains. Born with The Sight, she was the town's only witch, now that Una Gunn had passed on a week after her one hundred-and-fourth birthday.

"I've done two readings and the tower card came up both times." She paused, as if expecting him to respond.

Lucas obliged her. "And the tower card supposedly means?"

"An unexpected shock or disaster is going to completely change my darling Lark's life."

Lucas didn't believe in second sight, Ouija boards, or any other kind of hocus-pocus. He'd also never bought into the idea of Santa Claus or the Tooth Fairy so there was no way he'd believe a deck of pretty picture cards could predict the future.

"Where is she?" he asked.

"In New Orleans. She did a Christmas Eve concert there tonight and is booked for a Christmas matinee, then another night show."

"And the reason you're calling me is?"

"You're an FBI Special Agent."

"I left the Bureau seven years ago." Actually, it had been seven years, two days, and seven hours.

"I refuse to believe you don't still have connections there. Besides, you loved my niece."

He sighed. "That was a long time ago, Zelda." And he'd been a far different man.

"Some things, time can't erase. I realize you don't get out much, but did you happen to hear that Lark's divorced?"

"That would have been hard to miss." The tabloid headlines had screamed the news at him for weeks whenever he'd gone into town to buy groceries.

"She was still with that son of a bitch Cody Armstrong when she was home for the Highland Games this past May. Which, I noticed, you didn't attend."

"I was busy."

Zelda didn't bother to challenge the statement. "She didn't say much about her marital situation while she was here, but it was obvious she was miserable." She paused. "Your name came up."

Dammit, just the idea that she'd been thinking of him caused a spike in Lucas's heartbeat. Lark had been his first love, as he'd been hers. He'd had other lovers over the years; having become an expert at hit-and-run relationships, more than he could count. But no other woman had ever touched his heart.

"There may be a lot of water under the bridge between the two of you, but I refuse to believe she's the only person with regrets," Zelda conjectured.

Lucas didn't answer.

"I don't know exactly what happened when she took

off for New Orleans to be with you before you went off to war, but anyone could tell that you broke my baby girl's heart, Lucas McCloud."

"I know." And he'd slashed his own to ribbons in the process.

"However, since I understand that you were only, in your foolish, hardheaded male way, trying to protect her, I'm willing to forgive you. Now, I need you to call the New Orleans police department," she said briskly. "No one there will tell me a blessed thing, and I can't get any information from any of the hospitals."

"Doesn't Lark have a cell phone? Did you try that?"

"Of course I did. It doesn't answer and I keep getting sent into voice mail."

"Perhaps she turned it off so no one would wake her up with a middle-of-the-night phone call."

"My memory must be going in my old age, because I don't recall you being such a smart-ass," Zelda shot back. "I know your mama brought you up better than to treat a lady with sarcasm."

"Yes, ma'am, she did," he agreed, feeling about eight years old again.

A chorus girl turned successful mystery writer, Lark's aunt Zelda was a combination of Auntie Mame and Dolly Parton. She also was the most strong-willed individual Lucas had ever met.

"Have you spoken with any of the other family members? Maybe they've heard from her," he suggested.

"I doubt it; we're scattered all over the globe this holiday. My baby girl's in trouble, Lucas, and I need you to find out why." Her usually self-assured voice wavered.

"I'm sure everything's just fine," he said. Something sounding suspiciously like a sniffle came across the long-distance line. Christ, was she crying? "But I'll call NOPD and see if they know anything."

"Thank you, darling. I knew I could count on you. Oh, and Lucas?"

He stiffened at the suddenly sympathetic tone, guessing what was coming.

"It wasn't your fault," she said softly.

Knowing there was no point in saying he had no idea what she was talking about, Lucas said nothing.

"Even as a little boy, you were always shouldering responsibility for others, but it's time you moved on," she said. "No one blames you for what happened that summer, darling. Least of all Lark. She adored you."

As he had her.

Recalling the stormy August day everything had turned dark and ugly still tore Lucas apart.

Having already taken enough strolls down memory lane for one night, he hung up.

Twenty minutes later, Lucas was sitting at the heavy kitchen table built from pine grown and harvested on McCloud land, wondering how the hell he was going to tell Zelda that not only had her niece been involved in a shooting that could have taken her life, but a call to an old friend from his days in the FBI revealed something NOPD hadn't even picked up on yet: Dr. William Guest—an anesthesiologist who'd lost his medical license after being arrested for kidnapping, assault, false imprisonment, and twice stalking Lark—had escaped from prison.

* * *

There had never been any question that William Guest would be a doctor. As soon as he could reach the faucet with a step stool, he'd been taught to scrub his hands for ten minutes with the stiff-bristled brush.

At three he was already visiting the hospital as William Senior strode down the hallways like visiting royalty with his entourage of assistants. Despite disgruntled muttering from nurses and lower-pecking-order physicians, he'd scrubbed and entered the operating room for the first time at twelve, where he'd witnessed his demanding father slam an overhead light against a resident's head for not moving fast enough.

That was the day William decided that one of the reasons his father had become a surgeon was so he could scream obscenities and throw instruments in the OR. So long as too many of Dr. William Guest's patients didn't die on the table, no one dared call him on his behavior.

During a family Thanksgiving dinner during his internship, William had made the mistake of mentioning that the chief psych resident thought that he could have a strong career in psychiatry.

His father, who'd been carving the turkey at the time, reacted with the speed that had made him the fastest closer of all the surgical residents at Johns Hopkins back in 1965. He drove the scalpel-sharp carving knife through his wife's Irish lace tablecloth, deep into the cherry wood of the table.

"No son of mine's going to become a goddamn head-shrinker," he'd bellowed. "They're all quacks and as nutty as frigging fruitcakes. Hell, I wouldn't send my dog to any one of them." A moot point, since, abhorring dirt or disorder, he'd never permitted William to have so much as a goldfish. "My son will be a surgeon. End of discussion."

As the physician swept an imperious gaze around the table at his in-laws and wife, none of whom were going to risk saying a word, William imagined pulling the knife out of the table and slicing his father's throat. The dangerous mood passed like a summer thunderstorm.

"Now, who wants white meat?" Dr. William Guest asked, unaware that in his son's fevered brain, blood was spurting from his severed jugular, turning the snowy white Irish lace tablecloth crimson.

Since he clearly had no choice about his future, William managed to complete his grueling surgery internship with the help of judicious self-medication. He was in his second year of residency, on a weekend trip home to visit his parents, when they'd both conveniently died in a house fire after his mother had fallen asleep while smoking a cigarette.

Before William Senior had even been put into the ground, his son had switched from surgery to anesthesiology. Since the patients were unconscious, he didn't have to deal with them. Also, anesthesiologists lived in a world of drugs, which made acquiring them for himself very easy.

Over the ensuing years, William had been asked to leave the staffs of various hospitals due to suspicions of drug use, but since it was considered bad manners to accuse a colleague of being an addict, he was able to take the popular "geographic cure." By moving from hospital to hospital, state to state, his past never followed him and by avoiding street drugs, he stayed clear of the law.

Until fourteen years ago, in Highland Falls, when he'd been arrested by that rube county sheriff. It wasn't as if he'd done anything wrong; after all, how could you kidnap and imprison your own wife?

He'd insisted that Lark Stewart could confirm that he—who had, by the way, given up a lucrative medical practice to center his entire life around his teenage bride—was no kidnapper. But once cops decided you were guilty, there was no reasoning with them.

He was initially charged with kidnapping, aggravated assault, and aggravated sexual assault, but fortunately his parents' death had left him a wealthy man, so a dream team of attorneys had managed to make the kidnapping charge go away. Unfortunately, a jury of ignorant, inbred mountain people found him guilty of the remaining charges, forcing him to spend the next eleven years in prison.

Six months after his release, the police, obviously on a vendetta, had burst into his Nashville home and arrested him for stalking Lark. Adding insult to injury, they released photographs of the inside of his house to reporters.

Of course the media had leaped on the story in a piranha-like feeding frenzy, forcing him to endure painful public ridicule. So he'd collected photographs of Lark Stewart—what was wrong with that?

He was her husband; it was only natural that he was her number one fan. So what if his walls were papered with images of Lark? She was away from Nashville most of the year and being able to see her in every room of the house helped ease the crushing loneliness he was forced to suffer while she was on tour.

But talking to the shrink had been like talking to a goddamn wall, making him think his father was right about them all being quacks.

While the uptight psychiatrist had kept any personal thoughts to herself, his new attorney had not minced words.

"The problem is," his lawyer said in their first meeting, "I doubt many members of her fan club have a dungeon in their basement or have cut and pasted pictures of her face, and theirs, onto naked bodies downloaded from hard-core, bondage porn sites, to make her look like their sexual slave.

"That, in itself, is not against the law," the lawyer droned on, "so long as the photos are for personal use and local jurisdictions don't make such sites illegal—which, by the way, some in Tennessee do. Where you got into trouble, Dr. Guest, along with violating the conditions of your parole by contacting Lark Stewart in the first place, was using the U.S. postal service and email to send those altered pictures to Ms. Stewart. That's a clear violation of the Interstate Stalking Act."

"You can't stalk your own wife," he insisted.

"There's never been a marriage license issued in any state of the union for you and Lark Stewart. And do you have an excuse for that pistol in your jacket when her security guards stopped you from going onto her bus?"

"It's a rough city. I was merely protecting her when those goons got in the way."

That's what a husband did, after all. Protect his wife.

He'd dedicated his life to Lark. And how had she demonstrated her appreciation? By swearing on the Bible that he'd been harassing her.

The first time she'd testified against him, he'd been willing to give her the benefit of the doubt. After all, she was just a teenager, who might not understand the sanctity of marriage. Especially one that hadn't been consummated, thanks to the untimely arrival of the sheriff and that crazy McCloud kid—who'd attacked him like a rabid dog. She just needed more training. More discipline.

But as he'd watched the cool young woman she'd become testify at his second trial in Nashville, William had seethed with rage. How could she betray him yet again?

He'd first seen Lark while lying on a motel bed in Knoxville, where he'd been attending a medical conference at the University of Tennessee, channel surfing as he drifted on a cloud of fentanyl scored from an appendectomy. A local news program was promoting a pretty young singer from Highland Falls with one of those corny "day in the life" bios.

He'd been about to flip past the broadcast when she pulled a carton of orange juice from her home refrigerator. Stunned, he'd sat bolt upright in bed, the shock of recognition scorching through his floating drug haze.

*Oh my God! Tropicana was the same brand he used! Without pulp!*

As he stared at the screen, Lark Stewart's remarkable golden eyes locked on to his, sending him a secret message.

*You're the man I've spent my entire life looking for, William. A powerful man who'll take care of me, protect me, and love me in exchange for my absolute devotion. Can you feel that we're soulmates? Destined to spend eternity together?*

"Oh, yes."

He'd wasted thousands of dollars on women paid to play submissive to his dominant. But when the discipline sessions ended, instead of feeling powerful, William was left increasingly frustrated.

Now that he'd finally found his sweet, innocent, little girl, he would become Lark Stewart's protector. He'd mold her, encourage her to bloom under his care like a flower that turns toward the sun for warmth, and when she became a star, he'd not only be her Master, he'd be her Number One Fan.

The moment the clip ended, he began haphazardly tossing clothes into a suitcase. Two hours later, he'd reached Highland Falls.

Unfortunately, things didn't go exactly as planned. Mistakes were made. But the long hours spent locked in a cell did give him more time to focus on his wife and to figure out a way to prove to her that fate had determined they'd be together.

During his first incarceration, he'd also learned that prison worked on the same sort of hierarchy as a hospital. The trick to success was to make friends in high places. So, the second time he was railroaded behind bars, he knew that as distasteful as it was to mingle with convict trash, he had to begin networking.

Next on his agenda would be using those contacts—and his inherited wealth—to escape from the hellhole of his prison cell.

Then, once he was free, he was going to teach his naughty little wife the meaning of "Until death us do part."

# 4

Seven years ago, suffering the mother of all hangovers, Lucas had walked into the CIRG—Critical Incident Response Group—offices at the FBI Academy in Quantico, Virginia, and surrendered his shield.

Then he'd listed his Stafford condo with a real estate agent and headed southwest to Tennessee.

To call the old McCloud farmhouse a wreck would have been charitable. Most of the windows had been broken out, the porch had rotted into the ground, and the chimney was crumbling. The inside was worse. The musty odor of mildew assaulted him as soon as he opened the door, the chestnut floors were as black and sticky as tar, and he could see the sky through the holes in the roof. The empty beer cans littering the filthy floor, and the obscenities scrawled on the rain-streaked walls were evidence that kids from town had been using the farmhouse as a hangout.

Lucas hadn't cared. Exhausted from driving straight through from Virginia, he'd tossed a sleeping bag onto the floor and pulled a bottle from the wooden case of Highlander's Pride he'd bought in town. Determined to drown the horrific images in his mind, he'd set about getting plastered with the same steely determination he'd once used to set up a sniper shot.

Eventually, many cases of Highlander's later, he'd quit cold turkey. He'd been on the wagon for two years, but what if he'd lost his edge? How could he ask Lark to trust him? How could he trust himself?

There'd been those in the Bureau who'd called him "Lupus McCloud" because of his lone-wolf tendencies. He'd never been all that good at playing with others. But now, for Lark, he'd try.

Unfortunately, he ran into a brick wall when he called the FBI field office in Louisiana. "We're up to our federal asses in alligators trying to protect the Port of New Orleans and all the refineries from terrorism attacks," the Special Agent in Charge said.

"Lark Stewart's already in the hospital with injuries from one attack. You *do* realize that your federal asses will be in a sling if she ends up getting killed in your fair city."

"Look, McCloud, I know you're not the kind to over-dramatize and I can appreciate your situation here, even if it's not real clear to me why you've gotten yourself involved." He paused, waiting for Lucas to fill in the conversational gap, which might work on civilians, but not with a guy who knew the drill.

The silence stretched. The SAC was the first to break it. "If Stewart's stalker had ties to any known terrorist cells, she'd be higher on the priority list. As the situation stands, we're just too short-staffed to take on a stalking case."

Since the first thing every FBI recruit learned was the phrase "the needs of the Bureau," Lucas wasn't all that surprised by the lack of support. "Ever hear of a little thing called U.S.C. 2261A?"

"Sure, the Interstate Stalking Act. I've got a wife and two daughters and can't count the number of gray hairs I've gotten worrying about the twins since they went off to college. But I've also read NCAVC's report to Congress, stating that one in twenty American women will be stalked in their lifetime. There's no way we can provide personal security for them all. Not to mention the fact we haven't gotten a call from NOPD asking us to even drop by the murder scene."

Lucas abruptly cut the conversation short and called NOPD, where the police chief was at least politically motivated enough not to want to risk a Red Ball celebrity murder case in his jurisdiction, and agreed to provide a cop to guard Lark's hospital room.

Then he went back out to his shop, unlocked a steel locker, and retrieved a metal box, which he put down on his tool bench. He sat down on a stool and stared at it for a long time. The winter woods were silent, the only sounds the *tick, tick, tick* of his watch's sweep hand and the tapping of rain on the old tin roof.

Finally he opened the padlock and, feeling a lot like Gary Cooper when he'd reluctantly pinned on that tin marshal's star again in *High Noon*, Lucas lifted the Glock he'd never planned to touch again from the box. Looked like he was going to Louisiana.

A steady drizzle fell from low, dark clouds outside Lark's hospital room window. In contrast to the gloomy weather, a peal of church bells sounded throughout the city.

"I've been going out of my mind with worry ever since the police called the hotel," Ryan Glazer said. Utilizing the talents that made him a good road manager, he'd brought a bag of Lark's CDs to the hospital, which he'd used to bribe his way past the No Visitors sign on her door. "Are you sure you're all right? That fugue thing sounds awfully vague. I think we should call in some specialists and get a second opinion."

"I spent the night with more specialists than you can shake a stick at."

"But you still don't know what happened after you left the arena?"

"No." Lark shook her head. "God, I still can't believe someone shot Danny. It's driving me crazy that I can't remember what happened."

The night floor nurse was a fan who'd kept her updated on his condition. Fortunately, the surgery had been successful, he'd been moved from the operating room to the Surgical Intensive Care Unit, and while head injuries were always iffy, the neurosurgeon was optimistic.

"You were going to go see a friend of his perform at some blues club in the Quarter," Ryan prompted helpfully. "The rest of the guys went to a strip club on Bourbon Street."

"The rest of the guys including you?"

A faint red flush rose on his neck. "I've never been that wild about the blues," he said offhandedly. "Since I've never been to New Orleans before, I figured I might as well check out the tourist attractions."

"And we both know how much you enjoy local color." He was always reading tour books on the bus.

"Absolutely. Besides, I was merely getting into the spirit of the season—it was a special holiday extravaganza featuring Kandy Kane and Holly Body."

Lark almost smiled. "Nothing says Christmas like a naked pole dancer."

"My thoughts exactly." He almost smiled back, then sobered. "Damn, you've no idea how I wish I'd gone with you and Danny."

"I'm glad you didn't. You could have been shot as well." She paused, summoning up the nerve to ask the question she'd been afraid to pose to the two detectives. "You don't think the police could possibly believe I shot Danny?"

"Of course not." There was not a hint of equivocation in his tone.

She wanted to believe that, but something in his blue eyes set off alarms. "What are you not telling me?"

He pressed his lips together. She could see the wheels turning in his head. "Ryan." She rubbed her suddenly tingling palms on the scratchy top sheet. "Give."

"Okay." The shoulders beneath his body-hugging black silk T-shirt shifted uncomfortably. Ryan Glazer had worked for her for eighteen months, been her road manager for seven, and Lark could count the number of times on one hand she'd seen him nervous. This was one of them. He exhaled a deep breath. "They asked about Cody."

"What about Cody?"

"About the audit."

"How did they know about that? As a matter of fact, how do *you* know about it?" The audit, which was due after the first of the year, was supposed to be confidential.

"You know how it is. Word gets around." He slipped his hands into the front pocket of jeans creased sharp enough to cut crystal. "It's hard to keep secrets when everyone's living in each other's pockets the way we do. Skye McIntyre has called you three times in the past two weeks, and since all the guys know Armstrong had sticky fingers, everyone just figured Skye found something suspicious in the books."

Skye McIntyre was Lark's accountant. Concerned about Cody's honesty herself, Lark had asked her to conduct an audit. "Interesting that none of the guys thought to share that information with me."

He shrugged again. "He was your husband. We all just figured you decided to look the other way, like with . . ." He closed his mouth, but not before the damage was done.

"Like with his women."

Visibly uneasy, Ryan jingled some change in his pocket. "Shit, Lark. I'm sorry. I know the guy's a sore subject."

"Let's just say he isn't my favorite topic of conversation," she said mildly. Another thought occurred to her. "Did they say anything that led you to believe he's a suspect?"

"No."

"Good. Because Cody is a lot of things, but he'd never try to kill anyone, and I'd hate for the police to waste time investigating him while the real shooter gets away. Dammit, I wish I could remember something." She raked her hands through shoulder-length chestnut hair that needed washing. "Maybe if I go down to the Quarter, something will come back to me."

"You've had a head injury. The doctor said you need to remain under observation for twenty-four hours."

"So come with me, and add observing me to all those other jobs you do so brilliantly."

"Dammit, Lark, isn't Danny being shot tragedy enough? I don't want you running off half-cocked and having a brain hemorrhage."

"I hardly believe that would happen."

"I'll bet Danny didn't believe he was going to end up with a bullet in his skull when the two of you headed off to that club, either."

That hurt. Lark sagged back against the pillow and dragged her hands down her face. The air in the room suddenly became charged. Lark glanced up, then drew in a sharp breath when she saw her own personal Ghost of Christmas Past standing in the open doorway.

# 5

The good news to Lucas was the uniformed cop, who would have looked right at home on the defensive line of the New Orleans Saints, seated outside Lark's room. The bad news was that the guy was so deeply engrossed in the wonders of nature portrayed in the annual *Sports Illustrated* swimsuit edition, Lucas doubted he'd notice if an entire team of stalkers marched right past him.

Forgoing the temptation to kick the chair legs out from under the guy, Lucas entered the room.

"Lucas?" Lark stared up at him.

"It's been a long time."

*Great opening line.* Relationships had never been one of his strong suits, but taking out bad guys with a Remington sniper rifle hadn't required people skills. And the city slickers who bought his furniture didn't mind that he refused to shmooze them. On the contrary, his sister told him that the ruder he was, the more "artistic" people found him. *Go figure.*

"You always were the master of understatement." Lark's eyes sparked with temper, which wasn't surprising, given what he'd done to her. "What are you doing here?"

"I don't suppose you'd believe I was in the neighborhood."

"Not on a bet." She gave him a very unLark-like look of disdain. "Look, Lucas, my guitarist, whom I loved like a brother, was shot in cold blood last night; I was tested for gunshot residue—"

"That's standard operating procedure. To eliminate—"

"Suspects so the cops can focus on finding the guilty party," she cut him off. "So I was told. But that didn't make the experience any less stressful. I've also got a frustrating case of amnesia that the doctors tell me will probably go away with time, but might not, which is preventing me from helping the police capture Danny's shooter. So I'd appreciate it if you'd just get to the bottom line and tell me why, of all the hospital rooms in all the world, you showed up in mine."

Lucas was surprised. And impressed. The Lark he'd known could be far more stubborn than her spun-glass appearance suggested, but she'd never been so blunt. Her voice, amazingly steady for all she'd been through in the past hours, belied the emotions swirling like smoke in her eyes, reminding him that of the three Stewart sisters, she'd always been the most complex.

Laurel, the quintessential firstborn, had inherited her father's pit-bull tendencies and was so outspoken, she could make Lucas's brusque manner seem warm and fuzzy by comparison. He almost pitied any congressman grilled by the *Washington Post*'s rising-star political reporter.

Lily, the baby of the family, had been the perky sister, with her cheerleader looks, friendly personality, and emotions as open as her warm and generous heart. She'd been the family nurturer, the one people had turned to in times of trouble.

Lark was the most introverted, yet she'd chosen a career that required her to go on stage and sing before thousands of strangers. With her sisters, what you saw was what you got. Lark had always kept her thoughts and feelings deep inside her, revealing them only to a chosen few.

He'd once belonged to that privileged group, before things had gone so wrong. Before he'd thrown her love away. Yet even with the 20/20 vision of hindsight, given the same circumstances, he'd do the same damn thing again.

"You've gotten tougher."

She folded her arms. "I've had to," she said simply. "Now, you're here because?"

"Zelda called me. She's worried about you."

"My aunt's on a ship in the Aegean." Her brows lowered over those remarkable whiskey-colored eyes. "And why would she call you?"

Definitely tougher, and damned if it didn't look good on her. "She had one of her feelings that something was wrong and hoped that with my Bureau ties, I could find out more about the shooting than CNN is reporting."

"CNN is reporting the shooting?"

"You've been the lead story on *Headline News* for the past eight hours," the man, who'd remained silent until now, informed her.

Lark shot a lethal, dagger-sharp look at a guy who looked like a life-size Ken doll in his trendy, black silk

T-shirt, pressed jeans and pearlized, ostrich skin cowboy boots that looked as if they'd never stepped in manure.

"I thought you shouldn't have to worry about the press with all you had to deal with," he said a little too smoothly. "The doctor and I held a press conference about an hour ago, assuring people your injuries were minor and that your thoughts and prayers were with Danny. Then I asked the media and your fans to respect your privacy."

Lucas waited for this new gutsy Lark to take the guy's head off for having not only kept something vital from her, but for having spoken on her behalf. Once again, she surprised him. "Thank you, Ryan. That was the perfect response. I suppose I'll have to make a statement, but I'm not really up to answering questions right now. Though now that the news has broken, I'd better start tracking down my gypsy family."

"Figuring you'd want to call them on Christmas, I took care of that a few days ago." He retrieved his PDA from the pocket of a shearling-lined suede jacket lying over the back of a chair, and tapped a few keys. "Lily's off on some unpronounceable North Sea island off the coast of Wales—"

"Hapus Marchoges Ynys," Lark supplied. "She and Ian are making a documentary about the matriarchal government's plan to cast spells, to stop NATO from conducting bombing runs there."

"Talk about tilting at windmills," Ryan muttered.

Lucas, who hated to think he and Dapper Dan might have anything in common, silently agreed.

"Your grandmother Annie's in Scotland, your father

and Jenny are in Hawaii, and Laurel's in Afghanistan covering the president's Christmas visit to the peace-keeping troops. Your aunt Melanie's in Charlotte, and your cousin Missy is spending the holidays with her father in Knoxville. I gave the numbers to the hospital switchboard operator, who's prepared to place the calls as soon as you feel up to talking with everyone."

"Whatever would I do without you?" Lark held up a bruised and scraped hand. "No, don't answer that. I don't want to even imagine the possibility."

Her fond smile chilled considerably as she turned back to Lucas. "I hate that Zelda was needlessly upset. With all that's happening around the world, you'd think the press would have something else to report."

"The media thrives on celebrity," Lucas pointed out. "But, like I said, she was upset before the news bulletins. She sensed something was wrong and asked me to track it down. And you did drop to second place behind an ice storm in Buffalo, but you'll probably regain the top spot as soon as some reporter uncovers the fact that your stalker's on the loose again."

Lark's hand flew to her breast. When she turned as white as the hospital sheets, Lucas realized this was yet another thing she hadn't known. Fear flashed in eyes that appeared even larger in her pale face due to the bruising of fatigue beneath them.

She dragged her hand through her hair, which, cut to skim her shoulders, was about eighteen inches shorter than it had been last time he'd seen her. The look, like the atti-tude, suited her. It was more grown-up, more sophisticated.

"William Guest was released?"

"Not released. Escaped."

Impossibly, she turned even paler. "How? When?"

"Nearly two weeks ago."

Ryan whatever-his-last-name-was exploded. "A stalker who kidnapped Lark, terrorized her, sent hundreds of threatening letters, emails, and sick, doctored sexual photographs has been on the loose for two frigging weeks and we weren't notified?"

We? Lucas wondered if Lark and the Ken doll were an item, then told himself it was none of his business.

"Apparently, as the warden said, mistakes were made," he said dryly. He had put his fist through his kitchen wall when he'd heard about Guest's escape. "And you are?"

"I'm sorry, I should have introduced you," Lark said distractedly. "Ryan, this is Lucas McCloud, from home. Lucas, this is Ryan Glazer, my road manager and one of my best friends."

A distinction that had once belonged to him. Even though he'd long ago thrown away any right to be jealous of any guy Lark was involved with, Lucas felt a sudden urge to throw Glazer out the window.

"How on earth did he escape?" she asked.

"Fairly easily, as it turns out. He was in a work-release program, assigned a job as an aide in a low-income nursing home, and just walked away."

"They put a psychopath like that on work-release?" Glazer's face had turned as red as a Roman candle; he looked on the verge of exploding.

Lucas knew the feeling.

"Six months ago, he petitioned the court for a new psych exam. The upshot was that he got himself labeled an antisocial personality rather than his original psychopathy diagnosis."

"What's the damn difference?" Glazer demanded.

"According to a former FBI profiler I checked with, while most criminals meet the criteria for antisocial personality disorder, the majority are *not* psychopaths. There's also another huge category of people who are psychopathic, but never get arrested."

"That's bullshit." Glazer raked a hand over a haircut which, if cut at James MacDougall's barbershop in Highland Falls, would probably be called a crew cut. Lucas suspected this spiky style, which was undoubtedly viewed as retro-something, cost a lot more than the ten bucks MacDougall had been charging for the past two decades. "You don't need a degree in psychiatry to know Guest's a dangerous psychopath."

"It wouldn't have been that hard for the guy to get hold of the test and figure out how to skew the results. Finn Callahan, the profiler, told me about an inmate in Oklahoma who got his hands on two different sets of tests, set up a consulting business in the prison library, and for a fee, coached other prisoners how to slant their responses to the questions.

"His medical degree also gives Guest skills not generally found in a prison population. Since he's supposedly been a model prisoner, it's not all that surprising that he got put into the work-release program."

Glazer cursed, then glanced toward the door. "I suppose this explains the cop out in the hallway."

"There's a police officer outside my door?" Lark was clearly surprised.

"I felt it'd be a good idea, given the circumstances," Lucas said.

"That's it," Ryan said. "I was going to bring this up to you before McCloud showed up, but I think we ought to cancel tomorrow night's show."

She shook her head, then flinched, as if wishing she hadn't. "Not on a bet. Unfortunately, since the doctor's refusing to release me until evening rounds, we're probably going to have to offer refunds for this afternoon's Christmas show, but tomorrow night I'm going to be up there on stage. As promised."

"Nothing like carrying 'the show must gone on' slogan to extremes," Lucas volunteered dryly.

"I beg your pardon?" Despite her bruises, even fighting the pain he could see in her eyes, she could have been a duchess, putting an errant footman in his place. "It must be the amnesia that has me not recalling anyone asking you for your opinion."

*Too bad, because you're damn well going to get it anyway.*

He may have been a sniper, but during his stint in the Bureau, he'd picked up some negotiating skills. Suspecting that laying down the law would only get her back up more, he folded his arms and tried a different tack.

"I doubt your doctor would like the idea of your dancing all around a stage with a class three concussion."

"And *I'd* like to back up the clock ten hours." Her smile was as brisk as the wintry day outside the window. "Looks as if neither of us are going to get what we want. And I quit dancing all around the stage when I decided I wasn't going to let anyone else make decisions for me anymore."

Glazer's openly curious gaze had shifted from Lark to Lucas, then back to Lark. He cleared his throat.

"Uh, I've already taken care of canceling today," he said with the caution of a guy walking through a conversational minefield. "If you're going to insist on performing—which is certainly your call," he said quickly, raising both his hands, warding off any verbal grenades Lark might lob his way, "I'll get on the phone to the security company we used at the arena and hire an off-duty cop for additional protection until we leave town."

She frowned at that suggestion. "I can't believe that's necessary. We don't even know where William Guest is. Surely he'd know that the police would be expecting him to come here. Wouldn't it be only logical that he'd take off in an entirely different direction?"

"There's just one problem with that reasoning," Lucas said.

"Which I'm sure you're about to share with me," she invited.

She wasn't going to make it easy on him. Hell, Lucas didn't blame her. "Delusional stalkers aren't logical. According to Callahan, they can go on for years fixated on one person." She may not want his opinion about going on with her show, but about this, she was damn well going to listen. "Putting them behind bars keeps them away from their victims, but they have a lot more time to fantasize."

"Which Guest was obviously doing." Lark seemingly put aside her aggravation with him long enough to consider the idea. "Since he started sending those letters as soon as he was released from prison."

"He's turning out to be a textbook case, all right. His new shrink probably thought spending several hours a week doing something useful would help direct his thoughts away from you."

She leaned back against the stacked pillows. "Do you think that's possible?"

Lucas had lied to her once before. He wasn't going to this time. "No. I think the guy's a wacko drug addict who should be locked up for the rest of his life. Especially since male stalkers tend to become increasingly violent over time."

"That's it," Glazer said abruptly. "This is *your* life we're talking about, Lark. What if the guy in Pirate's Alley was Guest? What if the son of a bitch was aiming for you, and hit Danny by mistake? Why shouldn't we believe he'd try again?"

"Surely you can't believe . . ." Her voice faded and Lucas could see her take another hit as she considered the unsavory possibility. "All these years, he's never threatened my life. The kidnapping was horrific and those letters and photographs were ugly and unnerving, but the only thing he's ever said—and kept saying—was that he believes I'm his wife."

"Unfortunately, men have been known to kill their wives," Lucas pointed out. "Peeping Toms and stalkers often escalate into murderers. And even if they don't, delusional erotomaniac stalkers—and Guest is obviously one of those—create an elaborate fantasy life and hang on tight to their delusions. They also tend to believe that they're above the law, since they answer to a higher power."

"Their own perversity," Glazer suggested.

"It's the center of the universe," Lucas agreed, not taking his eyes from Lark's. "Hell, over time it becomes their *entire* universe. Guest undoubtedly viewed your testimony in his trials as betrayal. Then, if he saw you out on the town with another man—".

"Danny's a friend."

"Friendship can cover a lot of ground, intimacy-wise."

"Okay, to be more specific, we're intimate friends," she allowed. "But we were never lovers."

"Guest's a nutcase who believes you're his wife because you spoke to him from the television and your song lyrics," Lucas snapped as temper, triggered by concern, whipped through him. "He's also an S&M freak with a dungeon in his basement—which I don't need to be a hotshot profiler to guess he built just for you." The more he thought about the sicko fantasizing his dirty little scenarios about Lark, the more he wanted to track the bastard down and beat him to a bloody pulp. And that was just for openers. "Do you really think he's going to make that distinction?"

"The police seemed to believe the shooting was a random street crime." There was reluctant, but growing doubt in Lark's voice.

"It could have been random," Lucas allowed. His gut, which he'd learned to trust, said otherwise. So had Callahan's. "But it's just as likely—maybe even more so—that you were the target and Guest's a lousy shot."

"Well, that's a pleasant thought." She pressed her fingertips tightly against her temples as if willing her memory to return.

Lucas watched, with admiration, as she pulled herself together again.

"That horrible man turned me into an emotional hostage," she said, her voice edged with a flinty determination. "Not just once, but twice." Her eyes blazed with a fire he'd only ever witnessed from her when they'd been making love. "I'm not going to let that happen again."

"That's my girl," Glazer said. He began massaging her shoulder as if he had every right to touch her. Lucas wondered where else on Lark's too-slender body those hands had been. "I'll call the company right away and arrange for bodyguards for as long as you're here."

"There's no need to call in additional security," Lucas said. "That's what I'm here for."

Glazer gave him a sweeping glance. "No offense intended, McCloud, but why should we believe you're up to the job?"

"I'm former FBI, I have a gun, and I know how to use it." He pushed aside his leather bomber jacket to reveal his shoulder holster.

Lucas had never planned to strap his weapon on again, but had also never been able to get rid of it. He suspected that Zelda would tell him that fate was playing a hand here, that he'd been destined to use it to protect the only woman he'd ever loved.

"I want to believe you and Ryan are overreacting," Lark said. "It *has* to have been a random crime. Danny and I were merely in the wrong place at the wrong time."

"In the interest of full disclosure, right now the cops tend to agree with you. There's no evidence your friend's shooting had anything to do with Guest's escape."

"You sound as if you don't agree."

"I've never trusted coincidence. Meanwhile, I'm not going anywhere. And neither are you." Lucas folded his arms and held firm. "I promised Zelda I'd bring you back home safely. And that's exactly what I intend to do." Then, mission accomplished, he could return to his comfortable life of isolation. "But don't worry, Duchess, you won't even know I'm around."

Lark seriously doubted that. Church bells continued to peal throughout the city, a joyous contrast to the fear gripping her heart. The feeling that she'd stumbled into some dark, parallel universe had turned absolutely surrealistic when Lucas had suddenly appeared in the doorway of her hospital room.

Except for the latent danger surrounding him like a force field, physically, he hadn't changed all that much: his body looked as hard as ever, but his jet hair, a legacy of his Irish and Cherokee roots, was longer than when she'd last been with him. His face was hard and his eyes were too old for his age. The tightness around them suggested he could be as mean as he needed to be, making her wonder what they'd seen.

Once upon a time, in another lifetime, Lucas had been her dearest friend. She'd been three years old the winter her mother died in childbirth during a mountain blizzard; Callie Stewart had been much beloved and many tears were shed by grieving townspeople during the funeral mass.

Lark had been confused and frightened when John Angus Stewart—who'd always reminded her of the giants in fairy tales, but her daddy was much more fun—collapsed on the short walk to the family cemetery and had to be physically supported by her uncles as they made their way past snow-dusted tombstones while sleet fell on the mountains from a low, dark December sky.

She wanted to run to him, to wrap her arms around her daddy's strong legs and sob herself, but her aunt Melanie, who'd rushed to Highland Falls from her home in North Carolina, had squeezed her hand. Not in comfort, but warning.

"Don't cry, baby," her mother's sister had instructed, the sugar of her southern drawl laced with cold hard steel. "It won't bring your mama back and there's no point in upsetting people more than they already are."

When Lark realized that they were going to put that pearly white box her mama was sleeping in into the frozen ground, the tears burning at the back of her lids began to flow. She'd been on the verge of throwing herself into that deep hole, when a boy just a few months older than she, with sad but comforting eyes the color of the darkest night, shook loose of his mother's hand, broke away from the group of townspeople who'd gathered to pay their last respects, and silently took her mittened hand in his bare one. At that moment, Lark had known that she'd be all right because Lucas McCloud would protect her.

Falling in love with him thirteen years later had been a glorious surprise. But even before that halcyon summer when her newly discovered feelings had blazed like a newborn sun, Lark had never contemplated a life without Lucas in it, because she knew he'd always be there for her.

Unfortunately, she'd been wrong. It hadn't been easy, especially after their New Orleans reunion when she'd believed she'd finally broken down those high, stone walls he'd built around his heart, and then he'd left her again.

And now, against all odds, Lucas was back.

The difference was this time Lark felt far from safe.

# 6

Thanks to careful planning, big bucks transferred into the accounts of two guards by a new attorney who was prone to looking the other way, plus fortuitously lax supervision during the prisoner work-release, William was no longer behind bars. That was the good news.

The bad news was that the clothes waiting for him were definitely lacking in style. Since he'd certainly paid enough, it was obvious he'd been cheated. Yet another instance of the lack of control in prison.

Once he'd escaped from under his father's bullying thumb, he'd always been successful in controlling his environment. Which was further proof, he'd explained to that quack of a prison shrink, that he couldn't be suffering from erotomania. By definition, erotomaniacs were mentally ill, horridly disorganized, and delusional. Would a mentally ill person be able to keep such detailed journals, chronicling every moment of his days? *I don't think so.*

The genius was that not only did he write his journal entries in secret code, he printed the letters so small that even if someone did get lucky and stumble on the key to the code, even the strongest magnifying glass in the world couldn't decipher the writing.

After parking in the lot of the Lakeside Shopping Center in Metaire, Louisiana, he took out the leather-bound journal. *Six thirty-two, p.m.* It was already dark but the battery-operated light on his pen allowed him to make the entry. *Arrived at mall. Intend to spend thirty-seven minutes shopping, which, allowing four minutes to walk to the store entrance, will have me back here at seven-sixteen p.m.*

He was priding himself on having entered Dillards at precisely six thirty-six, right on schedule, when a slim, leggy brunette appeared from behind a rack of men's sportswear and began walking toward him.

"May I help you?" The dulcet tones sounded remarkably like Lark's musical voice. The silver heart around her neck was a duplicate of the one he'd bought for their first anniversary. It came with a silver key, which William had kept for himself.

A thought flashed through his mind.

He'd been giving a great deal of thought to the idea of murder since that second time Lark had testified against him and had come to the conclusion that killing a person was a great deal like practicing medicine: both required calm hands, sure judgment, courage, and confidence.

Cutting open a human being was, at its most elemental, a primitive, brutal act. If an ordinary man stabbed a knife into another man's belly, he'd be convicted of murder and sent to prison. Yet William had been part of a surgical team hundreds of times when a physician wielding a scalpel did exactly that. The difference, he decided, was in the intent.

There was also the inescapable truth that human nature finds evil alluring. What man didn't secretly yearn to escape, as the prison shrink referred to it, his "internal policeman" and experience a full, unfettered life without society's controls?

His first month in prison, he'd witnessed the killing of one convict by another in the recreation yard over a carton of cigarettes. It had only taken an instant—the quick slash of a throat with a boning knife—but the high he'd gotten from watching that fleeting moment of power was stronger than any he'd ever achieved from drugs.

Murder, like learning to inject anesthesia into a vein, undoubtedly took practice. And who better to practice on than this woman who, if you took her out of that ugly navy blazer and put her in something more flattering, could almost pass for Lark Stewart?

"You're very efficient," he said as she raced around the men's department, gathering up clothes for him to try on.

"Thanks, I have to be. I'm working here to put myself through nursing college and it takes organization to juggle both balls." She flashed a smile as she handed him a package of briefs. "I graduate this June."

"Congratulations." Evie—named after Longfellow's Evangeline, she cheerfully informed him—was, indeed, like him, a very organized person. It would serve her well in the nursing profession, if she lived long enough to graduate. Which, if he had anything to say about it—and guess what! He did!—she wouldn't.

He charged a black suit, two white shirts, a muted gray tie, a Ralph Lauren cashmere scarf, a black sweater, two pairs of jeans, a leather jacket and pants, and assorted underwear on a credit card he'd been assured would be valid for the next thirty days.

After Evie had rung up the sale, he surreptitiously followed her to the second-floor restaurant where she ate alone, engrossed in a thick book.

Not wanting to make a mistake by rushing into murder without proper planning, he trailed her for the next few nights, chronicling her every move in his journal. Except for Christmas Day, which she spent with her family, he could have set his watch by her.

Assured that she'd stick to her schedule on his last night in New Orleans, he pulled his anonymous, black Ford Taurus rental up to her aging blue Honda Civic with the Nurses Make It Better sticker on its rusting bumper. He dropped a Ping-Pong ball—which he'd been assured would be sucked into the fuel line after she'd driven a few miles, then parked two rows away, outside the yellow glow of the parking lot light. And waited.

There were still two hours left until the store closed, but one thing he'd learned in prison was patience.

*Soon*, he promised himself.

Lark nearly burst into song when the neurologist finally showed up at evening rounds and signed her release.

"Turn your back," she instructed Lucas before getting out of the bed wearing the ugly hospital gown. True to his word, he hadn't left the room, his hulking silent presence intimidating doctors and nurses alike; even the NOPD patrolman stationed outside her door appeared more than a little cowed. Of course, that might have had something to do with the fact that Lucas had taken away his chair.

His gaze skimmed over her before he turned toward the door. "We grew up skinny-dipping," he reminded her. "I've seen your naked butt before."

"That doesn't count. We were kids then. And you threw away the right to see any part of my body naked a very long time ago."

Holding the gap in the gown closed with one hand, she picked up the overnight case Ryan had brought to the hospital and went into the adjoining broom closet-size bathroom to change.

Lark groaned when she viewed her reflection in the mirror over the sink. Her hair needed washing, she had two white butterfly bandages across her temple, and the deep purple shadows beneath her eyes looked like bruises. Actual bruises marred her forehead, her chin, and her right cheek; an angry scrape ran up her left. She'd inherited fair skin from her Scots Stewart ancestors, but her pallor now reminded her of Morticia Addams.

She was a mess. Ryan had also brought her makeup bag, but since she'd have to plaster her face with spackle to cover the bruises, she settled for a bit of strawberry-flavored lip gloss.

"Where's Ryan?" she asked when she came out of the room and found herself alone with Lucas.

"He went back to the hotel to let your band members know you're okay."

"I'm glad. He told me they all showed up earlier, while I was downstairs getting more tests, but the police wouldn't let them into my room to visit."

"People with head injuries don't need a lot of visitors. And guarding a witness is standard operating procedures in a high-profile case like this."

"I suppose so." She'd have to take his word for that, having never been involved in even a low-profile police case before. "Of course, I suppose the same could be said for guarding a suspect."

"True."

It was obvious that subtlety wasn't going to work here. "Is that what they're doing?" she asked the difficult question. "Do they suspect me of having anything to do with Danny's shooting?"

Dearly hoping he'd immediately give her the same supportive answer Ryan had, she was disappointed when Lucas merely shrugged. "Cops suspect everyone. It's in their nature."

"Is that a *yes* to me being a serious suspect? Or a *no?*"

"While they're not sharing the details of their investigation with me, I'd guess probably no, since you obviously didn't beat yourself up and from what I could tell, the guy doesn't have any defensive wounds that would indicate a struggle."

"You've seen him?" That was a surprise.

"When I first got here."

"Why?"

"Why do you think? To see if he could identify his shooter."

"He's only a few hours out of surgery." She had to ask. "Could he?"

"Not while I was there." He paused a beat. "He appeared to be unconscious."

"I thought he'd gotten through the surgery without any trouble."

"Yeah. That's what the doctor told me. But apparently he's developed complications."

"What kind of complications?"

"Some brain swelling."

"Oh, God." Could this get any worse? She flinched and wrapped her arms around herself. Something else he'd said sunk in. "What do you mean, 'appeared' to be unconscious?"

Lucas didn't immediately respond. He didn't have to. Lark was beginning to get a handle on how this new, armed, and edgier Lucas's mind worked. "Are you suggesting that you actually believe anyone could fake being unconscious in a hospital SICU?"

"Mind over body control isn't that unusual. It's possible to control your heartbeat, temperature, hell, there are even swamis who've been proven able to control their brain waves."

"Danny isn't a swami; he's a guitar player from Middle Tennessee. And even if he could pull off something like that, why on earth would he want to?"

"How the hell would I know? I *do* know there's no limit to peoples' innovation when it comes to crime."

If he actually believed that, she'd been wrong about beginning to understand him. He'd always kept things inside, but somewhere behind those emotional barricades had been a warm and caring heart. "You don't trust anyone, do you?"

"Not really." He took her overnight case from her hand and cupped her elbow. "Let's go."

She dug in her heels when he headed toward the door. "If that's really true, then it's one of the saddest things I've ever heard." She also couldn't quite decide whether or not to be annoyed or hurt that he might be including her in that sweeping statement.

"Then consider yourself lucky to have lived such a sheltered life, Duchess," he shot back. "Because in the real world, it wouldn't even make the top hundred."

"Just because I grew up in a castle doesn't mean I haven't experienced the real world," she reminded him quietly.

She knew they were thinking about the same thing—that sizzling August day Guest had come into her life—when his fingers tightened on her elbow. A sudden, deadly fierceness blazed in his eyes.

"Yeah. You have." Lucas's grip gentled. He blew out a long breath. "Now, since you've been complaining about wanting to get out of here, let's go."

"I'm not leaving until I see Danny."

"Dammit, Lark—"

"You got to see him," she reminded him pointedly. "Besides, you're the one who brought up mind over body. Maybe if he hears the voice of someone he knows, someone who loves him—"

"Anyone ever tell you that you're lousy at taking orders?" he gruffly cut her off.

"I've worked at it," she said sweetly. If he only knew how hard. "So perhaps you ought to stop barking them out like some marine drill sergeant."

"Drill instructor," he corrected.

"What?"

"Drill sergeants are army."

"Surely there are sergeants who are drill instructors in the marines."

"Sure. But they're not called drill sergeants. They're—"

"Drill instructors." Frustration snapped in her tone. "I get it. And I have better things to do than waste time arguing military terminology with you. Such as visiting my friend who may be lying unconscious in a hospital bed because he had the bad luck to go out on the town with me." She shook off his touch and walked out of the hospital room, leaving him to follow.

The lights making the SICU as bright as day were a direct contrast to Lark's thoughts as she stood beside Danny's bed, looking down at his wan face.

"He doesn't look anything like himself," she murmured, more to herself than to Lucas. She hadn't realized, until this terrible thing had happened, how much she'd come to count on his laughing blue eyes and broad grin. Smile lines fanned out from the corners of his closed eyes beneath his bandaged head. She touched them with a fingertip, only realizing after there was no response to the light caress that she'd unconsciously been expecting him to wake up. She'd never considered a life without Danny Murphy in it. And she refused to now.

"Hey, Sleeping Beauty," she said, infusing her voice with a cheery enthusiasm she was a long way from feeling. "We've got a gig tomorrow night. If you don't show up, we're going to have to switch Kenny from fiddle to guitar and you know what they say." She straightened the sheet, like a mother tucking a child in for the night. "If you're going to play in New Orleans, you've got to have a fiddle in the band."

The saying was really about Texas, but the Texas-Louisiana border wasn't that far away; perhaps her words would sink into his poor, wounded head and he'd wake up to correct her. Nothing. Only the *swish*, *swish*, *swish* of the respirator, and the *click* of the electrocardiograph connected with ugly wires to his broad chest.

"You're going to be fine." She lifted his limp hand from the sheet and laced their fingers together. "Heaven knows, we've been through worse things together. Remember that tornado in Omaha? I thought for certain we were going to end up playing the palace in Oz. And the food poisoning in Raleigh? And how about the time the bus engine caught fire?"

Of all the places they'd traveled, Monument Valley, Arizona, had been one of the most lonely. Since it had been two hours before another vehicle appeared out of the shimmering heat mirage, they were not about to turn down the driver's offer of a ride into Flagstaff. Even if they did have to ride in the back of the open truck, in a rainstorm, with three sheep.

"It was months before I could put on a sweater without imagining the smell of wet wool."

Watching him carefully, Lark thought she saw a bit of movement behind his closed eyelids. "I'm not belittling this problem, Danny Boy."

He'd earned the nickname not because of his own name, but because every year, on March 17, wherever they were on the road, after the performance, he'd sit up front with the driver, drink green beer, and sing the song for mile after mile until everyone on the bus was offering to pay him to stop.

"This is a tough one. But *you're* tough. Didn't you get us out of that bar alive after all those angry, drunk people dressed like Trench-coat Mafia members started throwing beer bottles at us?" What had their manager been thinking, booking them into a heavy-metal club?

She felt the sting of hot tears at the back of her eyes. Emotion clogged her throat. She swallowed. Bit her lip. Struggled for composure.

"You'll get through this, too."

A nurse wearing sunshine yellow scrubs appeared at her elbow. "I'm sorry, but you'll have to leave now, Ms. Stewart."

Lark was afraid to leave. Afraid that if she wasn't here to encourage Danny, he'd slip away from her forever.

"We're taking good care of him," the nurse assured her. "Actually, your friend is a very lucky man."

"We must have vastly different definitions of luck," Lark murmured.

"If you have to get shot in the head, the forehead's best because it's the thickest part of the skull," the nurse said. "And the surgeon, Dr. Washington, came over to us from Charity Hospital, which isn't just the oldest hospital in the country, it's one of the busiest trauma centers. He's had a great deal of experience with gunshot wounds."

When the nurse smiled encouragingly, Lark wondered what parallel universe she'd fallen into where people getting shot could be a good thing.

"His brain-wave activity is strong," the nurse continued. "So is his heart, he's being monitored carefully for brain swelling, and given antiseizure medication." She gestured toward the IV bag and tubing. "What your friend needs now is a chance to heal."

Translation: peace and quiet.

Convinced Danny was, on some level, aware of what was going on, and not wanting to upset him, Lark resisted the temptation to argue.

"Sleep well." She bent and brushed her lips against his dry, unresponsive ones. "I'll be back in the morning."

She could sense Lucas's silent disapproval of that idea. *Tough*.

She was priding herself on making it through the all-too-brief visit without falling apart when she made the mistake of pausing in the doorway and looking back over her shoulder, just as the nurse detached Danny from the respirator to suction out the tube.

"Oh, God." She leaned against the hallway wall and squeezed her eyes tight. When she opened them again, Lucas was still standing beside her, still as silent as the Sphinx. "He's going to be okay." She refused to allow herself to think otherwise. "There are people walking around America with bullets lodged in their heads. You hear about it all the time." Okay, so that was overstating her point, but she knew she'd read about just such a thing.

"It happens," he agreed. Lark appreciated Lucas's affirmation, but she couldn't help noticing that his words didn't match his expression. "He looked pretty good, all things considering."

Anger at whoever had committed this hateful crime combined with exhaustion to spark a flare of temper. "I hadn't realized you'd gotten a medical degree since the last time I saw you."

"I haven't," he said mildly. "But I've seen a lot worse."

In the war? Lark wondered. While he was in the FBI? "Did the person recover?"

"No."

"Thanks for the pep talk, McCloud." She shook her head and began walking back toward the third floor service elevator Lucas had commandeered. "I can't tell you how much better you've made me feel."

Neither spoke on the way to the ground floor, both pretending a vast interest in the numbers lighting up above the door.

"You could have lied," Lark said as the doors opened.

"No." His tone was steel. "I couldn't have."

As she left the elevator, Lark told herself that she should be grateful for his honesty.

Lucas led her down a long hallway to a door clearly marked Emergency Exit Only. "We'll set off an alarm," she warned.

"No, we won't." He pushed the metal bar. The door opened without so much as a squeak.

"I don't think I want to know how you managed that."

"Then don't ask."

A tan no-frills Caprice that even Lark could recognize as an unmarked police car was parked in a yellow zone around the corner. Her heart skipped a worried beat when the passenger door opened and a grim-faced Detective Deveraux climbed out.

"There's a horde of press camped out in front," he

explained. "We figured this would be the best way to avoid them."

Having suffered a momentary fear that he'd come to arrest her, Lark was relieved. "You'd think one of them would have thought to stake out a different door."

"A couple did. But as we speak, they're all running like lemmings in the opposite direction after the limo carrying a brunette plainclothes policewoman."

"That's very clever." She climbed into the backseat, Lucas right behind her.

"It was McCloud's idea. We just provided the decoy," Deveraux supplied.

"We've also had the crowd under video surveillance." Detective Jordan pulled the car away from the curb, easing into the lighter than usual night traffic on Perdido Avenue.

"In the event your stalker might show up," Deveraux explained.

"Do you think that's possible?"

Jordan shrugged. "Hard to tell. We're still looking at it being an aborted mugging, some guy trying to pick up some last minute Christmas cash. But since the hospital has security cameras, we decided to take advantage of them. We'd like you to come down to the station tomorrow and look at the tapes, see if you recognize anyone."

"Why don't you bring them to Ms. Stewart?" Lucas suggested in what Lark recognized as his take-charge FBI tone. "There's a VCR in the house's media room."

The two detectives in the front seat exchanged looks. It was Deveraux's turn to shrug. "Sure, we can do that," he agreed.

                      *   *   *

A week before returning to Highland Falls for her family's annual Highland Games, as she sat alone at a
damask-draped table set for two, waiting for her husband
to show up, Lark had come to the conclusion that life was
all about control. Those who possessed it wielded it over
those lesser mortals who didn't. Unfortunately, as impossible as it might seem to her fans, who only knew her
public persona, she fell into the second category.

By the time the flame of the candle had sputtered in a
pool of melted wax and the California Chardonnay was a
great deal lower in the bottle, she'd decided it was high
time—past time—for a change.

She knew it wouldn't be easy to break a lifetime of old
habits. She could remember putting other people's needs
before her own since that bleak and rainy day when she
was three years old. It hadn't been easy to keep from crying her eyes out at her mama's funeral, but she'd dutifully
done as she was told.

Afterward, her aunt Melanie had paused while
unwrapping the green bean and bacon casserole a neighbor had contributed to the funeral supper. "Your mama's
so proud of you, baby. Why, right this minute she's looking down from heaven, smiling with pride because her
Lark's such a good girl."

The words, etched into her memory, had been a
warming bit of comfort in those terrible days. It was at
that moment Lark had vowed to be the best little girl in
the world and always make her mama proud.

For nearly three decades, she had done her best to live
up to that promise. Everyone in Highland Falls always

said that Laurel might be the smart sister, and Lily the perky one, but Lark was the sweetest of the three Stewart girls.

"And mercy," her aunt Zelda declared loudly and often, "the child sings like she's channeling the angels."

That natural talent, along with a lot of hard work and a little luck that she'd always thought might be her mama's guiding hand, had made her rich and famous.

But somewhere along the road to stardom, she'd lost Lark Stewart.

"You have the power to change your life," Zelda had told her during her visit home, when Lark had been about as rock-bottom as she'd ever want to get. "In fact, darling, with a face and voice like yours, you could well rule the universe."

A St. Charles Avenue streetcar rumbled past, its wheels clicking on the metal tracks, drawing her mind back to the present and revealing they'd entered into the Garden District. They stopped in front of a huge, curved-iron arch at least fifty feet across; two stone gate-houses anchored the arch; a guard sat in the right-hand gatehouse, watching a football game on a small TV.

As Jordan flashed his badge to the guard, then drove through the gate, Lark thought that she didn't want to rule the universe. She merely wanted to control her little corner of it, which was proving challenging enough.

*7*

The Silver Saddle Saloon was located just outside Nashville's city limits and calling the honky-tonk a dive was like saying George Jones had a bit of a drinking problem. As he took a long hit of Budweiser to ease the pounding in his head—which wasn't being helped by the drummer who was trying to compensate for being bad by being loud—Cody Armstrong decided that when Garth Brooks wrote his breakout song about friends in low places, he couldn't have imagined this place in his worst nightmare.

In contrast to neighborhoods just a few blocks away, where huge, spreading oaks shaded wide front porches, there was no leafy shade to be found outside the ramshackle building. Used needles, broken glass from beer bottles, and discarded condoms scattered the narrow, dark alley; inside, where absolutely nobody knew your name, pathos mingled with the odors of smoke, sweat, flat beer, and bathroom disinfectant. The Silver Saddle held the unique classification of being home to the most on-site murders in three Middle Tennessee counties. That the regulars boasted of that fact said a great deal about the clientele.

The floor was covered with peanut shells and tacky with spilled beer. An acrid cloud of cigarette smoke hovered over the room, hazing the neon beer light above a bar mirror that looked as if it hadn't been cleaned since the days when Roy Rogers was singing "Happy Trails to You" while riding Trigger into the sunset.

It was amateur night, and the guy singing a cry-in-your-beer-woman-done-him-wrong song would never be mistaken for George Strait. The only thing he and King George had in common was the cowboy hat and the wannabe country star had a better chance of nailing Faith Hill than he would ever have of making it in the music business.

"Did you mean it?" asked the woman seated across the table from him. Tanya Kay Gilman had a body like Shania Twain and knew how to use it, which almost made up for the fact that her voice was ordinary.

"Mean what, sugar?"

"About me becoming a country star?"

It wasn't the first time he'd used that line to bed a woman and it wouldn't be his last. "You bet your bottom dollar, darlin'," Cody drawled, flashing her an encouraging smile. "If I can make a little hillbilly wallflower like Lark Stewart a star, I can make you the queen of Nashville."

"I'd rather have a record contract."

"When the folks down on Music Row hear your demo, they're going to be knocking each other six ways to Sunday trying to be the first to sign you."

She drew in a deep breath that had her breasts nearly

popping out of her sequined halter top. "I was thinking maybe I ought to get a makeover."

Cody gave her a long perusal from the top of her frizzy bleached perm down to the pointy toes of her red cowboy boots. "Now, what would you want to go doing that for? When you're perfect just the way you are?" It wasn't that she couldn't use one, but makeovers cost money. "Why don't you get me another beer, sweetheart, while I start comin' up with a plan."

He'd have preferred a shot—several shots—of Johnnie Walker, but thanks to Lark screwing him in the divorce settlement, he didn't have much cash to throw around these days.

She paused and glanced over at the bar. "Dallas says I'm supposed to collect your tab before I serve you any more."

The damn bartender had never liked him. If the bastard weren't a former Hell's Angel, Cody would have told him to go straight to hell without passing Go.

"Now, you know I'd love to settle up, but I forgot my wallet back at the motel." He reached beneath the table and stroked her smooth, bare thigh. "Why don't you take care of it for me, and I'll pay you back tonight." His teeth flashed beneath his blond mustache. "While we plan how we're going to launch your career?"

She hesitated again. In a bit of perfect timing, the next contestant got up and started singing a Lark Stewart song in a soprano so strident, ears would be bleeding before she got to the bridge.

The song, which Lark had written while she'd been an opening act on her first European tour, obviously helped remind the waitress exactly who it was who'd made the shy little nobody from the hollows of East Tennessee a star.

Tanya Kay beamed. As she walked away, hips swaying sexily in that too-tight, too-short skirt that had male heads turning all across the bar, Cody considered again how easy women were to manipulate.

He remembered when Lark had looked at him that way, as if he'd hung the moon. Of course, that had been before she'd started believing her press clippings. In the image *he'd* crafted for her.

Just thinking about his ungrateful ex-wife got his blood to boiling. Ever since she'd gotten it into her swollen head to divorce him, Nashville was treating him as if he were a SARS carrier. Doors on Music Row not only shut in his face, they were locked and double-bolted, and he was right back where he'd been when he'd first met her in a dusty Texas hick town, where he'd been riding broncs and getting his brains screwed out every night by a red-haired barrel racer from Tulsa.

It had taken some ingenuity to get past Dan Murphy, that damn cracker guitar player who'd hovered over her like a big brother guarding his baby sister's virginity, but by the time Lark Stewart's bus left Still Springs, Texas, three days later, he was on it.

He'd made her one of the biggest stars in the country music constellation, and what had she done? Dumped him flat, then turned everyone in the business against him.

With anger churning in his gut like acid, Cody fantasized how to make the bitch pay for destroying his life.

# 8

The New Orleans street was home to beautiful old houses in a parklike setting of spreading oaks and palm trees. Jordan brought the car to a stop in front of a two-story house with a round, wide-columned white porch.

"We'll be by at eight-thirty tomorrow morning," Deveraux said.

"Fine," Lucas responded before Lark could answer.

"I'd prefer nine," she said mildly. Thirty minutes didn't matter one way or the other, but she needed to establish some control over her situation and was already getting sick and tired of Lucas calling the shots.

"Works for me," Jordan said agreeably.

"So, where are we?" Lark asked as the police car drove away, taillights fogged by the night mist. Fighting an odd lack of balance, which the doctor had warned her might be a symptom of her concussion, she grasped hold of a wrought-iron railing as they climbed the front steps guarded by two stone lions.

"Audubon Place." There was a lockbox on the door. Lucas punched in the combination to retrieve the key.

"I realize that."

The iron arch had spelled out the street's name. She vaguely recalled Ryan mentioning that the private enclave of late nineteenth and early twentieth century houses had been developed as New Orleans's millionaire row.

"I mean, who lives here?"

"No one at the moment." He opened a wide door that led into a formal entrance hall illuminated by a huge crystal chandelier and dominated by a towering blue spruce, resplendently decorated for the holidays in white lights, gold glass ornaments, gilt-winged angels, and burgundy velvet bows. The walls had been painted the color of strawberry wine, the high ceiling was adorned with frescoes, and a grand, curving, iron-laced stairway Scarlett O'Hara would have envied, dramatically led up to the second floor. Fragrant greens wrapped around the hand-carved banister had been adorned with more bows. "It's up for sale."

"I didn't see a sign."

"It's an exclusive seven-figure listing on a private street that doesn't allow looky-loos. It doesn't need a sign."

So how did he know about it?

"The owner's an old friend who's spending the holidays in Aspen," he answered the question she'd been about to ask. "I wanted to find someplace Guest, if he is in town, and the press wouldn't think to look for you."

"How fortunate for us that you have such an accommodating friend."

Lark knew her jealousy was unfounded; she could hardly have expected Lucas to have joined the Trappist monks and taken a vow of celibacy. It was unreasonable to resent the woman who, in Lark's mind, was a sleek, sophisticated ultrarich divorcee whose ski outfits fit her tanned and toned body like a second skin. But that didn't stop Lark from hating her.

"Louis Gravier and I go way back. He owns a chain of Creole restaurants. When his daughter was kidnapped for ransom and held hostage during my first year in the Bureau, I was called in for the arrest. He was grateful, said if there was anything he could ever do for me, to just call. So I did this morning."

The relief that flooded over her upon hearing the house's owner was a man was more than a little discomfiting. "You told Ryan you were a *former* agent." She'd heard that he'd joined the FBI after serving in the marines, but knew nothing about the details.

"I left the Bureau seven years ago." Those frustrating shutters came down over his eyes again. "Let's go find the bedrooms. You look wiped out."

Lark had no intention of getting involved with this man again—*dump me once, shame on you; dump me twice; shame on me, and no way there's going to be a third time*. But it would have been nice if he appeared to be suffering a little regret over what he'd passed up.

Okay, not a *little*. She wanted him to suffer the mother of all gut-wrenching remorse. Though he'd become so good at concealing his feelings, if he *was* devastated, she wouldn't be able to tell.

Having no trouble detecting the No Trespassing signs he'd put up around himself, Lark decided she'd pin Lucas down about his mysterious past tomorrow morning, when her head didn't feel about to split in two.

"Want a lift?" he asked as they crossed the black-and-white marble floor to the staircase.

*Oh God, yes.* "I can make it," she said stubbornly, hoping it was true.

"Your call." His hand tightened on her elbow, practically holding her on her feet. They'd made it to the thirteenth step—she was counting—when he stopped. "This isn't working." He put her overnight bag down on the step, scooped her up, flung her over his shoulder, picked up the bag again and continued up the stairs.

"I don't recall this being how Rhett Butler did it."

"I'm no Rhett Butler."

"Now there's a surprise." He might not be a smooth talker, but he definitely had the dangerous, edgy uber-alpha part down pat.

"I can make it the rest of the way from here on my own," she said fifteen steps later, at the top of the staircase.

"You're not heavy." He continued down a hallway lined with oil paintings and lit by wall sconces. "Actually, you could afford to put a little more meat on your bones."

Well, that was flattering. Make that *definitely* not a smooth talker.

"You thought my old friend was a woman," he said when she didn't respond.

Could that possibly be amusement in his voice? Upside down as she was, Lark couldn't see his face. "What possible interest could I have in whether it was a man or a woman?"

"Beats me."

He carried her into a bedroom as dramatically decorated as the entry hall, put her suitcase on a low gilt and painted chest Lark figured cost more than her first tour bus, then lowered her back onto her feet.

"You feeling okay?"

"Dandy." She dearly hoped she could continue to stand on her own. "You can let go of me now."

He waited for a moment, undoubtedly to catch her in case she fell flat on her face, then began walking around the room closing the gold brocade draperies. "Louis had the manager of his French Quarter restaurant send over dinner. He said he'd leave it in the kitchen for us to microwave. I can guarantee it's the best food in town."

"It must be terrific, to pay for this place." There was a Christmas tree in this room, as well—a wax myrtle dripping gilded glass beads and draped in diaphanous white angel hair.

"Since the Graviers were one of the few southern families who banked their money in France during the War Between the States, I imagine old cotton revenues probably built the house. But crawfish etouffee, gumbo, and bread pudding pay for the upkeep."

Even having grown up in an eighteenth-century stone castle, Lark was impressed. Stewart's Folly, as her childhood home was known in Highland Falls, had been designed by her ancestor for visual impact. Privately, she'd always preferred simplicity.

"It's very kind of Mr. Gravier, but I think I'll pass. I'm not very hungry."

At Ryan's insistence, she'd managed to choke down a

few bits of dry scrambled eggs and a cup of tea at the hospital.

"It's hard to have much of an appetite when some maniac's playing the 'Anvil Chorus' in your head," he said.

"You sound familiar with the feeling."

"I've been there," he said simply.

"You've had a concussion?"

"Yeah," he said from behind those walls she'd once known her way around. But he'd reinforced them over the years, building them higher and seemingly impenetrable. "Pain's good. Reminds you you're alive. Want one of those Tylenol the doc sent home with you?"

"No." She shook her head, then wished she hadn't, when rocks tumbled around behind her eyes. "Since the last two didn't do any good, I think I'll sleep it off. It's silly, since all I've been doing is lying in bed, but I'm exhausted."

"Your brain's been bounced around inside your skull, it'd be surprising if you weren't beat. You'll feel better in the morning."

She certainly hoped so. "Where are you going to sleep?"

"In the room next door. Unless you're uneasy about sleeping alone in a strange place."

"I've spent most of my adult life sleeping in strange places."

"So you have."

"I didn't mean that the way it sounded."

He lifted a brow.

"About sleeping in strange places," she elaborated. "I haven't spent all these years having wild, anonymous sex on the road."

"I never thought you had."

Strangely, his quick response stung. "I could have, you know." Musicians were, after all, infamous for their sexual escapades. And groupies weren't just reserved for the male stars.

"No surprise there, either," he said agreeably. "Get some sleep, Duchess. I'll see you in the morning."

He'd made it to the doorway when Lark called out to him. "Lucas?"

He glanced back over his shoulder. "Yeah?"

"I realize I wasn't exactly welcoming when you arrived at the hospital, but I really do appreciate you going to all this trouble just to ease my aunt's concerns."

He gave her a long deep look. For a fleeting moment she thought he might actually be about to say something personal. *Perhaps even explain why he'd never come back to her after the war?*

"Okay," he said. Then left the room.

*Okay?* Lark blew out an exasperated breath.

She took her pajamas out of her bag, went into the adjoining bathroom, which had gilt applied to every surface it'd stick to, washed her face, brushed her teeth, then fell into bed.

She was asleep as soon as her head hit the down pillow.

Lying in the next room, struggling his damnedest not to get bogged down in might-have-beens, Lucas was not so fortunate.

# 9

A cold spell had swept into New Orleans from the north, dropping daytime temperatures into the forties. The nights were even colder and the heater on Evie Lelourie's ancient Honda, which was blasting cold air through the dashboard vents, wasn't helping. As she drove home across Lake Pontchartrain, Evie vowed that the first thing she was going to do when she got a job after graduating was buy herself a new car.

She prayed the Civic lasted until June; the floorboards were eaten through with rust, the engine hacked like a chain smoker with emphysema, and a bent wire hanger served as a radio antenna.

Making matters worse was a fog alert on the causeway. With the left lane cut off by orange cones, traffic had slowed to a crawl on the right. Evie had made it about halfway across the twenty-four-mile bridge when the ancient car began to cough.

"Don't you dare quit on me, damn you!" It always chose the worst moments to give her trouble.

Knowing that stalling in the bumper-to-bumper line of traffic driving blind was dangerous, she crossed into the left lane just as the Civic sputtered to a stop.

"I don't believe this!" She turned the key again. Nothing. Once more, with no results.

Snatching her purse from the passenger seat, she pushed her shoulder against the driver's door—which tended to stick—and began walking ahead toward the nearest police call box.

It was spooky out on the bridge. Engines rumbled from cars that passed by, ghostlike in a fog bank so thick, she couldn't see her hand in front of her face. A wet chill seeped beneath her coat, deep into her bones.

A raucous gull swooped down, so close, Evie could feel the flutter of wings. When she instinctively lifted a hand to protect her face, she wobbled on the brand-new, red high heels she'd bought just this evening. They'd been marked down for the after-Christmas sale and with her employee discount, impossible to resist. She reached out to brace herself on the concrete divider when a car slid up behind her and came to a stop.

Feeling edgy, she slowly turned and squinted into the spotlight glare of twin yellow fog lights.

All too aware of the danger this stranger represented—it hadn't been that long since a serial killer had targeted the women of Baton Rouge—Evie changed her mind and decided that a cell phone, not a car, was the first thing she was going to buy when she got out of school.

The driver's window rolled down. "Ms. Lelourie?" The disembodied male voice drifted toward her. The soft southern drawl sounded vaguely familiar.

"Do I know you?" She hated the way her voice sounded, like some freaked-out bimbo on a chick channel movie. Of course, being out in the middle of the world's longest bridge on a foggy night wasn't the most intelligent thing she'd ever done.

"You waited on me the other day in the department store. You were very helpful."

He opened the driver's door and came looming out of the fog bank, palms up, as to demonstrate he meant her no harm. She recognized the leather coat and cashmere scarf.

"Dr. Longworth?"

"Small world, isn't it? I was at the mall picking up a pair of running shoes and was headed back to my hotel. When I found myself stuck in traffic, I was wondering what on earth possessed me to stay across the lake." His smile was a reassuring flash of brilliance. "Now I realize fate put me on this bridge tonight so I could come to your rescue."

Evie began to relax. When she'd waited on him the other day, he'd casually mentioned having been recruited by Tulane from Johns Hopkins in Baltimore. Unfortunately, all his belongings—including his clothes—had burned up when the moving van caught fire somewhere in Alabama, which was why she'd been able to rack up her largest sale of the season.

The friendly, fifty-something doctor certainly seemed safe. Besides, she could freeze to death waiting by the call box for help to arrive.

"It's lucky you came along," she said.

Another winning smile. "Isn't it?"

Deciding not to look a gift ride in the mouth, Evie walked back to his car with him. He surprised her by opening the door with a gentlemanly flourish. Wow. How many guys did that anymore?

"That leather coat looks very nice on you," she said as he pulled the car into the traffic crawling across the causeway. "Are you enjoying your other things?"

"Absolutely. The retail world is going to lose a valuable personal shopper when you enter the nursing profession."

Evie smiled at the compliment. "So I guess you don't have a wife to help pick out your clothes?"

"I was widowed eighteen months ago."

"I'm sorry."

"So was I. It's still difficult to absorb. One day she was there, then the next day"—he snapped his leather-gloved fingers—"she was gone."

It didn't sound as if she'd been ill. "Was it an accident?"

"No, she was murdered."

She placed a hand on his arm. "I'm so sorry."

"This holiday season is proving especially hard," he said. "It's the first without her and I've been at loose ends, which is why I appreciated your being so nice to me." He leaned forward and turned on the CD player.

"You were easy to be nice to," she said as Lark Stewart's "If Wishes Were Horses" flowed from the speakers. "Not all customers are as friendly as you are. Especially this time of year, when everyone's so stressed out."

A little silence settled over them. He was the first to break it. "I like your heart."

"My heart? Oh," she said, as comprehension dawned, "this heart." She touched her fingers to the silver pendant.

"It's very pretty. Simple and elegant. Like its owner."

She was grateful the dark kept him from seeing her flush of pleasure. "It was a gift from my boyfriend. When I graduated high school."

Enveloped by night and fog in their own private world, she chattered away like a magpie, telling him all about how she'd wanted to be a nurse ever since she was a little girl putting Band-Aids on Barbie.

"Did you ever think about becoming a doctor?"

It was not the first time someone had asked the question; Evie didn't have to even think about her answer. "Not for a minute. Doctors may cure," she quoted the poster on her bedroom wall, "but nurses care. No offense intended," she said quickly.

"None taken. It'd be impossible for us doctors to do our work without nurses. I've never heard the difference between the occupations put that way before, but it's a very admirable view."

Evie was impressed again. Most doctors possessed God complexes and treated nurses like servants put on earth to answer their bidding and do all their dirty work. They always claimed to know exactly what was the right thing to do, even when they were wrong, and heaven help the nurse who'd dare argue with them.

Dr. Longworth appeared to be one of those rare physicians who not only respected nurses, but treated them as fellow professionals.

Caught up in sharing her enthusiasm for her chosen profession, it took Evie a few minutes to realize he'd taken a wrong turn after leaving the causeway.

"Don't worry," he assured her when she pointed his mistake out. "I know where I'm going."

Having grown up in south Louisiana, Evie knew how easy it was to get lost in the bayou, especially at night when it became a haunted maze.

"I really think we ought to turn around," she said as the tires crunched on the oyster shell roadway leading farther and farther away from civilization.

"It'll be fine."

When she belatedly remembered that the interior lights hadn't gone on when he'd gotten out of the car, or when he'd opened the passenger door for her, Evie surreptitiously tried the door handle.

"They're all locked," he said calmly. "It's a safety feature."

That was when Evie realized that things were *not* going to be fine. They were going to get very, very bad.

She'd taken some psych classes and worked in a hospital volunteer program with women who'd been raped, so she knew it was imperative to make him think of her as a person, and not some anonymous victim. She'd screwed up badly by getting into the car, but at least she'd already personalized the situation by telling him all about her school and family.

"You don't have to rape me," she said in an even tone that belied the sirens blaring inside her head. She decided to appeal to his physician's ego. "You're a very good-looking man. Lots of women would love to have sex with you."

"Do you think so?"

"Absolutely."

He glanced over at her. "Are you including yourself in that group, Evie?"

She swallowed past the huge lump in her throat as Lark Stewart's pure soprano segued into the old bluegrass classic "What Would You Give in Exchange for Your Soul," and fought to keep her eyes on his.

"Yes." An involuntary shiver rippled beneath her skin.

He seemed to consider that. "It's an appealing offer, but I think I'll pass." His eyes, glittering in the moonlight, were as flat and cold as an alligator's. "This isn't personal, Evie," he said pleasantly. Her heart clattered against her ribs as he pulled into a stand of tupelo trees, cut the engine, and took a hypodermic syringe from his inside coat pocket. "You're merely a rehearsal." The needle glittered evilly in the frail silver moonlight.

Evie refused to die without a fight. She still had too much living to do! She hit out with her left hand as her right grasped for her hobo bag she'd carelessly dropped on the floor when she got into the car.

She connected with his face, and her nails, though kept short for nursing, dug deep into his skin.

"Goddammit!" he roared. His hands, which had been around her throat, loosened for an instant, which allowed her to pull the canister of pepper spray from her bag.

His fist slammed her head back against the passenger window. Evie felt the jolt all the way down her spine, but driven by adrenaline, didn't feel any pain.

She lifted the canister, aiming it directly at her attacker's face, prepared to take the back drift of the pepper cloud herself, if that's what it took to escape.

Before she could depress the red button, she felt a needle jab against the back of her hand. Evie struggled against the swirling, numbing sensation. Her drugged mind blurred; forgetting the door locks, she reached for the door handle in her mind, but her hand, which felt as heavy as a stone, wouldn't obey her mental command. She opened her mouth to scream, but his strong, black leather gloved hands on her neck cut off all sound.

The man she'd foolishly believed to be her rescuer, leaned close, so close she could feel the breath on her face. A gust of breeze off the lake parted the curtain of fog for an instant, revealing eyes that glinted in the moonlight like razors.

"Good girl," he said in a silky voice more terrifying than his earlier shout. He ran one of those gloved hands down her hair in a mockery of a caress.

He was swimming in and out of focus, but Evie saw the deadly flash of metal, felt the cold slice of steel on her icy flesh.

Then she began free-falling through the darkness.

# 10

Lark dreamed, and in her dream she was a teenager again back home in Highland Falls. It was hot. Uncommonly hot for the first week in July, so hot that old-timers couldn't remember the likes of it. Turk's-cap lilies withered on short, spindly stems, creeks dried up, highland meadows, usually a vibrant mosaic of emerald grass and colorful wildflowers, were brown scars against the sides of the mountains, and ruby-throated hummingbirds waged life or death battles over those few stalwart flowers that had managed to bloom.

The drought became the only topic of conversation. Residents discussed it while getting haircuts at James MacDougall's barbershop and shopping for groceries at the Tartan Market; fervent prayers for rainfall echoed from churches on Sunday mornings; there was talk of hiring a Cherokee to perform a rain dance; and the proprietor of Forbes's Video Express got in half a dozen more copies of *The Rainmaker*, to meet increased demand.

Clouds teased the town by gathering together every afternoon. Then, refusing to grace the mountains with desperately needed moisture, they'd move on. An occasional storm would rumble through, offering little more than thunder. On the rare occasion one would bring rain, it was a brief, violent downpour that did nothing to solve the problem.

In stark contrast to the unrelenting sun, the inside of the abandoned McCloud farmhouse was one of the few places in Highland Falls that wasn't blazing. It was cool, dark, and isolated.

Lark was walking through the house, looking for Lucas, calling his name, when she heard a sound behind her. She turned, the smile of apology dying on her lips when she viewed the strange man who, despite the blistering heat, was clad head to toe in black leather, standing in the doorway.

"Hello, Lark darling," he said before she could ask who he was and what he was doing there. His eyes crawled over her like evil hands. "I've come. Just as you asked."

Lark had no idea what he was talking about, but every instinct in her body assured her it wasn't good. She raced for the door, but he grabbed hold of her flowing hair and yanked her off her feet. She flailed out at him, trying to fight him off, but he was so much bigger and stronger, that the battle was lost before it had begun.

He dragged her across the gravel driveway to the smokehouse. Still struggling, she sank her teeth into the back of his hand.

"Is that any way to greet your master?" He slapped her cheek with the back of his leather-gloved hand, hard.

Lark screamed.

Another slap to the other cheek made her eyes water. She was about to scream yet again, then instantly reconsidered when he pulled a lethal-looking knife from a sheath on his studded belt.

"This is hurting me more than it is you," he said, almost sympathetically, as he pulled a length of black nylon rope from a backpack. "But it's what you asked for."

The speed with which he looped the rope around her wrists and ankles suggested it was not the first time he'd tied a woman up.

"I d-d-didn't ask for this."

"Of course you did." His tone was mild. Patient. "When you begged me from the television to take care of you and protect you. Which I'm more than willing to do. And in exchange, you'll do whatever I order you to do, without hesitation or question, because a good submissive always trusts her master to know what's best for her."

"Please." Lark risked the whisper. "Let me go. I promise not to tell anyone."

"No, you won't," he said agreeably. He stuffed a nasty-tasting black rubber ball in her mouth, which he secured with an attached strap. "From now on, you'll only speak when I allow you to speak." Her stomach roiled as he trailed his fingers over the flesh he'd bruised. "And scream only when I tell you to scream."

He picked up the knife again and sliced open her sunshine-bright yellow T-shirt and lacy white bra.

"You're a blank slate, Little One." Appearing to have come prepared, he took a marking pen from the backpack. It was too dark inside the smokehouse for Lark to see what he'd written on her breasts. "We'll keep a running tally of your mistakes, so you can be reminded of them later."

Then maybe he wasn't planning to kill her anytime soon. His fingers curved around her throat. "You have so much to learn. But won't we have fun with the instructions?"

A black dread billowed inside her again as those treacherous fingers squeezed. White spots floated like moths in front of her eyes. Lark was a week away from her eighteenth birthday, and she was about to die.

Then, horrifyingly, he smiled.

"I'm not punishing you out of anger, Lark," he explained in that eerie, patient tone she found more frightening than the knife. "I may be strict, but I'm never cruel. Everything I do to you today—everything I'll do in the future—will always be done out of love."

She couldn't keep the tears from flowing. Bile rose in her throat as he bent and touched his mouth to her wet face.

"Now, I'm leaving you in isolation for a bit—a sensory time-out, so to speak—so you can ponder on ways to beg my forgiveness. But don't worry. I'll be back." He squeezed her breast, marred with ugly black lettering. "And then our new life together will begin."

Bound and gagged on the dirt floor in the dark of the smokehouse, Lark lost all sense of time. The hoot of an owl somewhere in the woods, the deep croak of frogs in the pond, and the echo of katydids suggested night had fallen. Her head throbbed. Her entire body ached and she was humiliated when she realized from the dampness between her legs that she'd wet herself.

She tasted blood in her mouth, heard something rustling in the corner, and screamed behind the gag as something that felt like a spider skittered across her bare thigh. She tried to see, but she could have been inside a tomb.

That thought led to another, more horrible one. What if the man never came back? Would she suffocate? Die a slow, lingering death from starvation? Her hammering heart leaped into her throat as something swooped down from the rafters. Oh, God, it was probably a bat. Maybe she'd go insane before she died. Maybe a bear would find her and tear her limb from limb.

More and more horrid possibilities bombarded her mind, and panic clawed beneath skin that had turned all cold and clammy. How long had she been here? Was anyone looking for her yet? If so, would they find her?

Realizing that she was her own best chance for survival, Lark fought to focus through the pain and fear clouding her mind and the inky blackness surrounding her. She tried to loosen the ropes around her wrists, as she'd seen innumerable times in the movies, but he'd tied her hands back to back, which not only made her arms feel as if they were being wrenched from her shoulders, but also prevented her from freeing herself.

Trying a different method, she flopped over onto her stomach and arched her back, inch by painful inch, until her fingers could touch her ankle ropes.

Her muscles burned as she struggled with the vexing knots. Sweaty and more and more exhausted, she refused to give up. After what seemed an eternity, she thought she felt the knots slide, just a little. That small victory provided a huge burst of optimism.

*I will escape!*

*I will survive!*

Hours passed. Her nails became ragged and bloody. She'd cried so many tears her eyes were dry and burning. But Lark continued to work the ropes.

Finally! The knots loosened; the ropes fell away.

She still wasn't home free. It wouldn't be easy, running with her hands behind her back, but she'd crawl to safety if that's what it took. She had just managed to stand up when the heavy plank door burst open, and a blinding shaft of sunlight hit her face.

She looked up, into the center of that bright white light, into the face of evil.

"Honey, I'm home," William Guest said mockingly.

It was the scream that woke Lucas. Grabbing his Glock, he tore into Lark's room. The room was ablaze with light—she'd left every lamp on—and she was sitting amid the tangled sheets, shaking like a leaf, her wide eyes unseeing and filled with terror.

His first thought had been that Guest had somehow managed to breach the security system. But Lark was alone with whatever bogeymen lurked in her nightmares.

As much as he wanted to rush to her, to take her into his arms, he was afraid any quick movement would only frighten her more. He slowly, carefully, placed the pistol on the nightstand.

"Hey," he said soothingly. "It's okay."

He sat down on the edge of the bed. "You're safe. It was only a nightmare."

Fear of escalating an already dicey situation warred with his need to protect. When he touched a soothing hand to her hair, she began fighting him with surprising strength for a woman who appeared frail enough to be blown away by a stiff gust of wind.

"Lark, it's okay." Capturing her windmilling arms, he anchored her against him as she continued to kick. "It's me, Lucas." Dodging a vicious knee aimed at his balls, he pinned her to the mattress.

Her frantic struggles beneath him gradually ceased. Her eyes slowly focused. "Lucas?"

"Yeah, Lucas," he confirmed. "I won't let anyone hurt you." He ran his palms over her shoulders and down her arms. "You're safe," he repeated. "With me."

"Safe." She let out a soft sigh of release. "With Lucas." When he rolled off her, she grabbed hold of his hand with both of hers. "I don't want to be alone."

How could any man refuse such a request? "I'm not going anywhere."

Hoping like hell she'd remember that this wasn't his idea in the morning, he pulled the sheets over them. Obviously exhausted, she sighed and slid instantly back into sleep.

Lucas lay on his back, beside Lark, staring up at the ceiling. Where had her mind been? Here in New Orleans? Or back in Highland Falls, that other time she'd come so close to dying?

She stirred restlessly. When he drew her against him, she cuddled closer, pressing her slender curves to his angles.

Despite all the changes in their lives, they still fit.

Lucas had feared they would.

# 11

Lark was back in the mountains, this time lying in Lucas's arms after having just made love. It had been wonderful, which wasn't surprising, since it always was. Even that first time, when they'd both been virgins, discovering the wonders of sex together. Then again, she thought with a smile as she cuddled closer, they'd both been very fast learners.

She pressed her lips against his bare chest, loving his musky male scent, so different from her own, and closed her eyes, enjoying the sound of the nearby creek tumbling over moss-covered rocks, the hoot of a barred owl somewhere in the woods, the musical peal of bells. . . .

*Bells?*

Jerked out of the lovely dream, she blinked her eyes open and found herself in a gilded room that looked as if it'd been decorated by Marie Antoinette. She was still struggling to get her bearings when her gaze landed on Lucas, clad in a pair of gray cotton boxer briefs, bent over her overnight bag. His skin was smooth as polished hardwood, the muscles long and lean and well defined.

He retrieved her cell phone from her suitcase, flipping it open as he straightened. "McCloud . . . Hey, Zelda. Yeah, I'm with her and she's doing real fine, all things considering." He turned toward Lark and held out the phone. "It's your aunt."

Lark was definitely awake now. The elastic waistband of the briefs fit snug just below his navel; with that six-pack abdomen, he could have easily appeared on the cover of one of her aunt's novels.

She took the phone, covering the mouthpiece with her palm. "Would you mind putting on some clothes?" Lucas had always been comfortable with his naked body. And there'd been a time when she'd loved looking at it. Touching it. Tasting it.

"Whatever you want, Duchess."

"What I want is for you to quit calling me that stupid name."

He shrugged.

"Hi," she said with forced cheer as he left the bedroom. "How are you, Aunt Zelda?"

"You know me," the voice on the other end of a crackly line responded. "I'm always fine. The question, darling, is how are you? I've been worried sick."

"I'm so sorry. I tried to call you yesterday to let you know everything was okay, but the operator said there was no way to get through while you were on the ship unless it was an emergency. Which it wasn't," she stressed.

"Well, I'm on land now. I jumped ship in Kefalonia."

Lark was not surprised. The quintessential individualist, her aunt had never been one to travel with a group. "Alone? Or is it true what they say about shipboard romances?"

"Don't I wish," Zelda scoffed. "When I get back to Highland Falls, Kenny Gardner—you remember him, Lark, he's that tall drink of water I used to go dancing with every so often? He recently opened Smoky Mountain Travel, down in Asheville, and let me tell you, he and I are going to have ourselves a little chat about him booking me on a geriatric cruise. With the exception of the captain, who saved me by inviting me to sit at his table, everyone on that damn tub was over sixty-five. And even if I had been interested, the women outnumbered the geezers ten to one."

"I can't imagine that would have been a problem for you," Lark said. "And maybe it wasn't a mistake. Perhaps Kenny didn't like the idea of setting you up with the competition."

Silence. Lark had never before known her aunt to be at a loss for words.

"No," she decided. "I'm sure that's not it. Before his mama moved in with him, Kenny simply liked to kick up his heels on Saturday night, and since I'm the best dancer around, it was only natural he'd invite me to go to the VFW hall with him."

Lark seriously doubted that was the case. As she'd told Lily this past summer, if their aunt ever looked up from her computer, she'd notice that nearly every man—some half her age—walked into walls whenever Zelda Stewart sashayed by on her long, former showgirl legs.

"Well, I'm sorry you aren't having a good time."

"I didn't say that. The ship's band wasn't bad, the scenery's spectacular, and the local color is wonderful. I've been trying to come up with a plot that'll land my

Highlander on one of the islands so I can set a book here."

"I'm sure you'll think of something."

"I probably will. If for no other reason than to write this trip off."

Zelda had been audited for the past four years. Each time the IRS agent had spent an entire day going over her Schedule C line by line, only to declare the government owed her a refund, then ask her out to dinner.

"I'm coming home," her aunt announced.

"Please don't cut your vacation short on my account. You still have another week left and who knows, now that you're off the U.S.S. Senior Citizen, you might meet some sexy Greek."

"The Greeks may be sexy, but they're chauvinists. Can you see me letting some man tell me what to do?"

Lark had to laugh. Sure, the day pigs sprouted wings and started dive-bombing Highland Falls. "I'm not suggesting you get married—"

"Good Lord, I should hope not!" Just when a relieved Lark thought she was off the hook, her aunt turned serious again. "According to the news, you could have been killed."

"Also according to the news, Cody divorced me because I was pregnant with an alien's baby."

"That was the same trashy tabloid that also ran a story about that survivor of the *Titanic* being found on an iceberg with Bat Boy. Besides, Lucas told me that William Guest may be the shooter."

Lark shot Lucas—who'd returned in black jeans and a black shirt he hadn't bothered to button—an annoyed look. "Lucas doesn't seem to realize he's no longer in the FBI. He sees threats and conspiracies around every corner."

He gave her a level look, appearing unwounded by her accusation.

"Don't be flippant," Zelda scolded. "You know I won't stop fretting about you until I can see for myself that you're safe and sound."

"I'm fine," she repeated. Since the alternative was unthinkable, Lark was still trying to believe that. "Unfortunately, Danny's still unconscious, but the nurse assured me that his vital signs are strong and he's got too strong a spirit not to beat this and get better. And the only thing wrong with me is a headache from a minor concussion and some scrapes and bruises."

"I'm very relieved to hear that. But I need to see for myself that you're all right." There was more crackling on the overseas line. "Dammit, the signal's breaking up. I swear, two cans and a string would be more efficient than the Greek phone system. Take care, darling; I'll see you in a couple days. Now, put Lucas on."

Appreciating the irony of her aunt complaining about chauvinistic males while sending Lucas McCloud to New Orleans to practically put her under house arrest, Lark knew there was no point in arguing. Zelda could make a pit bull look ambivalent.

"You were in my bed," she accused, after he'd promised her aunt he'd look out for her, then hung up. She raked a look over him. "Nearly naked."

"Not uninvited."

Lark's memory was still distressingly foggy. Wondering how she could possibly forget something like that, she wondered if she might still be suffering a lingering result of her concussion.

"You had a doozy of a nightmare," he filled in the gap.

Damn. She'd thought she'd put those behind her forever after Guest had been arrested that second time. She supposed it wasn't that surprising that discovering he was on the loose again would bring them back. As visions of last night's terrifying dream stirred in her mind, she belatedly noticed the ugly red scratches on the back of his hands. "Did I do that?"

"It's no big deal. I've gotten a helluva lot worse trimming brush. When I told Zelda I'd watch out for you, I signed up for twenty-four/seven. If you have any more nightmares, we'll handle them together."

The need for control battled with a powerful relief that she wasn't alone. Which worried Lark. "How long are we talking about?"

His eyes went black, thunderheads before a storm. "As long as it takes."

As Lark had told the neurologist, she was not the kind of person to get hysterical. She'd been born the quiet sister in a family that thrived on drama. Laurel had never hesitated to tell others, including her two younger sisters, what to do, but both Lily and Lark knew she'd throw herself in front of a runaway train to protect them. Having chosen a career in investigative reporting, which was bound to make enemies, Laurel was probably the most likely of the three of them to find herself somehow mixed up in a crime.

Lily, the youngest, was the perky chatterer everyone fell in love with at first sight. Lark had often suspected Lily had taken on the role of family cheerleader due to misplaced guilt since their mother had died giving birth to her. It had taken Lily a while to find herself, and if she had a flaw, it was allowing other family members to take advantage of her nurturing personality. This past year she'd surprised everyone by marrying a globe-trotting documentary maker.

Being in the middle, it had been easy for Lark to get overlooked, but she'd discovered early on that she could win a little attention for herself if she sang. Her aunt Zelda swore she'd known every word to "Stand By Your Man" by the time she was three; by eight she was causing hardened coal miners and hardscrabble farmers to weep with her rendition of Dolly Parton's "Coat of Many Colors." On Sunday mornings, while wowing parishioners of St. Andrews church with her choir solos, she experienced a pride that was far from pious.

Reserved by nature, something magical happened to her when she got before an audience. It was as if a switch flipped inside her, turning her into another Lark—one who could command the stage and make people respond exactly as she wanted. There were times when she marveled that the performer *Rolling Stone* magazine had described as possessing Stevie Nicks's talent for creating musical poetry and Loretta Lynn's natural charm was living inside ordinary Lark Stewart from Highland Falls, Tennessee.

Her mama had been a singer, too. Her father loved to tell the story of how he'd walked into a smoky club on

Savannah's riverfront and immediately fell in love with the slender brunette who was gaining fame by disproving the old adage that "white folks" couldn't sing the blues.

Choosing to surrender the spotlight to her artist husband, Callie Stewart quit singing professionally when she'd married the larger-than-life artist, John Angus Stewart. Her sister, Lark's aunt Melanie, insisted Callie had never regretted her decision to focus on the more traditional roles of wife and mother, yet Lark often secretly wondered if she might be living out the dream of a woman she could barely remember.

Lark had spent her first years in Nashville in relative anonymity. She sold a few songs, though not as many as she would have liked, since there were a lot more men singers than women. Also, the pendulum of country music was constantly swinging back and forth between traditional and pop sounds.

When she'd first arrived, record executives had been looking for more crossover, pop-style "countrypolitan" tunes. In these more uncertain times, she'd found a growing audience for the type of songs she preferred: songs that addressed life issues as old as the mountains she'd grown up in.

She and Danny had just finished up a bus tour of rural country rodeos—where she'd met Cody—and she was recording her thousandth demo tape for yet another wannabe songwriter, when her agent called to tell her that one of his clients had undergone an emergency appendectomy in Italy. If Lark could get to Rome by the following morning, she'd have a gig opening for a star-studded European country music tour.

It was the opportunity of a lifetime.

The first singer, who'd obviously overindulged in the local wine, drunkenly staggered out onto the stage and incoherently mumbled his lyrics, resorting to a tuneless humming when he forgot them completely. His guitar playing, as he tortured the high, lonesome Bakersfield sound, was off-key and listless.

The Italian audience, who'd paid a great deal of lire to attend the concert, began to boo. Instead of leaving the stage, the singer cussed out the angry fans, screaming at them that he wasn't going to go away until they applauded—which only made the situation worse. By the time the bouncers stormed the stage and dragged the drunk away, the mood was verging close to World War III.

Lark had never been more nervous. There appeared to be more people in the arena than in her entire home-town, and every single one of them was in an ugly mood. Knees shaking, with nothing but her guitar between her and the riled-up crowd, she walked to center stage and began to strum the opening chords of "John Anderson, My Jo," an old Scots ballad about growing old with your true love.

By the time she reached the end of the second stanza, the people in the first few rows had quieted down. The silence spread, seat by seat, row by row. In less than two minutes, the arena was as hushed as a cathedral.

Her confidence began to build, burning off her jet lag as she segued into "The Lady of Kenmure," then "False Lover Won Back." By the time the final chord of "Gin I Were a Baron's Heir" hung on the air, Lark felt as if she and the audience shared a single heart.

The silence lingered for a moment. Then the audience slowly began to clap, seemingly one person at a time, then more and more, until the booming applause rolled over the rows of seats like thunder over the mountaintops back home.

*Country Weekly* magazine, who'd sent a reporter to cover the tour, had been effusive in its praise, claiming no female singer since the late, great Patsy Cline could play an audience like the Tennessee Songbird had. Her career had skyrocketed when she returned to the States, and Lark soon realized that becoming a celebrity meant surrendering her privacy.

Everything she said or did was scrutinized and dissected by a media who survived by feeding a seemingly ravenous public. After spending years pursuing the spotlight, she'd become pursued by that same spotlight.

Lark had discovered the truly dark side of fame when William Guest reentered her life after being paroled. When the letters and photographs began coming, she'd felt as if he'd taken her hostage a second time. She couldn't sleep, couldn't eat, and couldn't stop looking over her shoulder. The panic attacks she'd managed to conquer so many years ago had returned with a vengeance. It had taken every ounce of strength she'd possessed to go on stage every night, never knowing if her stalker would be in the crowd. If he'd try to get to her. To hurt her.

Although she'd tried not to show it, when Lucas had dropped his bombshell about Guest's escape, the old fear had attacked with monster claws. Every nerve in her body began screeching for her to run, as fast and as far as she could.

*But she wasn't going to run.*

*Not this time.*

Lark knew that people often underestimated her because of her tendency to be reserved around strangers. Having grown up in a part of the country where manners mattered, she was unfailingly polite and hated conflict; she'd come to realize that one of the reasons she'd put up with Cody so long was because he was so willing to wade into fights for her. Unfortunately, by their six-month anniversary, she'd realized that he had a flashfire temper, held grudges until doomsday, and mostly picked fights solely for the sake of fighting.

She'd begun to speak up for herself even before deciding to divorce him, and was getting better at it. In the beginning, whenever she'd felt herself getting pressured against her will, she'd ask herself *What would Laurel do?*

By the time she'd showered and blown her hair dry, she'd decided that there was no way her older sister would put up with Lucas running the show. If he was right about her being in imminent danger from Guest, then she had every right to be in on the decisions.

Following the enticing scent of coffee downstairs, Laurel walked down the Scarlett O'Hara staircase into a large, spacious kitchen. The rain had moved on during the night; sunlight was streaming into the room, bathing yet another tree—a southern pine decorated with miniature copper cooking utensils and carved wooden farm animals—in a warm golden light.

"Your friend certainly went all out with his decorating." She could almost imagine Nat King Cole seated on one of the wrought-iron barstools at the granite counter, crooning about being home for Christmas.

"Louis doesn't believe in doing anything halfway," Lucas agreed. "You should see the place the years it's on the charity Holiday Home Tour. It's sort of Charlie Brown meets King Louis the Fourteenth."

His comparison of the house to Versailles was an indication that at least about some things, they still thought alike. Not wanting anything in common with Lucas, she forced her mind back to what she'd come downstairs to say. "We need to establish some ground rules."

"Fine." *So long as they were his rules*, Lucas decided.

He took a flowered porcelain cup and matching saucer from one of the cupboards, poured coffee from the carafe, and handed it to her.

"You have to stop thinking of me as some helpless victim."

"That's easy, since I've never thought of you that way."

"And I don't want you keeping things from me, like when you and those two detectives got together and planned to hide me away in your friend's house."

He nodded, reasonably okay with that one. "You want input, you got it." He went back to stirring the batter he was mixing in a red ceramic bowl. "I'm making waffles if you want some."

"I'm not—" she paused, as if realizing arguing about whether or not she was hungry would only sidetrack the issue she seemed determined to discuss. "That would be nice, thank you. And I'm not talking about input. If you really believe my life's in danger, I have every right to be an equal partner.

"That's a deal-breaker," she said when Lucas didn't immediately respond.

"It's also unreasonable." He flipped open the lid of the Belgian waffle iron, poured in some batter, shut the lid, then refilled his own gold-rimmed cup, which was ridiculously delicate, but he hadn't been able to unearth any mugs in any of the cherry cupboards. "For chrissakes, Lark, you wouldn't let me tell you how to sing; why the hell should I let you tell me how to do what I do well?"

"That's a valid point." She cocked her head and considered it for a moment. "All right, you can be in charge."

"You always were the most sensible female in your family." Having won his point, Lucas could afford to be gracious.

"Since I'm feeling generous toward you for having come all this way to ease my aunt's concerns, I'm willing to take that as a compliment, rather than a criticism against the Stewart women."

"That's exactly how I meant it."

"There's also one more thing."

He ground his teeth. "What?"

Appearing completely undeterred by his hard look, Lark stuck out a determined chin. "I get veto power."

"No way." He'd been told he could be intimidating. Unfortunately, it appeared no one had informed Lark of that fact.

"Way. I refuse to cower in the corner like some hysterical maiden in distress while you get to play Sir Galahad."

"Damn. Don't tell me that all that time I spent polishing my armor was wasted."

When she didn't offer even a hint of a smile at his

weak attempt at humor, Lucas realized she wasn't budging on this sticking point.

Okay, he could work with this. He'd let her have her damn input, and if she did balk on anything, he was a helluva lot bigger than she was. If push came to shove, he could tie her to the four posters of that gilded, canopied bed upstairs.

When that idea proved unreasonably appealing, he dragged his rebellious mind back to the issue at hand.

"Okay, it's a deal."

She extended a hand and rewarded him with the smile she'd withheld. "Then we're partners."

Despite the scrapes, her hand felt lady-smooth and soft in his. It was a hand created for holding dainty cups, but it had also been strengthened from years of guitar playing and her fingertips were calloused.

Contrasts, Lucas thought again.

"Partners," he agreed.

# 12

Unfortunately, the interview with the detectives Jordan and Deveraux didn't go any better than it had at the hospital. After watching the hospital security tapes three times, Lark couldn't see anyone who looked even the slightest bit familiar. Nor did any of the mug shots they'd brought with them ring a bell. When Deveraux suggested hypnosis, Lucas jumped in to veto the idea. Lark knew he was trying to protect her from remembering more horrifying details of that day in the smokehouse, but wanting to help find Danny's assailant, she agreed.

Still nothing.

"There's only one thing left to do," she said after the detectives had left with the hypnotist.

"Yeah. Get you back to Tennessee ASAP."

"I still have a show to do." She put up a hand, forestalling any argument. "That's not negotiable. I have a lot of fans counting on me to be up on that stage tonight. I'm not letting them down."

"I strongly doubt they'd expect you to make yourself a target for Guest," he countered. "You realize that I'm bigger than you."

"Of course I do." She stuck out her chin. "But I'm a lot tougher than I look."

"So why don't you tell me something I haven't figured out for myself?" His gaze didn't soften, but his lips quirked, ever so slightly, at the corners. He skimmed an openly masculine appraisal over her. "We can wrestle for it," he suggested, his tone turning as rich as the pralines sold in gift shops throughout the city.

Alarms sounded inside Lark when she felt the unwelcome stir of old embers warming. "That's no fair. As you've already pointed out, you're bigger than I am."

"My point exactly." He moved closer, until they were standing toe to toe. "It's for your own good."

Lark had to tilt her head a very long way back to look him in the eye. "I've heard that before." Damned if she'd give him the satisfaction of knowing that he still could still have an effect on her by stepping back. "Most recently when a now former record producer suggested I cut a CD of show tunes to expand my fan base." Cody had been all for the idea. Lark had fired the producer the same day she'd filed for divorce.

"You know there's a big difference between tough and being pigheaded."

Color flamed in her cheeks. "Pigheaded?"

His eyes didn't waver from hers. "Just calling them like I see them, Duchess."

"Then you need to get your eyes checked, because I prefer to think of myself as tenacious. And my name's Lark. Do you think you could remember that?"

"I'll make you a deal. I'll remember to call you by your name, if *you* can remember that I'm here in New

Orleans in the first place because some wacko stalker's escaped prison and may be trying to kill you."

"That's a little difficult for me to forget," she said dryly. "And the point I was going to make, before you decided to start throwing your weight around again, was that I need to go back to where Danny was shot to see if it triggers any memories."

He folded his arm. "No way."

"You really need to work on building your vocabulary," she said helpfully. "That 'no way' phrase is becoming overused."

"May I ask a question?"

Although she thought she detected a hint of sarcasm in his tone, she gave him a little "go ahead" wave with her hand.

"Are you always this argumentative?"

"Absolutely not. Are you always this bossy?"

"Hell, no. Mostly I try to stay out of other people's lives. Maybe we just bring out the worst in each other."

"Or the best," she surprised them both by suggesting. His masculine assertiveness might get on her nerves, but Lark knew he was only concerned for her safety.

There was a pause as Lucas considered that idea. "I suppose that's one possibility."

"I'll go get my coat," Lark said, deciding to take advantage of the little window of opportunity when his tough-guy former Special Agent demeanor slipped a bit. "If we leave right now, we'll have time to check out Pirate's Alley before visiting the hospital."

The same frustration that was written across Lucas's face smoldered again in his eyes, but since he was, indeed, a great deal bigger than she was, Lark was glad he didn't physically stand in her way when she left the kitchen.

Despite the gravity of her situation, Lark nearly laughed. She really was getting better at this assertiveness stuff every day.

Unwilling to risk not being able to find a cab if they needed one in a hurry, Lucas had a rental car brought to the house, then spent what seemed to Lark to be an unnecessary amount of time driving around in circles the short distance from the Garden District to the French Quarter, constantly checking his rearview mirror.

"I think anyone trying to follow us would be dizzy by now," she offered after he'd taken yet another cruise down Royal Street.

"It's called taking precautions," he said as he glanced yet again into the rearview mirror, before pulling into the public lot next to Jax Brewery.

"I suppose they taught you that at the FBI Academy?"

"I picked up a few things there over the years," he said negligently.

"Are you sure you didn't work for the CIA?"

"I believe I'd know the difference." He shot her a look. "Why?"

"Because every time I bring up your time in the FBI, you dodge the issue. Anyone would think you were a spy."

He pulled into a space. "Anyone would be wrong."

He checked the mirror one more time, then opened the driver's door.

Blowing out a frustrated breath, Lark followed.

Despite the bright winter sun that had brought everyone outdoors, a stiff breeze off the river made the air bone-piercingly cold.

"I thought New Orleans was supposed to be hot," she complained, pulling her gloves out of her pocket as they crossed Decatur Street on the river side of Jackson Square.

Despite the chill, artists had set up easels and lined up paintings along the fence, tarot card readers were doing a brisk business, and street performers were entertaining crowds of tourists dressed like Arctic explorers.

"It's the moisture in the air." Lucas took her elbow as they dodged a man decked out in a green elf outfit wobbling by on a unicycle while juggling bowling pins painted to look like snowmen. "High humidity increases the conduction of heat from the body, so you feel colder."

"Thank you for the meteorological lesson, Mr. Wizard." Her tone was a great deal drier than the air.

"No problem. Next lecture we'll learn how to make a model volcano."

*Damn.* Yet another unwilling stroll down memory lane; her fourth-grade science project entry had been a plaster of Paris volcano that had taken the two of them three days to build.

"Aunt Melanie sure wasn't happy about me ruining that new blouse she'd bought me for the finals," Lark remembered aloud. It'd been splattered with the red food coloring they'd added to the baking soda and vinegar mixture for a lava effect when the volcano had exploded.

"But you won a blue ribbon," he reminded her.

A blue ribbon that had seemed extra special since because she was the "arty" Stewart sister no one, even her own family, had expected her to make the county finals. But she had, thanks to Lucas's help.

Like so much of New Orleans, Pirate's Alley, a one-block long street between the Cabrillo and St. Louis Cathedral—where William Faulkner had lived when he'd been writing his first book—was a place of legends and lore. Lark vaguely remembered Ryan telling them all that some stories, disputed by historians, had slave sales taking place in the cathedral's pretty little St. Anthony's Garden; other tales told of gentlemen defending their honor in duels behind the garden's iron gate and pirates using the alley to transport their stolen treasure.

"I have trouble believing that pirates would want to spend all that much time between a church and prison," she said. Ryan had informed everyone that the Spanish prison had once been located behind the Cabrillo and public executions had taken place in the square.

"One point on which we're in perfect agreement."

A brass band, playing a jazzy rendition of "White Christmas," marched down the street, followed by an open fringed carriage. In a jaunty display of holiday spirit, both driver and mule were wearing red Santa Claus hats. The passengers, a couple about her and Lucas's age, appeared fixated on each other, oblivious to the driver's tourist guide spiel and the festive atmosphere surrounding them.

The man's dark head lowered at the same time the woman lifted her lips. When they kissed, Lark felt a distant tug. It took her a moment to recognize the feeling, but when she did, the realization that it was envy was less than comforting.

She'd always been able to picture scenes while writing song lyrics. Now, a vision of riding in the black carriage beneath a huge white moon shimmered in her imagination. Harness bells jingled, hooves clattered on the cobblestones and stars glistened like ice in the sky overhead. Lucas's arm was around her and he was looking down at her as if she were the only woman he'd ever wanted. While she looked up at him as if she wanted to be that woman.

He dipped his head and at the first touch of his lips on hers, a soft mist rose in her mind, banishing any thoughts of killers lurking in dark alleys.

Without warning, the seductive image tilted, like the facets of a kaleidoscope, and suddenly she and Danny were walking arm in arm, cutting through Pirate's Alley to the club where his friend was playing. The band jokester, Danny was rattling off a riff of very bad Christmas jokes.

*"And the number one Santa pickup line is: That's no candy cane in my pocket, sweetheart. I'm just real glad to see you."*

*Lark shook her head. "I'm convinced your sense of humor stopped maturing at age twelve."*

*"You're probably right. Know why Santa is always so jolly?"*

*"No." She sighed. "But I have a feeling you're going to tell me."*

*"Because he knows where all the naughty girls live. . . . And speaking of girls, what do the female reindeer do when Santa takes the male reindeer out on Christmas Eve?"*

*"I haven't a clue."*

*"They go into town and blow a few bucks." He flashed a*

wide grin. "Why don't Santa and Mrs. Claus have any children?"

"Because the North Pole would be too crowded with all those elves?"

"Nope. It's because Santa only comes once a year and when he does, it's down the chimney."

She punched his arm. "That's just sick."

"A sick mind is a terrible thing to waste," he countered easily, and went off on a long riff about the differences between snow men and snow women.

The jokes were more stupid than dirty, and she and Danny were both giggling when she saw something move in the corner of her eye. Still smiling, Lark turned—then froze as a man in black loomed menacingly out of the shadows. The gun in his hand flashed metallic in the fog-diffused glow of the nearby streetlight.

"Danny!" Her fingers tightened on his arm.

Still smiling, Danny turned toward the man. There was a pop, like a champagne cork being pulled from a bottle.

A bright streak flashed; Danny sagged.

Lark flung her arms around him, trying to support him, but his heavier weight pulled them both down.

Her knee cracked against the cobblestones, sending a shock of pain all the way up her spine.

A scream bubbled up in her throat. Run! her fevered mind screamed. But her legs could have been frozen in concrete. She stared up in stunned disbelief and fear at the hooded assailant.

"Lark?" Lucas's fingers curved tightly around her arms as Lark swayed. "What's wrong?" His dark eyes scanned the crowd, as if searching for whatever she'd seen that had caused such a sudden physical reaction.

"I'm okay." She took a deep breath of the damp, icy air. "Oh, my God. It's really working, Lucas." As frightening as the memory had been, it was better than that sense of loss caused by the amnesia. "I remember being here with Danny." She looked around at the bustling scene that didn't seem at all dangerous. Then again, she reminded herself, appearances could be deceiving. "It wasn't as busy as now." She took in the three towering spires lancing into the clear blue sky. "Most of the people were headed to the cathedral."

"Makes sense. Given the time the shooting was called in, people would have been headed to midnight mass." He skimmed his knuckles up her cheek. She'd begun to get color back into her face, but now she'd gone pale as snow. "We need to get you somewhere warm. You're shivering."

"Of course I am. It's freezing." There was an unnatural brightness to her eyes that suggested her chill had nothing to do with the weather. Fear, he diagnosed. And a rush of adrenaline caused by whatever flashback had just played in her mind. The problem with recovering memories lost to traumatic stress was that you also got hit with the feelings that went with those memories.

"Which is why you can tell me about it over coffee."

He took her to the Café du Monde, which was open twenty-four hours a day, except for Christmas and the occasional hurricane. Since the inside of the café was packed, they had to sit outside, but the plastic sheeting walls and the heaters made it comfortable. He'd worried that they might be swarmed by fans, but without makeup, and lacking in any "I'm a famous person, look at me" attitude, she moved unnoticed through the crowd.

"The police think he shot at me, too," Lark said after she'd shared the memory over steaming mugs of *café au lait*. "I don't remember that part, but Detective Jordan said he missed and hit the building, so all I got hit with was brick fragments." She absently touched the bandaged wound she'd managed to somewhat conceal with a fringe of bangs she'd cut with a pair of surgical scissors borrowed from a helpful nurse before leaving the hospital. "They found the bullet on the street. The next thing I remember, after Danny falling, is riding the streetcar to the Canal Street station."

Witnesses had put her on the inbound car from Lee's Circle, where the statue of the Confederate general astride his war horse faced defiantly north. Neither Jordan nor Deveraux had any idea how she'd gotten there in the first place, but the prevailing theory was that after escaping the assailant, she'd wandered through the darkened streets in a daze before boarding the green St. Charles Street car back to the more bustling Quarter.

"So your assailant *was* a male." He studied her over the rim of the heavy white mug.

"I think so." A frown of concentration furrowed her brow. "At first I couldn't see him. It was dark and foggy and he was dressed all in black. Maybe I just assumed it was a man." He heard the doubt creep into her tone. "I suppose it could have been a woman with a deep voice."

"You're probably right. Most women, given an opportunity to plan a murder, prefer poison, and although they're catching up with the men when it comes to more violent crimes, Murphy's shooting doesn't have the feel of a female M.O. And since Guest hasn't given up his obsession with you, it's probable that he's still into black leather."

She stared down into her own mug, as if seeing the frightening scene played out in the light brown depths of coffee. She looked up at him, her eyes grave.

"God, I hate it that I can't remember his face."

He reached out, skimmed a hand down her hair and assured himself that it really wasn't touching. "Give it time."

"I also think I'm afraid."

"It's about time."

"Not of Guest. Well, him, too. But I think mostly I'm afraid of remembering."

"That's typical for traumatic amnesia. It's your brain's way of protecting you from reliving a stressful situation." There'd been a time when he would have welcomed a case of amnesia to keep the ghosts—especially Aaron Bragg—at bay.

"That's the same thing the doctor said." She sighed. "You know what's ironic?"

"What?"

"Before the Christmas Eve show, I was congratulating myself on regaining control of my life. I'd changed my show to a format that I felt comfortable with, I'd left a marriage that should have been declared dead at the altar—"

"From the outside looking in, at the beginning, before your husband's affair got plastered all over the covers of those tabloids, you seemed happy enough."

"Appearances can be deceiving. I learned during those days that I'm a lot better actress than I could have imagined.

"It was a terrible time," she admitted quietly. "When Guest was released from prison, I started reliving all those old fears I thought I'd finally managed to overcome after that summer. I'm embarrassed to admit it, but I felt safer having Cody around."

"Hiring a full-time bodyguard would have probably been cheaper."

"Unfortunately you weren't around to suggest that when I got married." Irritation—at her ex-rat of a spouse or him, or perhaps both of them—crackled in her voice like ice.

"I had my reasons."

He pushed the plate of beignets toward her, silently encouraging her to eat. Although she should be starving, she'd only picked at her waffle this morning and while fried dough might not exactly appear on any diet's list of approved foods, at least the powdered sugar might give her a buzz to counteract the exhaustion he could see in her eyes and on her face. Her lovely, heartbreakingly bruised face.

"What you had was a rampant case of hormones run amok," she said. "We both did." Lark looked away, toward the river, where a white Mississippi paddle wheeler, draped in greenery, was docking. "I suppose sending a soldier off to war with mind-blowing sex is a tradition going back to that first battle when prehistoric men threw rocks at one another."

"Any tradition that involves mind-blowing sex is definitely worth keeping." He wondered if she'd had mind-blowing sex with Armstrong and decided from the way she'd described her marriage, probably not. It might be small of him, but Lucas was glad about that.

Tourists were pouring off the boat and into the café. Lucas reached across the white table and took her hand in his. "And for the record, what we had was a helluva lot more than runaway hormones."

He felt her tense. Lark picked up a puffy beignet with her free hand, and bit into it. "We were kids," she said finally. He tightened his fingers when she tried to tug her hand away. "Sometimes those days seem like a thousand years ago."

*And sometimes they seem like yesterday*, he thought. His second thought was that he was standing on the edge of quicksand. One false step and they could both be in trouble.

"I was in Vegas," she volunteered after another brief pause. "Opening for Brooks and Dunn. My name was on the huge marquee outside the hotel, I had a real dressing room, with my name *and* a gold star on the door, there'd been lightbulbs around the mirror, and I didn't smell of diesel fuel when I went up on stage."

"I have a difficult time believing you could ever smell like an eighteen-wheeler."

"Diesel fumes are part of living on a bus," she said. "I was so excited. I was back from playing in Italy, where I'd gotten a lot of attention, and it looked as if all those years of hard work were finally paying off, when the two dozen blood-red roses were delivered." She shivered again, this time, Lucas suspected, not from the cold. "The card was signed, 'With love and devotion, from your husband.' "

"Who'd just gotten out of prison." He brushed a thumb over her scraped knuckles.

"Yes. Cody showed up about five minutes later. I was still shaking." She shook her head. "His timing was perfect. He proposed, I accepted, and four hours later, an Elvis impersonator declared us man and wife."

"You were married by an Elvis impersonator?" He'd missed that, which made sense, since he'd pretty much cut himself off from the outside world in those days.

"A dead ringer." She made a sound of disgust. "And not the sexy, 'Love Me Tender' king of rock and roll, but the fat, sweaty, banana-and-peanut-butter-sandwich-eating, sequined jumpsuit Elvis."

"Now there's an image."

"One I've tried to put out of my mind." Lark pulled her hand free and busied herself with brushing the snowy powdered sugar that had fallen onto the table back onto the white plate. "Although I hate to admit it, I'm not even sure Guest was the sole reason I married Cody. Once my career started off into the stratosphere, I became afraid of dropping that brass ring I'd finally managed to grab hold of."

"Seems like that'd be a fairly normal reaction. It's a lot easier to stick to your guns when you don't have anything to lose."

"Well, it was odd and totally unexpected, since I'd wanted to be a big star for as long as I could remember." When she licked some sugar off her fingertips, lust took on claws, and it was all Lucas could do not to put those pretty manicured fingers into his mouth.

"I never had a single doubt you'd make it."

An answering smile died half-formed on her lips.

"I hadn't realized how angry I still am at you," she said, seeming a bit surprised at the notion, which had him suspect that as tough as she'd become, deep down inside, she was still the same little girl who'd always gone out of her way to avoid conflict. "Which is odd, since I've never been one to hold a grudge." *Another understatement.* "Not even against Cody." She took another sip of coffee. "So much for magic," she muttered.

"Magic?"

Her scowl suggested she hadn't planned to say the words out loud. But now that she had, she'd piqued his interest. "I borrowed Zelda's *Book of Shadows* and used one of her spells to banish you years ago," she said.

*"Book of Shadows?"*

She shrugged. "It's hard to explain. Mostly, I suppose, it's like a witch's cookbook."

"Interesting. Was eye of newt and wing of bat involved?"

"I'm not allowed to share the secrets of the Craft with nonbelievers. If I told you, I'd have to kill you."

"I thought there was some witch's code about not hurting people."

"And it harm none, do what ye will," Lark quoted the wiccan code her aunt had taught her. "But Zelda's the witch," she reminded him. "Not me."

"So there's no reason why you can't tell me about the banishing spell."

"Of course there is." Her sharp smile glinted like a witch's blade. "I don't want to."

"At least tell me if it involved you getting naked beneath a full moon."

"Why would you think that?"

"Because it's an appealing image." He leaned back in the chair, crossed his legs at the ankles and allowed his mind to conjure up a mental picture of Lark wearing only perfumed and powdered flesh dancing in the moonlight.

"All I'm going to say is that it involved fire. A lot of it. You were reduced to ashes. Then stirred into water and poured down the drain."

"Sounds like that should have done the job."

"You'd think so, wouldn't you?" She polished off her cooling coffee. "Apparently, one of those pesky ashes escaped to live another day. And now that you're back in my life, I'm discovering that I'm not ready to give up my mad."

"I don't blame you," he said agreeably as he pushed back from the table. As he imagined sprinkling powdered sugar all over her body, then licking it off, Lucas decided mad was better than ambivalent. "You gonna tell me when you get unmad?"

Lark stood up, brushed the last of the sugar off her hands and pulled on her gloves. "You'll be the first to know."

They no sooner were back on the street when someone called out her name. That drew the immediate attention of a group of tourists who'd been clustered around a fire-eater. So much for anonymity.

Less than thrilled with the attention, Lucas was forced to wait while Lark signed autographs on checkbook registers, pages torn from guidebooks, and the brims of several baseball caps and assured the fans that she was fine and Daniel Murphy was making a strong recovery.

"The police are continuing with their investigation," she said as she posed for a picture with an old geezer who was ninety if he was a day. From the blissed-out smile on the guy's face, Lucas figured he could probably now die happy. "And we're all hopeful that Danny Murphy's assailant will be behind bars soon."

They were back in the car, driving uptown to the hospital, when Lucas stopped for a red light and glanced over at Lark, seated beside him, rubbing her forehead.

"Headache back?"

"No." She sighed.

"It must get old, not having any privacy."

"I wanted to be famous. It's part of the deal."

"You don't have to be so accessible."

"Yes," Lark corrected as the light turned green, "I do. Those people back there at the square buy my records because we've made a connection through my songs. I may have more fame, and the money that comes with it, but we're the same under the skin—we have the same hopes, the same dreams, have suffered the same heartbreaks. The day I forget that and start believing my own press is the day I might as well hang up my guitar and quit singing because I'll be out of the business anyway."

She leaned forward and hit a button on the radio, set to a classic country station. As if backing up her argument that country music was all about people suffering the same heartbreaks, Patsy Cline began belting out "Crazy."

Perfect.

"'Worry,'" Cline sang in her signature full-bodied voice, "'why do I let myself worry? Wond'ring what in the world did I do?'"

Talk about identifying. Just like in those famous lyrics, Lark had been crazy for thinking that her love could hold Lucas. She'd been crazy for trying, crazy for crying. And, she reminded herself firmly, she'd be crazy for setting herself up to suffer through it all again.

# 13

Lark's spirits lifted a bit at the hospital, after the SICU nurse informed her that Danny had regained consciousness earlier that morning.

"But he's not awake now?"

"No," the woman said, sending Lark's emotions plummeting again. "He had a brief seizure, which isn't unusual with a head injury. But he's responding much more to stimuli, so all in all, we're very positive."

Lark stood at Danny's bedside again, trying to find something positive about his appearance. "I think he's got more color in his cheeks," she murmured to Lucas. His skin was as waxy as it had looked last night.

"Seems so," Lucas agreed. "It hasn't been that long, Lark. You have to—"

"I know." She exhaled a short, frustrated breath. "Give it time." She'd never considered herself an overly impatient person. Then again, she'd never been in a situation like this one.

She bent down, brushed a kiss against Danny's beard-stubbled cheek, and thought she felt a movement in the muscle beneath her lips, like an attempt at a smile.

"You're going to do great," she assured him robustly. "We'll take some time off." She'd been thinking about cutting back anyway. Now she was more than thinking about it. Since her career had taken off, life had become a blur of hotel rooms, arenas, and interstates, performing a grueling two hundred and eighty shows a year. Nothing like having a friend shot in the head and facing death to trigger a change in priorities. "No more touring all fifty states every time a CD comes out."

She skimmed her fingers down the side of his face. "We'll experience real life for a change, catch some movies in a real theater instead of having the DVD skip a scene every time the bus hits a pothole. Maybe, if we're in the mood and something comes to us, we'll write a few songs, but we're not going to push things. Life's too short." A lump rose in her throat. "And you're too special to me."

She glanced up at the wall clock. She really should get back to the house if she was going to have time to rest before tonight's show.

*Priorities*, Lark reminded herself as she pulled up a chair beside the bed, took hold of Danny's hand and began softly singing about empty highways, homesickness, and broken hearts healed by the revivalist powers of endearing friendship.

"Leaving Lonesome Town" painted such a vibrant picture of small towns across the country that listening to it, Lucas felt as if he'd been traveling those blacktop roads right along with her.

Her style was one Lucas had grown up listening to, a living embodiment of a tradition that grew out of the mountain highlands of Appalachia, which in turn had come from the old songs brought over on ships from Ireland and Scotland; her themes were the timeless ones of love, helplessness, loss, faith, and family, seen through a modern lens, while still harking back to a time before songs were written for their potential to sell units.

Her voice turned husky as it faltered a bit on the bridge. Her eyes were moist when she looked up at Lucas, then back down at Murphy. The guitar player still looked like hell warmed over, but his lips had curved upward into a faint smile and his fingers appeared to tighten on hers.

Damned if she wasn't getting through to him.

Which wasn't all that surprising. Lark Stewart was the kind of woman who got under a man's skin, all the way into his heart, and stayed there.

"He's going to be all right," Lark insisted as they walked back down the hall from the SICU.

"It's looking encouraging," Lucas allowed. "I'm glad for you."

"I know." He'd always wanted her to be happy. Which was why she'd never understood how he could have broken her heart. But she wasn't going to dwell on that right now, not while her optimism had taken the edge off her mad.

They'd nearly reached the elevators when her cell phone rang.

"It's me," Ryan said. "We've got a problem."

"Why don't you tell me something I don't know," Lark said with a sigh. "What's wrong now?"

"There's a blizzard in Chicago."

"It's winter in Chicago. I'd be more surprised if there wasn't a blizzard. Why is that our problem?"

"Because the sound engineer we used on Christmas Eve took advantage of us canceling yesterday's show to fly to visit his family in Little Rock. He was planning to get back in time for tonight's show, but when they grounded all the planes at O'Hare, it caused a backup logjam throughout the system."

Lark had experienced the same thing innumerable times, which was only one of the reasons she hated to fly.

"Surely he's not the only sound engineer in New Orleans."

"No. But, but the new guy just moved here from Denver, and the equipment in the arena's not exactly the same as what he's used to in the Red Rocks Amphitheater, so he wants to do his own sound check, just to make sure he's got it right. I was going to call one of the guys to come in and take care of it, but I didn't want you to think I was trying to make decisions for you."

Lark managed a smile at the idea that she'd managed to intimidate him. Intimidating men had always been Laurel's talent.

"I'll be right there." A perfectionist, she'd always done her own sound checks and saw no reason to change things now. "And would you ask the guys to come in anyway? I have something I want to say to them."

There was a brief hesitation on the other end of the line. Lark suspected Ryan was waiting for her to tell him what, exactly, she wanted to talk about. But what she was planning to do was bound to come as a surprise and she wanted to break the news to her band members herself.

"I thought you were going to get some rest before tonight," Lucas said after she'd flipped the phone closed.

"I am. But they need a sound check and the arena's nearly right around the corner. It won't take long; we can swing by on the way back to the house."

When he'd realized that Lark was, unfortunately, dead serious about going through with her performance, Lucas had called NOPD and made certain that extra cops had been assigned to the arena. But the damn complex was still a logistical nightmare.

It was bad enough that the arena was connected to a hotel, shopping mall, and the Superdome, but with the Sugar Bowl being played in a few days, workers, tourists, and football fans had turned the place into a human anthill.

"You're going to need a full search," Lucas informed the events manager, who was on the scene when Lark arrived for her sound check.

"That's ridiculous," Lark objected. "We've sold over eighteen thousand tickets. Even if I'd be willing to have every ticket holder patted down or screened with a metal detector, which I'm not, people would have to start arriving hours early to get seated in time for the show."

"And your point is?" Lucas asked.

"It's overkill."

"We could do a visual search." Ryan suggested the compromise. "Check coats, bags, containers. That sort of thing."

Lark frowned. "I hate that idea."

Even back in the early days, when she and Danny were playing those venues in the boonies, she'd wanted to make the show special. Something fun that would take people's minds off their everyday lives. Through all the incarnations of the performance, she'd tried to keep that mind-set.

"It's done all the time now, Ms. Stewart," the events coordinator, a forty-something woman wearing a St. John's dress-for-success red knit suit, assured her. "We've become especially security conscious since the terrorist threats. Our crew's gotten very good at moving lots of people through the turnstiles very quickly and efficiently."

"If you all will excuse us for a moment," Lucas said, "Ms. Stewart and I need to talk." Gripping her arm, he dragged her away from the others.

"I realize it's going to take a major effort, but you have to stop being so damn dictatorial," Lark complained when they were out of hearing distance. "I'd also appreciate it if you wouldn't manhandle me."

His fingers flexed; black brows dove ominously low. "I wasn't manhandling you."

"What do you usually call it when you give a woman bruises?"

"A mistake." He jammed his hands deep into his front pockets. "I'm sorry if I came on too physical, but forgoing additional security is not an option."

Lark tossed her head. "You're not the boss of me." Terrific. Sounding like a petulant twelve-year-old was a great way to get him to treat her like an adult.

"I damn well am the boss when it comes to your safety," he reminded her. "Either you go for at least a visual search, or you're not going to get up there on that stage tonight."

So whatever happened to veto power? "You're just ticked off that I've acquired a mind of my own."

"Wrong again, Duchess. You always knew your own

mind—or you never would have made it in the music business. What I'm pissed off about is that anyone so damn bright can act so damn stupid."

"Now you're calling me stupid?" Lark's voice rose up the scale.

"Hell, no. If you'd just shut up and listen for a minute . . ."

Lucas dragged a hand down his face. Took a deep breath. "I take back what I said about you being the most logical of your sisters." He leaned forward, seeming to tower over her even more. "Getting up on that stage without adequate security is goddamn stupid and no way do I need any more damn ghosts in my life," he ground out through gritted teeth.

Surprised at both his unexpected flare of anger, along with the unexpected glimpse behind his well-constructed parapets, Lark opened her mouth. Closed it. Studied him silently.

"What ghosts?"

He shrugged, looking as if he wished he'd bitten his tongue off before letting those telling words escape. "They're not important. Forget about them."

"Too late. You already let them out of the bottle. Or box, or whatever."

He shot a look at the little group that was watching them with undisguised curiosity. "This is neither the time nor the place for a personal discussion."

She shook off his touch, turned on her heel and walked a few steps around a corner, knowing he'd follow, then turned back to look up at him. "Okay, we no longer have an audience. So, give."

"Pigheaded," he muttered.

"Tenacious," she countered, squaring her shoulders.

They stared at each other.

Lark didn't need her aunt's ESP to know that those ghosts he'd made the mistake of mentioning were hovering between them, dark and ominous.

"It's not fair," she complained on a frustrated huff of breath. "You know all about my life, but I don't know anything about what you've been doing these past years."

"There's not that much to tell."

"Fine." She folded her arms. Tapped a foot. "Then it shouldn't take that long to catch me up."

He cursed. "We can catch up later," he said.

"Later, when?" His gruff tone had suggested when hell froze over might be an option and Lark refused to wait that long.

"Hell, I don't know." He plowed a hand through his hair. "After the concert."

"Do you promise?"

"Yeah." He shrugged. "Sure."

Although he didn't seem at all thrilled with the idea, Lark was somewhat mollified. For now.

She glanced at the watch the record company had gifted her with when her first album went platinum. "We're wasting time. Why don't you go arrange for that extra security I seem to have no choice but to accept, while I do the sound check?"

"Fine. So long as you stay in sight."

"You really are too overprotective," she huffed.

"Maybe I just like looking at you."

The energy sparking between them, around them,

had suddenly become so palpable, Lark was surprised it wasn't setting off the arena's sprinkler systems.

"Lucas—"

"Shh." He touched a fingertip against her lips. Then, with his eyes still on hers, he lowered his head and replaced the finger with his mouth. Her breath shuddered out as he slowly—with that same devastating control he seemed to do everything else—nibbled his way from one corner of her mouth to the other.

His lips were cool; the emotions they stirred were anything but. Desire rippled beneath her skin. Unfurled in her blood. Lark breathed him in, tasting the rich flavor of coffee and a deeper, darker taste that set her pulse to pounding.

The kiss, which had her toes curling in her sneakers, ended far too soon. A faint whimper of protest escaped her lips when he lifted his mouth from hers.

"What was that for?"

"For you." He stroked her hair with a hand which, heaven help her, Lark suddenly, recklessly, wanted to feel all over her body. Then he surprised her even more by smiling, slow and easy. "And for me."

*Be strong*, Lark told herself firmly as her mutinous heart turned over. *Whenever you feel yourself weakening, remember how you cried all the way back to Nashville the last time you got carried away kissing this man.*

"Well, don't do it again."

The members of the band had arrived and were waiting with Ryan when Lark and Lucas returned.

After assuring everyone that she was, indeed, okay,

Lark got down to business. "First of all, I want you to know how much I've enjoyed working with y'all," she began.

"Oh, oh," Kenny Clark, a fiddle player from Stone Mountain, Georgia, said. "Sounds as if we're about to get the shaft."

"Not at all," Lark said quickly. "It's just that I've been thinking it's time for a change."

"Definitely the shaft," Marcus Nichols, the steel-guitar player, agreed.

"You're all jumping the gun," she complained. "There's no way, after all the miles we've traveled together, that I'm going to just cut you loose."

"What kind of change?" asked Chase Carpenter. The drummer, who'd begun his music career in the Seattle punk rock scene, did not appear to be expecting good news.

"What happened to Danny got me thinking about life in general," she said.

"Oh, oh," Kenny repeated.

"Always a mistake," Chase said.

"Don't be so negative," she countered. "Danny nearly getting killed has driven home the fact that the world—and life—doesn't revolve around the music business."

"Try telling that to the record label," Chase muttered.

"That's exactly what I'm going to do," Lark agreed. "I've decided to scale back. Sort of a 'less is more' thing."

"Scaling back as in cutting back?" Kenny's brows, below an unruly mop of rust-colored curls, carved deep ridges in his forehead.

"That's exactly it," Lark said. "Instead of being on the

road fifty weeks a year, I've decided to do fewer performances, but make each show special."

"They're already special," Kenny said. "How many shows are you talking about?"

"About a quarter as many as we've been doing now."

"My wife's fixin' to have a baby," Marcus complained. "No way can I get by on twenty-five percent salary."

"You won't have to." She'd been thinking about this for some time; the shooting had just proven the impetus. "You guys are the best band in the business; I'm still going to want you to back me up, if you still want to, after you hear my idea. But whichever you decide, it's time you went out on your own." She could feel them tense up and knew they were expecting the worst. "Which is why Danny and I are going to produce your album." The first without her standing out in front.

"Danny's in a coma," Chase reminded her.

"It's not exactly a coma." She wasn't exactly certain what his official medical condition was, but didn't want to get sidetracked. "But he's going to be recovered in time to show up at the studio."

"And if he doesn't?" Chase asked.

"He will." There was no way Lark could allow herself to think otherwise. "Meanwhile, while we're waiting for him to get back on his feet, we can start finding you some songs."

"Are you saying you're quitting performing?" Ryan asked, clearly surprised.

"No, I'm saying I'm going to cut back. I'm taking some time off, writing new songs, working on the new format."

"You cut back on touring and those guys in those fancy executive offices wearing those thousand-dollar boots will think you're flat-out nuts," Kenny said.

"Or more likely, they're going to think you're just hinting at leaving so they'll renegotiate your contract," Ryan warned.

"Well, then," Lark said, "you're just going to have to convince them otherwise."

"Me?" Ryan looked surprised. "I'm just the road manager."

"Not any longer. I'm promoting you to manager." She'd been without a manager since separating from Cody. "If you want the job," she said, surprised when he didn't immediately leap at what a lot of people might consider the opportunity of a lifetime.

"Uh, sure." She didn't blame him for being surprised; they'd all been through a lot of changes these past months. "If you're sure that's what you want."

"Absolutely. You're a marvel, Ryan. I've no idea what I would have done all these months without you and while it'll be difficult to replace you as road manager, I can't think of anyone more capable of keeping all the balls in the air than you." She smiled encouragingly. "And there's no one I'd trust more."

"Whew." He blew out a long breath. "Well, when you put it like that, how can I turn the offer down? I'm flattered, Lark. And I'll try my damnedest not to let you down."

"If I thought you would, I wouldn't have made this decision," she said. "Now, here's my idea. As you've all probably noticed, the radio's chock-full of testosterone these days."

"The women have been sort of nudged off the charts," Kenny agreed.

"You say nudged, I say muscled." There'd been a time, not so long ago, when women singers had ruled the Nashville roost. These days you'd have to have been living in a cave not to notice that three-quarters of the air time was being given to male artists. "Now, I'm not going to fret about it, because we all know that these things are cyclical—the industry swings one way, then it swings the other. Meanwhile, I'm also not going to sit back and just ride out the storm. I'm taking control."

"By cutting back?" Ryan asked, clearly puzzled.

"Exactly. I'm going to create a venue celebrating the things women care about," she responded. "A concert tour featuring a Who's Who of female singers."

"Like Lilith Fair?" Chase asked with blatant skepticism.

"Exactly."

Lark's first big break, which had gotten her noticed by that agent who'd sent her to Rome, had been when she'd appeared in the female-only music festival that derived its title from the Old Testament name of Adam's first wife—who'd been dumped, then banished from Eden for being too headstrong, to make room for Eve.

"Lilith Fair was right up there with Lallopalloza when it came to drawing fans," she said.

"It also only lasted three years," Kenny reminded her.

"Unfortunately, that's true." It had been steam-rollered by the more powerful commercial forces of angry male bands, and bubble-gum pop groups, and girl singers who'd been convinced by greedy promoters that the way to sell music was to appear half naked on magazine covers.

"But these are different times. Men got most of the strong 9/11 songs, but they're not the only ones who care about patriotism. A lot of the soldiers fighting around the world are women, but just because they fly helicopters and drive Humvees doesn't mean that they've surrendered their femininity at the army base gates. They want the same things every woman does. What we all—men and women want, even if the men are often not introspective enough to admit it: home, hearth, family, love, country, peace. The things we've been singing about all along."

"So you're not going to go all militant feminist on us and start singing guys-are-all-assholes-and-deserve-to-die songs?" Chase asked.

"Of course not." If she'd been going to write those kind of songs she would have done it immediately following her divorce. He really had to ditch that negative old punk mentality.

"And you promise you won't suddenly make us start playing that sappy New Age fairy stuff?" This from Marcus.

"I'm not changing the music," Lark insisted yet again. She glanced over at Lucas, who was leaning against the wall, ankles crossed, arms folded, seeming to be enjoying watching her try to win them over. "I'm merely changing the venue for a while. I also have an Academy Award–winning documentary maker on board."

Lark had shared her idea a couple of months ago with Lily, who had mentioned it to her husband, Ian, who'd professed interest in filming the tour.

"Give us a minute, okay?" Kenny asked.

Lark nodded, then watched as they walked to the back row of seats and got into a huddle.

"They'll do it," Ryan predicted.

"I hope so," Lark said. Watching them, she was unsurprised that Chase appeared to be the holdout.

"It's just that they've had a lot of change this past year."

"Who hasn't?" Lark murmured.

"Speaking of which, I'm really jazzed about you making me your manager."

"You deserve it. It's too much for me to handle and I need someone I can trust in charge of the big picture."

She'd been making all the decisions on her own since leaving Cody and had discovered that worrying about leasing agreements and venues and negotiating with the label on everything from cover art to liner notes was not the least bit conducive to creativity. How much easier things had been on the Mud and Dust tour. Before she'd gotten famous.

*Be careful what you wish for.*

They were coming back. Lark crossed her fingers behind her back.

"We've come to a decision," Kenny said. Then paused. He'd always been the dramatic one of the group.

"And?"

"Though Chase is afraid it's going to cut down on his groupies, since Lilith Fair tended to draw a lot of lesbian fans, we decided that any tour that's mostly chicks can't be a bad thing."

Lark exhaled a relieved breath and decided this was no time for a lecture on political correctness. "Terrific!"

There were hugs all around.

"It's going to take a lot of planning, but I think the key is to make it an event. Something special, so we'll only tour June to September."

Not only would she pick up the summer fair-going crowds, women singers trying to balance families and careers would be able to tour with their kids during the school vacation months.

"That's going to be more difficult to fund, since the odds of all the artists you want being on the same label as you is probably slim to none, which means you're not going to be able to get the suits in the executive offices all that excited about writing expense checks," Ryan suggested.

"I've already thought about that." Late into the night for several months, actually. Danny's shooting had simply provided the impetus for her to act on those thoughts. "Tours are already depending more and more on corporate sponsors. We just need to get a high profile company who wants to reach more women, like NASCAR's Winston Cup markets to smokers."

"A chick sponsor," Chase said.

"The Kotex Country Classic," Kenny suggested.

"The Tampax Acoustical Twang Tour," Marcus offered.

"All strings," Chase said, quickly jumping onto the chick joke bandwagon.

"Very funny." Lark's tone was dry, but she couldn't hold back the smile. Joking was definitely preferable to the out-and-out resistance she'd feared. "I've some ideas in mind," she told Ryan. "We need to contact those corporations who've asked me to sing for their conferences and sales meetings in the past. Let's get together after the first of the year to brainstorm and see what we can come up with."

"Absolutely," he agreed.

Unlike Chase, Lark was an optimist by nature. Granted, she'd been disappointed from time to time, but she'd long decided that while pessimists might be proven right, optimists had a lot more fun and the occasional regret was better than going through life with a negative attitude.

Which was why, after she finished up her sound check, she felt as if things were beginning to look up.

Until a hand from behind settled on her shoulder.

"Hello, Lark," the all-too-familiar voice said, cutting through her like a knife.

# 14

Lark slowly turned to face her ex-husband. A young woman dressed in purple leather hung on his arm; her skirt barely covered the essentials and fit like a surgical glove.

"This is a surprise," Lark said calmly. And not a good one. "I didn't realize you were in New Orleans."

He shrugged shoulders clad in the fringed leather jacket she'd had custom-tailored for him last Christmas.

"Hey, Danny was a friend of mine. Why wouldn't I come see how he's doing?"

*Maybe because you hated him and were jealous of our friendship?* "He's not allowed visitors."

"So the dragon of a floor nurse said. I'll bet you got in, though."

Lark didn't bother to respond.

"This is such a tragedy," the woman with Cody said with a west Texas twang. Her exaggerated sigh almost made her breasts pop out of the leather bustier she was wearing beneath her matching fitted jacket. The avid expression in blue eyes lined like a raccoon's was anything but tragic. "I wrote some lyrics about a musician's murder

on Music Row on the flight in from Nashville. It's a duet.
I'm hoping to get Kenny Chesney to sing the male part."

"Uh huh," Lark said noncommittally.

"This is Tanya Kay Gilman," Cody said. "I'm producing her new album."

"How nice for both of you." Lark wondered if the
brassy blonde had any idea what she was getting into.

Tanya Kay lifted her pointed, foxy chin. "Cody says I
have the best voice in country music." *Better than yours.*
The unspoken challenge hung on the air, along with the
acrid odor of cigarette smoke emanating from the
woman's clothes and hair, which didn't bode well for any
future career. Smoking was not beneficial to a singer's
voice. "I'm going to be a huge star."

"Congratulations." *Run*, she mentally warned Cody's
potential new meal ticket. *Run very fast and very far.*

"We need to talk." Cody took hold of her elbow, in
much the same way Lucas had done. But her former husband's touch made her skin crawl. How had she ever
stood to have his hands on her? "Somewhere private."

"There's nothing to talk about." She shook his hand
off. "Both our marriage and our business partnership are
over, Cody."

"It's not fair, dammit. After all I did for you."

"It was a two-way street. You got as much out of my
career as I did. Or perhaps more."

"What the hell does that mean?"

"I'm having an audit done of the last two years of the
corporation's books."

"Are you accusing me of skimming?"

"I'm not accusing you of anything." *Yet.* "As for your

income, you'll continue to earn producer royalties."

Despite its reputation as Music City, Nashville was, in reality, a songwriting town. Record companies made their money by album sales, but songwriters and producers got paid every time a radio station played a song for the life of the copyright. If a song became a golden oldie, the songwriter was set for life.

"Hell, most of those songs are eventually going to disappear. Then what am I supposed to do?"

"Go back on the rodeo circuit?" she suggested sweetly. "Or perhaps find a real job?"

"Cody has a real job," the other woman said. "Managing me. Don't you, honey?"

"Shut up, Tanya Kay." His hands fisted as he turned back to Lark. "I had a job, goddammit. Until you decided you'd outgrown the guy who made you the star you are."

"I don't remember your voice on any of the tracks," she snapped, angry at him, but even more angry at herself for ever getting involved with this man who, in the beginning, had played her like a Gibson Granada Hearts and Flowers banjo.

"I was the one singing, Cody. I was the one who was constantly putting out the fires you'd start by alienating everyone in the business. I was the one humiliated in public by that bimbo who lied and told the world she was pregnant with your child; I was the one who sang that duet with you about forgiving my man in front of a worldwide television audience at the Grammys.

"*You* were the one who, after swearing everlasting fidelity on a Barbara Walters Oscar special, started sleeping around with a tambourine player."

He shrugged. "So, I slipped."

"It was more than a slip, and we both know it. You were a chronic adulterer. It's the chase that excites you, Cody. Once you've gotten a woman, you lose interest."

Thankfully, it no longer hurt. Lark no longer felt anything toward Cody Armstrong.

"Maybe you weren't very interesting," Tanya Kay suggested.

"Yeah," Cody drawled, his narrow-slitted eyes moving over her in a way that made her skin crawl. Why ever did she find this man the least bit appealing? "Did you ever think that if I did lose interest, it was because I wasn't getting what I needed at home?"

"That's no way to talk to a lady," Lucas, who'd come up behind Lark, said in a low, dangerous voice.

Cody was forced to tilt his head back to look a long way up at Lucas's dark glower. "Who the hell are you?"

"Lucas McCloud." His tone was deceptively mild as he slipped his arm around Lark's waist. "You know, Armstrong," he said conversationally, "there are two hundred and six bones in the human body. And unless you want to discover how it feels to have every one of them broken, I suggest you leave. Now."

Their eyes clashed—Cody's swirling with hatred, Lucas's taking on a deadly warrior's glint. Cody was the first to look away.

He shot a furious gaze at Lark. "We're not through."

Radiating with repressed fury and frustration, he dragged Tanya Kay, who was tottering on the skyscraper stiletto heels of her thigh-high boots, down the theater aisle.

"I thought you said you were going to get her to give us some money," she complained in a strident whine.

"Would you just shut the hell up?" he yelled.

Lark sighed. "I need some air." She'd once known a keyboard player from L.A. whose method of loosening up before a performance was to screech like a banshee. For the first time, she thought perhaps there was something to be said for scream therapy.

The icy winter air instantly cleared her head.

"You okay?" Lucas asked.

"Of course." No, she wasn't. She and Cody had fought a lot at the end of their marriage, but never had she seen such . . . *murder* in his eyes.

"Want me to go shoot the son of a bitch?"

His matter-of-fact tone unnerved Lark nearly as much as her ex-husband's anger.

"Of course I don't want you to shoot him. You're not serious, are you?" She stared up at him, trying to get a handle on the stranger he'd become. "Please tell me you're joking."

Lucas folded his arms and leaned a broad shoulder against the outside wall. "I gave up joking when I joined the Bureau. It's bad for the image."

"And here I thought that was just an exaggeration perpetrated by the movies."

"Most stereotypes have some basis in reality. Would *you* trust your life to a joker?"

She would trust her life to him. Unfortunately, as she looked up into his shielded dark eyes, Lark realized that it was her heart that was once again in peril. "I wish you hadn't lied about us being involved."

"I didn't lie. We *are* involved."

"Not in the way you led him to believe." She sighed. "After I'd decided to divorce Cody, I found out he'd been secretly selling information about my personal life to the tabloids." The honeymoon shot he'd taken of her sunbathing topless on a beach in Mexico had, for a time, been one of the top ten downloaded internet pictures. It still pricked her ego that she could have married such a lowlife. "He's probably on the phone right now; they'll have us lovers by morning."

"Now there's an idea," he murmured in a deep, potent drawl. Lark caught the quirk of his chiseled lips, the sexy, wicked glint in his eyes, before he ruthlessly pulled the smile back.

Looking back on those four years she'd spent with him, Lark had realized that by marrying Cody Armstrong, she'd been seeking not only safety, but stability.

She'd been blessed with a wonderful family, but before his recent marriage, her father had gone through women so fast that by the time she'd reached her teens, Lark had quit bothering to learn their names.

Her aunt Zelda, whom she adored, had been divorced twice and had publicly sworn off men in favor of her work. Her other aunt, Melanie, was still bitter about *her* husband walking out on her to begin a new family with a much younger, less high-maintenance woman.

Lark had been determined to do whatever it took to keep *her* marriage together. Not wanting to rock the boat, she'd repeatedly turned a blind eye to Cody's behavior. When she'd finally decided to get a divorce, she hadn't known who she was angrier with—her lying, cheating, conniving husband, or herself.

"You had your chance." She kept her eyes on his. "Two chances, as a matter of fact. When we were kids, and again in New Orleans. It's not my fault you blew them both."

"Last I heard, it was three strikes and out."

"That's baseball. Not life."

"There are some people who'd argue that baseball is life. Would groveling help?"

"I have a difficult time imagining you groveling."

"I'm male. The willingness to grovel for sex is a genetic trait."

Steeling herself against the appeal of his surprisingly droll humor, she lifted her chin. "We were talking about baseball."

"A guy's gotta have priorities."

Laughter drifted across the arena parking lot. They watched as two teenagers walked hand in hand toward a turquoise 1960s Cadillac that could have belonged to Elvis. The girl was chattering away a mile a minute; the openly besotted look on the boy's face, as he opened the passenger door for the pretty young blonde, suggested he wasn't hearing a word she was saying.

"Take him, for example," Lucas said. "There's not a teenage boy in the world who wouldn't crawl butt naked over broken glass for sex."

"But you didn't have to."

On the contrary, it had taken her seven months after their first mind-reeling kiss, to talk Lucas into making love to her. It hadn't been that he hadn't wanted to. But even then he'd wanted to protect her, and had argued that if she got pregnant she'd never achieve her dream of stardom. At the time, she was frustrated by what she'd considered an over-amount of caution. Now, looking back on all the ways she'd tested his resolve, as only a teenage girl bent on seduction could, Lark wondered at his willpower.

"No, I didn't," he agreed. A cold breeze lifted her hair and blew it across her face. Lucas brushed it away, his fingers skimming her cheek as if he still had every right to touch her. "But I would have. In a heartbeat."

*Uh oh.*

"Hell." His voice was low and rough. "Do you have any idea what you do to me?"

"I wasn't the one who brought up sex," she reminded him breathlessly.

"But you've been thinking about it. The same way I have."

She thought about denying the accusation, then reminded herself how destructive lies were to a relationship. Not that she and Lucas had a relationship.

Of course they did. She just couldn't figure out what it was.

Lark noticed that the Caddy's windows were already steamed up, felt something curl tightly inside her, and was appalled to realize she was jealous of a teenage girl.

"Whatever happened to your car?" she asked. He'd bought a wrecked Mustang from a junkyard in Bristol and had spent two years restoring it, planning to sell the muscle car to pay for college.

"Dad wasn't worth much, but at least he brought in a

disability check from that bad-back scam he pulled off when I was a kid. Once he got sent off to prison, that money stopped coming." His tone had turned tight and rigidly controlled. "Mom's salary at the funeral home wasn't enough to make ends meet, so I sold it when I joined the marines."

They'd had it all planned out: she was going to pursue her music career while he earned a business degree at Vanderbilt so he could manage her career. They were going to have children she could sing lullabies to; they were going to travel, exploring the wide world beyond the mountains they'd grown up in. They were going to grow old together, remaining lovers and best friends for the rest of their lives.

And then a serpent in the form of William Guest had arrived in Paradise. Less than two weeks later, Lark left Highland Falls for Nashville, while Lucas headed south to Parris Island for boot camp.

Lucas saw her shiver and decided this wasn't the time or place for a heavy discussion. "We'd better get back inside before you freeze. And, returning to the unpalatable subject of your ex-weasel, I understand you don't want to give the tabloids any more fodder about your personal life, but would you rather they reveal that I'm hanging around to keep you safe from Guest?"

"I'm hoping the police catch him before the press finds out he's escaped and makes the connection. The last thing I need is for people to find out I need a bodyguard."

"The last thing you need is to end up shot in the head like Daniel Murphy."

"You don't pull any punches, do you?"

"I can't afford to. And you can't afford me to."

She'd always been surprisingly logical for such a creative person. He watched her agile mind sifting through the options before finally deciding he was right.

Because he'd been dying to taste that full, luscious mouth again, even knowing it would be a major mistake, he caught Lark's chin in his fingers, and with his eyes locked on hers, took it.

She stiffened for an instant. Then her lips opened on a shuddering breath that had him half wild with the desire to touch. Even in the darkest depths of his alcoholism, Lucas had never wanted a drink like he wanted Lark at this moment. Never *needed* a drink like he needed her.

*God grant me the serenity to accept the things I cannot change; the courage to change the things I can, and the wisdom to know the difference.*

When he'd first gone on the wagon, the serenity prayer had been the only thing keeping him from diving back into the bottle. He realized he'd internalized it when he could admit that Lark represented yet another addiction.

His feelings for her were not going to change. Which meant he was just going to have to figure out how to deal with them. Later, when the blood wasn't pounding in his ears and the front of his slacks wasn't bulging out. When he could think again.

She met him, passion for passion, her hands fisting in his hair, her body straining against his in a way designed to fan the flames. She moaned when he nipped her lower lip; shuddered when, desperate for her, he spun them around and pressed her against the building.

"You taste the same," he said against her mouth. Like heat and honey, sex and sin. She also packed more of a kick than his old Remington.

"But I'm not the same." Lark eased back. Her eyes were dark and grave and revealed a wariness he could identify with. "I told you not to do that again."

"You didn't mean it."

"Now you're a mind reader?"

"It wasn't your mind I was reading a minute ago." Irritation stormed over need. Since it kept him from groveling, Lucas welcomed it. "Hell, yes, I wanted to kiss you, and the fact that before you remembered to complain, you were practically swallowing my tonsils, tells me that you wanted to kiss me right back. So what's the problem?"

She turned her back on him. Folded her arms in an unconscious gesture of self-protection. "I told you—"

"I know. You're still mad. But mad can make for some damn hot sex."

"We're not having sex."

"Not right now," he agreed, denying the ache in his groin.

"Not now, not later. It'll only complicate things."

"Don't look now, Duchess . . . Lark"—he corrected when she shot him a blistering look over her shoulder—"but things are already damn complicated."

"It was only natural curiosity." Her teeth bit into her lower lip. "It's been a long time, anyone would wonder."

"Makes sense to me." Lucas suspected that a lot more than curiosity had been responsible for the punch that kiss delivered, but reminding himself that his goal was to keep her alive, which he couldn't do if she decided to send him back to Tennessee, he wasn't going to argue the point. "So, did you satisfy your curiosity?"

"Yes." She began walking back to the others.

"And?"

"And what?"

"You going to tell me how I scored?"

"Women don't keep scorecards."

"You're forgetting that I have four sisters. Of course women keep score. So, how did I do? And please be kind. Even we manly males have delicate egos."

"I suspect yours is armor-plated," she muttered. "And I suppose it was okay."

"Just okay?" That hurt.

"Nice."

"Nice?" He rubbed his chest where his heart had just taken a direct hit from her verbal dart. Fluffy kittens were nice. A beer on a hot summer day, popcorn at the movies, those things were nice. He wanted to be a helluva lot more than *nice*.

"Very nice," she amended.

"I can do a lot better than that. How about we kick those kids out of that Caddy, climb into the backseat, and I'll show you."

"Why don't I just take your word for that."

She heard someone call her name, turned, and saw Ryan, who'd come out of the arena, headed toward them.

"I know you want to get back to the house," Ryan said, "but since I'm still technically your road manager, I thought we'd better go over the list for tonight's meet and greet." He handed Lark a computer-generated list of names.

"Is that what it sounds like?" Lucas asked.

"A few VIP fans are brought backstage after the show," Ryan explained when Lark failed to respond. Obviously she was giving him the silent treatment. "Any local politicians who want their pictures taken, members of the local fan club—"

"No," Lucas cut him off.

Lark glanced up from reading the names. "What did you say?"

"I said, No." He plucked the paper from her hand and wadded it up. "There's going to be no meet and greet tonight. You'll do the show, then get the hell off the stage. Then we're going back to Tennessee."

"I'm not leaving New Orleans while Danny's in the hospital. And I always meet with fans after a show." When she reached for the list, he stuffed it into his jacket pocket. "It's one of the perks they get for paying their fan club dues."

"Glazer here can hand out autographed pictures and T-shirts."

"They get those anyway." She held out her hand. "Give."

"Nope." When she lunged for his jacket, he grabbed her by the arm and dragged her toward the rental car he'd parked in the yellow zone in front of the arena. The police card he'd stuck beneath the windshield wiper had prevented it from being towed. "She'll be back in time for the show," he called back to Ryan, who was watching with his mouth agape. "Meanwhile, you're in charge."

# 15

Lark fumed all the way back to the house. Seething, she slammed the car door, then was frustrated when she had to wait for him to unlock the interior door from a garage spacious enough to house a new-car dealership. She marched up the stairs, into the bedroom.

"You're pissed," he diagnosed, catching the door as she went to slam it, too.

"You damn well right I am." She turned on him, her hands curled into fists. "I have never, ever wanted to hit anyone before. Not even when I found Cody screwing that woman in my bed in my bus. But I want to slug you."

"Go ahead and take your best shot." He jutted out his jaw.

"Lucky for you, I don't believe in violence." Her fingernails were digging into her palms; ignoring the sting, Lark focused on her fury and bumped her temper against his. "I told you, I already made the mistake of getting mixed up with a man who controlled my every move. In case you haven't noticed, he's not around anymore."

"Actually, he seems to be."

"That's not what I mean!"

While she wasn't as obsessive as Celine Dion, who didn't speak a word to anyone on the days she performed, Lark usually tried to prevent straining her voice before a concert. Now her shriek risked shattering every piece of French and Irish crystal in the house.

"You have no right to start dictating to me about who I see and when I see them." She jabbed a finger against the hard wall of his chest, hard enough to chip a nail. "If I want to invite the entire damn city of New Orleans backstage after the show for a drunken orgy, there's not a damn thing you can do about it!"

"What to bet?"

"Bet." Lark tossed up her chin. She might as well have been wearing a sign: Dangerous Curves, Proceed with Caution.

Lucas was sick and tired of being cautious. He gathered up her hair; drew her head back. "You want to host yourself an orgy, sweetheart, you may as well begin right here and now."

The shock was hot and instantaneous as his mouth captured hers, the explosive taste of lust rocking them both. Her body jerked. Stiffened.

The air, ripe with passion, thickened.

Lucas's need to claim her overwhelmed prudence; he closed a hand over her breast; the low sound—half purr, half strangled sob—that rose from her throat sent raw, animal lust whipping through him.

He dragged her down, wrestling her onto the bed. Hunger warred with control; need battled reason. There were no words, no soft lovers' sighs. Only blurred movement as he dragged her sweater over her head. She bucked against him, cursed him even as he took the kiss deeper. Darker.

His teeth nipped at her throat, his lips streaked over feverish flesh.

She slapped her hand against his chest, but when his mouth clamped ravenously on her breast, devouring her, her fingers splayed and grabbed his shirt front and she twisted—no longer in anger, but need—atop the brocade satin spread.

"I'm furious at you."

"I know." He yanked down the zipper of her jeans, shoved a hand beneath the waistband of her panties, then lower, through the soft curls between her legs.

She was already hot. Already wet.

"I want to hate you."

"I know," he repeated. "Tell me to stop, right now, and I will."

"You know I can't do that." She kicked off her shoes, moved her feet up and down the back of his legs. "Oh, God, I want you inside me."

When she tried to attack his jeans, he caught hold of both her slender wrists with one hand and lifted them over her head as he used his superior strength to press her deeper into the mattress. "Not yet."

He stroked her quivering belly, dipped a kiss in her navel, touched his tongue to her sizzling flesh and was vaguely surprised when there was no answering hiss of steam.

She was trembling in anticipation, breathing through gasps and moans as he parted her silky, outer lips, then used his thumb to spread the moisture, teasing, tantalizing, tormenting her as he drew sensual circles, skimming closer and closer to, but never quite touching, her clitoris.

Her body arched, her thighs fell open in erotic invitation. *More.*

Oh, Jesus. His erection had gone from distracting to flat-out painful. He grit his teeth, fighting back the urge to surge into her.

"Don't move." His voice was ragged with lust as he pressed his open mouth to the inside of one of those long smooth thighs. If she touched him he'd be a goner. He nipped at her hipbone. "Just feel."

She let out a long, slow breath of pleasure as he made love to her with his hands, his fingers slipping smoothly into her.

She was tight and hot and, at least for this one stolen moment in time, his. "Lark. Look at me." He wanted to watch her go over the edge.

Her eyes, heavily lidded and slumbrous with desire, slowly opened. Then widened as he pressed deeper.

"Please." Her inner muscles clutched at him. "Don't . . ." Despite his admonition to hold still, her body twisted, her hips rose with his next thrust. "Don't stop."

"I wouldn't think of it." The wicked stroke of his thumb brought her to a quick, shuddering release.

*More.*

Her body went limp, but refusing to give her an opportunity to recover, he yanked the jeans down her legs and used his mouth on her, piercing her with his tongue, feasting voraciously. When his teeth nipped, tugged, then scraped on that ultrasensitive nub of tangled nerve endings, Lark climaxed again with a sharp strangled cry.

*More.*

He lightly blew on her, cooling her before taking her up again. And this time, when she came, it was Lucas's name she called out.

Much, much later, she was lying bonelessly beneath him, her breathing ragged, her heart pounding against his chest. "Well, that certainly beat the hell out of very nice." Her words were slurred, as if she were drunk. "And it went a long way to burning away my mad."

He smiled against her stomach. "You saw through my subterfuge."

"It wasn't very subtle." She combed her fingers through his hair. "But it was good."

He nibbled at the little crease between her bare thigh and her hip. "We aim to please."

"There's just one problem. You didn't—"

"Don't worry about it." He was sure he'd be able to walk again. Someday soon. Maybe, if he was lucky, by the next decade.

"But—"

"I left Highland Falls in a hurry." Lifting his head from the silken pillow of her body, he viewed the worry in her eyes. "I wasn't expecting things to take this turn, so I didn't come dressed for the party, so to speak."

"Oh." He could practically see the wheels turning in that gorgeous dark head. "But surely your friend has something—"

"He does. I found a box in the bathroom. But they wouldn't work."

"Why not?"

"I realize you women say that size doesn't matter—

which I think is mostly a crock to protect our egos—but sometimes it does." He moved against her, letting her feel the extent of his need. "They're too small."

"Oh." A spark of anticipation lit up those spectacular eyes. "Well." Her hand slipped between them, her splayed fingers stroking, measuring. "There are other ways."

They'd certainly explored them all once upon a time.

"It's okay. You need your rest and when I make love to you, I want to be able to do it all night long, and not have to worry about remembering to get you to the arena on time."

"You said *when*. Not *if*."

"Any problem with that?"

She didn't hesitate. "No. But I still feel bad you didn't enjoy yourself."

Lucas laughed at that, slid up her body and kissed her frowning lips. "Wanna bet?"

Because she still felt too good beneath him, was still too tempting, he rolled off her, onto his back. "Damn." He shook his head. "And to think some guys settle for a mirror over their beds."

Following his gaze upward, Lark took in the mural, which last night she'd been too exhausted to notice. Barely veiled nymphs and goat-footed satyrs were romping in a sylvan glade, enjoying what, from the free-flowing wine, appeared to be the drunken orgy she'd threatened him with. The one they both knew she'd never partake in.

Erotic energy pulsed from the oversize scene drenched in rich, bold colors.

"It's actually an excellent example of a nineteenth-century English mythological scene," she said. The sight of a satyr biting a buxom brunette nymph's neck brought back the still vivid sensation of Lucas's teeth scraping down her throat.

"And here I'd always thought those Victorians were supposed to be straitlaced." He tilted his head, studying a particularly sensual twisting of naked bodies beneath a waterfall. One especially bestial satyr was lifting the skirt of a flushed, half-naked maenad, while another lasciviously rubbed a hugely oversize penis between her plump breasts. The maenad—a mythical wild woman—appeared in the throes of ecstasy.

"That's what they wanted people to think," she said. "But Bacchanalian figures were popular subjects long before that, especially with the Flemish in the sixteen-hundreds. In fact, Rubens's satyr paintings remain some of Europe's most influential images of violence and erotic emotion."

Lark was discovering that studying such a painting when it was hung on a white wall of a brightly lit gallery was vastly different from taking in such a rawly sexual scene while lying on a rumpled bed beside a man whose jeans you'd been about to rip off in a frenzy of erotic emotion. Her body was beginning to feel all hot and bothered again. "Titian, Bellini, and Picasso all painted images based on Ovid's calendar of Roman rituals."

Lucas turned onto his side, lifted himself up on one elbow and studied her with an entirely different interest than how he'd looked at her just before dragging her down to the bed. "I suppose you learned that from John Angus."

"No. Since my father would never let anyone in his studio, I didn't learn about art at home." Their faces were so close together, all she'd have to do would be to lean forward, just the teensiest bit . . .

"But there's a lot of downtime while touring," she continued, trying not to get lost in those midnight-dark eyes. "Danny would hit the golf courses and I'd go to museums before a show. Then I wanted to understand more about the paintings I was seeing, so I signed up for an art history course online. One thing led to another, and pretty soon I was taking a couple classes each semester. He teased me about studying all the time." Lark smiled softly at the memory. "He calls me his Roads Scholar."

Lucas returned her smile. Then ran a hand down her hair. "You need to get some rest."

She stretched, feeling like a sleek cat that had indulged in a particularly rich bowl of cream. "I'm already more relaxed than I've been in months."

"Good." He dropped a light kiss on her lips. "Then you shouldn't have any trouble falling asleep."

"I need to be at the arena to change and get made up by six."

"I'll get you up in plenty of time," he promised.

Lark was floating on soft clouds of lassitude. "Okay," she murmured.

She was out like a light before Lucas shut the door.

"You look really, really hot," Lucas said, staring at the glamorous star who'd taken Lark's place in the dressing room. She'd always been lovely, but the woman standing in front of the mirror was enough to make any red-blooded male swallow his tongue.

"Thank you." She leaned forward toward the mirror, dipped the tip of her pinkie into a small pot and smoothed color over her parted lips. "I don't normally wear a lot of beads and glitter, but it seemed appropriate, being the holidays and all."

"Every man out there is going to thank you for wearing that outfit."

The top was some thin, sparkly red material that she'd tied below her breasts, revealing a mouth-watering display of porcelain flesh she'd dusted with some sort of powder that made her skin glisten like diamond dust. The ankle-length skirt, of the same fabric, clung to her slender curves like a lover's caress and was slit high on the hips on either side. Christ, her legs went all the way to her neck.

"How about you?" She put her hands on her hips and made a slow turn, showing off the merchandise. When she came back around to face him again, Lucas fantasized untying that knot. With his teeth. "Do you like it?"

He took her hand and put it against the fly of his jeans. "What do you think?"

His voice was rough as ten miles of bad mountain road.

"I think you'd better go shopping for those party clothes," she said, her voice vibrating with husky promise.

It should be illegal for a woman to sound like warm honey poured over hot sex; he also suspected it was against the law in several states for a woman to go out in public looking as if she'd just spent a long afternoon heating up silk sheets. She slowly ran her tongue around those full, glossy lips she'd painted the color of a ripe strawberry. Skimmed a scarlet fingernail down the front of his shirt.

"Soon."

Her slow, saucy smile was one Lucas suspected had been on Eve's lips when she'd sashayed up to Adam with that red, ripe apple and suggest they try something different for dessert.

"ASAP," he agreed.

Her whiskey-hued eyes packed the punch of a barrel of Highlander's Pride. When the blood fled his head, flooding hotly into lower regions, Lucas struggled to remind himself the reason for his being here in New Orleans.

Hell with it; his charge was to keep her safe. Close by. Which was, he decided, as he drew her into his arms, exactly what he was doing.

She melded against him; twined her arms around his neck. Just as he was about to kiss her, there was a knock on the door.

"Go away." Lucas's growl was that of a wolf warning an intruder away from his den.

"Sorry." Ryan opened the door. "As much as I hate to interrupt, Lark, we're at your two-minute warning."

He'd no sooner spoken, when Lucas's cell phone chimed.

"Damn." He whipped it out; his expression, when he saw the number on the caller ID, darkened.

"I've got to take this," he said. "I'll be right back.

Meanwhile"—he shot Ryan a hard look—"don't let her out of your sight."

"Yessir." Ryan snapped a quick salute. Lucas did not appear amused.

"Your old friend sure doesn't have much of a sense of humor," Ryan said after Lucas had left the dressing room.

"He's not as grim as he seems," Lark said, as she and Ryan headed down the corridor toward the stairs leading to the stage. "He just has a strong sense of responsibility." The biggest understatement yet.

"I've been picking up on some really powerful vibes. Were the two of you an item?"

"We were friends since childhood. Then, the summer between my junior and senior year in high school, I fell madly in love with him."

"How about the big guy?"

"You'd have to ask him." As close as she and Ryan had become, Lark was uncomfortable discussing Lucas with him.

They were standing in the curtains to the right of the stage, waiting for the warm-up act to finish their set. "I would, if I wasn't afraid he'd shoot me."

Before she could respond that Lucas would never do such a thing, she felt a familiar stir in the air and saw Lucas headed toward them. His jaw was set hard, his mouth pulled in a harsh line, and the way his long stride was eating up the pine floor reminded her of a Texas Ranger about to face off a gang of outlaws. He should have been wearing his pistol slung low on his hip, gun-slinger style.

Lark feared he wouldn't be looking so grim if Danny's assailant was behind bars. *Oh, God.* What if he'd died? What if she had moved to the top of their suspect list?

"What's wrong?"

"Guest was spotted six miles from here at a mall store in Metaire."

# 16

Lark stared up at him as if she'd never heard the word. "A mall?"

"Yeah. A woman employee has gone missing and the manager of the men's department remembered Guest because he was the week's high spender. He picked him out of a random group of photographs, though he said he looks as if he's packed on some muscle since that mug shot was taken, and he's dyed his hair brown."

The color drained from Lark's face as the ramifications of that idea hit home.

The warm-up band left the stage; the audience began to chant for Lark. "Maybe you ought to send those guys back up on stage and we'll get you out of here."

"No." She stiffened her spine. Drew in a deep breath. Let it out. "All those people have come here to see me."

He shrugged, understanding how important this was and knowing that short of handcuffing her to that nearby steam pipe, there was no way to stop her. She'd been born for this.

"Break a leg."

Lark smiled, understanding that this wasn't easy for him, but appreciating that he knew that singing was as vital to her as air.

She lifted her hands to his shoulders, and lifted her lips to his. "For luck." Then walked out onto the stage to a roar of applause.

She didn't ignore what had happened on Christmas Eve. It was obvious that the shooting was in everyone's mind; best just to deal with it right off, then hopefully move people's focus to the music.

Standing at center stage, she kept her words brief; assured the crowd that Danny's prognosis was good, offered thanks for the notes and flowers that had begun flooding into the hospital, and asked for their prayers and positive thoughts.

The house lights, which had been brightened for her comment, dimmed. She sat on a high stool, crossed her legs, which revealed a dazzling amount of leg, and bathed in a single spotlight began with "Thunder in the Dark," an original ballad that was bitter and sweet, sunlit and shadowy, simple and mysterious. It was a song of jealousy, and despair, and the dark and violent depths ordinary people can be driven to in the name of extraordinary love.

If Billie Holiday and Neil Young had gotten together to make a love child, it would have been Lark Stewart. Her voice was smoky, intimate, and Lucas doubted there was a person in the room who didn't believe she was singing it directly to them. It was the kind of voice you listened to at two in the morning on a blues and jazz station, when you were feeling down and lonely and tempted to drown your troubles in a bottle of cheap booze.

A dangerous voice, he thought as the last notes of the song drifted away. A dangerous woman.

Switching styles on a dime, she slid off the stool, and launched into an upbeat tune that had the arena rocking as her fans began clapping along with the rockabilly beat.

When Lucas had first known her, first fallen head over heart in love, she'd been too shy to speak to strangers. She'd developed a patter, talking to the audience, the mood changing from sunny to serious, depending on what song she was introducing. She'd had them in her hand from that first chord and continued to work them like a faith healer at a tent revival.

Ryan, proving that while he might look like Ken, he was definitely efficient, had filled her in on some special occasions, and she took the time to congratulate a young couple on their marriage (while suggesting with a sassy wink that they might have better things to do than share their honeymoon with 17,000 strangers), take note of a couple who were celebrating their fiftieth wedding anniversary, and earned huge applause by having all those serving in the military—and their families and loved ones—stand up so everyone could thank them for their sacrifices.

When she sat back on the stool again to sing a song about loving a soldier boy, the ethereal purity of her voice soaring over the arena brought several in the audience to tears. Hell, Lucas could feel his own damn eyes getting suspiciously moist. She had a way of connecting with people and any man who loved Lark would have to practice generosity because he'd always have to share her with strangers.

"They love her," Lucas said.

"Absolutely adore her," Ryan said. "There are basically three types of performers. Those who try to push the envelope too far, either due to their own creative demons, or for publicity, those who do it simply for the paycheck, and another, smaller group who make music with the goal of leaving something great behind when they're gone. Lark definitely fits into that third category."

Lucas could not disagree.

Lucas could tell Lark wasn't happy about not being able to visit with fans after the show, but reluctantly she allowed that Ryan was capable of soothing their disappointment. She was quiet in the car on the drive back to the house; he suspected it had more to do with the missing woman than the fact that she had to be exhausted after singing her heart out.

"Do you think he's killed her?" she asked as they entered the house.

"I don't know."

"Of course you don't. But what do you think?"

"It's only been a few hours since her parents reported her missing. She might be all right."

"She might not be dead," Lark said, bypassing the stairs to go into the kitchen. "But if Guest has her, she's not all right."

"Maybe it's just a coincidence." He took the milk carton from her hand. "Sit down, I'll pour. There's a box of bread pudding I can heat up."

"That sounds wickedly decadent."

"Like some pretty ladies I know," he said.

Her eyes smiled a bit at the compliment, but her mouth was pulled into a firm line. "You promised you'd tell me," she said. "After the show."

"So I did." Unwilling to risk the whiskey sauce, he nuked the pudding in the microwave for her, cut a piece of pecan pie for himself, then poured two glasses of milk. "How about taking these into the library?" he suggested.

The furniture was heady and oversize, the sofa and chairs covered in cordovan red leather studded with brass nailheads. Hunting prints of horses and hounds hung on the bird's-eye maple paneled walls that gleamed from years of oil being rubbed into the wood.

Lucas lit a fire, then sat down beside her on the leather sofa. "I don't know anything about the music business, and you could never be anything but great, but I like that show you did tonight better than that flash and dazzle show you were doing last year," he said.

"You sound as if you've seen it," she said, surprised.

"I drove down to Chattanooga when you played at the McKenzie Arena."

"I suppose you just happened to be in the neighborhood?" She repeated what he'd said when he'd shown up at the hospital.

"What do you think? I went to see you."

"But you didn't come backstage." Lark wasn't going to allow herself to wonder how things might have changed if he had.

"I didn't feel I had the right."

"You were wrong." Deciding to deal with their rocky past later, she took a bite of the rich, sweet, liquor-drenched pudding and nearly moaned. "Did you suffer? That night you came to the Chattanooga show?"

"Like the damned."

She grinned and touched her lips to his. "Good."

"It was my fault," Lucas said after the brief, sweet kiss ended. "What happened to you back then. Guest never would have gotten his hands on you if I hadn't stormed out and driven down to Asheville the night before."

They'd had a foolish teenage fight after Melissa Jackson, a bottle-blond senior whose reputation was dirtier than week-old snow, had sashayed up to Lark in the shampoo aisle of Duncan's Pharmacy and informed her that she'd had sex with Lucas.

At first Lark hadn't believed it. He wouldn't do that, she'd insisted. Not *her* Lucas. With a smirk on her glossy lips, Melissa had reached into her purse and pulled out a Polaroid of Lucas standing beneath the falls, naked, full frontal and blatantly aroused. When Lark rushed to the market and confronted him in the stockroom where he'd been opening boxes of canned vegetables, he'd refused to deny having been with Highland Falls's teenage slut. Instead, he'd gotten furious that she could so easily mistrust him.

"There was no way you could have known what would happen," Lark said. Even now, her palms went clammy thinking back on that day. "I should have had faith in you."

Much later, Melissa's best friend told her how Melissa

had followed them around town for two weeks to get that shot of Lucas so she could get back at Lark for appearing on that Knoxville television station. Lark had known that Melissa was already jealous of her—the other girl had been a bad loser after Lark had beat her out for the part of Annie Oakley in the school's spring musical—but she never could have suspected that Melissa would go to such lengths to break Lucas and her up.

"You wouldn't have been at the farm if you hadn't gone there looking for me," he repeated. "That sick son of a bitch never would have gotten you alone. You went through hell, Lark. And it was my fault."

Lark was appalled Lucas could look at it that way—but not terribly surprised, knowing the boy he'd been. And seeing the man he'd become.

"You couldn't have known that a psychopath had been tracking me for days, Lucas." No one ever had expected anything bad to happen in Highland Falls. Until that hot, hot summer.

"You can't have it both ways," she insisted quietly. "You can't tell me not to feel guilty about Danny, then turn around and blame yourself for what happened to me."

"That's different."

How strange it was that she'd be the one trying to reassure him when it had always been the other way around. "Would you care to explain how?"

"Hell, I don't know." He plowed his hands through his hair. "It just was."

"Is that why you left? Because you were feeling guilty?"

"Maybe. Partly. But like I said, my mother and sisters needed the money after my father got hauled off in handcuffs."

The week before William Guest had taken her captive, FBI agents had descended on Highland Falls to arrest Jed McCloud for mail fraud and racketeering, after he'd bilked dozens of churches throughout the South in a phony investment scheme for a religious resort retirement community.

"That explains why you joined the service. It doesn't explain why you broke up with me." Back then she'd pushed, prodded, begged, even resorted to tears, but he'd never given her a reason.

"If we'd stayed together I would have ruined your life."

"You *were* my life." Whatever happened between her and Lucas, Lark wouldn't make that mistake again. "It was unfair of me to depend upon you for my happiness." She shook her head. "Then again, during all my soul-searching over the past months, I've realized that depending on others had become a lifelong habit."

"I didn't go to Nashville with you, Lark," he reminded her needlessly. "You went alone, which took one helluva lot of guts."

"I was running away."

"Okay." He acknowledged the possibility. "I can buy that. It only makes sense that you'd want to get away from a place—and the people—who represented so many bad memories."

"You could never be a bad memory."

"There was also no way I was going to let you arrive

in Nashville under the cloud of being involved with the son of the new poster boy for white-collar crime."

"I wasn't *involved*. I was in love."

"I know. Which was why I had to break it off. You were meant for big things, Lark. I would have been just one more obstacle in your way."

"You know," she said dryly, "if I put that much bullshit into my lyrics, I'd still be waiting to be discovered. If you felt that way, why did you spend the night with me in New Orleans?"

He slanted her a look. "You shouldn't have to ask that question."

"It wasn't just for the sex?"

"Hell, no."

"I didn't think so." She'd hoped not. But sometimes in the middle of a lonely night, she'd wondered.

"Sex is easy to come by, especially in a city like New Orleans. If that's what I'd been after, I wouldn't have been sitting alone in that bar." He put his glass on the table in front of the sofa, turned toward her and put both hands on her shoulders. "When you walked into that pub you flat-out took my breath away." His eyes roamed her face. "You still do."

His words made her pulse jump. "You treated me like Typhoid Lark when I sat down at your table."

"I was trying—"

"I know. To protect me. Didn't it occur to you that it'd hurt me even more when you left the next morning without a single word?"

"I left you a good-bye note. And my dog tags."

"Ah yes, the universal symbol that a man still respects

you in the morning. Forget flowers and phone calls—nothing touches a woman like a pair of marine issue dog tags." She still had them, hidden away in a secret drawer of her jewel box.

"You know, if you weren't raking me over the coals, I might find this new attitude of yours somewhat amusing."

"We need to talk about this," she insisted. "To get it behind us. Do you have any idea how I felt after you played Houdini and disappeared from my life for thirteen damn years?"

"Angry? Used? Betrayed?"

"Bull's-eye. Give the man a Kewpie doll." Lark was surprised to find herself getting riled up at the memory. Anger, like tears, were something she'd always tried to avoid. Anger led to confrontation, confrontation to fighting, and fighting, as she'd learned the hard way, could lead to very bad things. "And let's not forget heartbroken."

Lucas grimaced and dropped his arms. "It seemed like a good idea at the time. I was headed off to war—"

"So?" She gave him her sternest look. "My grandmother fell in love with a soldier during World War II. He was captured by the Italians leading the assault on Sicily, but after the war was over, he returned to Scotland for her."

James Stewart had just happened to arrive in the Scottish Highlands the night before Annie was supposed to marry another man, but Lucas didn't need to know that.

"It wasn't the same. I was being sent off to kill people."

"So was my grandfather."

"Being a sniper requires a different mind-set than an ordinary soldier."

"My grandfather James was no *ordinary* anything." Lark folded her arms. "He was one of Darby's Rangers, the original tough guys who were the forerunner of the Army Rangers. And what makes you think I couldn't understand that war can get ugly?"

"That's the point, goddammit!" A log fell in a shower of sparks. Lucas jumped up and shoved it back into place with a heavy iron poker. "You were the kindest, most gentle person I'd ever met." He threw his body back down onto the couch. "I didn't want to be responsible for any more ugliness touching you. I wanted to protect you!" His eyes glinted.

"Interesting how the *P* word continues to be an ongoing theme between us," she said. "Did you ever think to ask me if I wanted your protection?"

"No, because it wasn't your decision to make. And I left without a word that morning because it would have been unfair to ask you to wait for me."

"It wasn't a very long war," she pointed out.

"No one knew that going in. Don't forget all those threats about flaming ditches of death. Afterward, I didn't come back to you because I didn't want to subject you to the man I'd become."

"You helped liberate a nation."

"I also executed fifteen men without a single qualm."

She hadn't known that. "You were a marine. It was your job. More than a job, it was your duty," she pointed out.

Lucas's shrug could have been agreement, or the surrender of that point.

"When I first showed up at Parris Island, I discovered that being able to nail a squirrel at a thousand yards made me a top candidate for scout sniper school. After the war, I taught other jarheads to shoot while I cobbled together a college degree so I could join the FBI as a sniper when I returned to civilian life."

His mouth twisted in a mockery of a smile. "It seemed shooting people was the only marketable skill I possessed. I didn't want to saddle you with living with a killer."

"It must be difficult," she murmured, "carrying the responsibility of the world on those manly shoulders."

The comment had been meant to encourage a smile. When it didn't, Lark's heart softened.

"You should have given me the choice," she said quietly. When he didn't respond, she tried again. "Did you ever shoot anyone who wasn't armed?"

"Hell, no."

"Aren't FBI snipers brought in on hostage situations to rescue innocent people?"

He jerked his shoulders. "That's the goal."

"Were you good at your job?"

"Yeah." It wasn't conceit. He *had* been the goddamn best. Until that debacle in New Orleans.

"Well, then, it seems to me that there are undoubtedly a great many people out there grateful for your marksmanship skills."

He wasn't surprised that Lark would argue in his favor. She'd always been as faithful as a puppy—which was why he hadn't given her the choice so many years ago.

"We wouldn't have worked out." He tried yet another tack, no longer sure which of them he was trying to convince. "If you'd gotten stuck being a serviceman's wife, getting dragged around the country from marine base to marine base, you never would have been able to launch your career."

"It would have been more difficult," she admitted. "But I certainly wouldn't have thought of myself as being 'stuck,' and we'll never know whether we could have made it work, Lucas, because you were a coward."

His jaw jutted out. "No one has ever called me that."

Not since his father taunted him for being a sissy when the bone was jutting through the skin of his forearm. From then on, Lucas had kept his fears and pains to himself. Which, he'd learned when researching alcoholism, could have contributed to him having ended up a drunk. Personally, his diagnosis was that he drank to forget the bad stuff. When the blackouts became the bad stuff, it had been easier to stop.

"You were afraid to trust that what we had was real enough to overcome whatever problems we might have faced. And, although I hate to admit it, I'm equally guilty for letting what we had slip away. I should have followed my heart and tracked you down again when you returned home from the Gulf, but my wounded pride kept me from going after you. I'd never had to pursue a boy before."

"Now, there's a big duh."

She shot him a frustrated look. "But more importantly, until you left Highland Falls, I'd never had to chase *you*. You were always there for me, Lucas, for as long as I could remember. Then one day you weren't, and I figured you'd decided you'd outgrown me."

She lifted a hand to his chest. "You didn't just break my heart, Lucas. You shattered it into a million pieces. It took me a very long time to gather them all up and put them back together again."

Lark had always gotten along with everyone: the jocks, the nerds, the wallflowers. She treated the kids whose parents were in upper management at the distillery exactly the same way she did ones like Lucas—kids from the wrong side of the tracks.

But even when she'd fallen in love with him, he'd been pragmatic enough to understand that in real life, the odds were stacked against a happily-ever-after ending between a princess and a lowly commoner.

"I'm not going to deny still having feelings for you, because it'd be a lie," she said, in the soft voice that still haunted his sleep. "But there's also no way I'm going to let you put me through that again."

"How about you break mine?" he suggested. "Then we'll be even."

She frowned. "I'm serious, Lucas."

"I know." He framed her face between his palms and touched his lips to her brow. "I won't push you, Lark. And I won't hurt you."

She was everything Lucas had tried to force himself to forget, and more. Everything he'd ever wanted in one delectable package. He didn't know where in the hell they were headed, but the one thing he was sure about was if he lived to be a hundred, he'd never feel for any other woman a fraction of what he felt for his golden-eyed girl.

# 17

The moon was a thin silver sickle as the shooter lay prone on the roof of the building, the familiar weight of a Remington rifle pressed hard against the hollow of his shoulder, his cheek resting against the wooden stock.

The target was pacing back and forth in front of the window. A head shot into the cerebellum could instantly short-circuit the central nervous system. A body shot took longer to do the job, perhaps twenty seconds from the time the bullet ripped through the heart to clinical death, but it was a better money shot—especially with the guy dancing around all over the damn place like he was and time running out.

Lucas's finger caressed the trigger as he placed the crosshairs on his target's chest.

One shot. One kill.

The gunshot shattered the heavy night like a crack of lightning. It was followed by a blast of thunder.

The blood was everywhere, spattering the walls, soaking into the rug, pouring out of a wound the size of a man's fist. A teenage girl lay in the midst of all that crimson blood, as limp and boneless as a rag doll.

* * *

Lucas was on the floor, Lark on her knees beside him, her eyes wide and frightened. "Lucas?"

"Do you smell it?" God, why couldn't he get it out of his head?

"Smell what?"

"The goddamn blood. The death."

"There's no blood, Lucas." Her palms were on either side of his face. "No one's died. You were having a nightmare."

Her voice was a distant chime of reason in the chaotic fog of his mind. He shook his head to clear it. He wasn't back in that room of death. He was here in Audubon Place. With Lark.

"Lark." He breathed her name like a prayer. "Lark." Like a mantra.

"You had a nightmare." She drew him closer, her hand stroking the back of his head. "You must have thrown yourself out of bed."

Although it hadn't been easy, since Lucas was still unwilling to risk an unwanted pregnancy, after their long talk they'd gone to bed in separate rooms again.

"Christ." *The woman's in a world of hurt, if she's depending on a nutcase like you to protect her from anyone. You can't even take care of yourself.*

He pressed the heel of his hand between his eyes and leaned his head, which felt as if it were splitting in two, against the box springs. "I thought I'd gotten rid of these goddamn headaches when I quit drinking."

"Apparently not." She stood up and went into the bathroom. He heard the tap turn on, off, then she returned with a glass of water and two white tablets. "Here's some aspirin."

They'd probably work as well as a peashooter against a grizzly, but he nevertheless took the pills to make her happy.

"Sorry about waking you up." He pushed himself to his feet and bit back a curse as the room began to spin.

"You're not the only one with ghosts," she reminded him as she put a slender arm around his waist, encouraging him to lean on her.

"Come back to bed and we'll talk."

"I don't need—"

"Yes," she cut him off firmly. "You do. There's still something between us, Lucas. I suspect it's those ghosts you mentioned and conveniently didn't bring up earlier. And we need to get them out in the open, because we deserve this second chance."

It wasn't easy to talk about it. He'd always known it wouldn't be, which was why he'd never tried before. In an attempt to set the scene, he told her about the war, about low-crawling through the minefields and barbed wire on the Kuwaiti border.

"The marine engineers used fiberglass mines to clear a path for troops to get through. There were mines as far as you could see, lines and lines of them, some half buried, some lying on top of the sand. We came in right behind the engineers, to hit the Iraqis who were moving through the trench lines.

"When the oil fires began, visibility sank to zero. A marine was assigned to walk in front of each tank to keep them from running into each other and we were working without radios so we wouldn't risk giving away our position—which left everyone literally in the dark."

"It sounds ghastly."

He shrugged. "If it was fun I suppose they wouldn't call it war. There's this cadence we used to march to in sniper training—*Hey, hey, Captain Jack, Meet me by the railroad track, with your rifle in your hand, I want to be a killing man.*"

"Catchy," she said mildly. "But I doubt it's got top-ten potential."

Not willing to share that for a long time it had been at the top of his own personal hit parade, playing over and over again in his mind for years, he brushed over the details of the military kills. At least they were righteous, only killing men who were trying to kill him.

"After I got out of the service, I joined the FBI Hostage Rescue Team. We were part of the Tactical Support branch of CIRG—headquartered in Quantico. Our main mission was to be prepared to deploy, within four hours of notification, to any location where we were needed to conduct a rescue of U.S. persons or others illegally held by a terrorist or criminal hostile force. Our motto was *Sevare Vitas*—To Save Lives, which always struck me as ironic, since a sniper's job is to end a life."

"They weren't exactly model citizens," Lark pointed out. "They were murderers." She'd remained quiet during most of his pained monologue, but couldn't let that go. "Or would have become murderers if it wasn't for you. They were not innocent people, Lucas."

"The last one was."

He admired the way she didn't flinch at what he knew had to be an unwelcome surprise.

"She was a nineteen-year-old girl," he revealed.

Lucas closed his eyes, but it didn't help. He could still see Becky Ellis's glazed blue eyes and blood-caked blond hair. So goddamn much blood.

"She was taken hostage by this spree killer who'd already killed four people. The negotiators had been talking to him for hours when I showed up. Sniper protocol calls for shooter isolation, so snipers have spotters, who listen in on the action and say when it's time to pull the trigger. Jack Barnes was my spotter that night. We'd worked together in the Gulf and trusted each other.

"I wasn't listening to any of the talk, because it'd be too easy to get emotionally involved. In order to be a sniper, you have to stay focused on one thing. The target. If you learn anything about him, maybe that he's going through a bad divorce, got a kid with cancer, anything like that, you might hesitate to pull the trigger. And even an instant's hesitation can make the entire operation go south.

"Later, after this ended badly, Jack told me the sociopath bastard had warned that if we shot him, he'd shoot the girl."

"Don't the bad guys always say that?"

"Yeah. Sort of like guys on death row claiming they're innocent until the moment the executioner pulls the switch." Lucas exhaled a weary sigh. "Usually it isn't much of a threat, since most criminals aren't nearly as fast with a gun as they think they are."

"Or as fast as you." She eyed him intently, as if really

looking at him for the first time. *What the hell did she see?*

"No. I was always faster." Three shots in three seconds—not that he'd ever needed the second two.

"But this sicko scumbag had a plan we didn't know about. Something Jack didn't notice. Couldn't have noticed." That had been the official ruling, which had satisfied the paper pushers and the politicians but sure as hell hadn't made either one of them feel better. "He'd rigged up a twelve gauge shotgun with fishing line. If he went down, the gun went off."

The realization widened her eyes before she could stop her reaction. Her face, already pale in the moonlight, turned ghostly.

"He killed the girl?"

"Yeah. Afterward, her father made of point of telling me he and her mother didn't blame me."

"How could they?"

"It was my job to get her out of that situation alive, dammit." He slammed a fist into his palm. "The first thing you learn at the Academy is a 'T' zone shot—that's an imaginary area that covers the eyes and nose. The goal is to put one round right between the eyes, which instantly shuts the criminal down. I'd hit a ninety-eight percent the week before on the range; if I'd only risked it that night . . ."

"It sounds as if the shotgun still would have gone off when he fell," she pointed out. "Life's messy, Lucas. Messy, often unfair, and sometimes even dangerous. But there's nothing to be gained by dwelling on what-ifs." She put a hand on his arm. "Is that it?"

"Yeah." He was raw. Drained. "I'm done."

"Want to bet?" Twining her arms around his neck, Lark drew him down to her.

"This isn't a good idea." God, he wanted her. "I still haven't gotten out to a store."

"Don't worry about it." Her luscious lips plucked at his. "According to *The Times-Picayune*'s music critic, the Tennessee Songbird—which would be me—is a creative genius." She kissed his throat. His chest.

"Lark." Her name vaporized on his lips. He sucked in his stomach as her mouth skimmed a hot wet path over his torso. Then lower still.

When she circled his penis in her hand, then touched her tongue to spread the pearly semen that had beaded up on its tip, Lucas tangled his hands in her hair and surrendered as she demonstrated exactly how creative this Tennessee Songbird could be.

# 18

Lark came into the kitchen, her hair still damp from her shower, smelling of soap and herbal shampoo and wearing a short red silk robe that had Lucas vowing to stop at the A&P on the way to the hospital. Last night had been amazing, but as inventive as they'd been, it still wasn't the same as being inside the hot moist flesh of a woman's body.

Not that he wanted any woman's body. He wanted Lark. With a need so powerful, it bordered on obsession, allowing him to almost understand Guest's unrelenting desire.

"Thank God, you made coffee," she said. "I think I love you."

"You were always a cheap date," he said as he handed her a cup filled to the gilt rim. He'd found the chicory-flavored coffee in the freezer.

"You are," he said, as he feasted his eyes, "the most unconsciously seductive woman on the planet. If you'd lived two hundred years ago, you would have been burned at the stake."

"Don't be silly." She tossed her hair over her shoulder.

"They never burned witches in New Orleans." She drained the cup, then went to work on the buttons of his shirt. "They celebrated them."

He reached over and turned off the burner beneath the copper pan. "Who needs *pain perdu?*"

He took her in his arms, lifted her up onto the antique French farm table, and moved between her thighs.

His lips were chapped. She thrilled at the roughness as they brushed against hers. When they skimmed down her throat to nuzzle at her bared breasts, she felt as if she were melting, just like the butter he'd been heating to put on the Cajun French toast.

His hands cupped her bottom, pulling her closer to the edge of the table, holding her against him, tormenting them both by rubbing her against his arousal. The rasp of denim against her tingling flesh was one of the sexiest things Lark had ever felt and she was about to suggest that they just throw caution to the wind, at least this once, when the phone rang.

"Ignore it," she suggested on a moan as his teeth nipped at the cord in her neck.

From the way he paused, just for a moment, she thought he might actually cave in. Then the damn doorbell chimed as the phone continued to ring.

"Hell." He heaved a sigh and backed away. "That's got to be Deveraux and Jordan. Anyone else would've been stopped at the gate." He bent and picked up her discarded robe. "You'd better take care of the phone." He took hold of her hand, pressed a kiss against her palm that sizzled through her bloodstream. "I'll get the door while you get dressed."

The phone call was from the hospital. Danny had regained consciousness and was booked on a medevac flight back to a convalescent home in Nashville. Doctors expected a full recovery.

The bad news was the look on the two detectives' faces when Lark came downstairs to share the good news with Lucas.

"They pulled a woman's body out of the lake this morning," Lucas revealed.

There was an ominous flutter in the pit of Lark's stomach. "Is it the missing salesclerk?"

"Yeah," Deveraux said. "And we've just added murder to the other charges against Guest."

"You can't be sure it was him," Lark said.

He pulled out a photo. "This is the woman on Christmas Eve."

The snapshot of the pretty brunette with the infectious smile had been taken in front of the cathedral in the French Quarter.

"She looks like you," Lucas pointed out.

It was only a coincidence. "A lot of women have brown hair. Undoubtedly thousands in New Orleans alone. What was her name?"

"Evangeline Lelourie. Her friends called her Evie."

Evie. She'd have a lot of friends, Lark thought. She cared about people; you could tell from the warmth the camera had captured in those light brown eyes.

Looking closer, Lark gasped as she saw the hammered silver heart Evie Lelourie wore on a chain around her neck. It was a twin of the one she'd received from a fan for Christmas two years ago. And not just any fan, but the man claiming to be her number one fan, Dr. William Guest.

It was not an unusual piece of jewelry; you could probably buy one just like it all over the country. It was another coincidence, that's all.

But as her eyes met Lucas's, Lark remembered what he'd said about not believing in coincidence.

"And this is a morgue shot of her after Guest got through with her."

The coffee she'd drunk churned in her stomach. Lark had to swallow hard to keep it from coming up again. The young woman's face had been horribly battered, her body bruised. Red lines, which looked as if they'd been drawn with a knife blade, crisscrossed her arms, legs, and torso. But as bad as all that was, what made Lark feel as if she were about to throw up—or faint, or both—were the words carved into her breasts.

They were the same words William Guest had written on her with that marking pen.

*Naughty Lark.*

# 19

Lark hated flying. The very first thing she'd done after separating from Cody was to sell the jet he'd insisted they buy.

It was more than flying. She'd discovered her fear of heights when she'd been six years old and a classmate had dared her to walk across an old swinging footbridge high over Little Pigeon River. By the tenth step she'd gotten so dizzy, she'd ended up crawling the rest of the way. But she'd won the bet.

Wanting to get her out of New Orleans as soon as possible, Lucas had reluctantly allowed Ryan to pull the strings that would find a plane for them to hire, during a week it seemed every jet in the country was already booked for holiday and football championship trips.

"It was looking grim," he told them. "Then one of the deputies who worked the arena told me the sheriff's department confiscated a plane last week in a drug bust. They're planning to use it to search out marijuana fields from the air."

His easy smile flashed. "Turns out the sheriff is, natch, a true-blue Lark Stewart fan, and was tickled pink at the idea of loaning the Tennessee Songbird his plane."

"That's very sweet of him, but—"

"Hey, darlin', you want to take the bus back with the rest of the guys and me, that's copacetic. A plus to this idea is that the plane's small enough to land at Highland Falls's airfield. If you take a commercial jet you'd land in Asheville, which means you'd still have to drive up into the mountains at the end of the trip. I knew you'd have some qualms about flying in a small plane, but I asked the sheriff to have it gassed up, just in case."

Lark was torn. She was a white-knuckle flier, and for good reason, since history was filled with performers who'd died in plane crashes. Aaliyah, Patsy Cline, John Denver, Otis Redding, Rick Nelson, Jim Reeves, Buddy Holly, and all those members of Reba McEntire's band came immediately to mind. But the past days had been exhausting, and the idea of going all the way to Highland Falls by car, even with Lucas driving, wasn't the least bit appealing.

"I don't want taxpayers footing the bill. I insist on paying a fair commercial rental fee."

"I already told him that, which, since the county budget's in a bit of a shortfall, made him real happy. I also assured him that if you decided against flying, we'd reimburse the department for the fuel and the time the pilot has been standing by."

"Please tell me the pilot's not ninety years old with a leather helmet and white scarf."

"Would I do that to you? Travis Hickman's a former navy pilot who flew a bunch of missions in Desert Storm. He's one of those hotshot top guns, like Tom Cruise in that movie."

"The description 'hotshot' doesn't exactly inspire confidence."

Lark preferred her pilots to be between fifty and sixty, silver-haired men with steady temperaments who had put their risk-taking days behind them. The kind who could land a 747 with a dead engine in a cornfield during a thunderstorm, after a close encounter with a UFO clipped off a wing and lightning had set the tail on fire.

"Oh, hell," she said. "Isn't life about overcoming your fears?"

"I suppose that's up there somewhere. A few notches below hot jungle sex with the Dallas Cowboy cheerleaders."

"One of these days you're going to meet someone you want to have exclusive jungle sex with, settle down, and have a bunch of little Glazers running around."

He grimaced at the idea. "Bite your tongue." Ryan's fear of commitment was well known. It also made him a perfect road manager, since he never felt guilty about leaving a wife and children at home.

"We're taking the plane," Lucas said in a gruff voice that didn't encourage argument. Wanting—needing—to be back home, Lark reluctantly agreed to the plan.

William Guest's new credit card matched his new driver's license; it was amazing what you could get in prison. Sex, drugs, liquor, women, a host of new identities—you name it; if you had enough money, there were ways to get it. If the government really wanted to fix the economy, they'd hire convicts to teach them about supply-side economics.

The security at the airport was tight, as it always was these days, but there were no outward signs that anyone was looking for him. William felt no stress, no anxiety, as he joined the crush of postholiday travelers walking past the newsstands, the take-out Cajun food counters, and souvenir stands selling Tabasco sauce and grinning plastic alligators. He even thanked the woman at the X-ray machine who'd complimented him on his scarf.

"It was a Christmas present from my wife," he said.

"Lucky you." She returned his smile and waved him on his way.

The flight was, unsurprisingly, delayed. He was sitting in the gate, idly watching CNN while keeping an eye out for airport cops and chronicling events in his journal, when a photo of Lark appeared on the screen.

"This is a photograph taken by a tourist approximately an hour after Daniel Murphy's shooting," the pretty blond anchorwoman told viewers.

Cut to a woman with blond helmet hair. "She was just strolling down Bourbon Street, big as life, wearing these green Christmas tree earrings," she reported breathlessly with a magnolia southern drawl. "Even though I'm a huge fan, I didn't recognize her right off, because I'd never thought Lark Stewart would wear such tacky jewelry."

This from a woman wearing a red *Voodoo Love* T-shirt.

"Why, I do believe that's Lark Stewart, I told Leon— he's my husband; we've been married twenty-five years, which is what we're doing in New Orleans, it's our silver anniversary, so I told Leon that I thought we ought to do somethin' more special than the usual Lobsterfest at Red Lobster we've done every other year—"

"But the woman you saw was, indeed, Lark Stewart," the reporter broke into the breathless explanation.

"It surely was." She bobbed her head in the affirmative. "I was going to tell her that she had this big ole stain on the front of her dress, because the poor little thing was actin' like she didn't know—of course, I had no earthly idea that it was blood—but then she crossed the street, and one of those carriages came between us, so I just settled for taking this picture."

The photograph flashed back onto the screen, this time appearing behind the anchorwoman's shoulder.

Static electricity began sparking in William's head, shorting out the reporter's voice. "Thank you *crackle crackle crackle* that eyewitness *spark*. A spokesperson from *crackle crackle* Quarter police *crackle* revealed that *crackle* currently *crackle crackle* undisclosed location."

He was straining to hear the words over the static when, just as clearly as it had begun, the noise suddenly cleared.

"Ryan Glazer, Lark's road manager, refused to reveal her whereabouts. But he did not deny reports that she's returning to Tennessee." The reporter flashed a brilliant smile at odds with the topic of her report. "Back to you, Bob."

Knowing his wife as well as he did, William had suspected that she'd go running back home after what had to have been a terrifying incident.

His lips curved in a small, secret smile. *Perfect.*

# 20

Travis Hickman was six feet tall with short-cropped, sun-streaked hair, emerald green eyes, and a jutting jaw that looked as if when they'd been handing out Y chromosomes, he'd gone back for seconds. Being cramped into the small cockpit with this top gun deputy sheriff and Lucas, Lark figured she'd be more likely to succumb to testosterone poisoning than dying in a plane crash.

"Miz Stewart." His grin was quick and disarming. "You've no idea what an honor this is. I lived in Nashville for a time and used to go see you whenever you sang at The Bluebird Café."

"Thank you, I'm flattered." The café had gained a worldwide reputation for presenting the best in acoustical music. Stars like the Sweethearts of the Rodeo and Kathy Mattea were discovered at The Bluebird, and Garth Brooks had nailed down his first record contract there. "And please, call me Lark. You sound as if you're originally from out west. Wyoming?"

"Close," he confirmed. "I grew up on a Montana ranch. Since distances back there are a lot different from here, I grew up flying before I could legally drive." His eyes smiled. "Mr. Glazer said that you're not a real fan of flying."

"It's not my favorite thing to do," she admitted. "I never have figured out how two tons of metal stay in the air."

"Neither have I." He chuckled at her stricken expression. "Just kidding. I majored in aeronautical engineering at the Academy."

"That'd be the Naval Academy," Lucas said.

"The very same." He gave Lucas a measuring glance. "Let me guess. You were one of the bold, the brave, the few, crazed devil dogs."

"Somebody's got to keep the world safe so you wingnuts can play up in the sky with your toys," Lucas countered. "British Field Marshal Montgomery said a marine should be sworn to the patient endurance of hardships," he told Lark. "Like ancient knights. He also said it is not the least of these necessary hardships to have to serve with sailors."

His mild tone didn't fool Lark; he was enjoying himself. It was the first time she'd seen him almost relax. A woman could read every *Cosmopolitan* magazine ever printed, study self-help relationship books until she went blind, and tune in to every episode of *Sex and the City*, and still never entirely comprehend the male mind. One thing that she *had* learned while traveling with a male band was that for some inexplicable reason, insults were a male bonding ritual.

"Is the weather going to be a problem?" she asked. It had begun to rain. She'd already taken a Dramamine, which would help keep her stomach steady during a bumpy flight, but it wasn't doing much for her anxiety.

"No sweat," he assured her. "I just called for an update and the freezing level's going to be far above where we're flying, so we won't be in danger of picking up any ice. As for any rain or snow we might run into, that's what instruments are for. I've been forced to land on carriers in ice, rain, fog, and snow, and I've always gotten in."

Lark was grateful when he included her in the exterior flight check, explaining what he was doing as he ran his hands all over the plane, wiggling the movable surfaces on the back of the wing and tail, checking the oil level, touching, listening, and even smelling for potential problems by opening the fuel tanks and sniffing for the sharp gasoline smell.

The pace of his hands was quick, but never too fast to worry her. Less fearful than she'd been when she'd arrived at the airfield, Lark finally climbed aboard the plane. Though not as nervous as she usually was, she turned down his invitation to sit in the copilot's seat, preferring to give that "honor" to Lucas.

Travis's quiet confidence continued to soothe her as he flipped switches and pushed levers. Her nerves took a spike when they began taxiing down the runway. Unwilling to watch her link with the earth pass away, she closed her eyes during takeoff.

"You doing okay?" Lucas asked, glancing behind him.

"Ask me that after we land."

"After what you've gone through the past few days, this'll be a piece of cake."

Lark certainly hoped so.

The voices coming from the plane's radio spoke at an astonishing pace, the mind-numbing streams of static-tinged jargon sounding like a foreign language.

Rain swept over the wings and the sky became bumpier as they climbed through the pewter clouds. After they leveled off, Lucas and Travis started talking about their time in the Gulf War. Or rather Lucas was responding in monosyllables, letting the more gregarious pilot do all the talking.

Since eavesdropping on the men wasn't going to give her any hints about what had been going on in Lucas's life during the time they'd been apart, Lark took a pen and notepad out of her purse, began writing down the lyrics Lucas's kisses had started running through her mind, and tried to forget that she was twenty thousand feet above solid ground.


The snowfall began so innocently, there was no reason to suspect it would make the record books. Just a few flakes, no larger than the head of a pin, flitting through the gray branches of winter-bare trees. If you happened to blink you might miss them entirely.

Even when those spotty flakes began to cluster together, no one in the small mountain town on the Tennessee-North Carolina border saw any reason to worry. After all, the weather forecast had been for cold and overcast with occasional flurries in the afternoon, a not unusual occurrence for the Smoky Mountains in December.

Still, concerned about possible ice on the remote back roads of the mountain hollow, the principal of Highland

Falls's Andrew Jackson elementary school sent the children home early. With gleeful shouts they burst out of the red brick building as if shot from a cannon, mufflers flying behind them like colorful flags, mittened hands scooping up the powdered-sugar snow dusting the playground.

The town's highway department, which consisted of Donald MacKenna and his battered old four-wheel-drive Ford F-350, leaped into action. Grateful for an opportunity to prove that he'd gotten the job because of his work ethic, rather than nepotism—his brother-in-law just happened to be mayor—he began spreading salt over every road within the town limits.

The snow gradually, steadily picked up. When fat white flakes began floating down from the sky like feathers shaken from a goosedown quilt, the Tartan Market experienced an afternoon run on essentials like popcorn, cocoa mix, candles, and toilet paper; the shelves of the Forbes's Video Express began to empty; and in kitchens all over town, hearty stews began bubbling on stovetops.

By midafternoon the sky had darkened to the color of slate, and the moisture-laden clouds began pressing down like heavy iron anvils. Streetlights, their sensors set to come on at sundown, flickered on hours early. Mothers began calling red-cheeked children indoors and some began bringing in extra wood for the fire.

"Last time I saw a sky this dark in the middle of the day was right before the blizzard of '92," Jamie Douglass told Doris Larson as he lowered the American flag outside the Tartan Market.

"It's fixin' to be one grandpappy of a storm," predicted Doris, who dispensed mail and gossip from her post office in the back of the grocery store.

Deciding to close down early before the roads turned too icy to make it up her steep driveway, she began cashing out her stamp box. Whoever had made up that slogan about mail being delivered in all types of weather had obviously never spent a winter in Highland Falls.

Wishing she'd taken Ryan up on his offer for some Valium, Lark dug her fingernails into the buttery leather seat and tried not to think about being stuck in a tin can bucking its way through the season's first storm.

But whenever she forced her thoughts away from crashing, her mind drifted to Cody. How could she have ever married him? Because, she told herself for the umpteenth time, when he'd proposed the night her stalker had sent two dozen blood-red roses to her Las Vegas dressing room, suddenly the risk of being alone seemed worse than the risk of marriage.

She hadn't been looking for a long-term relationship, but she had been at a low and lonely point. Her sisters were off living their own lives—Lily studying art in Italy, Laurel determined to top Woodward and Bernstein in Washington.

Lark had stopped going home, because she'd grown so weary of people coming up to her on the street to tell her that they kept listening for her on the radio and asking when she was going to become a star. She'd even started to doubt her dream of getting discovered. Then Cody Armstrong fell off a bucking bronc and into her life. From the moment she'd met him, at that rodeo in the wide, flat landscape of west Texas, he'd possessed the talent to know exactly what she'd wanted—needed—to hear.

He'd also professed to be the only person in a cut-throat business to care about her, and, blinded by the glow of romance, she'd actually believed that. Even after his girlfriend had lied and told the world she was pregnant, Lark not only accepted his tearful words of contrition, she'd apologized for paying too much attention to her career and not enough to her marriage.

In hindsight, she realized that Cody had begun working to cut her off from everyone who cared about her from the day they met.

After a lighting mistake in Wichita, he'd insisted her road crew was lazy and made too many mistakes. By the time they got to Albuquerque for the state fair two days later, the entire crew had been replaced with men hand-picked by Cody. Kyle O'Donnell, the drummer who'd played with her on several demos, had tried to warn her that Cody was bad news.

"Lord knows, who you marry is none of the band's business," Kyle had said. "But because we love you, we thought you ought to know the guy's alienating everyone who works for you."

"O'Donnell's always had a thing for you, darlin'," Cody had claimed when Lark had approached him about attempting to get along better with her band members. "Now, I can't blame him for that, because you're a beautiful, talented woman. But you can't let some vindictive doper drummer ruin what we've worked so hard to build up."

Since Kyle had two young children and a wife he openly adored, Lark was sure Cody was mistaken about the so-called "thing." She was also convinced that his drug accusation was wrong. Until Kyle was busted at the Abilene airport for narcotics possession three days later.

When the tabloids leaped onto the story and began implicating Lark in alleged drug use, Kyle quit the band. She'd tried to talk him into staying, even offered to pay his lawyer, but he'd been adamant about wanting to protect her reputation. Too late, she suspected that Cody had set Kyle up for the bust to get rid of him.

She'd called to apologize while she'd been home for the Highland Games. He'd assured her that there was nothing to forgive, that he'd never blamed her for his troubles. But Lark was much harder on herself than he'd been.

*So many mistakes.*

The thick, steely clouds were blocking the sun, turning the cabin so dark that the only illumination was the gentle red glow of the instrument panel. Outside the oval window, Lark could barely see the flashing red-and-green wing lights.

"Isn't that snow?" she asked, when a white feathery substance began hitting against the windshield.

"Yeah, but don't you worry," Travis replied. "All the instruments are working. That's what they're for—to help navigate through bad weather."

He still sounded confident, but watching him carefully in the dim light, she saw the frown deepen between his brows.

"What are you doing now?" she asked as he flipped a switch.

"De-icing the engine inlet cowl. Just as a precaution."

If she was going to be terrified, Lark wanted to know the reason. "Please don't patronize me."

"All right." He didn't take his eyes from the instrument panel. "This storm's getting a little dicey. But we can deal with it."

Having spent too many years with a perpetual liar, Lark had learned to listen to what someone *wasn't* telling her. "But?"

"There's a little icing on the wings, so I'm going to lose some altitude. Hopefully the temperatures down lower will be above freezing."

"Isn't that dangerous?" The clouds were keeping her from seeing the mountains she knew were below them.

"It's more dangerous to stay where we are. The air collects lots of extra water when it's lifted up the mountain slope by the wind, which means it can hold more ice. But we'll be okay."

Lucas unbuckled his seat belt, squeezed between the front seats to sit down beside her, and took both her icy hands in his. But even that didn't stop Lark's nerves from jangling like the old civil defense system siren Jamie Douglass still tested once a year, in the unlikely event a Russian missile might ever target Highland Falls. The cold war might be over, but Jamie, who'd ridden a tank into the City of Light to liberate Paris and had returned home with a French bride, believed in remaining vigilant.

"Why can't we just go above the storm?" she asked Travis.

"The clouds are stacked too high and we've been

fighting headwinds for so long, we've used a lot of fuel."
The smile he shot over his shoulder was obviously meant
to reassure her. It failed.

"There's an old saying in the military," Lucas murmured as Travis began talking pilot jargon again on the
radio. "'The navy rules the night.' He doesn't need to see
where he's going. It'll be okay."

Needing to believe that, Lark watched as Travis
scanned the instrument panel continually, keeping the
wings level and the airspeed steady, even as they began to
descend. As when he'd done his preflight check, the pace
of his hands was quick but competent.

Clouds continued to hide the ground and sky; the
atmosphere in the cockpit grew more intense.

The plane bumped low over the mountain ridges as
Travis took it lower still, seeking warmer air. The static-
tinged voice coming from the radio was their only link to
the snowy, mountainous world beneath them.

"Okay." Travis blew out a long whistle. "We're out of
the woods."

The relief was dizzying. Lark hadn't even realized
she'd been holding her breath until she let it out on a
long whoosh. "Remind me when we land," she instructed
Lucas, "that I'm never, ever flying again."

# 21

Lark's 1800s farmhouse didn't suit William's modernist tastes, with its white clapboard siding, black shutters, and slate roof, but at least it didn't scream out "new country-music money," unlike the surrounding Tara wannabe estates with swimming pools in the shapes of cowboy hats, boots, or guitars.

Her security was laughingly simple; she really should be more careful. Didn't she know that every cell block in the country held Alarm Avoidance 101 seminars? Name a system and you could find someone inside who knew how to get around it.

The casual mélange of primitive farmhouse furnishings was a far cry from the hard-edged leather, glass, and steel with which he'd furnished his architectural homage to Frank Lloyd Wright, and a chimpanzee with a fistful of crayons could do better than the trite regional folk art paintings. But even as he cringed at an angel weathervane over the fireplace, William reminded himself that Lark's lack of sophistication was one of the reasons he'd fallen in love with her.

He went into the upstairs bedroom with its high ceilings and French doors leading out onto a balcony, lay down on the four-poster bed, and waited for his wife to arrive home.

William Guest's escape, along with her imminent return to Highland Falls, had both good and bad memories bouncing around inside Lark's head like the steel balls in a pinball machine.

Since the flight was already making her nervous, she tried to concentrate on the good, which had her thinking back on a gilded day the summer of her sixteenth year. She'd gone to Firefly Falls with the usual crowd, and people began leaving by midafternoon. It was the Fourth of July weekend so everyone in town was gathering in the town square for barbecue, Sousa, and fireworks. By unspoken agreement, Lark and Lucas stayed behind, sharing a lazy day talking about everything and nothing.

They'd always been comfortable together. Although she was often tongue-tied with people other than her sisters, she could tell him anything. Over the years she'd poured out all her personal hopes and dreams. It was only later, looking back on those days, when she'd realized how little of his own thoughts and plans he'd shared with her.

They were lying on their backs on the flat rocks by the edge of the pool, beneath the falls. Too old for skinny-dipping in mixed company, she was wearing a red, white, and blue bikini that tied at the side with perky little bows. Lucas was wearing cutoff jeans and as she cast surreptitious sideways glances at him, Lark wondered why she'd never noticed how beautiful his body was.

He reminded her of those marble statues lining the grand hall of Stewart's Folly. No, not marble, she considered, taking in his darkly tanned chest, his long, muscular legs. Marble was too cold. Bronze, she decided as her hands itched with the need to touch.

They'd just slipped back into the sparkling green pool to cool off when he playfully—as he'd done a gazillion times in the past—grabbed her ankles and yanked her beneath the water. Whenever one of them dunked the other, there'd be lots of splashing and laughing.

But not this time. Today was different. Instead of shoving him away, after a brief, feigned resistance, she flung her arms around his neck while his long fingers grasped her waist, pulling her against him.

He took her mouth, his tongue invading, arousing, creating a heat so intense, Lark was amazed the water didn't begin to boil around them. He was so strong. So hard. His chest crushed her breasts, his broad hands cupped her bottom, dragging her against his lower body, letting her feel his need.

The roar in her head was more intense than that of the falls cascading over the rocks overhead. Lark couldn't think. Couldn't breathe. But still, she wanted more. Much, much more. She wanted everything.

She locked her legs around his waist, moving desperately against him. Blood bubbling, lungs screaming, they'd burst to the surface in an explosion of need when Travis's deep voice, announcing their impending landing in Highland Falls, jolted Lark back into the present.

The world outside the window was a swirling sea of white, obscuring any sign of the town.

"They've plowed the runway," Travis assured her, anticipating her renewed attack of nerves. "It'll be a no-sweat landing."

Easy for him to say. Lark didn't believe there was such a thing as a no-sweat landing; a belief that was soon confirmed.

"Shit." Travis's tone was frighteningly grim as he began flipping levers. "We've got ourselves another little problem." His frown deepened. "Seems we've developed a fire in the exhaust system."

"A fire?" Her voice cracked.

"I won't know until we're on the ground, but I'm guessing it's breached the firewall, crossed over, and severed the fuel lines. I'm going to have to set her down."

Lark stared out at the swirling white snow. She thought she saw a lick of flames, but hoped it was a trick of her imagination and the setting sun. They were finally coming out of the clouds, low enough that she could see the ancient rounded mountaintops of the Smokies. Draped in snow, they looked like whitecaps rolling across an unending ocean.

Having grown up in these mountains, Lark knew that they could be murder on small aircraft. There were tales of planes disappearing and once, when she and her sisters had been picking wildflowers in the woods, they'd come across the wreckage of a private plane that had gone down in a winter storm in the 1960s, long before they'd been born.

"It's not that different from landing on a carrier

deck," Travis said. "The trick is to turn parallel to the mountains and land in a valley. It should be a piece of cake, but you might want to put your pillow in your lap, then bend forward and put your face in it."

As Lark did as instructed, Lucas put his arm around her, drawing her close.

"I'm slowing down to minimum speed." It was hard to hear Travis over the wild drumming of the blood in her ears. "The next sound you hear will be the gear going down."

*Wrong.*

The next sound was a strident, ear-splitting electronic voice calling out, "Sink rate!"

The gear lowered with a horrible grinding sound. Lark buried her face deeper into the foam pillow and shut her eyes so tightly she saw stars.

They hit the ground, bounced, then hit again. Lucas's hold on her tightened. The brakes squealed; the jet shuddered so hard Lark's bones rattled.

There was a furious screech of metal and the right wing slammed against a tree. The plane veered so hard to the left as the wing was sheared off, that Lark's head would have struck the window if Lucas hadn't had her pressed tight against him.

There was a sound like gunshots as the cables holding the rudder in place snapped loose. Pain pulsed in her temples, her ears, behind her eyes.

Then the left wing hit something, and the impact violently flipped the plane over. The cabin lights flickered once, then a second time, then went out as the jet skidded on its roof over a frozen pond.

The nose of the fuselage plowed into a snowdrift with a force that rattled Lark's teeth, yet kept going for what seemed like an eternity. Finally it hit a boulder, the metal crumbling into accordion folds as it shuddered to an abrupt stop.

# 22

The blip had been cruising along John Harding's air traffic control screen at twenty thousand feet for a few miles before it began to flash, which was his signal to accept the handoff from Knoxville. The pilot had gotten himself in a bit of nasty weather that had resulted in some clear icing on his wings—never a good thing—but had calmly reported that he was going to try flying lower to get beneath the stacked ice-filled clouds.

He'd found the warmer air he'd been seeking and leveled out. Harding relaxed.

Ten minutes later, he was watching the fluorescent blip descend to ten thousand feet as the pilot made the approach into Highland Falls. Nine thousand. He momentarily lost the jet when it descended behind what he guessed was a small rise in the terrain, then reappeared, only to disappear behind another rise. This time the jet didn't emerge.

Harding waited ten seconds. Then ten seconds more.

*Shit.*

The scope continued the blip, but Harding knew that

was merely computer conjecture. After another half-dozen sweeps, the radar confirmed his worst fear. The damn thing had vanished.

"I have a possible downed aircraft," he said with studied calm, which was air traffic controllese for "Christ on a crutch, I think the frigging damn plane crashed."

The low hum of voices around him stopped.

Where the hell was it?

Harding made an LKP mark on the radar screen, signaling the last known place, then, following FAA protocol, stood up so his supervisor could take his place.

Ten minutes later, an ALNOT—Alert Notice—had been issued and John Harding was standing outside the break room door, sucking Marlboro smoke deep into his lungs.

After ten years as an air traffic controller, he'd just lost his first plane.

They were upside down.

"Lark." Lucas's deep voice was gentle, but insistent. "We've got to get out of here."

"We've stopped." Lingering fear clogged her voice. She'd died a thousand deaths since the plane had gone out of control. "And we're still alive."

"So far." He quickly unfastened his seat belt, dropped down, and tugged at hers. It had jammed. Outside, bright orange flames began to lick at the window. "We need to get out before what's left of the plane goes up."

He pulled a Swiss Army knife from his pocket and cut through the strap, then eased her down to keep her from falling.

"We need to help Travis."

He was slumped in his seat, his head at an angle that didn't look natural.

Lucas pressed his fingertips against the pilot's throat. "He's dead." He pushed the door open with his shoulder.

"Are you sure? Perhaps—"

"I know dead." Lucas's brusque tone made her believe him. His fingers dug into her waist as he thrust her out of the plane, sending Lark sliding down the fuselage into deep snow. Right behind her, he yanked her to her feet and began to run.

He was a great deal taller than Lark, and, unlike her, was wearing practical boots. It was difficult to match his stride and she stumbled twice. Each time, he pulled her up fast and ran again.

They were about fifty yards from the jet when the explosion rocked the mountain. When the blast hurled them to the ground yet again, Lucas threw himself on top of her as a huge fireball exploded into the twilight red sky.

After three hours of watching CNN for any news about the New Orleans shooting, and waiting impatiently for Lark to return home, William began to prowl the house, going from room to room, touching her things: a blue-and-white spatterware pitcher on the dining-room table, the colorful American ironstone pottery in the kitchen, the weathered old checkerboard set in the library.

Growing increasingly impatient, he returned to the bedroom and roamed the room, opening various drawers and boxes, exploring their contents. He'd just dipped a finger into a jar of pink night cream when *Headline News* reported that Lark wasn't returning to Nashville, but had instead chartered a plane to take her directly to her family's Tennessee mountain home.

Furious, he backhanded a row of antique perfume bottles and sent them flying. A bouquet of floral scents rose from the shattered glass.

Rage boiled inside William's veins like hot lava; he picked up a ladder-back chair and threw it across the room, shattering a standing floor-length mirror in the corner.

He'd had a plan, dammit, meticulously thought out! First he'd been going to tie her to the four posters of her bed and rape her, atop the pretty sunshine-and-shadows quilt.

Then, he was going to pour the kerosene he'd bought at a busy Pilot station over her naked body and punish her for her betrayal. Slowly, methodically, so she'd fully understand the gravity of her crime. He'd make her beg for her life. Then he'd use the blue-and-red Titans lighter he'd picked up at the station's mini-market to give his traitorous wife a Viking funeral.

Now she'd spoiled everything. Well, if he couldn't kill her right now, at least he could leave her a message.

He retrieved the jerrican from the trunk of the car. He'd learned in prison that kerosene was the fuel of choice of the professional arsonist. Gasoline, with its lower flash point, was more dangerous; anyone using it as a fire starter risked becoming a human torch. Kerosene took longer to get going, but since it didn't burn up the oxygen like gasoline, it made for a hotter fire.

Kerosene was like the Energizer bunny of fuel—it just kept burning and burning and burning.

Chuckling at his little joke, he drenched the bed, then spread a trail of the accelerant throughout the house.

He stopped at the front door, then stuck a match and tossed it onto the pile of pretty kerosene-drenched bras and panties he'd taken from her dresser drawers. It took longer than he'd thought it would, but just when he began to worry he hadn't bought enough fuel, the small flames licking at the frothy bits of silk and lace caught.

*Whoosh!*

A vast column of fire rushed up the stairs, greedily eating the hand-carved banister. The fire spread, room by room, like a row of dominoes falling.

He was driving away from the house when the explosion rocked the car. The sight of Lark Stewart's house engulfed in orange flames, black smoke billowing from the roof, made William smile.

"Next stop," he murmured with heady anticipation, "Highland Falls."

"It's going to be all right," Lucas assured Lark as ashes began to drift down from the sky like black snow.

Lark wasn't certain anything would ever be all right again.

She felt the weight of his body ease as he stood up beside her. "Come on."

Despite the adrenaline racing through her body, Lark couldn't move. "Where?"

"Believe it or not, there's something positive about this," he said. "We're not that far from my place."

"Your place?" She hadn't even known he'd moved back to Highland Falls.

"I moved to my great-grandfather's farm after I came home."

The old homestead was about twenty miles outside town; she and Lucas had spent a lot of time there during their teenage days. They hadn't been farming.

Dark memories of the farm stirred in the deep recesses of her mind. She hadn't been to the farm since that summer. She wasn't certain she had the courage to go there now.

"I've always read you're supposed to stay with the plane. So searchers can find us."

Like Dustin Hoffman's aviophobic character in *Rainman*, Lark knew a great many crash stories. She also knew that survivors had a sixty percent survival rate if they were rescued within eight hours. After that the odds plummeted; after two days, the rate dove to ten percent.

"Even if they know we're down, there's no way anyone could get a search party going before dark," Lucas said. The sun, shimmering blood-red in the blue haze of the burning fuel, was already sinking below the mountaintops. "And that's *if* this storm blows over into North Carolina. I can understand why it's not your first choice, Lark. But it's our only choice."

"We're in the middle of nowhere. How do you plan to find the way?"

"I know every inch of this mountain. Plus, my watch is equipped with a compass, an altimeter, and GPS."

"I didn't know they made watches like that." They

both knew she was stalling. But to go back to that place she almost died . . .

"There are some on the market, but they're so thick and clunky only card-carrying geeks will buy them. This one's a prototype I've been testing for a guy I know who develops high-tech stuff for the Pentagon. I'll get us there, Lark." His rugged face was smeared with smoke, his expression grim but determined. "You have to trust me."

"I do." As she looked back at the burning skeleton of the plane, tears stung her eyes. "Until this month, the only two people I've ever known who died were my mother and grandfather. I barely remember my mother, and Grandpa James was in his eighties and had cancer, so in a way, it was a blessing when he passed. Now Danny was almost killed, and two other people are dead because of me."

"You can't let yourself think that way, Lark—it's a dead-end road leading straight to hell. Besides, from what Travis said before we went down, the crash was due to mechanical failure. Knowing how to make a plane catch on fire in midair is not something your average stalker would know how to do. Even a stalker turned murderer."

"It doesn't matter." She was trying hard not to cry, knowing that breaking down would only waste valuable energy. "Travis is dead because of me. If it wasn't for me, that plane would still be parked in the hangar back in New Orleans."

"Lark." Lucas's hands curled around her shoulders; his tone was gentle, but firm. "We'll deal with survivor guilt later." He scooped her off her feet. "Right now, we've got to get moving."

"I wish you'd stop carrying me around like a sack of potatoes." *I hate feeling weak. And helpless. And whatever you do, don't let go of me.*

"Objection noted." He kept walking. "And this is where *I* point out that you'll never make it through the snow in those silly girlie boots."

"Had I known I was going to be hiking across the Smokies in the middle of winter, I would have worn damn steel-toed Doc Martens."

Lark hated confrontation, but now, dammit, she wanted a fight. *Needed* a fight.

"Besides, you're a fine one to talk. You're not exactly dressed like Nanook of the North, either." His sexy-as-hell leather bomber jacket and black jeans weren't nearly warm enough for a winter storm.

"It's good to get pissed off," he said approvingly. "Keeps the blood flowing."

It was getting dark, the temperature was plummeting, and the wind-driven icy snow felt like a storm of needles against her face. Lark knew Lucas was right. Even if he did shorten his steps to accommodate her stride—which would only slow them down—she'd never be able to stay in the deep footprints his boots were making in the snow drifts.

She'd once heard Willie Nelson tell about having to perform the night after his mother died. His point was that sometimes the only thing a person could do when tragedy struck was to keep on keeping on. Which was pretty much what Lark had been struggling to do ever since those cops had put her in the back of their patrol car on Christmas Eve.

*Keep on keeping on.*

But how much was one person expected to endure?

The events of the past days were threatening to crash down on her, but Lark desperately feared that if she allowed herself to dwell on Deputy Travis Hickman's death right now, while their lives were still in danger, she'd fall apart. And this time, perhaps there'd be no putting herself together again.

*Keep on keeping on.*

As Lucas trudged through the snow, Lark forced herself not to look back.

# 23

The McCloud farmhouse, built from local stones and timbers that had been harvested to open up land for farming nearly two centuries earlier, was set on a rise above a creek. During spring, when snow began melting from the mountaintop, the water flowing over the rocks could become a torrent, but now it had frozen into a shimmering silver ribbon.

The barn, where she and Lucas had made love on a bed of straw in the hayloft, was still standing; it appeared to have been recently reroofed and painted a traditional red. Her wary gaze drifted to where the smokehouse had once stood.

*He loomed over her, huge and threatening, his eyes gleaming like twin coals in the dark. The rope dug into her wrists and ankles. When he reached out to touch her, she screamed behind the gag covering her mouth.*

"It's gone," Lucas said. "The first thing I did when I came back was burn it to the ground." His lips twisted in a mockery of a smile. "Okay, the third. First I got stinking drunk. Then I passed out. The next morning, I burned it down. Then I got drunk and pretty much stayed that way for the next few years."

"I drank for a while, too," she volunteered as they crossed the frozen creek. "When my marriage began falling apart. I quit when it seemed to be getting out of hand." Since deciding to divorce Cody, she'd never once wanted the numbing effects of alcohol.

"That happens."

"Yeah." They reached the front door.

*"Lucas? Are you here? I hate it when we fight."* She *searched the empty rooms, then, not finding him, turned to leave . . .*

Lark's throat worked painfully as she swallowed. "Could we wait just a minute?"

"Sure." Seeming to understand her need to stand on her own two feet, he set her down on the covered porch.

*Run.*

Lark took a deep breath. Another. "Okay," she whispered.

Walking into the house was like walking into a meat locker; the air was as cold as outdoors, and frost had created icy white doilies on the windows.

Lucas flipped a switch beside the door, but no lights came on. "Power's out." He took a book of matches from his pocket and lit a lantern on a nearby table. "The storm must've knocked down the lines."

"Does that mean the phone's not working, either?"

He picked up the receiver and held it to his ear. "Yeah, it's out. And there's no cell tower close enough to get a signal."

"So we can't let anyone know we're here?"

Surely Travis had filed a flight plan, which meant that when the plane didn't show up at the tiny Highland Falls airfield, people would know they'd crashed. Her family would be frantic when they heard the news.

"Not until morning, when hopefully, if the storm slows down, I can take the snowmobile into town." He struck another match on the stone fireplace, using it to light a trio of fat utilitarian candles on the mantel. The logs had already been set for a fire; he touched the match to the kindling, which caught immediately.

Lark was shivering and her teeth chattered so violently she was afraid they'd shatter.

"Unfortunately, I'd planned to go into town to buy more gas for the generator the morning Zelda called. The good news is that since the power goes out a lot out here, I had Donald MacKenna build a double-sided fireplace on the wall between the bedroom and bathroom when I was remodeling the place. And the water heater works on propane, like the stove, so there should be plenty of hot water."

He gestured toward a door she remembered led to a room that had, during their teenage days, been home to innumerable spiders. "Let's get you into a warm bath."

The bathroom was definitely a man's room. There were no wallpaper flowers, no fragrant soap shaped like roses or seashells, no dishes of scented potpourri. The towels were a muddy shade of brown Lark suspected had been chosen for their dirt-hiding ability.

He lit the wood stacked in the smaller stone fireplace, then twisted on the faucet. As steaming water began flowing out of the tap, Lark was immensely grateful the pipes hadn't frozen.

"I'm going to go light the stove so we can heat up some supper," Lucas said. "Holler if you need anything."

The fire was already beginning to warm the air in the compact room as Lark stripped off her black coat, a style similar to one Audrey Hepburn had worn in an old movie. The sleeve had been ripped from the shoulder when Lucas had pulled her out of the plane, and she doubted it could be repaired.

*Reality alert. A ruined coat is the least of your concerns.*

"You're alive," Lark reminded herself as she peeled her sweater over her head, then unhooked her black-lace bra and hung them both over the shower rod to dry. "No complaining allowed."

Lucas knocked on the door. "You doing okay in there?"

"I'm fine." She began peeling her ice-encrusted jeans down her legs.

"I'm leaving some clothes outside the door. The storm's really starting to kick up, so I'm going out to get more wood."

She heard the front door open, then close as she yanked the jeans off her frozen feet. Next came the panties, which she hung up next to the matching bra.

After wrapping her hair in a towel, she lowered herself into the old claw-footed tub. The steaming water came up to her shoulders, and as her body began to thaw out painfully, she flinched. But at least the pain was a reminder she was alive.

Unfortunately, Travis wasn't. Lark leaned her head against the high back of the tub and closed her eyes, mourning the top-gun pilot who'd survived a war, only to die because of her.

*    *    *

Lucas lifted the ax above his head and brought the blade down, sending the pieces of split log flying. *Thwack.*

He didn't need any more wood; the neatly stacked maple, apple, and oak was stacked up to the rafters. What he needed was a goddamn drink. A stiff shot of whiskey dumped into a mug of beer, a boilermaker created solely for the purpose of getting quickly, ruthlessly drunk.

*Set up another round, bartender, and keep 'em coming.*
*Thwack.*

Lucas didn't believe in all that much—an improvement, he figured, from those lost years when he didn't believe in anything—but there was one axiom he'd come to accept. Drunks lie. Not just to the world, but to themselves. The fact that he was doing so now warned that he was on a slippery slope, perilously close to sliding back into old bad habits.

Hell, he didn't really need a drink.

What he need—*thwack*—was Lark. He wanted to run his hands over her slender curves; wanted to touch every inch of her body, taste her fragrant flesh, bury himself deep in her warm, welcoming warmth.

*What you need, dammit, is to keep focused on the goal.*

Which was keeping her safe.

He placed one of the pieces of split log upright on the stump. *Thwack.* As kindling went flying, Lucas came to the unwelcome realization that after all these years, after all the effort to drive Lark Stewart from his heart and mind, he loved her still.

After the debacle in New Orleans, he hadn't wanted

the responsibility for anyone ever again. But, dammit, he wanted Lark—too much for comfort, too much for sanity.

He attacked another log and wondered how the hell he was going to get through the hours until morning.

Lark was shaving her legs with a razor she'd found in the medicine cabinet, when a memory began playing in her mind.

*The moon moved from behind a cloud, cutting through the fog before disappearing again, but in that suspended heartbeat of a second, Lark saw his face.*

*Horrifyingly, she recognized him. They both froze.*

*Fight or flight—which to do?*

*She heard another pop. Saw another flash. Felt something burn its way across her forehead.*

*Knowing that staying where she was would get her killed, Lark scrambled to her feet and began to run. For her life.*

Sitting in the cooling bathwater, she struggled desperately to recall the murderer's face. But his features, along with what had happened next, were still a blank slate.

"Don't push." She soaped the washcloth and began scrubbing. "It'll come back." She couldn't allow herself to believe otherwise.

When her skin gleamed pearly pink, she rose from the cooling water, wrapped a towel around herself, and retrieved the clothes Lucas had left for her.

The wool socks climbed nearly to her knees and the fleecy gray sweats were far from stylish, but blessedly warm. She pushed up the heavy sleeves; when the baggy pants slid down her legs, she rolled the waistband over several times and hoped they'd stay up.

She wiped off the steam-fogged mirror and frowned at the angular face looking back at her. The bruises were turning an ugly shade of yellow, and there was a new lump where her forehead had hit the back of Travis's seat. Unfortunately, her cosmetics bag, along with her purse and her clothes, were toast.

Studying her reflection, Lark wondered if Lucas would still even be interested in making love to her, looking like she did.

Of course he would. The same way she wanted to make love with him, despite the fact that getting involved with any man, especially one with whom she had such a long, complex history, was the last thing she needed right now.

Unfortunately, need and want were turning out to be very different things.

# 24

Lark wandered through the empty rooms as if in a fog. Thanks to the crackling fire Lucas had started, the house, which was familiar and foreign at the same time, was beginning to warm up. Lucas's parents had never lived there, and when she and Lucas had first started using it as a hideaway from the rest of the world, it had been a mess.

The second time, she'd insisted on bringing out buckets, mops, and old rags. By the end of a day of hard work, the windows had gleamed, their bare feet hadn't stuck to the floor, and wildflowers had bloomed in an old tin coffeepot on the kitchen table Lucas's great-grandfather had made for his bride.

The house was yet more evidence that Lucas had changed. Who would have thought that the teenage boy who'd griped about wasting time polishing glass when they could be making love would have grown up to be so neat? The main room—a combination kitchen/living room/dining room—had originally been four smaller rooms, and by replacing the upstairs bedrooms with a loft, he'd created a towering cathedral ceiling. The tall windows and skylights brought the outside in.

The house was as meticulously clean and tidy as a Swiss kitchen; there were no magazines cluttering the coffee table or kitchen counter, no photographs; no candid snapshots of his family or any photographs of women on his nightstand. The only personal touch in the house were the bookcases on either side of the stone fireplace—an eclectic mix of fiction and nonfiction that had been shelved in alphabetical order by author. A voracious reader, Lark liked knowing they had something in common besides a rocky past, hormones, and murder.

Drawn to the warmth, she sank down onto the rug in front of the fire, drew her knees to her chest, and rested her forehead on them as exhaustion came crashing down on her.

God, she was so tired. Mentally, physically, and emotionally. Her body felt as if it'd been used as a punching bag, her brain had shut down, and dual impulses—the need to be strong versus a desire to curl into a ball and sleep forever—battled within her.

The tears she'd been fighting for days finally won, spilling out of her eyes to run in silent rivers down her cheeks. Her shoulders, weighed down by guilt and grief, shook beneath the oversize sweatshirt. She wrapped her arms around herself to keep from breaking apart.

The door opened on a gust of icy air, and she was only distantly aware of Lucas dumping the wood into the box beside the hearth.

"Go ahead, baby." He sat down beside her and held her tight as she began to sob. "Get it all out."

Pressing her face into his sweater, Lark allowed the

hot tears to flow free. Racked by anguish, she clung while his strong hands stroked her back and he murmured words of comfort against her hair.

Cody was in a shitty mood. After the business opportunity of a lifetime had dropped into his lap, he'd cowboyed up and flown to New Orleans, where Lark was performing. All he needed was a few thousand bucks—okay, fifty thousand, but hell, Lark could write that out of petty cash—but when he'd tried to hit her up for some of the money that should have been his in the first place, the bitch brushed him off like he was some panhandler begging for loose change, then sicced her pit bull of a boyfriend on him.

"Women," he muttered as he tossed back a glass of Jack Black, enjoying the burn. "You can't trust 'em and you can't kill 'em." *At least not and get away with it.*

Among those on his personal hit list would have been that tight-assed banker he'd just met with. He'd dressed for business in a gray western-cut suit, black shirt, dress boots, and Calgary Stampede buckle. He'd said all the right things, explained the earning potential of the rodeo stock business, along with the collection of shiny silver buckles he'd started winning when he was fifteen. Explained how rodeo was in his blood, being how his daddy was a wrangler. No one knew bucking horses like Cody Armstrong, he'd told her.

She should have considered it her lucky day. The Rocking R Ranch supplied stock to rodeos all over the South, from Texas to Florida. Trace Tremont, the guy who'd started the company back in the '60s with two broncs and an ornery Brahma bull who'd just as soon kill you as look at you, had sworn he'd never sell out. Tremont had always been a man of his word.

But, as Cody had explained to Miss High and Mighty Moneybags banker, after Tremont dropped dead of a heart attack, his daughter had put the ranch up for sale and four of Cody's old rodeo pals were offering him a twenty percent cut of the business.

"You've probably heard the ranch's slogan—Born to Buck," he'd said.

"I don't believe I have," she'd said.

"Well, it's the God's honest truth. Don't think of this as me askin' you for a loan," he'd said. "Think of it as Cody Armstrong offering you the best investment offer of your career."

"I'm sorry." She hadn't even bothered to open the manila envelope of documents he'd brought with him. "But I'm afraid I don't know anything about livestock management."

"You don't have to." He'd flashed his boyish smile, the one that had coaxed more than one barrel racer out of her Wranglers. "You'll have me."

"I'm sorry." She held the envelope back toward him.

*Here's your hat; don't let the door hit your ass on the way out.*

Now, as he sat at the bar in the Silver Saddle, trying to drink every damn female he'd met into oblivion, Cody couldn't stop thinking about how all his problems were Lark's fault.

He'd had a damn good career going for himself before she'd come along, and hell, he was probably the only cowboy on earth who didn't even like country music. Like the Rocking R's broncs, he'd been born to buck and raise hell, but he'd given up the rodeo circuit to concentrate on making Lark a big star.

Okay, so she might have had one hell of a natural-born talent. But the fact that she'd gone back to just standing up on stage singing her songs without any flash and dazzle was proof that the girl didn't have any head for business. She was probably already starting to realize the mistake she'd made.

Just maybe, he'd take her back, Cody considered magnanimously as he staggered out of the Silver Saddle. But first he'd make her crawl.

"I'm sorry," Lark said when she was finally cried out.

"Hey, you're entitled. You're having a lousy week." Lucas kissed the top of her head, then gave her face a critical study. "Feel better?"

She felt helpless. Vulnerable. Embarrassed.

Because it was too tempting to hide in his arms, Lark moved a little away from him.

"I hardly ever cry." She swiped the sleeve of the sweatshirt across her wet face.

"Perhaps you should more often." He took a hand-kerchief from his pocket and dabbed at the tears with an amazingly gentle touch for such a large man. "It's not good to bottle stuff up inside."

"Like you don't."

He shrugged, pleased with that small spurt of emotion. A heart he'd given to her years ago, the same one he hadn't even realized he still possessed, had ached while she'd wept like a child in his arms. "It's different for guys. We're supposed to be strong and silent."

"Which is probably why men don't live as long as women."

Another tear escaped. Even heavy with fatigue, her red-rimmed eyes were still the most beautiful he'd ever seen. Understanding the need for space, he held out the handkerchief.

"Thanks." She wiped away the silver streak. Blew her nose. And once again struggled for that composure she'd always worn like a second skin. Except when they'd been making love. "I thought my father was the only person in the world who still used these things."

"Rachel's a very vocal member of the Sierra Club. She sends me a box every Christmas to keep me from killing trees."

"God, that brings back memories." Good ones, from her ghost of a smile. She tucked the handkerchief into her sleeve. "Do you remember her and Laurel getting into that fight over newsprint?"

"Yeah, in the seventh grade. Rachel was angry about Laurel expanding her weekly paper from four pages to six."

"Your sister accused her of killing trees for gossip and broke her printing press," Lark recalled.

"Yeah, but *your* sister got even by telling the world that Rachel McCloud stuffed tissue in her bra before the middle-school cheerleader tryouts." Because he couldn't be this close to Lark without touching her, Lucas began to knead the lingering tension out of the back of her neck.

"So how is Laurel?" he asked, wanting to take her mind away from the horrors that had made her weep. "Whenever I go into town to pick up my mail, Doris tells me she's still playing Lois Lane."

"With a vengeance." Lark rolled her neck. Closed her eyes. "She tackles journalism with that same mad saint's obsession that had her writing that story about the school board hiring the principal's cousin to be prom photographer without allowing competing bids."

She breathed out a slow shimmering sigh of pleasure. She'd always been a sucker for neck rubs. "How many other people would get a kick out of being falsely accused of being Anonymous when *Primary Colors* was published? When I asked her this summer how she dealt with all the stress of her work, she told me she's taken up kickboxing."

"That's good to know. I'll be sure to keep out of her way next time she comes back to town."

"I think you're safe. She's always liked you." She was all but purring now. "I was thinking perhaps I should take it up."

"Now there's an idea. Though I think yoga's probably more your style."

She opened her eyes. Narrowed them. "Are you accusing me of being wimpier than my sister?"

"Are you kidding? Hell, the past few days you've proven that you're as tough as they come." He paused a significant beat, then skimmed a long slow look over her. "I was just remembering how flexible your body can be."

Color drifted prettily into too wan cheeks. The chemistry was so still there. If he'd shown up in New Orleans for any reason other than Danny's shooting, Lucas thought, they'd have already been to bed.

He started to push himself to his feet. "The fire in the stove should be hot enough by now to make coffee."

Lark caught his arm. "I don't need coffee."

*What I need, what I want, is you.*

The words hovered unspoken between them.

He looked down at her hand on his sleeve. Then back at her face. His eyes were as serious as Lark had ever seen them, but studying him as intently as he was studying her, she could see the banked lust in them, as well.

All too aware of the precious gift of forgiveness she was bestowing on him, Lucas took his time, tantalizing her with slow hands and soft kisses.

He kissed her wounded brow. Her cheek. Her throat. He stripped the oversize sweats off her body, then touched her everywhere, watching her eyes turn dark and slumbrous, steeping himself in her tastes, her textures.

As he kissed her with all the emotion he'd only felt toward her, with all the feelings he'd locked up inside him for so many years, Lucas found her body even more glorious than he'd remembered.

She was, he thought, as she arched against him, her body silhouetted by the flickering firelight, perfect.

They rolled over the rug, arms and legs entwined.

Breaths tangled. Lark's flesh grew slick beneath his mouth; Lucas's blood pounded beneath her lips.

As desperate as he was to be inside her, Lucas didn't have to remind himself to be tender. Even as a part of him wanted to take, to plunder, another, even stronger part of him reveled in her soft sighs, her faint moans, the way she moved so fluidly beneath his touch.

Her hands stroked over his shoulders, his back. When he pushed her smooth thighs apart with his palms, her nails bit into his shoulders.

Her face was flushed with vibrant life; her eyes gleamed like molten gold in the firelight.

He sheathed himself in the condom he'd retrieved from the bedroom while she'd been in the bath.

"Now." His voice was raw.

"Now." It was little more than a whisper, but easily heard in the snow-muffled silence.

With his fingers on her hips, he covered her mouth with his as he slid slowly, inch by inch, into her. She sighed his name, her breath a warm breeze against his lips as her body welcomed him. Embraced him.

Then she twined her long bare legs around his hips and Lucas was lost.

With a sound between a groan and a growl, he pushed her knees back so he could thrust deeper. Harder. Faster.

Any earlier desire to soothe was scorched away by the shared madness of need.

Rising to meet him, Lark bowed her body and matched him stroke for stroke as he pounded into her like a man possessed, driving them up a cliff of no return.

Hearts pounded in rhythm, jackhammer hard, jackhammer fast as they tumbled over the edge together.

# 25

Zelda Stewart knew that if anyone could protect her niece, it would be Lucas McCloud. But sometimes bad things happened, and mortals couldn't always outtrick fate.

Although she had always enjoyed traveling, the bulletlike rat-a-tat of the icy snow hitting the window of the jet winging its way through the night toward Asheville, North Carolina, exacerbated nerves already on edge.

There was something else underlying the jet lag and worry.

She closed her eyes, leaned her head against the back of the seat, shut out the steady drone of the engines, and focused.

It wasn't apprehension. Not trepidation. Nor fear, though she'd certainly felt both of those in the past three days. It was something else; something she couldn't quite put her finger on. *Restlessness?* That came close. *It's only natural; you've been sitting on your ass for hours trying to get home.*

That still wasn't quite it.

Zelda's fingers curled around the moonstone, worn to

protect night travelers, suspended from a slender silver chain around her neck.

The stone warmed. In anticipation, she decided. But of what? Or whom?

She slipped the necklace off and rotated it in her hand, gazing at the white "moon" inside that had given the stone its name.

Many in Highland Falls had viewed her as Una Gunn's logical successor, but Zelda's powers had never been as strong. Or, as the old woman had suggested, perhaps the fault was not in the strength of Zelda Stewart's sight, but the strength of her focus.

She'd be the first to admit she had the attention span of a rambunctious toddler. But there were so many things she wanted to do, places to see, and people to meet before she passed on into her next life it was difficult to concentrate on a single thing and her snappy response in the past had always been that she'd been multitasking before multitasking was cool.

Patience had never been Zelda's strong suit. It wasn't now.

*Focus, dammit. You're a witch. How hard could it be?*

She took a deep breath. Another.

*Focus.*

A shadow of wings moved across the stone moon, swift and silent. In Celtic lore, the owl was a servant of the Crone Goddess, the Goddess of Wisdom. Vocal in November, the night bird heralded the winter death of the Goddess, then fell silent until February. Rather than the ill omen many believed, the birds led those wise enough to follow out of the darkness toward the light.

As the pilot announced their approach into Asheville, Zelda decided to take the vision as a sign that Lark would soon be emerging from the terrible darkness William Guest had brought upon her.

Harlan Boone was waiting when Zelda exited the jetway. She'd once loved Harlan with every fiber of her being and she'd never doubted that he loved her as well. When he'd chosen duty over love, Zelda had been unable to hate him for the decision. She couldn't have given her heart to any man who'd chosen the easier, less honorable path.

Looking into his grim face, Zelda tensed.

"What's happened?"

She hadn't realized her hands had fisted until he'd uncurled her fingers. He flung her carry-on bag over his shoulder and looped an arm around her waist. "Let's go find someplace to sit down," he suggested in a mild tone she wasn't buying for a moment.

It had been years since Harlan had put a hand on her. The last time, they'd both cried.

"I've been sitting for what seems like days. Tell me now."

He knew her well. He always had. He didn't sugarcoat it, just stated it flat out, as she herself would have done. "Lucas and Lark's plane has gone missing."

"It's crashed?" Her knees buckled. "Where?"

"Somewhere west of Highland Falls." His arm tightened around her, literally holding Zelda on her feet.

"You don't know exactly where?" Vast areas of the mountains were literally impenetrable. If the plane had gone down there . . .

"The plane didn't carry a transponder, because it was private, so all they have to go on is the LPK—the last place it showed up on radar."

"Oh, my God." She pressed a hand against her chest. Somewhere in the mists clouding her mind, an owl hooted. "Harlan." Her other hand clutched his arm. "I'm the one who sent Lucas there to bring her home."

"Which is why she'll be okay. Searchers will begin looking for them at first light, and the Civil Air Patrol will start an air search as soon as this snow stops." He drew her close and pressed his lips against her firecracker red hair. "Lucas was a marine, babe. He'll keep Lark safe."

*Babe*. Memories—good and bad—rushed back, swirling with fears and hopes and other feelings too complex to sort out while she was so wrung out.

"They're alive." That single thought managed to slice through the darkness like a shaft of sunshine through a thunderhead. If her darling Lark had died, she would have felt the blow to her heart. Because a very large part of her would have died, as well.

"Hell yes, they are," Harlan said in a robust, encouraging tone. "Now, let's get you to Stewart's Folly so you can be there to welcome her home."

Her legs had regained their strength. Her head began to clear. "I'm glad you're here," Zelda said as they waited for the rest of her baggage to arrive.

His gunmetal gray eyes warmed. "Me too."

They were tangled together, arms and legs entwined, Lucas still buried deep within her. Lark lay bonelessly beneath him, her hands stroking the damp, cooling flesh of his back while he sprawled over her, his lips against her throat.

She wasn't sure she'd ever be able to move again. Didn't think she'd ever be able to talk again. It was taking all her concentration just remembering how to breathe.

How could she have forgotten this? The passion that burned like a fever in her blood, the pleasure so intense it bordered on pain, the dark, heady thrill of surrender.

"Well," she managed, "that was certainly worth waiting for."

"I had more control when I was seventeen."

"Do you hear me complaining?" She pressed her hands against the ridge of muscles running from Lucas's broad shoulders to his waist.

It had been a very long time since she'd enjoyed the strength of a man's body on top of hers. Even longer since she'd wanted a man. Just thinking back on those rough hands that had demanded so much from her had her skin warming up all over again. With the exception of that desperation-driven night in New Orleans before he'd gone to war, he'd always been so tender, so gentle, treating her as if she were made of spun glass. "And you definitely took my mind off being afraid."

She felt his low chuckle. "I wish I'd known it was that easy the day you screamed about those spiders in the bathroom."

That memory made her shudder. "A spider the size of a fist is not exactly an aphrodisiac."

"It was the size of a dime, but I can see your point." He rolled over, taking her with him. "On the other hand, danger can be one hell of an aphrodisiac."

"Since I find myself hating every woman you've ever been with, I'd rather not know if that knowledge comes from personal experience."

"I've never felt about any woman the way I feel about you."

That statement, straightforward and unembellished, caused her heart to turn over in her chest. Lark wasn't foolish enough to believe she and Lucas could pick up where they'd left off, but in the soothing afterglow of lovemaking, she allowed herself to believe they could somehow forge a new beginning.

"I've never felt this way about any other man, either." She cuddled closer and sighed happily. "I had no idea I was multiorgasmic."

A rough, utterly pleased laugh burst from his chest. "You realize that you just gave my ego one helluva boost."

"I know." Feeling ridiculously blissful, she leaned forward to lose herself in the sweet, dreamy mating of lips. "I can feel it." He was hard and full again. *And all mine*, she thought giddily.

"While I'd love to take credit for your newly discovered sexual prowess, it's not me," he said. He framed her face in his hands; his thumbs skimmed along her jaw. "It's us."

"Us," she agreed as she rolled over on top of him. "Together."

# 26

There'd been a time when Lark had been everything to Lucas. He would have given his life for hers. As he heated up something for supper, Lucas knew he still would.

After refusing her offer to help fix dinner, he suggested she sit at the table while he worked. He held up two cans of soup. "Which one?"

"The minestrone," she decided.

"Minestrone it is." He opened the can and poured the minestrone into a pot.

"I remembered something while you were outside," she said. "About the man who shot Danny."

"Oh?" Lucas asked with studied casualness.

"I recognized him."

"Recognizing someone and knowing them can be two different things."

"I know." She briefly squeezed her eyes tight, as if trying to force the vision.

"Did Armstrong ever threaten you?"

She blinked at the out-of-the-blue question. "Not physically. Why?"

"Then the guy never laid a hand on you?"

"I wouldn't have stayed married as long as I did if he'd been abusive." Her eyes widened. "Surely you don't suspect Cody of having shot Danny?"

"At this point, we shouldn't be ruling anyone out. Your ex-weasel didn't look real happy about your cutting off the gravy train. Does he own a gun?"

"I don't know. He used to."

"What kind?"

"A handgun."

"Pistol or revolver?"

"Pistol. I have no idea what kind," she said, anticipating his next question. "All I know is that it was ugly and I hated it."

"I don't suppose you happen to know if he had a permit to carry concealed."

"Actually, I do, because I made him apply for one."

Lucas had been counting on that. The Lark he'd once known had refused to jaywalk in a town with so little traffic, it had only a single traffic light. Which flashed yellow.

"Then it should be a snap to find out the caliber."

Her brow furrowed. "I wouldn't want you doing anything illegal on my account."

"Attempted murder's illegal." He found some crackers in the cupboard.

She shivered. When she recovered quickly, he wondered if she was already compartmentalizing the crime. She'd always put things in little boxes, locking them away somewhere deep in her mind. He'd watched her do it with her mother's death.

When she'd testified at Guest's first trial, everyone

had been so impressed that a teenager could be able to maintain such poise under such terrible pressure. Watching her, Lucas had known that she'd locked the psychopath away in one of those mental strongboxes.

She'd done the same thing to a lesser degree when she'd tracked him down in New Orleans. Looking back on that night, he suspected they should have discussed what Guest had done to her, if for no other reason than to try to put the horror behind them. But no more eager than she to ruin what could be their last night together, he hadn't pushed.

"I hate all this." She got up, found his stash of paper napkins and began setting the table. "But I like the idea of us being a team again."

He liked that she was smiling. Pleasing Lark still pleased him. "Me too."

"Cody wouldn't shoot anyone." She opened a drawer and took out two spoons. "He's too much of a coward."

"It doesn't take much guts to pull a trigger." He might not be a legendary profiler like Finn Callahan, but he'd had a lot of experience with individuals who'd blow a life away as easily as stepping on an ant. "How did you get hooked up with a loser like that in the first place?"

"Because you refused to marry me."

"Score one for the Tennessee Songbird." Little bubbles were forming around the edge of the soup.

"I'm sorry. That was unfair. It was just rotten timing. I won't lie and say it was easy getting over what had happened to me here," she said as he poured the soup into a bowl, then put it, along with the crackers, on the table. "I spent a lot of years looking over my shoulder, I tried never to go out at night alone unless someone was with me, and I still sleep with the lights on."

"Yeah. I noticed."

Fury and guilt that for years had been all tangled up with loving thoughts of Lark, had slammed back when he'd seen her sitting in the midst of those tangled sheets in the Audubon Place house, every light in the bedroom blazing.

"We've got coffee, cola, or water," he said.

"Water. If I have any caffeine, I'll be awake all night." He watched as the thought of the lights being out suddenly occurred to her.

"There's a fluorescent lantern in the bedroom. The batteries are fresh, so it should run all night."

"Thank you," she said as he pulled her chair out for her. "I tell myself it's just a habit, like any other, and that I'm too old to be afraid of the dark, but I've never put it to the test."

When Guest had attacked Lark here at the farm, she'd ended up being locked in the dark smokehouse for nearly twenty-four hours, which must have seemed an eternity.

"By the time I came back from Rome, I'd stopped feeling like a victim, and I was beginning to enjoy life again," she said quietly. "The first time I heard my single being played on the car radio, I pulled off Briley Parkway and parked in an Albertson's lot to listen. It was one of the most exciting moments of my life, and I'll probably never buy groceries again without thinking about it."

"I was driving home from a weekend fishing trip." He, too, had pulled off the road, wanting to flag down passing cars to tell them to switch their radios to WDVX.

"You remember?"

"Hey, can't forget anything that important. The consensus was that you were going to become the hottest thing on the planet. Which I'd figured out a long time before that."

She smiled. "I did a call-in interview with them." The station had championed bluegrass and traditional country music long before anyone had seen the movie *O Brother, Where Art Thou?*

He knew. He'd taped it, and later decided he must have a vicious masochistic streak when he kept playing it over and over again until the tape had finally broken.

"The record company was doing this big coordinated publicity push. My picture was on the cover of *Country Music Weekly*, I did a lot of call-in interviews with radio stations, and CMT did a bio piece on me. After all those years, my ship had finally come in."

She picked up her spoon and stared into the minestrone. "I'd begun to distance myself from Cody, because, for various reasons, including some strange vibes I got when Lily came down from Florence to visit us in Rome, I didn't think we were going to work out."

She put the spoon down again. "But then Guest was released from prison, and began stalking me and sending me those horrid letters and emails."

"That'd be bound to take the fun out of your newfound fame." She needed nourishment. He hadn't seen her eat enough to keep a sparrow alive since he'd shown up in New Orleans. "Change your mind?"

She finally glanced up.

"About the soup. I can heat up the chowder."

"This is fine." She looked back down at the minestrone as if seeing it for the first time.

"How would you know? You haven't tasted it."

"I'm not all that hungry." She pushed the bowl aside.

He moved it back. "If you don't eat, I'll get distracted worrying about you."

"That's emotional blackmail. And bossy."

"Probably," he allowed without an ounce of remorse. He reached across the table, picked up her spoon, and held it out to her.

"I'm not surprised you went into law enforcement."

"There's something to be said for getting paid to be a bossy emotional blackmailer."

"I was referring to the way you were always taking care of others." Faint frown lines creased the smooth skin between her brows. "I don't think any of us appreciated that enough at the time."

Lucas was uncomfortable talking about himself. "Eat," he repeated.

"Bossy," she muttered as she finally took the spoon from his outstretched hand.

# 27

William came up with a new plan on his flight to Asheville. Which, if he did say so himself, was his most inspired yet. He was carefully detailing it in his journal when a head popped up over the top of the seat in front of him.

"Hey, Mister. How come you got a lollipop?" asked a bespectacled brat with hair the color of boiled carrots. "You're a grown-up."

Not wanting to call attention to himself, William took the fentanyl sucker out of his mouth and put on the smile he used to calm a pediatric patient he was about to put under for a tonsillectomy. "Grown-ups like candy, too."

"Not my mom. She says candy gives you cavities."

*Little four-eyed shit.* "I suppose that's true," he said agreeably. "Which is why it's important to always brush after eating."

"That's what Mom says. I'm in the No Cavities club. Dr. Baden took my picture and put it up on the wall."

"Good for you." He returned to writing.

"You can't brush your teeth on an airplane."

Feeling the amused looks of the surrounding passengers, William forced yet another winning smile while he pictured opening the jet's door and pushing the kid out. "We're going to land soon."

"Oh." The kid processed that. "Can I have one?"

If this wasn't his last sucker, William would have been tempted to give the brat one, so the drugged candy would knock him out and shut him the hell up.

"Andrew." A woman's voice from the aisle seat took on a warning note. "Don't bother the nice man." She turned around and flashed a bright smile that backed up her son's claim about her oral hygiene diligence. "I'm sorry," she said.

"No bother."

"We're coming back from visiting my sister in San Diego, and it's been a long day."

"Perfectly understandable." Her hair was a dark russet, but her eyes were the same golden color as Lark's. He wondered if they were related in any way. Everyone knew mountain people all intermarried, and there were a great many redheads in the Stewart family.

"We went to Sea World," Andrew said, as if William could possibly be interested. "I got to feed sea lions dead fish." He wrinkled his nose. "They were real smelly, but it was cool."

"How nice." He enjoyed a vision of chopping the annoying brat into pieces and feeding him to some sea lions.

"We got to sit in the front row at the show, and this killer whale—that's just their name, they really don't kill people like sharks do—splashed us." His eyes went wide behind his Harry Potter glasses. "We got all wet. It was way cool. Wasn't it, Mom?"

"Way cool," she agreed with saintly patience. She tugged on the back of his yellow San Diego Chargers T-shirt. "Now sit down. Why don't you color a picture of Wolverine for Grandpa?" she coaxed.

"Okay," he agreed with the same enthusiasm he'd displayed toward killer whales. "Wolverine's Grandpa's favorite mutant," he told William. "What X-Man do you like best, Mister?"

William clenched his teeth.

"Andrew." His mother's tone revealed she'd just given up on sainthood. "Sit. *Now.*"

"Okay." He threw himself back down with a mighty huff. "Geez," he complained. "I've had a long day."

An elderly woman across the aisle smiled, amused. William was not.

His irritation escalated when he finally arrived in Highland Falls, only to find that Stewart Castle, which the financially strapped family had turned into a five-star hotel, was closed to the public from the middle of December to January 25, when it opened again with a gala Robert Burns Birthday Bash ball.

Rage roared through his veins as he read the sign on the tall wrought-iron gate shutting him off from the massive, castellated limestone building. The photographs he'd cut out and pasted on his wall hadn't done Lark's childhood home justice. If he hadn't felt on the verge of exploding, he might have been impressed by the battlements, arrow slits, tall Gothic windows, and square Norman towers.

If any of those damn magazine articles had ever mentioned that the goddamn castle wasn't open three hundred and sixty-five days a year, he would have planned accordingly. If he'd known she was coming here, instead of staying in Nashville where she belonged . . .

*If, if, if. If wishes were horses, beggars would ride.* His father had always said that. But his father had been burned to a crispy critter in the conflagration the fire marshal had ruled an accident.

Oh, lighting one of those scented candles his mother bought by the dozen and putting the flame to the draperies had been satisfying. And watching flames shoot out of the windows of the massive mock Tudor house had given him a hard-on. But there was a remoteness to his parents' death, a separation that wasn't nearly as satisfying as he'd expected. It hadn't even really been murder. More an accident waiting to happen.

Evie should have been a different story, but he'd miscalculated how much fentanyl to inject, so it had been over too fast. He'd have to lower the dosage next time. *Better yet, give his wife several smaller injections, enough to keep her sedated while he took her in all the ways he'd dreamed of during those long, lonely nights in prison. But alert enough that she'll know exactly what's happening to her.*

He'd missed the pleasure of watching that awareness of impending death in Evie's eyes, just as he'd missed it with his parents.

*Third time's the charm.*

Calmer now, he turned on the car's dome light, took out his Waterman, and carefully wrote the amendment to the killing plan into his journal.

As he drove back to the inn he'd passed on the way through town, William was smiling.

The snow had stopped falling during the night, and the view outside the farmhouse's windows looked like a Christmas print from Currier and Ives. The woods were beautifully inviting in the rosy pink, early morning light; the black of the tree trunks and branches contrasted with the bluish white of the snow dusting the boughs and shawling the ground.

" 'The woods are lovely, dark and deep,' " Lark murmured. She had no trouble at all imagining the old man in his red plaid coat and bright green muffler, the horse-drawn sleigh, the jingle of harness bells, the soft sweep of wind and downy snowflakes.

" 'But I have promises to keep,' " continued Lucas, who'd come up behind her. He looped his arms around her waist and rested his chin on top of her head. " 'And miles to go before I sleep.' "

"I used to think that poem was about death." Lark leaned back against the solid wall of his chest. When she'd first read it in high school, she'd found it terribly melancholy.

"I've always thought Frost wanted us to identify with our responsibility to trudge on despite obstacles. Our responsibility to live."

"Why am I not surprised you'd view the theme as one of responsibility," she said dryly. The smile she slanted up at him took any criticism from her words. "I've never been out here in the winter. It's so hushed and beautiful. Perhaps he was talking about how we don't take time to appreciate the nature surrounding us."

"Even the horse senses there's something wrong with stopping by the snowy woods, because he's been trained by humans to keep plodding on."

"Exactly." She loved that they were so in sync, just as they'd once been. "Promises to keep could be a metaphor for how busy life had become during urbanization, even back when Frost wrote it. Why else would he mention that the man who owns the woods has moved to a house in the village?"

She sighed as she considered the relentless pace her own life had taken these past years. "I think he's telling us to slow down so we can watch the woods filling up with snow. Metaphorically speaking."

"Makes sense to me." He turned her in his arms, got lost in her gorgeous gold eyes, and felt his own life pause. "I've always been a big fan of nature." The pleasure of just looking at Lark was one of the world's great wonders. He brushed a kiss against the corner of her lips. "How about we go back to bed and appreciate it together?"

Her eyes glittered. "You keep coming up with ideas like that, and I just may let you be in charge." She went up on her toes, pressing her smiling mouth to his.

There were advantages to being cut off from the rest of the world, Lark had decided, when the shrill demand of the phone shattered any immediate plans for a lazy winter morning.

"Guess we're back in business." Lucas didn't sound any more thrilled about it than she was. "Keep that thought," he said as he crossed the room and snatched up the receiver.

"McCloud." The tension that had steamrollered over

his easy, seductive mood was palpable. "Oh yeah. She's definitely alive and well. Better than well," he said, his gaze sweeping over her in a way that suggested the untimely interruption hadn't dented his desire. He held out the receiver. "It's Glazer."

She took the receiver from his hand. "Ryan? How on earth did you get this number?"

"The difficult, we do immediately. The impossible takes a little longer." He always said that when he pulled off some near-miracle. "How are you, really? I've been going nuts ever since the news of your missing plane became front-page news."

"Oh, damn. I was afraid of that." She sank down onto the couch; outside the window a red fox had come out of its den, a flash of color in the black, white, and blue world. "The phone lines were still down when we went to bed last night, there aren't any cell towers this far from town, and we've been snowed in."

There was a slight, significant pause on the other end of the line. She wondered if it was due to the mention of her and Lucas going to bed.

"Well, you've no idea how immensely relieved I am you're okay," he said. "McCloud was being straight with me, right? You really *are* okay?"

"I'm fine." Though the way Lucas was looking at her had the teenage heart she'd discovered deep inside her doing somersaults. "And now that the phone's working, I've got to find all the various members of my family to tell them the same thing. Could you do a favor for me?"

"Absolutely." How like him not to ask what that favor might be.

"Could you prepare a press release saying that Lucas and I survived the crash without injury? But please wait to send it out until you hear that the sheriff's notified Travis Hickman's family."

Another significant silence. "Are you saying he's dead?"

"He died in the crash," she said flatly, then gave him a brief description of events.

"God, that must have been terrifying. Especially given your fear of flying." She heard him draw in a deep breath heavy with regret. "And I hate to be the one to tell you, but there's something else."

"I'm almost afraid to ask."

"There was a fire." Another pause. "Hell, there's no good way to say this. Your house burned down."

Shock reverberated through her. "My house burned?"

Lucas turned from rebuilding the fire. Frown lines furrowed his forehead, bracketed the mouth that had thrilled her during their long night of lovemaking.

"To the ground. The official report hasn't been filed yet, but the fire marshal told me he's going to rule it as arson."

"It was Guest." Her flesh goose-bumped.

"I hate the idea like hell, but I think McCloud's right," Ryan agreed. "Which could mean he sabotaged the plane, too. You're damn lucky McCloud was with you."

She managed a wobbly smile at that. "Yes," she agreed. "I am. I don't think I would have survived without him."

"God moves in mysterious ways. Tell the big guy that I'm buying him a thank-you drink—and the biggest steak in town—when I get to Highland Falls."

"I thought you were planning to spend New Year's in St. Barts frolicking with beach bunnies."

"The beach will still be there. So will the bunnies. Lark, you're not only my employer, you're my closest friend and you've come close to dying twice in the past week. I need to see for myself that you're doing all right. Besides, I've been thinking for a long time that it might be fun to visit your little castle in the hollow." The wry humor she was used to hearing in his voice had returned.

"I don't want you to cancel your vacation on my account, especially since this latest mess dumped so much extra work on you."

"I'm glad to help."

"You're still the same Eagle Scout you were back in Idaho."

He'd obviously been proud of his scouting badge, having included it in his résumé. During that first interview she'd learned that he'd grown up poor on a potato farm. Like Highland Falls, the small community didn't have a lot to offer intelligent, ambitious kids, so he'd left home to seek employment in the cities. It was a situation Lark could identify with; unlike her, however, Ryan never seemed the least bit homesick.

"How about a compromise? You go romp with the bunnies, and then come skiing here in the mountains. You haven't lived until you've celebrated Robert Burns's birthday with a bunch of wannabe Highlanders."

He laughed at that. "Sounds like a plan. Watch out for black cats, darlin', don't walk under any ladders, and I'll see you at the bash. Now, let me speak with McCloud."

Suspecting what he was going to say, Lark handed the receiver to Lucas.

"Don't let her out of your sight," Ryan instructed on a far sharper tone than he'd used when speaking to Lark.

"I have no intention of that."

"Good. Then we understand each other."

"Absolutely." Conversation over, Lucas hung up, then drew Lark back into his arms. "Now, where were we?"

# 28

"I want you to teach me how to shoot," Lark said.

The out-of-the-blue statement startled Lucas out of the lazy pleasure that had settled over him after making love to Lark. "What?"

"I need to learn how to shoot a pistol."

"No, you don't. That's my job."

"You can't always be with me."

"Wanna bet?" He pulled her closer and gave her a deep, drugging kiss designed to take her mind off guns and her stalker.

"You're trying to distract me," she murmured against his mouth.

"Absolutely." He plucked at her lips. "Is it working?" He sighed when she stopped kissing him back. "Apparently not."

"This is important to me, Lucas."

"I can tell that." He sat up against the headboard of the bed his grandmother had been born in. "But it's not necessary. You don't even have a gun." And wouldn't, if he had anything to say about it.

"I've not a single doubt that you'd throw yourself in

front of a bullet for me. But what if you actually have to do exactly that?" She sat up as well. "What if he shot you trying to get to me? Wouldn't I stand a better chance if I at least knew the fundamentals of shooting your gun?"

"That's quite a scenario, right out of some woman-in-jeopardy chick-flick. If you ever get tired of writing songs, perhaps you ought to give Hollywood a try."

"I hate having to even think of such horrible things, but if there's anything Guest has taught me, it's to expect something far worse than I could imagine." Her brow furrowed. "This is important to me, Lucas." She laced the fingers of her left hand with his and looked him straight in the eye. "I don't want to fight about it."

"Me, neither." Lucas pinched the bridge of his nose and felt himself caving in.

Ten minutes later, bundled up in layers of fleece, they were in the woods. The empty minestrone can sat on a low stone wall. Also standing on end atop the wall were some of the logs Lucas had split.

"First thing to remember is that all guns are loaded," he said, taking the Glock out of his belt holster. "Even if you've just taken out all the bullets, you need to treat them as if they're loaded."

"I know that from the NRA education posters they used to put up in school every fall, before hunting season."

"Just don't forget it. Second, never turn around with an unholstered weapon and never point at anything or anyone you're not willing to destroy."

She cringed at that.

"You're the one who wanted to learn to shoot," he reminded her. "We're not talking about toy cap guns from Wal-Mart, here. This is the real thing. You know that old bumper sticker about guns not killing people—"

"People kill people."

"That's it. And the ugly truth is that people routinely use guns to kill people. Which, if, for some reason, you ever did end up facing down Guest, you're going to have to be mentally prepared to do. If you don't honestly think you could take his life, without hesitation, we're going to stop right now, because all we'll accomplish is to make your situation more dangerous by giving you a false sense of security."

Lark realized that it was one thing to fantasize or dream about shooting her stalker, another thing entirely to face the prospect while holding a gun in her hand.

"I could do it," she decided.

"Okay." He didn't sound thrilled with her answer. "The next thing is to always be aware of what's in the background. Look to see what's going to stop the bullet if you miss the target, which you'll probably do."

"I shot skeet with Daddy a couple times," she said. "I was actually pretty good." Even better than Laurel, who was accustomed to being the family overachiever.

"Handguns are tougher to aim than shotguns. And shooting at clay pigeons is a lot easier than shooting at someone who's shooting back at you."

"Point taken. When do we get to the actual shooting?"

"You wanted to know how to operate a weapon. First you need to know the basics of gun safety. Anything in front of the line of fire is the danger zone."

"Danger zone," she repeated. "Got it."

"That's where your weapon must be pointed whenever it's out of the holster. Conversely, the safe zone is everything behind the line of fire. It's where you want to keep all your body parts."

"I believe I could have figured that part out."

"People shoot themselves all the time. I once worked with an agent who'd shot himself in the foot, trying to beat Matt Dillon to the draw at the opening of a *Gunsmoke* episode."

She lifted her right hand. "I promise never to play quickdraw against a television."

He rolled his eyes. "Smart-ass."

"And only this morning, you were telling me how much you like my ass," she said sweetly.

"I do. A lot. Which is why I have every intention of keeping it safe. We'll start with dry shooting. Without bullets," he answered the question she'd been about to ask.

"If you're not going to let me have bullets, how will I know whether or not I hit anything?"

"We'll get to that. First you need to learn the proper grip." He held the Glock out to her. "Take it in your left hand."

"I'm right-handed."

"I know. You're going to use your left hand to place it into the web of your right. That's the soft part."

"All my parts are soft," she said saucily.

He wanted to smile. Lark could see it in his eyes, the slight quirk of his lips. Lucas actually seemed to be lightening up a bit. She liked knowing that she was making a positive difference in his life.

"So you say." He ran his palm over her shoulder, then

down her side, skimming the side of her breast. "How about we go inside and check it out?"

"Good try." His light touch, meant to tease and arouse, did both. "But you're not going to sidetrack me that easily." She placed the gun's grip between her thumb and first finger. "Like this?"

"Exactly."

When he moved behind her, she could smell the faintly musky scent of male beneath the tang of the soap. *Concentrate on the gun! Not the man.* "You may never have noticed, but when you point your finger, it's on the same line as your forearm. The weapon should be the same." And he covered her hand with both of his and lifted them to demonstrate.

"That's not very difficult," she murmured.

"It's a lot harder when you're in an actual shooting situation. When you're threatened, your body reacts to stress by producing adrenaline. Which is why the next thing we're going to cover is learning how to breathe."

"Newsflash, McCloud—I already know how to breathe."

"That may be, but shooting isn't hardwired into our brains, so you've got to learn how to reprogram your lungs for a shooting situation. The brain and the eyes are not only two of the biggest users of oxygen, they're also two of the most important organs in shooting, so we've gotta be sure they're getting lots of it."

"I've just figured it out. You've got a sneaky plan to drag this lesson out until Guest dies of old age."

"Don't I wish. Just remember, you're the one who wanted to play Annie Oakley."

"I'd rather play Sydney from *Alias*. She has a sexier wardrobe." She smiled flirtatiously over her shoulder.

Lucas didn't smile back. Obviously, he didn't believe in combining work and play. Which made sense, Lark allowed, since shooting people for a living was about as far from singing to them as a person could get.

"You know the feeling of being out of breath?"

"Of course." Then, because she couldn't resist, "I feel that way every time you look at me."

He briefly closed his eyes. Then forged on. "That feeling isn't due to a lack of oxygen, it's due to your body detecting an excess of carbon dioxide."

"Actually, it's anticipating your hands on me."

When he let go of her hand to drag his own through his hair, the gun barrel immediately dropped down by the oversize boots she'd borrowed.

"See," he said. "That's how people shoot themselves in the foot."

"It's heavier than I thought it'd be," she muttered.

Since she could feel her nose getting as red as Rudolph's, and was beginning to lose feeling in her toes, Lark got down to business, learning how to purge her lungs, to do a deep inhale while she lifted the gun, exhale again as she aimed, before finally taking a normal inhale.

After he'd made her repeat the sequence several times, he finally decided she was ready to learn how to pull the trigger. Still without bullets.

"I'm going to use my middle finger? Every TV cop I've ever seen uses the index finger."

"So do most real cops. Who, on average, only hit their targets fourteen to seventeen percent of the time."

"Really?" That was an unsettling statistic. Especially if you happened to be a bystander to a shootout.

"Really. There's this guy who developed a different way in World War II, after studying real gunfighters, figuring they'd know their firearms. Wild Bill Hickcock used a method where he extended his index finger along the barrel and pulled the trigger with his middle finger. Not only does it make the trigger pull feel lighter, which is good, because of the way hand tendons work, but also the aim's more accurate and you don't get the gun wobble you do the other way.

"Another plus is you don't have to worry about using the sight, which I don't have time to teach you, and most cops don't remember to do in an actual situation, anyway. All you do is point at the target. Where you point is where the bullet will go."

With his hands over hers again, he arranged her fingers in the proper position. "Try it."

She pointed her index finger, which was extended along the side of the gun barrel. The gun followed her aim, just as he'd promised. "It's that easy?"

"Shooting's never easy. But the police departments who've switched to this method have brought their accuracy rate up to around ninety-eight percent."

"I'll take that in a pinch."

"In your dreams, sweetheart. You'll be lucky to hit the side of that barn."

"Shooting takes hand-eye coordination, breathing control, and technique. You've taught me the breathing and technique." She held out her hand. "Now give me some bullets, so I can demonstrate what a good student I am."

Lucas still didn't like this idea. Shooting at a target that was standing still and didn't shoot back was one thing. In a real-life situation . . .

But Lark wouldn't be faced with a real-life situation, he vowed. He'd made sure of that.

He showed her how to load. It was obvious she didn't like handling the actual bullets, but he wanted her to fully understand, as well as a civilian ever could, how real shooting wasn't playing cops and robbers. It wasn't fun when people—even the bad guys—died. And it damn well wasn't pretty.

*Crack!* The first shot went wide, hitting the tall earth berm behind the stone wall.

"Try using both hands." Lucas reached around her again and arranged her left hand over her right in the Weaver shooting position, with all the fingers below the trigger guard and her weak hand thumb lying over the top of her strong hand thumb, forming a cross. "And remember to keep your elbow and wrist locked."

*Crack!* This time a piece of log went flying.

"I did it!" She spun around, her face wreathed in a dazzling smile.

"You also just risked shooting me in the gut."

"Oh." The smile washed off her face. "Right. Never turn around with a loaded weapon," she repeated.

She let out a breath. Drew one in again, turned back toward the targets, and went through the breathing exercises he'd taught her.

*Crack!* The blue minestrone can sailed off the wall. *Crack!* A red-and-white cream of chicken followed. *Crack!* The baked bean can was history.

Obviously pleased with herself, she lifted the barrel and blew, looking like Wild Bill after facing down outlaws on the streets of Abilene. This time she pointed the Glock at the ground as she turned toward him. "Well?"

He took the gun from her hand. "Those cans will never give anyone any trouble again."

"I did it! I did just what you told me, and it worked."

"You did, indeed." Not wanting her to get too cocky with false confidence, he turned, aimed, and sent the rest of the cans into the air, clearing the wall in five seconds.

"Wow." She took that in. "I guess I need a bit more practice."

"What you need is to get back inside before your fingers freeze, fall off, and turn useless."

She nodded. "Good idea, Deadeye." She waited until he'd reholstered the Glock, then went up on her toes and brushed her lips against his, their breaths mingling. "We can light a fire and warm each other up in the tub before we take that long snowmobile ride into town." She put her palm over the front of his jeans, stroking, arousing. "And since you were so nice to teach me to shoot, I'll show off a little eye–hand moves of my own."

"Have I ever told you I love the way your mind works?"

Lucas put his hand to the back of her head, took the kiss deep, and felt her surrender to it.

Then held her hand as they walked back to the farmhouse.

# 29

Highland Falls's sheriff's office was on the third floor of a red brick building still referred to as the "new" courthouse. The old one, built out of native stone after the Revolution, had been turned into a museum/library/welcome center.

The roads were clear in town, but Donald MacKenna and his snowplow hadn't yet made it out into the hinterlands. Lucas parked the snowmobile they'd ridden across the snowfields in front of the building.

When Lark had been a very little girl, the elevator—which dated back to the 1950s—had been operated by Eleanor Cartwright who, in another time, would have been described as a spinster. Eleanor had taken her "career" very seriously, calling out the floors as if she were announcing the various levels of heaven. After her death at eighty-three, the elevator had gone to self-service, but there were still those who insisted that they'd seen Eleanor Cartwright's ghost, sitting on her tall three-legged stool, warning riders to "step back from the doors" and to "watch your step."

The moment the steel doors closed behind them,

Lucas pulled her into his arms. "Your lips are cold," he murmured against her mouth.

"Now there's a surprise, since it's twenty degrees in the sunshine."

"Let's see what we can do about warming them up."

The kiss was slow, warm, and meltingly soft. Their breaths mingled. Became one. Lark was thinking that she could have floated up to the third floor all by herself when the elevator dinged and the doors opened.

"Want to take a ride back down to the lobby?"

"It's tempting." *Too tempting.* "But I think we'd better pass," she said as they exited into a hallway as vacant as the lobby. No government business got done between Christmas and New Year's, and Lark guessed that the blizzard was keeping many people at home.

"Does Stewart's Folly still have that snazzy old-fashioned elevator?" As children, they'd spent hours riding up and down in the small ornate cage. Later, when they became lovers, he'd used the back stairs to sneak up to her bedroom.

"It was still there a few months ago. Why?"

"I used to fantasize about taking you in that elevator." He confirmed her suspicion as they walked toward the office at the end of the hallway. "Up against the bars, your legs around my waist, me deep inside you."

Lark could feel the color sparking in her cheeks; Lucas was the only man she'd ever known who could make her blush. "Me too."

He stopped in his tracks and stared down at her with lust in his midnight eyes.

"When I called Harlan to tell him we were on our way

into town, he said your aunts are waiting in his office for you. The others will be arriving later today."

"They're probably frantic." *Nearly as frantic as I am to feel your hands on me.*

"They know you're safe with me." When his hungry gaze settled on her mouth, she nearly moaned with need.

*There's nothing safe about you, Lucas McCloud.*

He skimmed a thumb around her lips, which parted in anticipation. "Christ. Do you have any idea what it does to me when you look at me like that?"

Her breath and her heart hitched as the caress traveled down her throat, warming the rest of her. "The same thing you do to me when you look at me the way you're looking at me right now?"

"Yeah." He blew out a long breath. "If you're talking about feeling like Mount Vesuvius."

"That's it." Every cell in her body felt about to explode. "Maybe we should stop looking at each other," she said in a whimper when he bent his head and nuzzled, his clever mouth finding that sensitive spot behind her ear only he had ever discovered.

"Ladies first." He nipped at her earlobe. "Or we could just quit trying to fight it. . . . God, you smell good."

"It's your soap."

"It's a lot sexier on you."

"We can't do this," she said breathlessly. *Touch me.* "Not here in a public hallway."

His sigh was a warm breeze against the hollow in her throat. "Good point." He took her hand and led her to the nearest door, which was, like most other doors in Highland Falls, unlocked.

"We can't," she repeated, her tone making the protest a hundred and eighty degrees away from *no*. "Someone might come in."

"It's the holidays." He pulled her into the room, shut the door. Flicked the lock. "Besides, how many folks do *you* know who want to come to the tax collection office?"

Without giving her time to answer, he pressed her back against the wall and crushed his hungry mouth to hers, feasting on her while he yanked down the zipper on the heavy parka.

"Hurry," she gasped against his mouth, ripping at his jacket. "Oh, God, please hurry."

Swallowing her moans, he pulled the parka off her shoulders, jerking it halfway down her arms, restraining her as effectively as ropes.

Lucas had never been into forcing a woman. It had never even entered his head as a fantasy, perhaps because at the FBI he'd seen too many cases where women had been left shattered—or dead—by men who felt the need to dominate in a sick attempt to validate their masculinity.

Now he was stunned by a primal need to take. To claim. It wasn't the same, he tried to reassure himself as lust stripped away control. Lark wasn't surrendering; she was demanding. Her avid mouth was as ravenous as his; her body strained against his.

Her hips bucked when he cupped the heat between her legs. She cried out, then shattered as he pushed his fingers into that tight, wet warmth.

The cell phone on his belt chimed. They both ignored it.

"Please, Lucas." Her breath was coming in ragged gasps as she ground against his hand. "Hurry."

The cell phone chimed again. He tore his mouth away from hers long enough to punch it off and hurled it across the room, then pulled her jacket the rest of the way down and sent it flying.

Her arms free, Lark yanked at the first metal button on his jeans. "Dammit," she said as she tore at the next, "haven't you ever heard of a zipper?" Three more to go.

"I'll burn every pair of 501s I own," he vowed. Frantic and needy as she, he pushed her hands out of the way and yanked the jeans open.

She kicked away the sweatpants and panties that had pooled at her feet.

As soon as he was free, he lifted her up and dove into her heat, using his weight to pin her against the wall.

They came together, quick, violent climaxes that forced Lucas to slam a hand against the wall to keep from collapsing to the floor and taking Lark with him.

Afterward, a shaky laugh bubbled out of her. "I can't believe we did that. You're right."

"About what?" he asked, waiting for his legs to become functional again.

She slid her legs down his until she was back on the floor, but didn't release her hold on his shoulders. "It's like being teenagers again. I haven't made love standing up since that time in the janitor's closet, when we ducked out of graduation practice."

"I seem to remember you telling me afterward that we were never to speak of that little interlude."

She'd been terrified, hot, and all too willing. Now that

Lucas thought back on it, she'd complained about his jeans then, too.

"Just because I was embarrassed doesn't mean I didn't like it. A lot." She went up on her toes and touched her mouth to his. "I'm probably the only woman in the world who gets turned on by the smell of Mr. Clean."

He laughed on what little breath he could muster up. "I'll buy a case of the stuff this afternoon," he promised as he bent and picked up her clothes.

"I think we've just proven that's not necessary." She pulled her pants back up her legs. "Chemistry was never our problem."

"You'll get no argument from me on that." Where the hell was his goddamn phone? *Eureka!* He located it on the windowsill behind the desk.

"I've never had sex without all sorts of complications," Lark murmured. "This is a first for me."

The hot flash of anger her words generated surprised him. "It would be, if that were the case. But this situation is rife with complication."

"Because of Guest," she agreed. "But if you take him out of the equation—"

"No." He caught her by the chin. "In case you've never noticed, control's all tangled up with responsibility. You want to grasp control of your life—all aspects of it, including sex—and that's fine and dandy with me, since I think it looks real good on you. I also don't mind you using my manly body for hot sex. But I'm not into playing games."

"Damn," she murmured. "There go my plans for that strip poker game this afternoon."

"No need to get hasty. I'm nothing if not flexible."

Her smile spread slowly. "You've already proven that."

"Believe me darlin', you haven't seen anything yet." She'd always brought out a side of him he'd forgotten existed. Despite the very real threat of Guest, Lucas was almost feeling like the carefree seventeen-year-old he'd never been. "But it was never just about sex, Lark," he said, getting serious again. "Not even when we were hormone-crazed kids, and it damn well isn't now."

"I know. But it's not the same as then, Lucas. It's different, because we're different."

He heard the strain in her voice, knew he put it there, but couldn't be sorry for it. Having left too much unsaid in the past, he damn well wasn't about to make that mistake again.

"We're older," he agreed. "And hopefully wiser, since we've both gone through a lot of stuff." *Talk about your understatements.* "Look at me, Lark," he insisted quietly when she dropped her gaze. Her eyes, when she lifted them back to his, were wary. "The thing is, none of that stuff matters. Because the road, however rocky, was always leading right back here to where we began."

He caught her wrist, lifted the soft underside to his lips, and felt her pulse leap. "I loved you, Lark. Whatever else you may think of me, of what I did, don't ever doubt that."

He loved her still. As they continued down the hall the short distance to the sheriff's office, Lucas decided that once Guest was either in custody or dead—and he'd prefer the latter—they were both going to have to get used to that idea.

# 30

The walls of the sheriff's office were painted an institutional gray and were lined with black metal filing cabinets piled high with manila folders. A recruitment poster—Exploring Law Enforcement, depicting a young man and woman in starched uniforms standing beside a patrol car, looking like the last bastion between the citizens of Highland Falls and the bad guys—was surrounded by bright crayon drawings from the students of Mrs. Tomlin's third-grade class, thanking the sheriff for the tour of the two-cell jail. A locked rifle rack shared wall space with posters of the FBI's most wanted, all of whom looked as guilty as charged.

There'd been a Boone in law enforcement ever since the county had gotten its charter. Harlan's great-grandfather, grandfather, and father had all been sheriffs. Harlan, who'd been the symbol of law in Highland Falls since before Lark was born, had won six straight elections, the last four of them uncontested.

Lark couldn't remember him ever wearing an official uniform, not that he needed to. Harlan Boone looked tough as a hunk of hickory, with broad shoulders and a rock-hard chest. He was an avid hunter and fisherman, and his rugged face, weathered by sixty years spent outdoors in the elements, made the hooded gray eyes beneath his dark brows appear ever more piercing.

A columnist for *The Knoxville News-Sentinel* had once written that Highland Falls didn't need a lie detector, since the sheriff's laserlike stare could get the truth out of a criminal a lot faster than any machine.

Those eyes warmed with welcome as Lark and Lucas entered his office. Zelda, who'd been pacing the Tennessee marble floor, gathered her niece into her arms like a mother bird sheltering a fledgling.

"Oh, baby," she said, her tears wetting Lark's neck, "we've been so worried about you."

"Worried sick," the other woman in the room agreed in a rich, North Carolina drawl.

Melanie Lancaster was the quintessential steel magnolia. Lark couldn't remember ever seeing an expertly streaked hair out of place and although her mother's sister had reluctantly given up white gloves for all but the most formal occasions, she always looked as if she'd stepped off the cover of *Town and Country*. Which was why it was such a shock to see her with mascara streaks on her cheeks and her salsa red lipstick mostly chewed off.

"I'm fine. Really."

"But those horrid bruises . . ." Zelda frowned as her gaze took in Lark's battered face.

"Aren't nearly as bad as they look," Lark assured her aunt.

"I have some Chanel coverup that'll do wonders," Melanie volunteered.

Lark smiled, grateful that there was at least one thing in her life that hadn't changed. "Things would have been a lot worse if Lucas hadn't been there."

Zelda swiped at her damp cheeks with the backs of her hands and bestowed a watery smile on Lucas. "I never doubted for a moment that you'd keep our baby girl safe, though I'll admit that my heart started having palpitations when Harlan told me about the crash."

"It must have been terrifying." Melanie shuddered. "Especially considering your fear of flying."

"The worst part was the pilot being killed." Lark shook her head. "I feel so guilty about that."

"The crash didn't have anything to do with you," Harlan said. "You and Lucas just had the bad luck to be on the plane when it went down."

"How do you know that? The NTSB couldn't have filed a report yet," Lucas said.

"They haven't even gotten to the scene yet. But thanks to your marking the GPS coordinates, a search crew is already on the way back from the site with Hickman's body. The Feds still have to inspect what's left of the jet before we get an official ruling, but we got a call this morning from the Orleans county sheriff's department. Seems a kingpin who'd been using the jet to bring drugs in from Central America wasn't real happy when the sheriff confiscated it in that raid."

"So he had it sabotaged," Lucas guessed.

"Revenge is an age-old motive," Harlan said. "Especially when there's so much money involved. I called your cell phone as soon as I found out, but I got sent into voice mail after a couple rings."

"The signal must have gone out," Lucas said mildly. He didn't risk looking at Lark.

"Devlin Watson opened up the *Herald* offices to put out a special midweek edition with Guest's old mug shots on the front page."

"I can't imagine the mayor's thrilled about the possibility of frightening away skiers," Lark said.

Although the summer Highland Games had always been the town's largest tourist attraction, three years ago, Jon Young and Luke Martindale had arrived from Colorado with plans to build a ski resort on Stewart's Mountain. Hating the big-city developers who seemed determined to turn the Appalachians into an upscale, Dogpatch-style theme park, building log cabins and condo developments with cutesy mountain names, many in town had opposed it. But eventually the former ski bums won the naysayers over with a resort that fit into the mountain as if designed by Mother Nature. From the opening day, the resort had brought both skiers and revenue to Highland Falls.

"The mayor's pissed at the situation," Harlan acknowledged. "The Chamber of Commerce isn't exactly doing somersaults either." He paused a beat. "Now, why don't you ask me if I care what they think?"

Zelda sighed and patted her breast. "I do so love a manly man." Now that she'd seen Lark was all right, she appeared to be getting her old spark back.

Lark felt a twinge of additional guilt that her sisters were also disrupting their lives to come see for themselves that she was safe. Their father's wedding during last summer's games had been the first time in years that they'd all been home at the same time, but she'd been so deep in the doldrums over her marriage that she hadn't been able to truly appreciate their time together.

Now, despite the less than happy reason for a family reunion, Lark was looking forward to being together with her sisters again.

# 31

"She seems to be handling this well," Zelda said to Harlan, after Lark and Lucas had left the office and Melanie had gone to the restroom to repair her makeup.

"She's a tough cookie." His gaze swept over Zelda in a very uncoplike way, the same way he'd done for years in her dreams. "Like the other women in her family."

"Lucas will keep her safe."

It was not a question, but he answered it anyway. "Absolutely."

"He was, after all, an FBI agent. And it's obvious that he still loves her."

"A blind man couldn't miss it," he agreed. He leaned back in his chair. "And this is undoubtedly an inappropriate time to bring it up, but I know just how he feels."

She studied him speculatively. "You've never said anything."

"I didn't have the right. I was a married man." Whose wife had spent years in a nursing home suffering from Parkinson's disease. "Abby and I took vows. And even if I would have been willing to ask you to wait until

I was free, I couldn't let myself think that way, because . . ."

He dragged his broad hand down his face.

"Allowing yourself to think about being with me was the same as wishing Abby dead," Zelda said.

"Yeah." His eyes were dark with the burdens he'd insisted on carrying alone for so many years. "I loved her from the time we were kids, Zelda."

"Just like Lucas loved Lark."

"Yeah," he repeated. Then he shook his head. "I shouldn't be talking with you about how much I loved my wife."

"Only because it isn't necessary. It was obvious to everyone how much you loved Abby, Harlan."

Hadn't Georgia Jennings, the RN in the nursing home, told everyone at the funeral supper how Harlan had continued to visit his wife every evening, long after Abby Boone was capable of demonstrating any response to her husband?

"What you and I had together"—he raked a palm over his short silver hair—"meant a helluva lot more to me than a one-night stand."

"I always knew that. And if you *had* been the kind of man who could sleep with another woman that easily, I wouldn't have fallen in love with you."

He gave her a sharp look. "You never said anything about love."

"Would it have made a difference?" The question had bedeviled her for years.

"Probably not."

He'd always been brutally honest. Even when he'd

dragged her away from sitting vigil at a sleeping Lark's hospital bedside, the evening after he'd rescued Lark and arrested William Guest. Insisting—unflatteringly—that she looked like hell and obviously needed a break, he'd driven her to the Barred Owl, where he'd convinced her to choke down a blue plate special.

Highland Falls being the small town it was, they'd known each other for years. Since Abby—the town librarian—was her closest friend, Zelda had been a guest in the Boone home many times and had admired what appeared to be a near perfect marriage.

Until that night, she probably could have counted on one hand the times she and Harlan had talked together alone, but as the night grew late and the tables around them emptied, it was as if a dam had burst inside her best friend's husband.

She'd let him talk, her heart going out to him as the frustration, anger, and fear he'd kept bottled up since he'd no longer been able to care for Abby at home, came pouring out. Finally, when they looked up and realized that the café staff was politely watching from the kitchen, waiting for them to leave so they could lock up and go home, they moved the conversation to the Jeep parked in the darkened lot.

Zelda could never remember who made the first move, but the first touch of lips was electric. The second was, amazingly, even hotter, and by the time he'd driven the two blocks to the Firefly Inn, they were ready to rip each other's clothes off.

No words of love had been spoken, no promises made. But as a pearly pink predawn light slipped into the room, they both knew things would never be the same. Neither of them had ever spoken of that stolen night of passion. But Harlan Boone would become the model for the time-traveling, crime-solving Highlander millions of her readers had fallen in love with.

Abby had passed on this fall, just as the leaves had been turning from green to crimson. The consensus was that her death had been a blessing, but if Harlan had experienced so much as a smidgen of relief, he'd never shown it.

"We'll catch that son of a bitch Guest," he promised now. "And after he's back behind bars where he belongs, you and I have some catching up to do."

Heaven help her, the way he could make her toes curl just by looking at her, made her admit it had been no fluke.

"Catch him quick."

His gray eyes glittered with steely purpose. "I intend to."

Any tourist to this hidden spot in the Smoky Mountains who expected to find coffees with exotic-sounding names or triple mocha caramel lattes was bound to be disappointed. Residents of Highland Falls drank their caffeine in large white mugs at the Barred Owl café across from the courthouse. The rest of the planet may be spinning at warp speed, but Delilah and Dave Parker, who ran the café, weren't eager to embrace change.

The buzz of conversation momentarily dropped off as Lucas and Lark entered the café, after Lark had gone shopping for clothes to replace the ones she'd lost in the crash. Every eye in the place followed them as they were forced to stop at all fifteen booths to share the story of the plane crash. By the time they got to the back of the room, they had an encapsulated version of their adventure down pat.

"Welcome home," Delilah said as she arrived at their table with two laminated menus, an insulated carafe of coffee, and two mugs. A bit more plump than she'd been in high school, her welcoming smile was as brilliant as when she led cheers for the Fighting Scots football team with Lily. "Miserable weather we've been having, though they're saying it's going to fair up by the weekend, which hopefully will bring in flatlanders—and their pocketbooks—for skiing." She plunked their mugs down, and without asking, filled them to the brim. "It liked to give everybody cardiac arrest when we heard about that plane crash; I'm really glad you're okay, but it sure was a shame about the pilot."

"A terrible shame," Lark agreed. Even if the drug dealer's sabotage turned out to be true, she'd always feel terrible about Travis Hickman's death. "So," she said, needing to change the topic, "how are the kids?"

"Doin' well enough. Jamie was one of the wise men in the fifth-grade Christmas pageant, and Mary Beth's got herself a sheep for this year's 4-H project. In the beginning David and I discouraged her because we thought she was too flighty to take care of it, but she's gained tons of responsibility. If we let her, she'd take that damn animal to bed with her, especially during this cold spell. I've told her time and time again that it's wearin' wool all over, but the way the girl frets, we're a little concerned about what'll happen when she has to sell it at the fair this spring.

"Dylan is in preschool; the teacher says he's smart as a whip, but I swear that if I have to hear that damn alphabet song one more time I'll go stark raving mad. Molly went crashing into her terrible twos last month and changed overnight from a little angel into that kid from *The Exorcist*. David says he doesn't care if we are Methodists, if she starts throwing up green pea soup, we're calling Father MacFarlane for an exorcism. And Cassie's cuttin' her first tooth, which kept me up all night, so I'm feeling a tad wrung out today."

"I'd be exhausted *every* day," Lark said. "I can't imagine how you juggle home, family, and running this place."

Delilah shrugged. "I've had some help around the house since David's daddy passed on this past summer, and his mama moved in with us. I never would've thought the old dragon and I'd get along together in the same house, but she actually likes to tidy up, and the babies just love their mawmaw to pieces. But even before she moved in, it didn't seem all that different from when I was living at home, takin' care of all my brothers and sisters and working here for my dad. Except David and I don't have to sneak into the meat locker to make out anymore, like we did back in high school," she said with a grin.

Lark laughed. David had been the star quarterback and they'd married during their senior year after Delilah had gotten pregnant, but unlike so many other teenage marriages, theirs seemed to be thriving.

"Speaking of high school," Delilah said as she handed them the menus, "it's like the good old days seeing you two sittin' in your old booth." Her gaze moved from Lark to Lucas, then back to Lark. "So, are y'all back together again?"

"We're just friends," Lark said quickly. Too quickly, she thought, when her friend's eyes narrowed.

"We're talking about it," Lucas said, surprising Lark by reaching across the table and taking her hand in his. He'd never displayed much affection in public.

Delilah studied the blush that rose in Lark's cheeks. "I always knew you two belonged together. It's good to know that sometimes things do work out in the end.

"Just hold your tater, Jared," she called out to a man at the end of the counter who was impatiently asking for his check. "I'd best be getting back to work. Irma Brown brought in some fresh baked goods this morning, so we've got apple and chocolate cream pies, carrot cake, and lemon squares. They all look great, and knowing Irma, they are, but the apple smells like heaven."

They ordered the apple pie, hot, with vanilla ice cream. Delilah returned to the kitchen, pausing to write a ticket for the man at the counter, whose carrot-hued hair she ruffled in her naturally affectionate way.

"She certainly seems happy," Lark murmured after taking a sip of coffee so strong, a spoon could have stood up in it.

"I guess she's found her niche."

"She never had any interest in leaving Highland Falls. And she always wanted a big family. She was probably the only girl in third grade who preferred Betsy Wetsy to Barbie."

"Well, she obviously got her wish. She and David have their own basketball team. So, how about you?"

"How about me, what?" She poured some cream from the stainless steel pitcher, added a packet of sugar, took a tentative sip, and stirred in a second packet.

"Ever think of having kids?"

"Of course. In the beginning, I was too busy trying to get my career launched. Then things just got so busy, I didn't think it'd be good to drag a baby all around the country on a bus."

As soon as she heard the words coming out of her mouth, she realized that they were Cody's, not hers.

"Some people do. And from what I hear, those tour buses are pretty tricked-out inside."

"They are, which is why I began to seriously reconsider the idea." Hadn't she argued that lots of entertainers, including the Dixie Chicks, combined careers with motherhood? Faith and Tim had started a baby factory even as their careers had skyrocketed. And Vince Gill and Amy Grant were currently touring with their precious little girl.

"But then I became wary about bringing a child into a marriage that I wasn't sure was going to last." She sighed and took a sip of the now too-sweet coffee. "How about you? Do you ever think about becoming a father?"

"I've always tried not to."

"Oh." Lark hadn't realized she'd been hoping for a different answer until her heart plummeted at his brusque denial. "I suppose you got burned out, practically raising your sisters on your own."

"That never bothered me, since it seemed normal at the time. But I wouldn't have a clue how to be a father. I didn't exactly have the best role model," he reminded her.

"If having good role models was a prerequisite for having children, the human race probably would have come to an end shortly after Adam and Eve," Lark said mildly. "My father has certainly never been in the running for the *Father Knows Best* Dad of the Year award. But Lily, Laurel, and I never had a single doubt that he loved us, which is far more important than whether he remembered to stop painting in time to show up at our recitals or knew our friends' names."

Conversation stopped momentarily as Delilah delivered the plates of fragrant pie, topped off their coffee, then left them alone again.

Lucas's eyes, which had been taking in everything and everyone in the restaurant during their conversation, suddenly narrowed. "We've got company."

Lark glanced over her shoulder as he pushed himself to his feet. "That can't be your mother." The trim woman in the emerald ski pants and royal blue parka looked younger and far less haggard than the woman she remembered.

"Yeah, it is. She's changed."

"Hello, Lark," Paula McCloud greeted Lark warmly after hugging her son, who towered over her. "I'm so relieved to see that you're safe. I've been worried sick about you both, ever since Harlan called me with the news last night."

"I wouldn't be alive if it wasn't for your son." Lark stood up and hugged the woman she'd once been furious at for failing to protect her son from her abusive husband. "You're looking well. And very chic," she said.

Paula skimmed a hand over hair that had changed

from mousy brown to a soft, flattering ash blond. "Thank you, dear. You're looking fabulous." It was a polite lie, ignoring the bruises. "But of course, you always have."

Paula glanced up at the tall, sandy-haired man standing beside her. "You remember Mr. Conway, don't you?"

"How could I forget?" Lark smiled up at her former teacher. "Your music classes were the best thing about school."

Hazel eyes warmed behind the lenses of wire-framed glasses. "That's a very nice thing to say."

"It's the truth."

"David and I were married this fall," Paula revealed.

"How lovely," Lark said, meaning it. "I hope you'll both be very happy."

"How long are you planning to be in town, Lark?" David Conway asked.

"I'm not sure. I just finished up my tour in Las Vegas, and had planned to take several months off to write. But staying at my Nashville house is no longer an option."

"We heard about it burning down, on *Good Morning America*," Paula said. "Is it true they think your stalker is the arsonist?"

"There's no proof yet, but it seems likely." Everyone in the Barred Owl was now tuned to the conversation. "Since I don't have anywhere else to go, I imagine I'll be staying in town until after the Robert Burns Birthday Bash on the twenty-fifth."

"Which means you'll be here for the school Winterfest fund-raiser, Friday night," Conway said. "We'll be having the usual food and game booths, singing, dancing, an exhibit from the art classes, that sort of thing."

"David, dear," Paula murmured. "I'm certain Lark has better things to do than spend an evening at her old elementary school."

"I wasn't going to ask her to spend the entire evening there, dear," he said quickly. Too quickly, Lark thought. "I don't mean to appear pushy, Lark," he said. "But I can't believe you'd want all those students to lose their music and art programs."

"Lose? As in shut them down?"

"Arts are always one of the first departments to be targeted during budget cuts," David explained. "We've always dodged the bullet before, but it looks as if this year could be our last. We've planned this fund-raiser, but it's the off season, the storm's keeping skiers away, and people have Christmas bills coming up. . . ."

He shrugged fatalistically.

"I'd love to help." How could she not?

"Maybe you could donate some T-shirts," Lucas suggested. "Some autographed CDs."

"Well, that's certainly a possibility." And something Ryan handled several times a month. "But I was thinking more along the lines of a concert. Nothing too elaborate, just an evening of songs in the gym."

"A concert would be terrific," David agreed. "But I'm afraid your price is a bit high for us to cover."

*What kind of diva did he think she'd become?* "I wasn't suggesting charging you, Mr. Conway."

He looked puzzled. "I wrote and asked about the possibility of you helping us out last year and received a letter stating that your base fee for charity events was ten thousand dollars plus a percentage of the profits."

Lark experienced a slow burn. "Obviously there's been some miscommunication. I've never charged for charity performances." *Damn Cody's greedy, cheating black soul!* "The least I can do is try to make it up to you this year."

"I don't think that's such a good idea," Lucas interjected. "Didn't you say something about needing to concentrate on writing the songs for your new album?"

"It's only one evening. Music was such a vital part of my life growing up, I want to do whatever I can to help out the kids."

"So write a check."

"That's an excellent idea. I'll do that as well." She took out a pen and scribbled her cell phone number on a paper napkin. "Why don't you give me a call at Stewart's Folly this evening and we'll work out the details?"

"Wow!" He looked as excited as if she'd given him the original sheet music for a lost Beethoven symphony. "Thanks, Lark. You always were my favorite student. And my most talented."

The women exchanged another embrace. The men shook hands, then the couple left to sit down at a table across the room.

"I thought we'd agreed that you'd keep a low profile until Guest's caught." Lucas was clearly less than thrilled by Lark's plan.

"A performance in an elementary school gymnasium is not exactly as high profile as singing 'The Star-Spangled Banner' at the Superbowl."

Which Lucas recalled her having done looking damn hot in low-slung, crimson leather jeans and a red, white, and blue spangly top that had reminded him of the barely-there bikini she'd worn that world-altering summer day at Firefly Falls.

"It'll still get in the *Highland Herald*, which is bound to be picked up by the AP, which will spread it all over the goddamn country."

"Well, then, aren't I fortunate to have you to protect me."

"Dammit, Lark, you could achieve the same thing by donating some bucks to the cause."

"It wouldn't be the same," she argued with an intensity that often surprised people who didn't know her well. "Anyone can write a check, Lucas. It's important that I show up in person, so that kids who may not have thought beyond these mountains might envision a wider world and a better future."

"Hell." He couldn't argue with that. Highland Falls was a lovely little town, but unless you were part of its thriving arts community, there weren't a lot of career prospects.

"By this time tomorrow, the paper will be out with the mug shots on the front page," Lark reminded him. "There's no way Guest will be able to get into the gym without someone recognizing him. And the reward will make people even more vigilant." Her family had offered $50,000 for information leading to William Guest's capture and Zelda had contacted the producer of *America's Most Wanted*.

"I still don't like it."

"I know." She patted his hand, which had curled into a tight fist atop the table. "Perhaps this will force him into the open," she suggested optimistically. "Then it'll all be over."

He sighed heavily, turned his hand, and laced his fingers with hers. "You're just trying to make me feel better."

"I am not." Laughter touched her eyes. "That comes later, when I get you alone."

She took a bite of pie so delicious she almost wept, and glanced across the room at the couple who could have been on their own desert island.

"Your mother's looking marvelous. I hardly recognized her."

"Marriage has been good for her." He knew she was trying to sidetrack the conversation, but nothing would be gained by arguing further. "She spent years under my father's thumb, and was just going through the motions after his arrest. Then she and David worked together on some Save the Smoky Mountain Air committee and to hear her tell it, things just clicked."

Like Lark, Lucas had been amazed at the changes in his mother. She'd cut the long, graying braid she'd worn for as long as he could remember, colored her hair a flattering blond, learned how to do her makeup from Irma Brown (who'd won a pink Cadillac a few years back for selling more Mary Kay than anyone else in this part of the mountains), ditched her drab gray-and-brown wardrobe, and started wearing bright colors.

She'd gotten her GED, was taking an online college history course and the last time he'd dropped by the house she'd bought with the music teacher, he'd actually caught her in a snazzy red leotard dancing to the oldies with Richard Simmons.

"It's as if a spaceship landed in town, beamed her up to the mother ship, then sent this alien down to earth in her place."

"Love's supposed to be transforming."

"So they say."

A little silence settled over them as they polished off the pie.

"Thank you," he said finally.

She glanced up. "For what?"

"For being nice to her."

"Why wouldn't I be?" He watched the awareness on her face. "I'll admit I never had a lot of respect for her after your father broke your arm. She should have protected you."

"Which would have been difficult, since she couldn't even protect herself."

She'd heard that argument from him before. After Lucas had reluctantly admitted how he'd suffered the injury, Lark had rushed to tell Zelda, who in turn had called Harlan, who'd immediately driven out to the McCloud house. Unsurprisingly, Jed denied abusing his son. Lark had been surprised when Lucas had backed his father up, insisting he'd broken his arm falling out of an apple tree.

Even more shocking had been the way he'd angrily accused her of betraying his trust. It had been the first of only two fights they'd ever had. It wasn't until they were teenagers that he finally told her he'd lied to protect his mother, who, knowing her husband wouldn't be locked away forever, had feared his wrath.

"She doesn't have anyone else to take care of her,"

he'd tried to explain with all the earnest conviction of a seventeen-year-old who'd had too much responsibility dumped on his young shoulders. At the time, Lark had considered Mrs. McCloud to be every bit as evil as her husband. Later, when Lark grew up and discovered that the world wasn't strictly black and white, and her own marriage taught her how difficult and complicated relationships could be, she'd come to recognize Lucas's mother as a classic abused woman.

"Well, I can certainly understand how easy it is to surrender power in a marriage," Lark allowed.

As she sat here in the booth where she and Lucas had exchanged so many hungry teenage glances, listening to Delilah and David's laughing banter coming from the kitchen, and gazing out the window at the silhouette of her family's castle standing over the town as it had for more than two centuries, Lark was reminded again of how life was a circle.

She and Lucas were being given another chance. And this time, they were going to get it right.

# 32

Unlike hospitals in larger cities, the security at Aberdeen Medical Center was remarkably lax.

*Lucky for you I'm not a terrorist,* Guest thought as he breezed past the receptionist who was sitting with her back to the front door, talking on the phone. From her flirtatious giggle, he suspected she was talking to a boyfriend.

"Good morning," chirped a silver-haired woman—a volunteer, by her pink-and-white striped smock and the cart of paperback books she was pushing. "Are you here to visit a patient?"

"I was looking for administration," he said.

"Oh, Mrs. Britton's office is right down the hallway," she offered obligingly, not bothering to ask who he was or what he was doing wandering the halls of the hospital without a staff or visitor's badge. "It's the fifth door on the left. I can show you the way, if you'd like."

"That's not necessary. But thank you, just the same."

"No problem," she assured him with a friendly smile. "Have a nice day."

The administration office had been decorated in

shades of blue and gray: a print of Monet's *Water Lilies* floated on lake-blue walls, and two blue chairs faced a gray steel desk that held stacks of manila folders, a computer, and a framed school photo of—of all the kids in the world—the mouthy brat from the plane.

The woman glanced up from the monitor when she sensed him standing in the open doorway. The nameplate on her desk read Angela Britton and her face registered surprise. "Well, hello. What a surprise to see you again."

"It definitely proves the old adage about a small world," he said pleasantly.

"Are you here to visit someone?"

"No. I'm Dr. James Wagner, from the state hospital licensing board." He entered the office and flashed an ID that wouldn't have held up if she'd taken the time to study it closely. Fortunately for him, no one ever did.

"Oh, dear." She frowned behind the lens of her black-framed glasses. "Is there a problem?"

"None at all," he assured her. "I'm just doing a routine inspection."

"We were just inspected." She gestured toward a certificate on the wall. "And as you can see, we passed with flying colors."

"Hmmm." Looking bureaucratically official, he opened the attaché case he was carrying, pulled out a metal clipboard, and leafed through a few sheets of paper. "You're right. Our records show that you do, indeed, have an impeccable record." His smile was friendly. "A ninety-eight percent compliance is very difficult to earn."

"We try our best," she said with unmistakable pride.

"I'm sure your patients appreciate the extra effort." He skimmed the papers again. "This is a new policy we're implementing. The agency selects a few hospitals at random for follow-up checks." Another smile. "If only everyone was as diligent as you, Mrs. Britton, we wouldn't need an inspection program."

She beamed. "Since this is your first time at Aberdeen, I'll be happy to give you the tour myself."

"Oh, you needn't bother."

"It's no bother at all." She began to stand up. "I've been reading billing records all morning and it'll be a relief to get away from the computer screen before I go blind."

"Thank you, but the guidelines, mandated by the state legislature," he tacked on, giving his visit additional legal authority, "require I observe conditions on my own."

"Oh." He could tell she was bothered by the idea of him wandering unattended around her hospital, poking into corners.

"You needn't worry about me disturbing any patients," he assured her. "It's not as thorough an inspection as last time. I'll be confining my inspection to the kitchen, the nurses' stations, and the med rooms."

"I suppose that'll be all right," she said.

"Feel free to call the agency if you have any questions," he volunteered helpfully as the intercom on her tidy desk buzzed. "Perhaps my superior can explain the changes better than I have."

"Oh, that's not necessary. You've explained them quite well." The intercom continued to buzz.

"Well then, since I can see you're a very busy woman and I don't want to take up any more of your time, if you'll just sign on the dotted line, I'll get down to business." He turned the clipboard and held it out to her.

Her handwriting was tidy and slanted to the left. "The cook begins serving lunch in the staff cafeteria at noon, if you'd like to stay and discuss anything you might have questions about after you've finished." Her confident tone suggested she didn't expect him to uncover any problems. "Wednesdays are meatloaf. Agnes makes the best you've ever tasted. She guards the recipe with the ferocity of a dragon protecting a treasure chest, but one of her tricks is using oatmeal flakes in place of the usual bread crumbs."

"The offer's tempting." He frowned thoughtfully and consulted the clipboard again. "But I've another inspection in Johnson City, and I'm running late. It took longer to get up the mountain than I'd planned."

"The storm has shut down roads all over. Perhaps next time."

"I'd love a rain check." He nodded toward the intercom, which had buzzed again. "I'd best let you answer that, while I get to work," he said, cutting off any further stalling tactic she might think up.

A shortage of nurses had become a national problem, and Aberdeen Medical Center proved no exception. The medicine room was empty and the cabinet unlocked—which was against regulations but was common practice, since no one wanted to go searching for a misplaced key.

It took only a moment to slip a stack of fentanyl patches into his briefcase. The patches, created for chronic pain, didn't give the same quick boost as an injection, but the theft would be less likely to be noticed than the bottles. Besides, as street dealers had long ago discovered, soaking the patches in water caused the drug to revert to its liquid state, which was why he'd applied to that nursing home for his prison work-release program. Elderly patients were often too ill, and in many cases too demented, to tell anyone they'd had their pain patch ripped off their backs.

He left the hospital, strolling past the blue-and-gray administration office, past the chatty receptionist who was still on the phone, through the double doors, and across the plowed parking lot where he'd parked in the visitor's slot.

Had it not been for Mrs. Britton, he'd be home free. He considered waiting for her to leave work and kill her, but decided it was a risk he couldn't take.

Fortunately, he'd had a great deal of time in prison to prepare for any contingency.

Thirty minutes later, back in his room at the inn, a bald man with gray eyes and a thin gray mustache smiled back at him from the bathroom mirror.

Last time they'd been together, Lily had been distracted by falling in love with Ian MacKenzie, Laurel had been in a bad mood because she'd believed John Angus was making a huge mistake, and Lark had been dealing with her crumbling marriage.

Now it felt almost like old times as she gathered with her sisters, aunts, and grandmother in the barrel-vaulted media room of Stewart's Folly for some cinematherapy.

"How about *The Way We Were?*" Lily suggested as she scanned the titles in the extensive film library.

"How about not," Laurel said. "I hate that movie. It's just one cliché after another: he's rich, she's poor, she's a brain, he's a jock, he's the drop-dead-gorgeous, blond Wasp, she's the frizzy-haired ethnic, he's red, white, and blue, and she's just annoyingly red. But they still spend the entire movie drooling over each other, then mooning over what might have been. If Streisand's character had half the brains the screenwriter keeps telling us she does, she'd realize ten minutes into the movie that he's a shallow jerk who doesn't begin to deserve her."

"Gee," Lily said mildly, "why don't you tell us what you really think?"

Laurel folded her arms across the front of the black, cowl-neck cashmere sweater she wore over a pair of tailored, gray wool slacks that could have come from Katharine Hepburn's closet. "Not that I have anything against nurturing my inner bitch, which that movie definitely does, but since it's the holidays, perhaps we should try something a little lower on the annoyance scale."

"We've got *It's a Wonderful Life*," Lily suggested.

"Sure," Laurel said. "Why don't you put it in the DVD player while I put on a frilly apron and whip up some cocoa and marshmallows à la Donna Reed."

"Gracious, you've become so cynical, living in Washington," Zelda murmured.

"No, I haven't. I was born this way."

Not a single person in the room chose to argue that statement.

After rejecting *Now, Voyager* ( Laurel was in testy week

four of nicotine withdrawal and refused to watch Bette Davis puffing away), *Jerry Maguire* (despite Tom Cruise's dazzling smile, Lark wasn't about to watch a movie where Dorothy-the-Doormat happily settled for being an extension of some self-centered man's all-controlling ego), and *Sleepless in Seattle* (Lily, who usually went along with everyone, insisted that if you were going to get all weepy over Deborah Kerr's jaywalking tragedy, you may as well wallow in the original *An Affair to Remember*), they managed to come to a consensus.

Two bags of microwaved popcorn and two six-packs of Vanilla Coke later, Lark pointed the clicker at the screen to eject the DVD.

"Oh, God, why didn't anyone remind me how much I hate *Legends of the Fall*," she sniffled.

"It's not that bad." Lily handed her the box of tissues they'd been passing around. "The scenery's great: Brad Pitt's got the best butt in Hollywood."

"And goodness, the way he looked, riding over the crest of the hill, those golden sun-gilded locks blowing in the hot Montana summer wind, made my heart go pitty-pat." Melanie fanned herself.

"The entire movie is an homage to Pitt's hair," Laurel scoffed, but didn't deny Lily's comment about the actor's butt.

"Nothing wrong with that," their grandmother, Annie, said with a deep, heartfelt sigh.

"And that glorious backlight turned those flowing locks into a religious experience," Zelda said.

"It's still a classic Peter Pan story," Laurel said.

"That's why it works." Lily blew her nose. "Deep

down in his heart of hearts, Tristan is just a lost little boy who could only be rescued by the purity of Susannah's love."

"Then he should have stayed around, instead of disappearing for years on all those manly adventures—where he didn't exactly seem to be pining away for his one and only," Laurel said.

Even when she wasn't on the verge of doing murder for a cigarette, Laurel had the toughest standards of the Stewart sisters when it came to men. Which, Lark considered, was perhaps why she was the only one of them who hadn't married.

"Men are not, by nature, monogamous," Melanie said.

"Ian is." Lily stalwartly stood up for her new husband.

"Of course he is," Laurel agreed. "It's obvious he adores you."

The Academy Award–winning documentary filmmaker, who'd returned to Highland Falls with Lily, was currently off in the game room shooting pool with Lucas, Lark's father, and Ian's father, Duncan MacDougall, who, as Melanie put it, was "keeping company" with Lark's grandmother.

Wanting to end the reunion on an uplifting note, Lark went looking for a second feature and came up with *Romy and Michele's High School Reunion.*

"Oh, that's a great slumber party movie," Lily said. "And so perfect, since you and Lucas are together again."

Everyone immediately agreed, even though Laurel complained the comedy would test her nonsmoking resolve, considering Janeane Garofalo's character invented a fast-burning cigarette paper for "the gal on the go."

"You're going to be in a bad mood whatever we choose," Melanie stated.

"No offense intended, Aunt Melanie," Laurel countered, "but you've been acting like a surly cat on a hot tin roof ever since Uncle Charles left."

The room turned deadly quiet.

"You're right," Melanie surprised them by acknowledging. Southern women were rarely willing to admit they'd made a poor choice in a man, since such an admission reflected badly upon themselves. "It has recently dawned on me that I've given Charles and his little truffle-making bimbo too much power over my life." She ran a hand down her sleek bob. "You know my house down in Charlotte."

"Of course," Lark said. Her aunt no longer lived in the home that had been in the Lancaster family for over a century, but refused to sell since it represented her last tie to the magnolia South of her birthplace.

"Well, when I went home for Christmas, I discovered termites had moved in. After the exterminator got through evicting them, I had this contractor come over to give me a bid to rebuild the front porch." Her cheeks colored. "The minute I saw that long, tall drink of water at my front door, wearing a sexy tool belt slung gunslinger-low over tight, faded jeans, I decided it was time to move on with my life."

Zelda burst out laughing. "Melanie's got herself a beau."

"I do, indeed." Melanie's smile was that of a sleek Siamese who'd just lapped up a bowl of sweetened whipped cream. "And with all the plans I have for that old house, I think I can probably keep the man around for the next ten years."

"You won't need construction projects to keep a man," Zelda said loyally. The two women could not be more different, but they'd both come to Highland Falls after the death of John Angus's wife and had forged a workable odd-couple relationship as they'd reared his three daughters. "So, what does he look like?"

"Well, as I said, he's tall. And lean, but not skinny; his body's all hard, rangy muscle. And he has this huge hammer," she tacked on, with a wicked light in her eyes.

"Melanie!" Eighty-two-year-old Annie Stewart giggled like a schoolgirl. "And here I've always thought you were such a proper southern lady."

"I was, for all the good it did me," Melanie scoffed. "When Charles left, my cousin Layla assured me that the best way to get over a man was to polish silver. All that got me was the shiniest ice tea spoons in the South. Times are changing. Did you know that Nieman-Marcus is actually selling white shoes after Labor Day? Oh, they may call it winter white, but my mother taught me that it just wasn't done. Of course," she reflected, "I doubt if Mama would've approved of a southern woman having hot sex with her carpenter in the front porch hammock, either."

"You didn't!" That surprised even Zelda.

Melanie tossed up a chin she'd kept firm with daily facial exercises—and a slight touch-up by a plastic surgeon's scalpel. "Well, it was night. And we finished indoors," she admitted. "But I let Brock take off my top right there beneath the porch light, where anyone driving past could see my breasts."

Zelda lifted her glass of Coke as the DVD started up. "To our own dear Melanie, the boobs of the New South."

"So that's why no men have hit on me in my kickboxing class," Laurel said ninety minutes later, as the credits rolled. "Who knew I needed a lavender patent-leather miniskirt, flowered spandex top, and turquoise boxing gloves?"

"Personally, I prefer the metallic minidress with the baby-blue cuffs and collar," Lark decided, choosing not to point out that strong-minded Laurel had intimidated men *before* she'd taken up kickboxing.

"I had a dress exactly like that back in the eighties," Zelda volunteered. "But mine was red."

Lark was laughing with the others when an unexpected emotion hit her like a sledgehammer from behind and caused tears to fill her eyes.

"What's the matter, darling?" asked Zelda, who seldom missed a thing.

"Are you worried about that horrid man?" Melanie asked. "If you are, you needn't be, because none of us will let anything happen to you." From the conviction in her voice she could have been Scarlett, holding up that turnip, swearing to never be hungry again.

"Things are looking much better," Zelda assured her. "I did a reading just before supper, and the six of swords came up. That's the one with the ferryman carrying the sorrowing woman and child across the water to the far shore," she explained. "The boat's moving from the rough water into the calm, indicating a move from difficulties to more peaceful times." She took Lark's hands in hers. "When I called Lucas from Greece, I was so afraid for you. But I can feel the harmony just around the corner."

"Me, too," Melanie, who'd never shown any interest in her sister-in-law's tarot cards, claimed.

"I've been feeling the same thing ever since I arrived home," Laurel, the family member least likely to believe in tarot cards, crystals, or wiccan magic, said loyally.

The tears swam. For a woman who never cried, Lark had certainly been making up for lost time the past few days. "I love you all so much."

They drew into a teary group hug that, at any other time, Laurel would have declared unbearably sappy. Their lives were so intertwined Lark would feel incomplete without her sisters. They were each others' mirrors and opposites, sharing the same DNA, the same family history, and the same hatred of those scratchy wool Christmas sweaters from their great-aunt Charlotte.

"I have an idea," Laurel said. "Something we can do instead of sitting around waiting for the men to take care of things."

She'd gotten everyone's attention.

"From the description that department store manager gave, Guest doesn't look anything like his old mug shots. Putting them in the *Herald* is a good idea, but we need a new photo we can put on posters."

"If someone had taken an updated photo, the horrid man would already be in custody and we wouldn't need it," Annie pointed out.

"True. But Lily's an artist."

"I failed painting," Lily reminded them. Indeed, she'd tried nearly every artistic medium before discovering a talent for filmmaking.

"You may not have been Mary Cassatt, but you were very clever with those pen and ink sketches," Zelda reminded her.

"It wouldn't hurt to try," Melanie said. "If you began with the mug shot—"

"Then tweaked it a bit to match the description," Lark said, catching on to Laurel's plan.

"And added a few years," Annie added.

"It might just work," they said together.

# 33

Lark had been telling herself and her family for years that her busy life was the reason she had only returned to Highland Falls a handful of times. Being with Lucas had forced her to accept the truth: she'd been afraid to confront her past. But as she lay in Lucas's arms in her old bedroom in the family wing of Stewart's Folly, listening to the high, lonesome sound of a train whistle echoing in the night, she remembered how, until that summer, she'd always found comfort in the ancient, gently rolling embrace of the Smokies.

She could not remember a time when she hadn't been singing. Music had been as necessary as air. She'd sung while walking to school, while picking blackberries, while wading in the pool beneath Firefly Falls—always singing, the music becoming a way to travel beyond the patchwork quilt of small Appalachian towns that stretched from Georgia to Maine.

She wrote her first song, a sad ballad about her mama becoming an angel and watching over her girls from heaven, the summer she turned seven. From then on, she'd taken brightly colored scraps of ballads, mountain legends, and stories she'd heard growing up, piecing them together with events from her own life and the lilt of harmony in her head into a new song that kept the connection with her roots.

To her, music had not only been a dream, but a way of life. Many singers, especially these days, seemed to be more attracted to the spotlight and stardom than the music itself. Call her old-fashioned—and Cody certainly had on more than one occasion—but Lark needed more. She needed to write from the heart, about emotions ordinary people experienced. Love and loss, pain and sorrow, friends and family. And most of all, she sang of home.

In Highland Falls, people didn't have to check out PalmPilots and appointment books when they went out visiting. They got together when there was a birth or a death in the family, a wedding, or a christening. And sometimes just when they felt the need to hear new stories, or even ones they'd heard dozens of times before.

Here in the mountains where she'd been born, music wasn't just something that came out of a radio; it was a bond the people had brought with them from across the sea, something they'd shared for centuries on front porches, parlors, and country fairs. And occasions like Winterfest, where they'd come together to save the music that was as vital to them as air.

It was good to be home, she thought on a blissful sigh. Even better to be home with Lucas. His slow, steady breathing revealed he'd fallen asleep. She cuddled closer and pressed her lips against his bare chest.

As she drifted off to sleep, Lark's last thought was that

despite William Guest lurking somewhere out there, she was happier than she'd been in years.

Damn her! William stared up at the darkened window, pornographic pictures of Lark with Lucas McCloud bombarding his mind.

He'd once loved the Tennessee Songbird more than life itself. There hadn't been anything he wouldn't have done for her. Nothing she could have asked for that he wouldn't have moved heaven and earth to get for her.

But that was before he'd discovered what a shameless slut she was. He'd stood on the sidewalk outside the café, rage and jealousy burning in his gut like battery acid as she'd covered her lover's wide, brutish hand with her smaller one. She was his, dammit. It infuriated him that the woman he'd put on a pedestal was nothing but a wanton whore, but whore or Madonna, he owned her. She might think she could escape, but they both knew that she'd never belong to anyone but him.

The bitch would pay for her betrayal. But not right away. First he'd punish her by taking McCloud away from her. He liked the idea of killing her lover in front of her. Then it would be her turn. First he'd tie her up. Gag her so no one could hear her screams. That way he wouldn't have to listen to her weep and wail for her dead lover.

But then he wouldn't be able to hear her beg for her life, either.

No matter. So long as he didn't blindfold her, he'd be able to read her penitence and terror in those wide, liquid whiskey eyes as he cut her with a razor blade—not deep enough to kill, just enough to draw blood and mark that pale porcelain flesh.

He'd brand her, cutting his name across her breasts. Just imagining it made him hard. And then, when she finally understood that she was his property, that he could do whatever he wanted to her, he would love Lark Stewart to death.

"Meet me in the library," the note that had been slipped into the pocket of Lark's parka instructed. "Come alone."

Lark recognized the handwriting immediately. Laurel had always tended toward intrigue.

"I have something for you," she said, as soon as Lark entered the book-filled room. She pressed a button on the desk. A sliding panel in the wall opened, revealing a hidden bookcase. She retrieved a small mahogany box from behind a book, whose glossy dust jacket, with a dagger dripping blood, suggested murder and mayhem, and held it out to her sister.

Lily opened the lid; a small silver gun lay on a bed of black velvet.

"It's a derringer," Laurel said.

"Where did you get it?"

"From the armory. It belonged to Great-aunt Edna."

Edna Stewart had been an early feminist and one of the black sheep of the Stewart family. Rather than marry, or even go to work at Highlander's, she used the recipe James Stewart had brought over from Scotland and turned to moonshining during the days of Prohibition.

"It's the gun she took with her on her runs to Kentucky and Georgia, but she never had to use it because she was the fastest driver in the mountains."

Lark remembered Zelda telling her those stories. "The government agents could never catch up with her." Apparently her son and grandson inherited her talent for speed; they became NASCAR drivers.

"Guest is just like Jason in all those *Friday the 13th* movies," Laurel said. "He might wear black leather instead of a hockey mask, but he's going to keep coming back, Lark. Until one of you is dead."

"Lucas won't let that happen." Lark had to believe that.

"I know he'd cut off his right arm before he'd let anything happen to you. But what if Guest shoots him like he did Danny Murphy? Then who's going to protect you?"

Lark had no answer to that. Hadn't she worried about that, deep down inside, herself? Which was why she'd made Lucas teach her how to shoot.

"Take it," Laurel insisted. "Just in case."

Assuring herself that she wouldn't need it, that she only wanted to keep Laurel from worrying, Lark took the gun from its case and slipped it into her pocket.

She planned to show it to Lucas, but then he'd caught her in the stairway on her way to her bedroom and kissed the small silver derringer right out of her mind.

John Angus Stewart, "laird" of Stewart's Folly, had arrived home like Napoleon entering Berlin. All that was missing was the blare of trumpets. Red-bearded and kilted, he was the very picture of a burly Highland warrior as he began the inquisition of Lucas McCloud, a glass of Highlander's Pride cradled in his huge hands.

If he'd wanted to appear intimidating, he couldn't have chosen a more suitable room than the armory packed with pseudo-baronial suits of armor, walls festooned with swords, carbines, and crossbows, and glass cases filled with pistols, thumbscrews, and other instruments of war and torture.

"So," he demanded, "are you going to marry my daughter?"

Lucas took a sip of seltzer. "No one could ever accuse you of not getting straight to the point."

"I haven't been a very good father." The older man rubbed his flaming red beard. "I never thought I had to. The girls had their aunts, after all, and I had my art." He tossed back the one hundred and twenty-six proof Highlander's Pride as if it were spring water. "My bride has recently suggested that I have a tendency to be self-absorbed."

Lucas had crawled on his belly through oil well fires in a Middle East war, but wasn't brave enough to touch that line.

"Although I've never spent a lot of time on introspection, I've come to the conclusion that she's right." John Angus refilled his glass. "Lark was on tour when she got mixed up with Armstrong. Zelda warned me he was trouble, Melanie thought he was a gold digger, and even Lily, who tends to think the best of everyone, didn't seem real taken with him.

"But I told myself that she was a grown woman, capable of making her own choices, and if she wanted some rodeo cowboy, well, I ought to just stay out of her way."

He rubbed a broad hand over his face. "Turns out that I screwed up big-time."

"People have their own reasons for getting married," Lucas said mildly. "I'm not sure anything you said would have made a difference."

"Perhaps not." John Angus took a thoughtful sip of whiskey and stared at a battle-ax hanging across the room. "But at least I should have done the fatherly thing and given Armstrong the third degree. Asked his intentions. Maybe brought him in here and put the thumbscrews to him during the interrogation." A smile crossed his lips; then he shook his leonine head with obvious regret. "Well, I'm not going to make that mistake again."

Lark might be right about him never being a candidate for the Father of the Year award, but Lucas knew he adored her—something he and the flamboyant artist had in common. "Lark's always known you love her. As for my intentions, yes, I'm going to marry your daughter."

"It's about time." John Angus put the empty glass down and folded his massive hands over a chest large enough to have its own zip code. "Does she know yet?"

"We've been a bit distracted to discuss details."

"Distracted by that goddamn Guest." Another scowl moved across the broad features like a summer storm. "I've done some trapshooting. Probably still have the shotgun somewhere around the place." He glanced around the armory as if considering various alternative weapons. "I don't suppose you'd be willing to bring the bastard here after you capture him, so I could blow his fucking nuts off?"

"Sorry." Lucas had promised Harlan he wouldn't do anything rash. Of course, they might have different definitions of what constituted rash behavior. Personally, he didn't think John Angus's suggestion was that out of line. Which could be why he no longer fit into the FBI system.

John Angus shrugged. "I didn't think so, but it was worth a try."

"I've been thinking," Tanya said, as she and Cody entered their room at the Firefly Falls Inn.

"Don't." He dumped the suitcases on the bed. "You're not very good at it."

She pouted. "That's not very nice."

He cursed beneath his breath. Women could be so damn sensitive, even without PMS. But even he could tell that had been over the line. "I'm sorry, darlin'," he said, wanting to cut the conversation off before it escalated to tears. "I've got a lot on my mind."

"Did you see that darling little chapel we passed when we came into town?"

"No."

"The sign outside advertised a special New Year's Eve marriage package."

"Good for them." He could see the lights of Stewart's Folly glowing farther up the mountainside. Was Lark there? And if so, how the hell was he going to get her away from that damn hulk, Lucas McCloud?

"I thought it might be a romantic thing for us to do."

"Us?" He stared back over his shoulder at her. "As in you and I?"

"The sign said there's no waiting period." She dropped her purse on the bed.

"There's also no reason for us to get married."

*Ah, shit.*

Her eyes were welling up with tears; the last thing he needed were waterworks.

What the hell had he been thinking, bringing her with him? He should have just left her in Nashville; now he was going to have to figure out some way to keep her happy until he could settle things with Lark.

"I made the mistake of marrying a partner before. Business and love just don't mix, sweetheart. I don't want us to end up the same way."

"I'm not Lark."

*No shit, Skippy.*

She smoothed a hand down her hair, which she'd had straightened and dyed back to brown. She'd changed her clothes and makeup, too, in an unsuccessful attempt to look like Lark.

"I'm out of cigarettes," he said. He also needed a drink. Bad. "Why don't you unpack while I run down to that pub we passed. Then we can go out and I'll buy you a steak."

"I'm a vegetarian."

"Pasta, then."

Deciding that women were more trouble than they were worth, Cody left the room. He did not look back.

# 34

"Alone at last," Lucas said as he pulled the SUV he'd retrieved from the farmhouse up in front of Stewart's Folly.

"I think it went well," Lark said.

He cut the engine. "You charmed the hell out of everyone. I doubt there's a man in the place who didn't want to take you to bed, and the amazing thing is, that all their wives seemed to want you as a girlfriend."

"That's one of those funny things about creating an image," she said. "Even if I could come off sexy—"

"If?" He arched a brow. "If you were any sexier, half the men in town would be in the cardiac care unit after that performance."

She shook her head. "I've never seen it."

"Sweetheart, you're a walking poster girl for the near occasion of sin."

Lark laughed. "That is so far off base. I'm probably the most straitlaced person in the music business."

Not that she'd ever been straitlaced with him; from the time her hormones had first kicked in, she'd never been able to think about Lucas, or look at him, without feeling as if she was burning up from the inside out.

"I know marketing people look for a sexy image, but since women buy most of the CDs and choose what concerts they and their husbands or boyfriends go to, it's never made any sense to get up on stage and make them feel threatened if their men enjoy my show right along with them. I don't want their husbands; I just want them to buy my songs."

"I'm sure you sold a lot of them tonight. And thanks to you, some kid out there might just be the next Lark Stewart."

"That's the best part of being successful." She smiled. "The ability to make a difference in people's lives now and again."

It was another thing she and Cody had argued about; he hated it whenever she took time to visit a children's or VA hospital, or appear at a charity event in some small town that couldn't draw huge crowds. Just thinking about how he'd tried to extort that ten thousand dollars from her former music teacher made her angry all over again. She was going to have to call her accountant right after the New Year and see how that audit was going. If he'd been embezzling from her, she was going to have his ass thrown in jail, even if it would land her right back on the front page of the tabloids.

But she was not going to allow Cody to ruin such a lovely night.

"Did you see Harlan?" she asked.

"I don't think anyone could have missed him. I've known him all my life and never knew he owned a sheriff's uniform."

"I think he put it on for Zelda."

"What does your aunt have to do with him suddenly putting on khaki?"

"Women can't resist a man in uniform."

He mulled that over. "Zelda and Harlan, huh?"

"Apparently they've been mad about each other forever, but since he was married, they couldn't do anything about it. Now they're making up for lost time. He asked her to go to Hawaii with him as soon as Guest is captured."

"Well, that's an added incentive to get the guy fast."

Lucas brushed his lips against hers. The kiss was as light as thistledown, but still made her feel as if she were being lit up inside with sparklers. His mouth rubbed over hers, lingering, then retreating.

Once. Twice. A third time.

Although the temperature was rapidly falling inside the SUV, Lark felt the familiar warmth rise inside her. Her lips parted on a throaty moan as she linked her fingers together at the back of his head and poured herself into the kiss.


The thick snow had brought out every snowmobile in Highland County. They raced back and forth across the snow, engines buzzing like angry wasps, their headlights cutting yellow swaths in the moon-brightened fields, plumes of snow thrown high behind them. Sparks from bonfires danced like fireflies in the night sky and Jimi Hendrix's "Star Spangled Banner" screeched from somewhere deep in the woods.

It was Saturday night—date night—and despite the

frigid temperatures, it seemed as if everyone who hadn't gotten tickets to hear Lark Stewart sing in the school gymnasium had taken to the great outdoors. The ski slopes were ablaze with floodlights and an impromptu hockey game had sprung up on the small frozen ice rink lit in the town square. As players madly chased the small black puck around the center of the ice, teenage couples skating hand in hand circled the edge, stopping every so often to share a brief kiss, breaths mingling like little ghosts.

The hot chocolate hut was doing a brisk business and everyone seemed to be having themselves a high old time. Everyone but the man who cut his snowmobile's engine at the top of the bunny ski run.

He never would have come to this hick mountain icy town if it weren't for Lark. The house she'd grown up in reminded him of Sleeping Beauty's castle at Disneyland. And just like Sleeping Beauty, she was going to be going to sleep for a very long time. The difference was, she wouldn't be waking up from any prince's kiss a hundred years from now.

He pushed the faceplate of his helmet up, felt the sting of ice crystals against his face and cursed her. His gloved hands were already turning numb, his booted feet felt like blocks of ice, and if she didn't get back from that damn concert soon, his dick was going to freeze and break off.

Finally!

When he saw the headlights headed down the long drive leading to the towering front door of the castle, he took the rifle out of the duffel bag and waited.

"Do you realize how long it's been since we've made love in the backseat of a car?" Lark asked.

"We've grown up. We don't have to risk getting arrested anymore."

"Harlan wouldn't arrest us." She unfastened her seat belt. "Besides, I'll bet he and Zelda will be doing the same thing tonight."

"I wouldn't be surprised. But I'll bet they won't be doing it in Harlan's Explorer."

"Probably not," she allowed. "Did I tell you about Aunt Melanie?"

When she leaned across the gear shift and pressed her hand against the front of his jeans, his erection stirred against the denim. "I don't believe her name came up."

The lowering of the metal zipper on the jeans he'd bought to replace the button-fly 501s sounded unnaturally loud in the stillness of the night. He was hot and hard and ready.

"She's taken herself a lover down in Charlotte. He's a carpenter. Apparently he's got this huge hammer." Her eyes danced with a wicked, feminine power as she curled her fingers around him. "And speaking of huge . . ."

Any control Lucas might have been holding on to disintegrated when she lowered her head and took him in her mouth, swallowing him deep. "Sweet Jesus, Lark." He hissed out a ragged breath as tongue stroked a hot wet trail up the length of his penis.

As good as it was, Lucas wanted more. He fisted his hands in her hair and pulled her head back. "I want to be inside you."

"Why, you must be psychic." She began wiggling out of her jeans.

Both flat-out insane with lust, they tore at the jeans, yanking them down below her knees, where the heavy denim was stopped by her boots.

"Don't bother with them." She straddled Lucas, impaling herself on his erection, the line between pain and pleasure blurring as she filled herself with him. Teeth clashed, tongues tangled. He kissed her deeply, devouring her, claiming her. She kissed him back hotly, demandingly.

Losing themselves in the heat, in each other, they moved together, body to body, heart to heart. The ride was long and hard, the release, when it finally came, explosive.

"Oh, God," Lark gasped as she collapsed against him, her forehead against his. "I wonder if there's a twelve-step program for sex addiction."

"If there is, I don't want to know about it."

"Me neither."

Lucas was laboring for breath and his heart was hammering hard enough to break ribs. Could a man his age die of a heart attack from too-hot sex? Well, there were far worse ways to go.

Their cooling bodies were slick and moist. Outside the steamed-up windows the breeze sighed in a stand of pine trees; an owl hooted.

As sanity slowly returned, he realized how humiliating it would be if the family came home and found them with their pants down around their ankles, and tried to muster up the energy to pull them up. "I want you again."

"Well, isn't that handy? Since I always want you." He could feel her smile against his mouth as she kissed him. "Maybe this time we can make it to the backseat."

"Inside." Although he didn't really want to ever move again, he reluctantly lifted her over the gearshift back to the passenger seat. "Where I can take my time making you scream, without having to worry about dying of carbon monoxide poisoning."

She stopped in the act of pulling her jeans up over her hips, which was every bit as sexy as when she'd wiggled out of them. "You're going to make me scream?" She looked interested.

"Absolutely." He slid his hand between the denim and skin before she zipped them and dipped his finger into her. "And you're going to love it."

They finally left the SUV and were nearly at the castle door when a crack, like glass breaking, shattered the night. As the wood above her head splintered, Lucas shoved Lark to the ground and threw his body over hers.

# 35

Angela Britton had been born in New York City. She'd grown up learning the fine art of ignoring everyone and everything around her. There were millions of people in Manhattan alone, and when you counted in the other boroughs, well, if you stopped to chat with everyone you passed, you'd never get anything done and the entire city would grind to a screeching halt. But she was also the daughter of a New York cop, who'd taught her that the world could be a violent place, and that the power of observation, combined with learning to trust her instincts, could mean the difference between life and death.

After she'd been married a few years, her husband, an editor for *New York* magazine, got it into his head to move back to the small nowhere town in the South Appalachians where he'd grown up, to concentrate more fully on his yet uncontracted novel.

"There's just too much distraction here," he'd complained.

"Excuse me, but that distraction just happens to be life," she'd countered. "Something I believe novelists are supposed to experience."

But he'd proven adamant, and since she loved him, she quit her job, packed up all her chic black clothes, and moved South.

She'd been in Highland Falls for three years. Amazingly, her husband had found a mentor their first week, when he'd wandered into the town's only bookstore the same day Zelda Stewart was autographing stock.

The older woman had taken him under her wing, recommending him to her agent and although under her guidance he'd thrown away the manuscript he'd been working on since his freshman year at Duke, the second had sold to a reputable publisher. While they certainly weren't talking Grisham money, he appeared to be on his way to being able to earn a living telling stories.

Life was good. But although crime was almost nonexistent in Highland Falls, she still possessed the self-protective instincts instilled by her father. So when, despite the newly shaved head, she recognized the man walking out of the Gothic Dragon pub with the young woman as the same man who'd been wandering around her hospital the day the fentanyl patch count came out short—and a dead ringer for that murderer whose face smiled out from all those posters the Stewart sisters had stuck up all over town, she whipped out her cell phone and dialed 911.

"Dammit, you need to go to the hospital."

"I'm fine," Lucas insisted yet again. "Which is more than I can say for my jacket."

"So now you're a doctor," Lark grumbled as she took

a brown bottle and some cotton balls out of the medicine cabinet. "And a jacket can be replaced." While there was only one Lucas McCloud in the world.

"It took ten years to get that leather that soft. And I don't need a doctor to tell me a shoulder scratch isn't serious."

"Excuse me, but in my world getting shot is serious." She'd never been so scared in her life. Not even when the plane had crashed, because then he'd been there to take care of her. Now it was her turn to take care of him, but he was proving less than cooperative.

"Don't look now, but you landed in my world when your stalker escaped. And I wasn't shot. It's only a graze."

"Shot, grazed, it's all semantics. And violence isn't your world anymore," she reminded him. "You're a furniture maker." And an exceptionally good one, if the furniture in the farmhouse was any example. "At the very least, you should be in bed."

"Now that, I'm not going to argue with."

She absolutely refused to laugh. "Have you ever been shot before?"

"Nope. And I wasn't shot tonight, either. It's only—"

"Yeah, yeah. A graze." She drew in a frustrated breath. "You could have been killed."

"It could have just as easily been you," he pointed out.

"No, because I have you to protect me. I don't suppose it could have been an accident," she suggested hopefully. "Perhaps a hunter?"

"I don't believe Fish and Game gives out a lot of licenses for winter midnight hunts."

"A poacher, then."

"How many deer walk in the front door of Stewart's Folly?"

"Okay, so it wasn't an accident." She poured the antiseptic onto one of the fluffy white balls. "But you're still not leaving here until I make sure that ugly bullet wound is cleaned out. I'm not going to be responsible for you dropping dead of sepsis."

She dabbed the wound with the cotton, then, worried it might not be enough, poured more straight from the bottle over his wounded shoulder.

"Shit!" He yanked away. "That stings like hell."

"You're lucky you're still alive to feel anything. Fortunately Guest trained to be a doctor, not a sniper."

"You're awful damn calm about this."

"I know." She was surprising herself. "I'd hate to think I've become adjusted to murder and mayhem, but I suspect I've just gone round the bend into deep denial." She tore the paper wrapper off a large cloth Band-Aid and covered the ugly, but admittedly not very deep, scrape. "I'll probably crack like ice as soon as this is over."

"Which isn't going to happen real soon, if I'm stuck here while you play Florence Nightingale."

"Harlan's the sheriff," she reminded him. "It's his job to track down the bad guys. You promised me you'd stay by my side and protect me."

"No fair, baby. You've been complaining about me hovering over you ever since I showed up in New Orleans, so it's a little late to play the maiden in distress card."

Headlights flashed against the wall. Lucas looked out the window at the SUV with the county sheriff's department seal on the door pulling into the circular driveway. At the same time, his cell phone rang.

"We've got him," Harlan said, anticipation of the hunt in his voice. "A witness identified him leaving the Gothic Dragon pub with a woman who looks a lot like Lark. Merlene, down at the inn, thinks a guy matching his description is a guest there. Problem is, she's vain and refuses to wear her damn glasses, without which she's as blind as a mole. But she sat up and took notice when he walked past her this evening with a newly shaved head. Seems she had a thing for Yul Brynner."

"I'll meet you there in five." Lucas yanked his blood-stained sweater back on over his head.

"Good. And I sent Lanny Wagner—he's my best deputy—over. Since the rest of the family's still at Winterfest, Lanny'll keep an eye on Lark."

"Thanks." He snapped the phone shut. "A witness just placed Guest leaving the pub with a woman and the desk clerk at the inn thinks he's a guest there," he tersely told Lark.

"But if Guest is at the inn, who shot at us?" *Surely not Cody?*

"I don't know. But there's a deputy parked outside so you'll be safe. I'll be back as soon as I can."

Lark wanted to ask him to stay. But the glint of determination in his eyes told her that even if she could use Lucas's strong sense of responsibility to keep him here, safe with her, it would always be between them.

Another part of her wanted to go with him. She wanted to be there when Guest was taken down. But one shooting lesson didn't make her an expert, she wasn't trained for capturing bad guys, and she'd never forgive herself if anything happened to Lucas because he'd been distracted worrying about her.

"Don't you dare get hurt."

"Never happen." The quick flash of grin made her worry he might actually be enjoying this. His kiss was hard enough to send her head to spinning and ended far too soon.

Lark stayed at the window, listening to the sound of his boots on the stairs. She heard the front door open, then slam. Then she watched as his taillights disappeared down the driveway, headed toward town.


At first Tanya Kay thought she was dreaming. No, not a dream, she thought, as she forced her heavy lids open and tried to focus on the man standing over her. She was bound, hand and foot, as Cody sometimes did when they were playing bondage games.

But this man wasn't Cody. This man she'd made the mistake of picking up in the pub, after going there to look for Cody, was evil.

"I gave you enough fentanyl to keep you from moving," he said conversationally. "You've been a very bad girl," he said, "yet there's something about you that appeals to me. I can't make up my mind whether to keep you or kill you."

His smile was that of the monsters from late-night movies.

Tanya opened her mouth and screamed. But the sound was only in her head and no one could hear her.

*   *   *

Shortly after Lucas left, the doorbell chimed "The Battle of Stirling" from *Braveheart*. Looking through the peephole, Lark saw Lanny Wagner and a man who was wonderfully familiar.

She flung open the heavy door. "Ryan!" She threw her arms around him. "I thought you weren't coming for another three weeks."

He hugged her back. "The islands were boring. All that sun, sand, and surf. And one can only drink so many mai tais."

The deputy cleared his throat. "Fella said you know him. Guess he was telling the truth."

"He certainly was. This is my friend and manager, Ryan Glazer. Thanks, Lanny. Since I'm not alone anymore, you can go on home now."

"That's okay." His smile revealed the flash of a gold tooth. "Harlan told me to stay outside until Lucas gets back, so that's what I'm gonna do."

"It's so cold out."

"The heater works," he assured her. "And my wife sent me off with a thermos of coffee."

"Let the man do his job, Lark," Ryan said goodnaturedly.

"All right. You be sure to come in if you get too cold," she instructed him.

She watched him lumber back to the SUV, then shut the door and turned to Ryan. "I'm so happy to see you!"

"I'm happy to see you, too. Though I have to tell you, this place is something else. I've seen pictures, but it's a little overwhelming in person."

"The Stewarts have always been given to grand gestures." Lark glanced around the huge great hall that looked as if it had been designed for royalty. It could be quite a culture shock for someone seeing it for the first time. The Stewart crest—depicting a winged pelican feeding its young—hung above the mantel at the far end of the hall.

"*Virescit vulnere virtus*," Ryan read the motto. "What does that mean?"

"Courage grows strong at the wound." Something she personally knew a little about. "Are you hungry?"

"Famished. I didn't want to take time to stop in Asheville."

She took his hand. "Let's go into the kitchen and I'll make you a sandwich. You won't believe all that I have to tell you."


Never a patient woman, Zelda grew increasingly tense as Laurel drove the family back to Stewart's Folly. When Harlan had hurriedly left Winterfest to arrest William Guest, he'd assured them all that Lark was well protected. Zelda dearly hoped that was true, but every instinct she possessed told her that something was very, very wrong.

The pain struck her chest like a bolt from the star spangled night sky as they drove through the tall gates of the castle. A sudden chill swept over her; her body was wracked by violent shivers.

"Aunt Zelda?" Lily's voice sounded as if it were coming from far away.

"It's happening," Zelda whispered.

"Oh, shit," Laurel said as she pulled up next to the

Suburban bearing the Highland County sheriff's department seal. The driver's door was open and Lanny Wagner was lying on the ground. The headlights of Melanie's Range Rover illuminated the crimson snow around his head. "What if Guest set up that sighting at the inn as a ruse to lure Lucas away from Lark?"

The others raced to the house while Zelda dropped to her knees beside the gravely wounded deputy, desperately hoping that even if he was too far gone to talk, she'd be able to sense what had happened here tonight.

*Focus!*

She was sitting in the snow, Lanny's bloodied head in her lap when Laurel appeared in the doorway, backlit by the chandeliers in the grand hall. She was flanked by Lily and Melanie. Zelda had never known her eldest niece to fear anything or anyone.

Until tonight.

Laurel's complexion was as white as the snow-clad mountains, her green eyes wide with dread.

"Lark's gone."

# 36

Not wanting to take any chances, after stationing Highland County's other four deputies at the entrance to the inn's parking lot, and having an ambulance standing by, Lucas kicked the door in and rushed into the room, Harlan right with him. Guest was standing over an obviously drugged woman, the nasty-looking scalpel in his hand glittering in the light from the overhead fixture.

He spun toward them.

"It's over, Guest," Lucas said with measured calm, his Glock pointed at the man who'd terrorized Lark for too many years. "Drop the blade and we can end this quietly."

"You don't get it, do you, McCloud?" He actually smiled. "It's not going to end until I have my wife back. The wife you're trying to steal away from me."

"She was never yours to begin with." *Give me an excuse.* "Never will be. Now, drop the damn scalpel before someone gets hurt."

Guest opened his fingers. Just as the scalpel clattered to the wood floor, he grabbed a blue-steel pistol from beneath the bed pillow and fired.

Lucas was quicker. Harlan, only a heartbeat behind.

Gunfire exploded, then everything went suddenly, deadly, quiet.

And when it was finally over, William Guest was sprawled on the floor, a scarlet bloom spreading across the front of his studded, black leather jacket.

"Case closed," Harlan said into the silence.

As the ambulances took Guest to the morgue and the drugged woman Lucas recognized as Tanya Kay to the hospital, Harlan began to seal the scene with yellow crime tape for the lab guys who'd be arriving from Knoxville in the morning.

Feeling a huge weight lifted from his shoulders, Lucas went outside to call Lark to give her the good news that she no longer had anything to fear from William Guest.

After her cell phone signaled "no reception," he was about to dial Stewart's Folly, when Cody Armstrong pulled into the parking lot with a squeal of brakes. The car skidded for a few feet, managing to stop just before plowing into the front of the building.

"There's nobody at the damn sheriff's office," he complained as he climbed out of the driver's seat.

"Maggie Knox works the night shift," Harlan supplied. "Calls come into her house since Highland Falls doesn't have a lot of crime. Or didn't, until this week," he amended, looking back at the taped-off motel room.

"Well, I've been looking all over for you two," he complained.

"Sorry. We've been saving your protégée's life," Lucas said. "Since you weren't around to protect her."

"Tanya Kay? Who the hell would want to hurt Tanya Kay?"

"Guest had her in his room," Harlan said. "He picked her up in the pub."

"Shit." He plowed his hands through his hair. "Did he hurt her?"

"He drugged her and she's a bit bruised up, but thanks to a witness who recognized him, we got to her before he cut her up."

"Cut her?" His face paled. "Christ." From the expression on his face, Lucas realized the guy actually cared. "How the hell did you guys let him get away?"

"We didn't," Harlan said, clearly affronted by the suggestion.

"He made the mistake of playing *Gunfight at the O.K. Corral* and came out on the losing end," Lucas said.

"Good." Cody nodded, satisfied. Then he frowned. "If Guest's dead, then who the hell is with Lark in the gondola?"

"The ski gondola?" Lucas's blood chilled.

"Yeah. I was headed past the ski resort on the way to Stewart's Folly, to talk to her about a business proposition and saw her and some guy getting into one of the gondolas, which was damn strange since she's scared spitless of heights."

"Goddammit!" Lucas shouted.

"I tried to call you on the cell, but the signal kept shorting out," Cody said as they raced for the SUV.

They stopped at the office only long enough for Harlan to open the gun rack, toss Lucas a rifle, then grab one for himself.

Then they drove, hell-bent for leather, to the ski lift.

\* \* \*

It had begun to snow again. Highland Falls, dressed in holiday lights, looked like a toy town from the gondola that was slowly making its way up the mountainside. For once Lark wasn't afraid of the height—because she was a lot more unnerved of the man pointing the gun at her. The same gun he'd used to shoot Lanny through the windshield as he'd sat drinking his coffee.

"I don't understand, Ryan. Why are you doing this?"

"I'm sorry, Lark. It's nothing personal, but I really don't have any choice. I've gotten myself into one helluva mess."

"Whatever it is, we can work it out." *Where was Lucas?*

"By the way," he said, proving that he still had the ability to read her mind, "Lucas is in town wrapping up your stalker case. Which I have to admit, turned out to be a convenient stroke of luck."

"Luck?"

"Like I said, I was in a helluva mess. But when the warden called from the prison with the news that Guest had escaped, I saw a way out. I figured the cops would automatically pin that shooting in the alley on your stalker, and that's exactly what happened."

"*You* were the one who tried to shoot me?" The idea was incomprehensible.

"I didn't have any choice. Danny saw me talking with one of the T-shirt vendors, and figured out that I had a deal working with the counterfeiters. That's what he was going to tell you Christmas Eve night. Naturally, I couldn't let him."

Her head throbbed. Her heart was pounding. "You tried to kill him for money?"

"That's why most people are killed."

"But you're talking about T-shirts!" *Calm down. Keep him talking. Give Lucas time to get here.* "How much money could that possibly represent?"

"Enough. When you factor in all the U.S. and the foreign sales—"

"Foreign?"

"Counterfeiting is a big business, Lark. There are dealers in China, Korea, Mexico—name a country and there's someone willing to set up shop and once you make that first deal, the rest get easier, because then the others hear you're open for business and they come to you. And T-shirts are only part of the deal. There's the scalping—"

Lark knew that he wouldn't be telling her all this if he intended to keep her alive. *Keep him talking.* "Ticket scalping?"

"Sure. Even Cody, who was pretty straight for an asshole, did that sometimes. It's a breeze; just have a third party buy up the seats, then sell them at triple the price."

"But one of the reasons we dropped the razzle-dazzle was to make tickets more affordable."

"Christ, Lark, this is a business. If you don't want to make money, you might as well have gone into social work."

"I make money." *A lot of money.* "Enough money."

"Now see, there's where you're wrong. It's never enough."

The gondola kept climbing the floodlit mountain. "If you kill me, the gravy train stops."

"Not really. If you remember, we revised your business plan after you ditched Cody. In the event anything happens to you, Skye and I have the authority to put the corporation into liquidation. And I've established several dummy companies in the Caribbean that'll receive payment for various services rendered."

"Skye would never enter into such a fraud."

"You're right. But she won't be a factor."

"Are you saying you killed her?"

"Not yet. I needed to take care of you before your memory returned. But she's next on my list."

*Oh, God.* She was in the middle of a nightmare.

"If Harlan and Lucas have captured Guest, you won't be able to blame this on him," she said.

"That's unfortunate," he said. "But we can work around it. Everyone knows you were depressed and drinking too much when you were home last year. The past week—Guest's reappearance in your life, Danny's shooting, that salesgirl's death, the plane crash—has been stressful. You couldn't take the pressure. So, you decided to commit suicide."

"By jumping out of a ski gondola?"

He shrugged. "The trouble with attempting suicide is that sometimes things don't work exactly as planned. This will. And there's no option of changing your mind at the last minute."

He knew so much about her. But he didn't know that no one who was really close to her would ever believe she'd go up on a mountain.

*Then again, that won't help if you're dead.*

Her bare hands were turning to ice. She slipped them into the pockets of the parka Ryan had let her grab as they left the house and felt the derringer she'd completely forgotten about.

"What the hell?" It was Ryan's turn to be shocked when she pulled the gun on him.

"I don't want to shoot you, Ryan," Lark said. "But I will."

"You don't have the guts."

"Yes, I do." She was surprised to discover it was the truth. "This has gone too far," she soothed. "We can fix things. It doesn't have to end this way."

"There's no other way for it to end," he said. "I'd rather die right here and now than go to prison."

Before she could think up a response to that, Lark was knocked against the gondola's side as it came to an abrupt stop.

"What the hell?" Ryan shouted.

The floodlights that had turned the mountain into day went out. And as they watched, every light in town flickered out, casting Highland Falls into darkness.

*You can't get emotionally involved*, the sniper's voice inside Lucas's head advised.

*Shut the hell up*, the man in love countered.

How the hell was he not supposed to be emotionally involved when the woman he loved was hanging high above a mountaintop with a killer?

When Zelda had called in about the wounded deputy and Lark's abduction, his heart had nearly stopped.

This wasn't going to be easy. Every rifle and scope had a drift, a microscopic misalignment of barrel, sights, and telescopic lens. Glazer's sudden arrival on the scene hadn't given Lucas the opportunity to zero-out this one;

Harlan had assured him that it'd been sighted, but with all the variables, a bullet didn't always hit where a scope said it would.

One thing in his favor was that there wasn't any wind tonight. More importantly, shooting through a scope was more art than science. And before he'd turned in his badge, he'd been the Picasso of snipers.

Words from the Marine's Creed echoed in his mind: *What counts in this war is not the rounds we fire, the noise of our burst, nor the smoke we make. We know that it is the hits that count.*

*We will hit.*

The rifle felt familiar and unfamiliar at the same time. Lucas set the crosshairs on his target's body. A green circle appeared on the front of Glazer's black parka.

*Please.* It was a one-word prayer to a God who, until Lark had come back into his life, he'd stopped believing in.

Lucas shut down, going deep into the Zen-like state that had once been so natural to him, a relaxation so complete that you neither breathed, nor held your breath. You just were.

*One shot. One kill.*

He'd once sworn never to shoot again. But with everything he held dear on the line, Lucas eased back on the trigger.

The shot echoed off the dark mountainside.

Then there was silence. And the soft, muffled sound of falling snow.

The lights were back on again as Lark flew off the gondola into Lucas's arms. "I knew you'd come," she said, laughing and crying all at the same time. "I never had a moment's doubt that I'd survive."

*That made one of us.*

She'd helped a lot by dropping to the floor of the gondola—in the duck-and-cover move Jamie Douglass had made them repeat every year during his civil defense warning exercises—when Lucas had the lights turned off.

"It's okay." He buried his face in her hair and pressed her face against his chest to keep her from having to look at the dead man Harlan and his deputies were putting into the ambulance to take to the morgue. "You're okay." He said it over and over again, like a mantra, a prayer of thanksgiving.

After the EMT shut the door to the ambulance and it drove away with lights off, Lucas kissed her, his lips roaming over her cheeks, her temples, her eyelids, her lips, tasting salt, not knowing if they were from her tears or his.

"I want to take you home with me. To the farmhouse."

"Yes."

His mouth brushed over her jaw. Plucked at the lips whose taste he'd never been able to forget.

"I've decided I want babies," she said as they walked hand in hand toward the SUV.

"Sounds good to me. Fortunately I've already promised your father I'll make an honest woman of you."

"My father?" God, he loved the way her eyes narrowed; loved the woman she'd become. "You told my father you were going to marry me?"

"Yeah. I did. You got a problem with that?"

Lark took a moment to consider, then laughed as she brought her mouth back to his. "Only that it took you so damn long."

POCKET BOOKS
PROUDLY PRESENTS

# OUT OF THE STORM

# JoAnn Ross

**Available in paperback Fall 2004
from Pocket Books**

Turn the page for a preview of
*Out of the Storm* . . .

Because I could not stop for Death
He kindly stopped for me.
                    —Emily Dickinson


The last day of Sissy Sotheby Beale's life was another Low Country scorcher. These were the dog days, when any canine possessing the sense the Lord gave a flea could be found sprawled on a veranda beneath a slow-moving, paddle-bladed fan.

Long after the blazing sun disappeared behind the towering twin alabaster spires of St. Elizabeth Cathedral—which marked the boundary between city and marshland—the humidity-drenched air remained thick enough to drink. As Sissy Sotheby Beale stepped through the French doors onto the hotel balcony, she felt as if she were walking into a sauna.

The sultry scent of night-blooming jasmine wafted up from the formal courtyard garden ten stories below; usually its sweet perfume bathed her in a heady sensual pleasure.

Not tonight.

Fingers of white-heat lightning danced on the horizon. Electricity from an approaching storm sizzled on her tongue, sparked beneath her glistening, damp skin.

A century earlier, Summersett's movers and shakers had

decided to mark the bicentennial of the city's founding with a mock sea battle which they'd hoped would bring much-needed tourist dollars to the town, still suffering economic deprivation after the Civil War. A huge success, Buccaneer Days quickly escalated into South Carolina's answer to Mardi Gras, allowing citizens to slip the reins of southern civility as they drunkenly reveled in Summersett's infamous pirate roots.

Bringing in more revenue than Savannah's St. Patrick's Day bash or Charleston's Spoleto Festival, Buccaneer Days was a nonstop extravaganza of parties, masked balls, parades, street fairs, a beauty pageant, and nightly sea battles.

And, because the original colonists had the unfortunate timing to arrive from England in the middle of August, there was always the heavy, unrelenting heat.

Sissy's short silk slip—the deep hue of a late summer rose, which complemented her magnolia-pale skin—clung to a body rigorously firmed by diet and daily exercise. Tendrils of blond hair, streaked just that afternoon at Dixie Belle's House of Beauty, trailed down her neck.

Cannon fire boomed from Summersett Harbor as wooden ships bearing either the tricolored Union Jack or black-and-white skull and crossbones kicked off the week-long celebration.

As a fringed black carriage carrying tourists on a Ghost and Graveyards tour passed on the street below the balcony, the bay horse's hooves clicking on the cobblestone street, Sissy climbed atop the railing.

From the Victorian bandstand at the center of Market Square, the Summersett Pops Orchestra had just broken into a rousing rendition of "Dixie," when Sissy spread her tanned, toned arms and flew off the balcony railing.

"What are we doing here?" Laurel Stewart asked the man sitting next to her in the presidential retreat's Evergreen Chapel.

"Praying for peace?" suggested Max Kelly, a reporter from *The Boston Globe*.

"Granted, it's an admirable goal, but given that the Weather Service has declared this the hottest summer on record, what made the White House decide that August would be a good time to hold yet another round of Middle East Road to Peace meetings? Couldn't the State Department find a road map that leads to Maine?"

She slapped at yet another mosquito that had sneaked in through the window screen. "And how come they all invited us here to participate?"

She had to raise her voice to be heard over the huge pipe organ's rendition of "The Song of Peace." According to her program, Israeli Prime Minister Yitzhak Rabin had sung the song with over a hundred thousand people at a peace rally in Tel Aviv minutes before his assassination.

"This, from the reporter who's always bitching that we don't get enough access when the president hides out at Camp David?"

"Like you think anyone's going to nail down a scoop here today," Laurel scoffed. "We're being herded around the place like a bunch of senior citizens on an If-It's-Wednesday-It-Must-Be-Camp-David bus tour from hell."

"Hey, it's not every day you can watch two world leaders knocking down ten pins in the Nixon bowling alley."

"Bowling for Peace," she muttered. "Now, that's going to catch on. I'm still trying to find out if those were new shoes they gave the prime minister, but no one's talking."

"Go get 'em, Lois Lane. That story's bound to get you a banner headline."

"That's my point, Max. There *is* no story here. At least nothing new, other than their refusal to release the president's scorecard and the Laurel dining room chef's diplomatic faux pas of serving sun-dried tomatoes with the beef tenderloin. I mean, really, no one's eaten sun-dried tomatoes since the Clinton administration."

"I thought they ate Big Macs."

"Cute." Actually, a big juicy cheeseburger sounded a lot better than the uninspired deli spread of sliced cheese and cold meat they'd laid out for the press in the mess hall. "It's an evil plot cooked up by the politicos to do away with us."

She felt the sting at the back of her neck and slapped again, an instant too late. "The gang in the White House is probably hoping the press corps will all be attacked by a swarm of West Nile virus–carrying mosquitoes, and drop dead before the election."

Unfortunately, the organ player wearing marine dress blues had just pounded out the last chord, leaving Laurel's conspiracy theory audibly—and loudly—hanging on the steamy air. The president and first lady, displaying impeccable manners in the front row, did not turn around. Neither did the prime minister.

Her peers were not as polite.

Pretending vast interest in the flags on either side of the linen-draped altar at the front of the chapel, Laurel ignored their evil grins.

Two hours later, she was back in the Clinton Room at the Cozy Country Inn in nearby Thurmont, soaking in the mirrored Jacuzzi, when her cell phone started playing the theme from *Jaws*.

*Buh dum. Buh dum.*

"No one's home." She took a long swallow of the frozen margarita she'd brought up from the pub and savored the icy tartness.

*Buh dum. Buh dum.*

"Undoubtedly some jokers wanting to rag me about my big mouth." Journalism was a blood sport; she'd do the same thing if it'd been Max who'd jammed his Bruno Magli into his mouth.

*Dum dum dum dum.*

Some people might be able to ignore a ringing phone. Laurel was not one of them. Splashing water onto the floor, she lunged for the phone she'd left on the sink.

"Oh, hell." The caller screen identified her *Washington Post* editor. She punched Talk. "Yes, Barry, I'm afraid it's true," she admitted, not bothering to waste time with hellos. "I insulted the entire White House in front of a foreign dignitary. You can probably read all about it in tomorrow's *Washington Times.*"

"That's already old news." He brushed it off. "Don't worry about it, I'm not calling to chew you out. I wanted to see if you've been keeping tabs on the AP wire."

"The Secret Service confiscated my computer and phone and held them hostage until we were finally released thirty minutes ago. Something about electronic bombs and homeland security."

Her body was draped in fragrant white froth from the bubble bath she'd dumped into the tub, and Laurel noticed she was dripping on the floor. "What's up?" she asked as she pulled down a towel and wrapped it around her.

"That's all they did?"

It was not unusual for Barry Yost to answer a question with a question. He was, after all, a newsman, more accustomed to delving for information than handing it out.

"Yeah, which was too bad," she answered, "because there's this really cute, hot new agent I wouldn't mind being patted down by."

"Did they return your computer?"

"Of course." There was the silence of dead air, and for a moment, she thought her phone had dropped the call. "Barry?" she said. "Are you still there?"

"There's been a leak."

She retrieved the margarita from the rim of the tub and took a sip. "There are always leaks in Washington. Which is probably why those Watergate guys were called plumbers."

"This one happens to concern the vice president."

"Oh, *hell*. Don't tell me someone else has already broken my story." She'd been promised an exclusive when her confidential, high-level source had brought the papers to her. The first of a five-part series was due to start tomorrow morning.

"Not exactly."

Silence descended again, thick and, this time, a little unnerving.

"Not exactly?" she coaxed, trying to ignore the little frisson of nerves that skimmed up her spine.

"The vice president's people are alleging that papers were stolen from their offices."

"That's certainly not unheard of." If the confidential report had been meant to be for public viewing, it wouldn't have had to be leaked.

"Yeah, but . . . shit."

Barry Yost was one of the most articulate men Laurel had ever met, which, in a city populated by glib-tongued politicians, attorneys, lobbyists, and fast-talking, charismatic television reporters, was really saying something. She couldn't recall ever hearing him at a loss for words. Until now.

"The story hasn't gone beyond rumor stage at this point," he said. "But your name's being floated around town as a suspect."

"A suspect?" Laurel's fingers tightened on the stem of the glass. "As in, someone thinks I'm the person who stole the report?"

Her nerves began screeching like the Civil Defense siren Jamie Douglass continued to test once a year back in her hometown of Highland Falls, Tennessee.

He blew out a breath. "Like I said, it's just a rumor, but—"

"Hold that thought." An unmistakably authoritative knock had begun hammering on her door. Hopefully it was room service with the steak she'd ordered.

*Oh, hell. It wasn't.* One look at the grim faces on the other side of the peephole, and the idea of being patted down by the new Secret Service agent—whose thrust-out jaw was wide enough to land Air Force One on, and who appeared neither as cute nor as hot as he had this morning—suddenly lost its appeal.

"I'll have to call you back, Barry. I've got company."

Laurel tossed back the margarita, threw on a robe, said a quick Hail Mary, then opened the door to face the inquisition.

"It could have happened that way," Derek Manning claimed, defending his jumper scenario as the four homicide detectives observed the broken female body sprawled on the hood of the black Suburban.

"No way." Caitlin Cavanaugh shook her head. "Even Wonder Woman wouldn't have been able to climb up onto that iron railing in four-inch Manolos. Some guy threw her over the balcony."

One of the high heels in question—flimsy bits of silver leather held on with a thin ribbon tie—was still on the dead woman's foot. Assigned to take the crime photographs, Cait lifted her 35mm Olympus and snapped the other, which had landed in the "Frolicking Nymphs" fountain ten feet away.

Having never understood how women walked in ice-pick heels in the first place, Detective Joe Gannon decided Cait's murder scenario sounded more plausible than suicide.

"Vic probably weighs a hundred and five, tops," Manning estimated. About the weight of one of his muscular, tree-trunk-size arms. Cait, who had a minor in psychology backing up her criminal justice degree, had long theorized that the bulked-up detective was overcompensating. "Could have been a woman doin' the tossing."

"Maybe a catfight," Lonnie Briggs suggested. His lips, beneath a mustache the color of a rusted-out skiff, twisted in a leer.

"Why am I not surprised you'd latch on to that idea?" Cait muttered.

On the days Briggs got to pick the lunch spot, he invariably opted for the harborfront Hooters. Little wonder his fifth marriage was breaking up.

Cait looked up at Joe, who'd remained typically silent since arriving on the scene that was beginning to draw a crowd. "Well? You're the Cop of the Year medal winner. What do you think?"

He slapped at the back of his neck. The damn sand gnats had been attacking like kamikaze bomber squadrons ever since he'd arrived on the scene. "I think I'll move to Maine."

Glacier-carved peninsulas, craggy seaside cliffs, icy waves, cool, crisp sea breezes, and the tart taste of an apple plucked right off the tree. If he left right now, then drove straight through up 95, he could probably be sitting down to a lobster dinner tomorrow night.

"Discounting the fact that you just happen to be a homegrown, deep-fried southern boy who'd freeze your very fine ass off by Labor Day, homicide's in your blood, Gannon. You'd be bored brainless investigating murder by moose before you were there a week," Caitlin predicted. "So, getting back to this case, do *you* think we've got a jumper?"

"Anything's possible."

He scanned the crime scene, his hands deep in the pockets of his humidity-rumpled gray slacks to keep from touching anything. One of the unwritten axioms of homicide investigation stated that the least competent cop would always be the first to arrive. Beat cop Dylan Thomas, son of an English professor at the nearby Admiral Summersett Military Institute, was the exception that proved the rule. Thomas had already cordoned off the crime scene and had begun taking the names of witnesses.

He'd also held firm when the owner of the SUV had demanded his vehicle back and the area cleared. No small feat, considering the Suburban was registered to the Secret Service. Two guys built like Coke machines wearing dark suits, with walkie-talkie earphones, were pacing impatiently on the other side of the yellow-and-black tape.

Since the vice president's advance team had been a royal pain in the ass since they'd hit town last week, Joe decided to let them cool their heels awhile longer.

It had been twenty minutes since the first 911 call had come in. Not enough time for the victim's smooth, golden skin to turn blue-gray or lividity to begin to set in. Her still-clear hazel eyes, more green than blue, stared unseeingly up at the night sky, giving no clue as to the last moments of her life. They didn't look depressed, or surprised, or frightened. They just looked dead.

A high-pitched whistle screeched from the old iron suspension bridge leading to Swann Isle, a palm- and pine tree–studded barrier island three miles offshore.

"Damn." Manning glared accusingly at his measuring tape as fireworks lit up the sky in a dazzling display of red, white, and blue over the water. Buccaneer Days wasn't about to slow down just because someone had discovered the hard way arms made lousy wings. "The point of impact is six feet from the building." He shook his shaved head in disgust.

Cait, who'd had a one-night stand with the detective after her divorce, had reported back that he'd also shaved his entire body. Which was a lot more personal information about the guy than Joe wanted to know.

"I can't hang around here all night investigating a frigging murder," Manning complained in a whine that sounded ridiculous coming out of a guy with an eighteen-inch neck. "I've got a hot date with a hard body."

"She could be a jumper who bounced off the side of the building after she was airborne," Joe surmised. The rule of thumb was that a body in free fall would land three to four feet from the takeoff point. "Her blown right pupil suggests a primary impact before she hit the SUV."

He tilted his dark head back, looking a long way up at the balcony. According to the desk clerk, the twenty-something woman had checked into room 1033 as Sissy Somers, from Charlotte. A check for a South Carolina driver's license had drawn a blank, which made Joe wonder about the slender gold band on her broken left hand. A woman meeting a man other than her husband at a hotel wasn't likely to check in under her own name.

"Jake and I tried counseling before the final breakup." Cait bent her knees to get a close-up shot of the wedding band. She'd always had a knack for sensing Joe's thoughts, which was one of the things that made her such a good partner. "The counselor suggested hotel dates to spice up our marriage."

"Guess it didn't work," Manning said.

"No shit, Sherlock." She changed the angle of the camera to capture the broken neck.

Cait's marriage to a vice cop had ended in divorce. They were both good people, who'd reluctantly decided that murder didn't make for scintillating pillow talk. Something Joe had found out for himself.

The woman's slip had twisted up, revealing a skimpy scrap of pink silk thong.

"A woman doesn't put on butt floss and hooker heels to attend a garden party," Briggs said.

"If she was trying to spice up a marriage, she definitely picked the right wardrobe," Manning agreed.

"How come the woman's always the one who has to make the extra effort?" Caitlin complained around the plastic pen stuck in her mouth.

She snapped a longer shot of the SUV, capturing the crowd of lookie-loos—every once in a while, you got lucky and caught a picture of the perp who'd stuck around for the fun—then scribbled the photo sequence in her notebook.

"Because they outnumber men. It's a competition thing," Briggs claimed. "Chicks need to attract males so they can get laid to keep the species going."

Cait made a low sound of disgust.

Joe suspected she was thinking the species would have been far better off if Briggs's mother hadn't attracted Briggs's father.

"Unless she's a Victoria's Secret model, that's sure as hell not everyday underwear," Manning pointed out. "Which fits the pattern of women prettying themselves up before they check out." He was still pushing for suicide, which wasn't surprising, given all the unsolved murders they were trying to juggle.

All summers in the South Carolina low country were hot, but this one was breaking records every day, and crime had escalated right along with the temperature. The hotter it got, the more tempers flared. Minor fender benders exploded into road rage, bar arguments became brawls, date rape rose in direct proportion to increased alcohol consumption, patrol cops couldn't keep up with the number of domestic disturbance calls which were increasingly leading to murder, and just last night, unhappiness about an umpire's "safe at home" call at a kids' baseball playoff game had started bullets flying.

"Jumping off a ten-story balcony is not exactly the way to leave behind a good-looking corpse," Joe countered.

One more twist in the air and Sissy Somers, or whoever she was, would have left a face print in the SUV's windshield. The investigative unit hadn't arrived to set up the klieg lights yet, but the flashing red-and-blue bubble lights from the cruisers illuminated a bit of pink on the dusty brick hotel roadway. Joe crouched down, picked up the lacquered tip of a fingernail, and slipped it into a glassine bag.

"It could still be a suicide," Manning insisted hopefully.

"Well, you're going to have to put your hot body on hold," Cait advised him as the medical examiner's white van arrived. "Because I've got ten bucks that says murder."

"This sucks," Manning complained.

As the sky overhead exploded in a grand finale that drew oohs and aahs from the crowd, and gave the broken, nearly naked body atop the waxed-to-a-mirror-gloss, black Secret Service Suburban an eerie, surrealistic look, Joe silently agreed with him.

Maybe he'd become a lobsterman, piloting his boat through the cool morning fog, setting his traps, returning to harbor in some small, picturesque little town of gray clapboard buildings. Unfortunately, if there was one thing he'd learned in a dozen years of homicide investigation, it was that appearances could be deceiving.

A lobsterman's life undoubtedly wasn't as uncomplicated as his fantasy. But as he swatted away another attack of vampire gnats, Joe couldn't help wondering if those Down-Easters had any idea how fortunate they were, breathing in the crisp scent of salty sea air instead of death and despair.

GET CAUGHT READING AT SEA

getcaughtreadingatsea.com

Join top authors for the ultimate cruise experience. Spend 7 days in the Western Caribbean aboard the luxurious *Carnival Elation*. Start in Galveston, TX, and visit Progreso, Cozumel, and Belize. Enjoy all this with a ship full of authors, entertainers, and book lovers on the **"Get Caught Reading at Sea Cruise"** October 17–24, 2004.

Mail in this coupon with proof of purchase* by September 1, 2004 to receive $250 per person off the regular **"Get Caught Reading at Sea Cruise"** price. One coupon per person required to receive $250 discount, subject to availability. Offer valid in the U.S.A. Void where prohibited. Sponsors not responsible for lost, late, illegible, postage due, or misdirected mail. Limit 1 per customer.

For further details call **1-877-ADV-NTGE** or visit **www.GetCaughtReadingatSea.com**.

PRICES STARTING AT $749 PER PERSON WITH COUPON!

Look for these other bestselling paperbacks from JoAnn Ross: *Out of the Mist, Magnolia Moon,* and *Blue Bayou*. And don't miss her new book, *Out of the Storm*.

*Proof of purchase is original sales receipt with the book purchased circled. (No copies allowed.)

**Carnival**
The Most Popular Cruise Line in the World!

---

# GET $250 OFF

GET CAUGHT READING AT SEA
getcaughtreadingatsea.com

Name   Please Print

Address                                    Apt. No.

City                          State           Zip

Email Address

**See Following Page for Terms and Conditions.**

**For booking form and complete information,
go to www.GetCaughtReadingatSea.com or call 1-877-ADV-NTGE.**

09629

# Carnival Elation

## 7 Day Exotic Western Caribbean Itinerary

| DAY | PORT | ARRIVE | DEPART |
|-----|------|--------|--------|
| Sun | Galveston | | 4:00 P.M. |
| Mon | "Fun Day" at Sea | | |
| Tue | Progreso/Merida | 8:00 A.M. | 4:00 P.M. |
| Wed | Cozumel | 9:00 A.M. | 5:00 P.M. |
| Thu | Belize | 8:00 A.M. | 6:00 P.M. |
| Fri | "Fun Day" at Sea | | |
| Sat | "Fun Day" at Sea | | |
| Sun | Galveston | 8:00 A.M. | |

---

## TERMS AND CONDITIONS

**PAYMENT SCHEDULE:**
50% due upon booking
Full and final payment due by July 26, 2004

Acceptable forms of payment are Visa, MasterCard, American Express, Discover and checks. The cardholder must be one of the passengers traveling. A fee of $25 will apply for all returned checks. Check payments must be made payable to **Advantage International, LLC and sent to: Advantage International, LLC, 195 North Harbor Drive, Suite 4206, Chicago, IL 60601**

**CHANGE/CANCELLATION:**
Notice of change/cancellation must be made in writing to Advantage International, LLC.

**Change:**
Changes in cabin category may be requested and can result in increased rate and penalties. A name change is permitted 60 days or more prior to departure and will incur a penalty of $50 per name change. Deviation from the group schedule and package is a cancellation.

**Cancellation:**

| | |
|--|--|
| 181 days or more prior to departure | $250 per person |
| 121 - 180 days or more prior to departure | 50% of the package price |
| 120 - 61 days prior to departure | 75% of the package price |
| 60 days or less prior to departure | 100% of the package price (nonrefundable) |

**US and Canadian citizens are required to present a valid passport or the original birth certificate and state issued photo ID (drivers license). All other nationalities must contact the consulate of the various ports that are visited for verification of documentation.**

We strongly recommend trip cancellation insurance!

For further details call 1-877-ADV-NTGE or visit www.GetCaughtReadingatSea.com

---

For booking form and complete information
go to **www.getcaughtreadingatsea.com** or call **1-877-ADV-NTGE**

Complete coupon and booking form and mail both to:
**Advantage International, LLC,
195 North Harbor Drive, Suite 4206, Chicago, IL 60601**